City of Burning Shadows

Book One of
Apocrypha: The Dying World

Barbara J. Webb

CITY OF BURNING SHADOWS
Book One of APOCRYPHA: THE DYING WORLD
Copyright © 2014 by Barbara J. Webb

Cover art copyright © 2013 by Jordan Grimmer
Cover design by Scarlett Rugers Design www.scarlettrugers.com

Published by Frontiers
Trade Paperback First Edition 2014

City of Burning Shadows
ISBN No. 978-0-6159792-1-2

2

For my parents, who surrounded me with books.

— 1 —

Day by Day

It's amazing how little anything changes after the end of the world. Coffee from the corner stand still costs more than it should. The motley huddle of kids on the corner of East and Ouliria still look like they might pull a knife if you stare at them too long. And it remains impossible to find a seat on the early morning train to downtown.

They used to call Miroc the city where even the gods wouldn't walk alone after dark. Now the gods are gone, I don't know what they toss around to scare the tourists, but the sentiment remains true. During the day, it's safe enough, long as you don't look too small or smell too weak, but you learn to keep your valuables under several layers and try not to push anyone who's bigger than you. Easier said than done on the crowded blue line. Especially what with me being human and most of the other folks riding in from this side of town being . . . not.

Giants and lizards and boneheads. Most places, those weren't the sort of people who'd pose a threat, but the ones who chose to slum in Miroc trended towards mean. Especially nowadays, now everything's fallen apart.

Anyone who thinks that riding the train in together every morning we'd find some sort of camaraderie has obviously never set foot on the blue line.

This morning, either the train was early or I was late. I had no choice but to jump on the closest car right before the doors slid shut, choking my way through the reeking cloud of stale sweat and exhaust. I slid myself between two lizards—the only space I could fit. Their armored bodies desensitized them to a bit of jostling, as long as you kept clear of their tails, making my spot uncomfortable, but safe.

The taller, green one looked down. He was at least a foot taller than me, and by human standards, I'm not a guy anyone would call short. I held eye contact just long enough to show I wasn't afraid of him, without staring so long it was a threat. It was a skill one developed quickly in this city if one wanted to survive.

I tried to ignore the way his elbow-spike dug into my back and checked the news on my NetPad as the train jerked along. I flipped through headlines of water protests, break-ins, assaults, and news of a hidden pocket of Ziflan priests that had been discovered by one of the gangs and dragged out into the street and murdered. The last story was more than I'd wanted to see. I slid the device back into my bag and spent the rest of the ride trying not to think about it.

Miroc was falling apart, and every single one of us on this train was locked in some level of denial. We were still going through the motions, commuting to jobs and friends and lives that on the surface looked little different than what they'd been before. Underneath, our city—our world—was crumbling. And if there was a way to stop it, it was going to take a better person than me to figure out how.

The lizards got off at my stop, and I hung back to let them get well ahead of me. Which gave me the perfect view of the ragged, half-starved teenager who darted out of a shadowy alcove between two long-dead vending machines and angled his path to intercept my big green friend.

Plenty of kids like this in Miroc. Plenty of wretched people of all ages. They were invisible to most of the folks who still had places to go and lives to live. I hadn't yet mastered the trick of blindness.

The kid wasn't subtle. He must have been desperate. He needled his hand into the lizard's robe, sacrificing finesse for speed, but the lizard had better reflexes than his bulk implied.

The lizard grabbed the boy by one arm and lifted him effortlessly into the air. I heard the boy's shoulder pop. Struggling like a fresh-caught fish, the boy scraped at the arm holding him, but it was soft fingers against scales and plates and there was nothing he could do. The few other people who had gotten off the train with us split around them and hurried on. Just another attempted robbery. Nothing to see.

"Little thief." The lizard leaned in and the thrashing boy banged his head against the horn's curling out from the lizard's forehead. "You know what we do with thieves?"

I couldn't watch this. I couldn't look away. Sudden bursts of violence were the new way of life in Miroc, and I should have been inured by now. I certainly knew better than to get involved.

The lizard switched his grip, and now his thick, clawed fingers were wrapped around the kid's throat.

There were two lizards, and they were armed. Swords on one hip, guns on the other. They were bigger than me, stronger than me, and the smartest thing I could do was to keep walking. It wasn't like this would be the first murder I'd witnessed in this station.

"Put him down," I said.

The second lizard—this one bronze with a faint pattern of stripes along his scales I might have found pretty in a different situation—flicked his hand at me. "Keep walking. This doesn't concern you."

He was right and I should have listened. Instead I raised my hand, called symbols of motion, force, and energy to my mind, and *pushed*.

Lizard number one staggered. Startled, he dropped the boy. The kid wasted no time. He ran.

I should have done the same.

In two strides, the big green lizard crossed the space between us and grabbed at me, his claws digging into my robe and the shirt beneath. He swung me around and slammed me back against the station wall. His amber eyes were inches from my own. "Do it," I choked out.

Another slam against the wall. My head cracked hard against the concrete, and for a moment, my vision grayed. I tried to push against his arms, the solid mass of his chest, but it was like trying to move a mountain.

The other lizard elbowed his friend. My captor's gaze twitched down, and he snarled in the back of his throat. "Priest," he spat, and dropped me.

They turned their backs and left me there. I pressed back against the wall, rubbed at my aching shoulder. My fingers traced across the rough patch of skin on my collarbone that had just saved my life.

Symbol of the Dark God. Usually it started more fights than it ended, so I tried to keep it covered. But my shirt collar had gaped open to reveal the tattoo, and I guess these two still held respect—or fear—for those of us who used to serve. Lucky me.

All the same, I was ready to get out of here. I stumbled through the turnstiles, up the stairs, and out into the bright desert sun.

Huddled clumps of beggars lined the early-morning street, accosting commuters, trying to scrape together enough cash for the day's water and shelter before the sun cleared the rooftops and the city became a furnace. Most of the beggars were human. We're not the most colorful inhabitants of Miroc, but what we lack in exoticism we make up for in numbers.

Without the temples and priesthoods, there was no place for people to go, no charity but that which they could scrounge up themselves. And the ranks of the desperate grew day by day.

As I shuffled through sand drifts that every day won ground against the sidewalks, I scanned faces I passed for anyone I recognized. Anyone from before. But strangers filled the street this morning. A small comfort, if only because I had no help to offer anyone if I had seen a friendly face.

My workplace wasn't far from the tube station—a building that had wanted to be a skyscraper in its youth, but like everyone else in this city had settled for something less. It was a good fifty years shy of modern, but it was clean and climate-controlled, and I was grateful for both.

I waved at the security guard and made for the elevator. The thirty-third floor had only one business listed on the wall directory: Price & Breckenridge, Legal and Investigative Services. My employers. The ones who had been good enough to take me in.

I wasn't first to the office this morning. The smell of coffee brewing welcomed me as the elevator door slid open. Talk about your comfort smells. Society might be disintegrating like a body rotting in the sun, but for one more morning, at least, we still had coffee and the water to brew it. I tried not to wonder how long that would last.

Iris was in the reception area, staring at the dripping machine as though trying to speed the brew with the heat of her impatience. Iris was like me, another displaced priest. Amelia Price collected us like strays.

This morning Iris's hair was magenta and her eyes were violet. Her nose looked longer than it had yesterday, her skin a more reddish brown. For good reason, Amelia requested Iris pass for human, but that didn't mean Iris had to be the same human every single day. And maybe Iris never managed what most people would call normal, but, shit, who does?

"Hey, Ash." Like all shifters, Iris managed somehow to smile with her entire body.

I joined her vigil by the coffee-maker. "You're in early."

I swear, the tilt of her lips didn't change a bit, but her smile became a frown all the same. "More like I'm still here late. I haven't been to sleep yet."

I gave a sympathetic groan. "Out spying last night?"

"Investigating," she corrected me.

"Another husband-thinks-his-wife-is-cheating case?" Tiresome and repetitive they might be, but these days, paranoid spouses were our bread and butter. Thicker on the ground than contract disputes. Less dangerous than other investigations. No one wanted to be the first to ask if these things still even mattered—if either love or money could hold their value as the world collapsed around us.

Old familiar patterns; people clinging to the past. As long as they kept paying us for our time, who was I to criticize? For most problems, we were still cheaper than the cops.

Iris didn't answer. Which meant her investigation was secret, above my pay grade. There were a lot of things around here I wasn't supposed to know.

The coffee finished dripping and I poured each of us a cup.

As I handed Iris hers, I caught her looking at me funny. "You okay?"

Her eyes were on my neck, and I stuck a hand back there. My fingers came away spotted with blood. Leftover from my encounter with the lizards. "I'm fine. No problem." I reached inside for a genuine smile. Iris could always tell the difference.

It wasn't convincing enough. Iris followed me back to my office.

Okay, technically it had been a storage closet before they'd hired me. Amelia had cleared some space and they'd squeezed in a desk. They'd even painted my name across the frosted glass door. Joshua Drake, nothing more. No fancy job title for the secretary/transcriptionist/file clerk. Not many of us "retired" priests had much in the way of marketable skills. I was lucky to be here, lucky to be able to run water and pay my bills and have someplace to come in out of the rain. Not that it rained anymore in Miroc. Like so many other things, sustainable living in the desert had gone right out the window when the gods went away.

My little desk was wedged into the far corner, with an old computer and a single chair. The rest of the space was claimed by filing cabinets, shelves, and tilting stacks of boxes and folders. It wasn't glamorous, but it was mine.

Iris leaned against the doorway, her soft brown skin darkening to a concerned black. "So what's going on?"

I'd been picking fights, but Iris didn't need to hear about that. She had harassments of her own to deal with. I'd walked away, so no reason to dwell, right?

And if I was being completely honest, my day had been rough even before I got on that train. "Another bad night," I shrugged. "No big deal."

"Again?" she asked. "Have you considered—"

"Yes," I snapped. "Doctors, pills, therapy, séances—whatever you're going to suggest, I've considered it. I'm fine, all right?"

The words came out harsh. Harsher than I'd meant. "I'm sorry, Iris, it's just—"

"Whatever, Ash." She stalked away.

I sighed. Iris was a friend, pretty much the only one I had these days. I'd have to apologize later. Once I wasn't so on edge.

Amelia Price had given me the file room to manage, a harmless enough occupation. And more than enough work, as slammed as P&B was these days. Every flat surface was piled high with files from recent cases, and these were just the public files, the information P&B would release to the press or the government if an investigation required it. The secrets, the proprietary details, those were all stored on the systems that only Amelia Price or Jonathan Breckenridge had access to.

There shouldn't have been anything back here to get me into trouble. Except that I'd been trained to find secrets other people wanted hidden. In my old life, before the Abandon, I'd been a research archivist for Kaifail's temple. I'd been one of the best. It wasn't a skill worth much now that society was falling apart, but it meant I was good at seeing the puzzle pieces hidden in otherwise innocuous documents, and I could read between the lines like a pro. I didn't know details, couldn't find much more than tantalizing hints, but I was absolutely certain Price & Breckenridge was involved in more than what they advertised on the door.

It was tempting, so tempting to reach for the tools my time as a priest had given me. To really focus, engage my mind, and most of all to touch once more the magic I was afraid I'd lost the knack for.

Except that I couldn't afford to lose this job.

Getting myself killed provoking fights was one thing. Starving to death in the street was a whole other. Not that I'd probably live long enough to starve. I'd be another headline: former priest of Kaifail beaten to death, or burned alive, or strung up with his intestines hanging out for the crows. People in this city were nothing if not creative in their punishments for those of us they blamed for the state of things.

All this was still fresh in my mind when the intercom on my desk pinged. "Mr. Drake?" The security guard. "There's a man down here asking for you."

Was there any way this could be good? "Who is he? What does he want?"

"Says he needs to see you. Says you know each other." The guard's voice dropped, whispering into his microphone: "He says he was a priest."

Just like that, I was back on my feet. "I'll be right down." Because I hadn't learned my lesson yet about getting involved. Because I didn't have enough to worry about these days. Most of all, because I thought it would be good to see a friend.

In other words, I hurried back downstairs because I was an idiot.

— 2 —

Bright and Dark

Thirteen gods, thirteen priesthoods, and not every one responded to the Abandon in the same way. Some withdrew into themselves, pulling away from the world until they were lost. Others fractured and imploded without the direct guidance of their deity to hold them together. One church—Jansyn's, of course—actually tried to find an answer, an explanation for why the gods had suddenly disappeared. They might even have succeeded if their Favored Son hadn't snapped one night and started . . . well, that's a different story.

We who followed Kaifail pretty much went on with business as usual. Kaifail had never had a direct hand in our daily lives. He'd never shown any interest in church politics or practices. You could say Kaifail abandoned his children back before it was cool. The church was ours even more than it was his, and so it survived the Abandon and even grew in prominence as the rest of the world started to crumble.

Put another way, we priests stepped up to assume the responsibilities Kaifail had abdicated. In his name, we continued to minister, to teach, to counsel. We spoke out, because it was our way. We continued to tell our stories as the world descended into nightmare around us.

All that accomplished was to make us a target. We couldn't

stop the fear. We couldn't stop the world from breaking. Mobs and violence, fires . . . even the temple burned at the end.

At least, that's how it happened here in Miroc. I have no idea how Kaifail's temples fared elsewhere in the world. All I know is, for all the scars I bear, I was one of the lucky ones. I had long since given up hope that anyone else had escaped.

Except there he stood at the security station. A face I knew well. "Micah?"

"Ash!"

I gripped his offered hand, a reflex, and squeezed it harder than was polite as a complicated storm of emotions ran through me. Relief that a friend—a fellow priest was still alive. And joy to see him. But deeper down, in that churning part of my soul that never seemed to quiet, I was pissed. "Where did you come from? Where have you been?"

Micah had obviously been through hard times. A jagged diagonal scar marred what had once been one of the handsomest faces in Miroc. It continued under his jaw, down his neck, all the way to the iridescent lines of his Bright God tattoo. His clothing, too, was new for him. He was dressed like me, in the light linen robes that were the best way to survive now that the true desert climate had enveloped the city. In those plain drapes of fabric, who would guess he'd once been the darling of Kaifail's stage, the shining jewel of Bright Kaifail's church?

He frowned, doubtless measuring me in the same way, taking in the new shape my nose had healed into and the scars that trailed rough dark lines across what had once been smooth brown skin. I'd accepted these changes as a small price to pay for the fact I could still draw breath. "It's good to see you," he said.

"I didn't know anyone else made it out. I thought everyone was dead."

"So did I. Until I saw your name in the directory."

I yanked my hand back. "You're here for Price & Breckenridge?" Add betrayal to the emotional soup in my head.

His smile faded. "I'm sorry. I can't pretend I'm not. Believe me, I'm grateful to find you, too."

"I've been here." A sudden roughness in my throat made it hard to talk. "I've been here for months. Where have *you* been?"

We'd risen together through the priesthood, both gifted kids from families who couldn't afford to pay for secular education. Micah's face and talents had drawn the attention of the Bright Church's scouts, while my own interests had pointed me towards the Dark Church's studies, but we'd remained close over the years. Despite what outsiders might think, there has never been enmity between the two sides of Kaifail's church. Competition, sure, and even a sibling-like rivalry, but we have always been one church, not two.

Which made it so much worse that it was Micah—that he'd only come here because he needed something.

Micah glanced at the security guard, who was watching our interchange with shameless interest. Micah twitched his chin to indicate we should step out of earshot and put a hand on my arm—a normal, friendly gesture that I jerked away from faster than I could think.

But when he walked a few steps away, I followed. "I've been in hiding," he whispered. "With people . . . people trying to help. Trying to *do* something."

It was hard not to read accusation into his words. "I'm done with crusades." I had to clench my fist to stop myself from compulsively running fingers along the scars that traced my arms, hidden under the loose sleeves of my robe.

"I know." Micah's tone was placating. "I feel terrible asking you for anything. I do. But we need help. We need your employers' help. I need you to—"

"No." I turned away from him, strode to the elevator, and pushed the button. Whatever was going on, whatever trouble, whatever crisis, I wanted nothing to do with it.

The elevator arrived with a ding. The door slid open. But Micah hadn't given up.

"Ash." His voice was soft. "There's no one else we can go to. And this is important. I can't tell you how much. Please. I don't know what else to do."

I stood with my hand on the elevator door. A couple more steps and I could leave him behind. Walk away. Abandon him to whatever problems had driven him out of hiding. Driven him to me.

"What do you want from P&B?" I asked without turning around.

"Just a meeting at first. My friends want to see a representative from the firm. It'll be worth Price's time to talk to us. We have information she's interested in. Information about the city council."

Gods-dammit, I was going to do this. "I'll talk to Amelia." I stepped into the elevator. "No promises."

The doors slid shut behind me, cutting off any response he might have made.

The door to Amelia's corner office was open, and I could see Iris inside, sitting on Amelia's desk, leaning in close to read what Amelia had up on her computer. On the touch-screen display that filled the wall to their right, a map of the city was displayed, marked with a number of circles and Xs. Whatever was going on had both of them frowning.

I lingered in the doorway, unsure if I should interrupt.

No question it was Amelia I needed to see. Jonathan Breckenridge was a brilliant attorney, and he had earned his name on the door a hundred times over, but P&B was Amelia's firm. Everything funneled through her.

Amelia's office wasn't the cluttered mess of my workspace, but, like Miroc, it had seen better days. The fountain that had once trickled soothingly in the corner stood dry and the potted ferns that used to soften the light from the wide, ceiling-to-floor windows had been left to die as the price of water soared.

Miroc had been a green city. Sure, no one was ever going to call it pretty, but once upon a time, it had looked alive, not baked brown by the desert sun. Through the thirty-third-floor windows, I had a clear view of scorched parks, cracked roads, and crumbling high-rises. High in the sky, fluttering shadows under the afternoon sunlight—the bird priests wheeled in the air, praying to a goddess who no longer answered. Not since the Abandon had their aerial dances brought the rains that used to keep this city lush and beautiful. Despite that, they were the only remaining priesthood no one in the city dared attack on sight. Because we never entirely give up hope.

And at the city's edge, untouched by the decay far below, the glittering glass dome of the Crescent stood serene and untouched. If we all dried up and blew away, would the Jansynians even notice?

"Are you here for the view, Ash, or is there something I can do for you?" Amelia's question startled me back to the present. She and Iris were both staring at me.

Stronger men than I have been lobotomized by one of Amelia Price's stares. "If you're not too busy, can I talk to you about something?"

Iris slid off the desk. "Might as well. We're nowhere with this."

Amelia turned a tight, but affectionate smile at Iris, then swiped her hand across the wall, sending it dark. "What is it you need?" she asked me.

Brevity was my ally. "A friend came to see me this morning. He wants to hire Price & Breckenridge."

"I'm sorry." Amelia's dismissal was quick and painless. "We don't have the resources to take on new clients right now."

15

And that was that. Easy and over. Until Iris got involved. "What friend?"

I tried to think if Iris had ever met Micah. She and I had crossed paths a few times before Iris had met Amelia and settled into the person she was now. Back then, Iris had spent a lot of her time working freelance for the university, tracking down random and obscure bits of information for the senior students. And on occasion for priests of Kaifail.

"Micah Talmadge. He was—"

"An actor, wasn't he?" Amelia asked. "I saw him in *Songs like the Ocean*. And that play about the Twins. He was really quite something." She paused, thoughtful. "What was it he wanted?"

"A meeting. He didn't say what about." I could have left it there. But no amount of petulance justified not giving Amelia the full story. "He said his employers knew something about the city council? Something you would want to know?"

Iris's head jerked up, like she'd been stabbed. Amelia's only response was to narrow her eyes. If I hadn't been looking straight at her, I would have missed it.

With the churches gone, Miroc's council was the only thing holding our city together. They regulated what water we had left, negotiated with the Jansynians for the trade deals we could still manage, and organized the various police and security forces that kept the city from erupting into violent chaos. "What's going on with the council?" I asked.

"Nothing you need to worry about," Amelia said smoothly. "But I think I will have you take that meeting."

Now it was my turn to be surprised. "Me? Shouldn't you send someone with experience? Iris or Josiah or—"

Amelia cut me off with a sharp shake of her head. "He approached you. He trusts you. Find out what he and his employers know—and, if you can, how they know it."

"Isn't there some kind of training? What do I say? What do I do?"

Amelia sighed, impatiently tapping her perfectly lacquered nails on the surface of her desk. "It's the end of the world. We've moved past probationary periods and promotion tracks. Ask questions. You know how to do that. Whatever they tell you, bring it back to me."

It sounded straightforward enough. It wasn't what I would have chosen to do, but Amelia was the boss and I couldn't say no. "I can do that."

Amelia waved her hand, finished with me. "Off you go."

Iris followed me out. "I can come with if you need me. Amelia won't tell me no."

The offer was beyond kind, especially after I'd snapped at her earlier. "Thanks, Iris. I appreciate it, really. But I should be able to talk to people without getting myself in too much trouble."

She shrugged, and her eyes whirled a cheerful rainbow of colors before returning to violet. "We'll see about that."

Bathed in the warmth of her friendly amusement, I went back to my office to call downstairs and tell Micah it was done.

No surprise the nightmares came again. The fight at the tube station, the stress of seeing Micah—I should have expected it.

Tonight I didn't dream of the riots. Which was a change, at least. If my subconscious was determined to make my nights a living hell, at least it was good enough to offer up some variety in its punishments.

We take the small comforts where we find them.

I was in an alley at night. The glass and concrete walls to either side of me reached claustrophobically high. The still-lucid sliver of my mind called out that I shouldn't be here, that I should know better than to be alone, after dark, in this part of town.

It wasn't enough to break the dream. Because I *had* been here. I *had* done this, even knowing at the time that I shouldn't.

"Hello?" my dream self called out, and my voice echoed all around, the word stretching and twisting and growing louder and louder until I had to cover my ears from the deafening thunder.

I'd come here looking for other priests in hiding. I'd come alone because none of the other survivors huddled at the temple were in any shape to walk the streets. But the little girl who'd stumbled in this morning—dehydrated, bruised, and cradling a broken arm—had said her mother and four other priests were trapped. They'd been spotted coming back from a trip out to find food. Their attackers had set fire to the building and the priests had been caught when the building collapsed.

Ellie was the girl's name. Alana was her mother. Alana had been one of mine, a priest of Dark Kaifail. I had to try to find her.

The bastards were waiting for me.

The blessing and curse of dreams is that they are not real. The pain I felt as they broke my bones, cut my face, caved my ribs— it was a shadow of what the reality had been. But the terror, the soul-deep anguish, the horrific loss—these things were worse for countless repetition and the knowledge I would never see any of these friends again—not the one I'd left behind in the temple; not the ones I'd come to save.

I woke to the echo of my own voice, a sobbing scream that no one but me was there to hear. Further sleep was out of the question. Once the nightmares started for the night, they'd keep coming back.

My apartment was small—a one-room efficiency—the best I could afford. These days, it wasn't space that ran up your cost-of-living; it was the utilities to make it habitable. Water wasn't the only thing that had become more expensive as Miroc limped closer and closer to being swallowed by the desert.

I stumbled over to the tiny sink that served both bathroom and kitchen functions and slid my hand over the panel that acti-

vated the small sconce above it. I dribbled water onto the wash-
cloth that hung on the wall and scrubbed my face.

Reflexively, I rubbed again at the rough lines that traced my
skin over my collarbone, across to my shoulder, several inches
down my chest. Kaifail's stone doorway, with the swirling vortex
in the center and the basic symbols of magic worked in all around.
I knew it well enough I only had to trace it with my fingers to see
it in my mind. This morning, it had gotten me out of a beating.
Other times, like the night I'd just been dreaming about . . .

Among the Thirteen, there were gods who taught tolerance
and love. Who guided their followers to forgive their enemies and
bear no judgment against those who wronged them.

Kaifail was not one of those gods. Which was good, because
I wasn't sure I could ever forgive those people. I wished them
countless nights of nightmares worse than mine and eternal judgment from whichever god they belonged to—whichever god they
had turned their backs on to commit atrocious acts against the
servants of all the Thirteen.

"Ellie," I said into the mirror. "Alana. Jason. Molly." I'd lost
them on that horrible night. When I woke up in the hospital, days
later, no one could tell me what had happened. In the months
of my recovery, I couldn't get in contact with them or any other
refugees from Kaifail's temple. So many friends and colleagues
and people I considered family—all gone. I'd assumed they were
dead, but seeing Micah today had opened up the possibility that
anyone could still be out there.

Amelia had found Iris, and Iris and found me, but who else
was looking for these lost souls, these broken men and women
who could be anywhere in the city, desperate and alone, con-
demned to their fate by the tattoo we all bore?

Kaifail couldn't help us. Or Kaifail wouldn't help us. It
amounted to the same thing. For years we had served him, and
then he and the rest of the Thirteen had disappeared without a
word of warning. They'd left the world to this dismal fate, left their

priests behind to bear the ire of a civilization slowly collapsing.

I couldn't bring the gods back. I couldn't save the ones they'd left behind. The best I could do was hope my friends found some kind of peace and shelter and fellowship as we all counted off the days remaining until the end.

—3—

Copper

Kaifail was a liar. I'm his priest; I can say that. And it's not like it was any great secret, especially to anyone who took thirty seconds to look.

For followers of the Bright God, lies were a way of life. They celebrated Kaifail the storyteller, the trickster, the scoundrel: the Kaifail who stole the secrets of magic as a gift to his children, who conned three different goddesses into believing they were his one and only true love. The Bright Church was full of itinerant storytellers, actors, artists, and politicians—crafters of fiction, every one.

Those of us who aligned with the Dark God, we venerated a different Kaifail. Our Kaifail hoarded puzzles and stalked mysteries but he was no more honest than his other face. Maybe priests of the Dark God didn't lie as often as our bright brethren, but that didn't mean we couldn't.

I didn't want to see Micah again. Didn't want to meet with his people. Had no interest in whatever they needed from Price & Breckenridge. But because Amelia had told me to, and because I still needed to pay my bills, I would go and I would listen and I would report back.

My apartment had no windows, but my bedside alarm informed me the sun was up and it was time to get moving. I had work to do. I dressed, packed up my NetPad and wireless and made for the tube station.

I transferred to the yellow line today, since I was headed for a different part of town. I rode to the last stop and still it spit me out with quite a few blocks to hike. I pulled up my hood as I stepped out into the glaring sunlight. I was alone on the sidewalk. Flat-faced warehouses offered neither canopies nor decorative trees for shade. Cargo trucks, the street's lone occupants, jetted clouds of smoke into air that was already hot enough to suffocate. This was the only part of the city where regular traffic still moved, and all these trucks were going in and out of one place. I squinted up at the most visible landmark, the shining expanse of glass and steel, high above the city, shimmering in the heat. The beating heart of Jansynian industry: the Corporate Crescent.

After us humans, the Jansynians probably had the highest population in Miroc—in the world—but you'd never know it by faces on the street. They kept to themselves, lived, worked, and played in their private, glassed-in and fenced-off complexes.

Mostly. As it turned out, I knew a great deal about the Jansynian city above because of one woman who had stepped down from the sky to be with me. Years ago, before everything fell apart. Our story was as old and worn as time. We'd been in love, but life had intervened.

And then the world had ended. So points for originality right there at the end. Still, a failing grade overall.

The Crescent was the one place in Miroc that hadn't changed since the Abandon and the subsequent collapse. It had always been its own world, a self-sufficient haven for those who belonged, an impenetrable fortress to those who didn't. The Crescent didn't seem to be suffering from any of the problems that plagued Miroc, but how would anyone know? I'd lived in this city all my life, and I'd spent three years intensely involved with a Jansynian woman, and I'd still never been any closer to the Crescent than this.

The city in the sky began a hundred stories above the street on which I walked. The outside was a shell of reflective, tinted glass, a sleek dome covering the Jansynian city that protected them both from the elements and any outsiders who might want in. A dozen different corporations each had their own enclave within, providing all the space their employees needed to work, live, and play. Most Jansynians were born in a corporate complex and never saw the need to leave. The Crescent had its own sources of food, water, and power. As Miroc starved and withered below, the Jansynians went on as they always had.

At no point had the Jansynians offered to share their bounty, but they at least had the good grace to ignore those who had taken refuge in what was quite literally their shadow.

Natives called it the Web. It had existed almost as long as the Crescent, but since the Abandon it had taken on a new life.

The city above was connected to the ground through one single, enormous lift. It was the umbilical cord through which all goods and all people moved back and forth between the Crescent and the freight yards on the ground. In between, a hundred stories of open air except for the spider's network of girders and cables that kept the city aloft and stable. Within these supports, in the Crescent's protective shade, a new arcology had sprung up. A tangled nest of canvas and plywood offered haven, if not safety, to a desperate community that grew larger every day.

As for the rest of this district, anything outside the protective shadow of the Crescent had already withered and died. Warehouses were useless when you had no goods to move and no way to get them anywhere. The only life, the only movement, was the line of traffic, like ants in a column, that travelled between the city and the Crescent receiving yard.

I crossed the street well before I reached the gates that opened onto Jansynian property. No reason to draw the attention of either the armed guards I could see, or the people watching through the cameras that kept a thorough surveillance on any space the

BARBARA J. WEBB

Jansynians claimed. I knew enough about how Jansynian security worked to know I didn't want to arouse the slightest suspicion I might be a problem.

Micah's instructions led me further down the decaying street and around a corner, to a long line of run-down warehouses. I spotted him at once, the only person in sight. He waved me over to join him.

And what a location he'd found. Even in this neighborhood of neglected, decaying warehouses, the one he'd parked himself in front of stood out.

Blowing sand had scoured away all but a few small patches of dull white paint. That same sand had formed rippling waves that ran up against the building on all sides. This close to the city edge, the desert was hungry. Broken windows hadn't been replaced or even boarded over, and one of the huge delivery doors along its side had broken off its hinges and gaped open at an angle.

"I'm so glad you came," he said.

"I wasn't given any choice."

A shadow passed over us and Micah flinched. He squinted up, no longer smiling. I followed his gaze, but it was only one of the bird priests wheeling in the air. By now, even I recognized the patterns of a rain prayer. "Let's go inside," Micah said. "Get out of the sun."

"Here? Really?"

He shaded his eyes and looked up again, but not at the bird priest. This time, his attention was focused on the inscrutable facade of the Crescent. "I'll explain inside."

The warehouse didn't look any better on the inside. The small windows at the top of the walls provided insufficient light for the space. Towering metal shelves stood empty—the ones that still stood—but cast even deeper shadows between. The sand had made its way inside and crunched under my feet as we walked. The air was stale and suffocatingly hot.

"Is this where you've been living?" I asked, horrified, despite myself.

"Oh no, not at all. But we wanted this meeting on neutral ground."

"Who's we? And why all the secrecy?"

"Copper will explain. But, please, Ash," Micah stopped, forcing me to stop with him. We faced each other in the gloom. "I know you're upset with me. I get that. But you're going to have to ease up. Copper, she's touchy. And about as thrilled to be taking this meeting as you are."

If this Copper woman didn't want the meeting and I didn't want the meeting, it seemed to me we could all just go home. "You came to me, remember? If you, or your people, don't want me here, I'm happy to leave."

Micah's tranquil facade cracked. "What's *wrong* with you? Why are you being like this? I thought you'd be happy to see me. I thought you'd be happy to help us."

"Happy?" I clung to enough professionalism not to raise my voice, but it was a struggle. "It's been a year, Micah. *A year* since the last time I saw another priest alive. To know you've been out there and never once tried—"

"Stop it," Micah hissed. "You don't get to be mad at me. Not for this. I'm not the one who just disappeared. All this time, I figured you were dead like everyone else, and then it turns out all along you've been working the sort of cushy job I didn't even know existed anymore? Do you know what I've been through? And you've just been—"

"It wasn't like that!" I was getting louder. I couldn't help myself. "I almost *died*, Micah. Six months in the hospital. Six months! By the time I got out, everyone was gone. The temple was gone. I couldn't find . . . " I couldn't go on. I didn't want to talk about this. Didn't want to think about it.

Micah's voice was flat as he spoke. "There wasn't anyone to find. You were lucky. Those last few months were a nightmare. Actors and librarians. That's all we were. How in the thirteen hells were we supposed to know how to disappear into the mean city streets? I wouldn't be here—I'll tell you that much—if it weren't for Copper. I owe her everything."

Actors and librarians. That much was true. Neither of us had been prepared for any of this. "What *is* this business? Why am I here?"

A sharp voice issued from above our heads. "Jansynians, Mr. Drake. That's what we're talking about. That's why you're here" I looked up, but couldn't make out more than a small shape on the shadowy catwalk above. "Stop wasting time chattering."

The shape retreated and I heard the sound of a door closing. I looked back at Micah, who stood contrite, the beginnings of a smile on his lips. Smiles had always come so damned easy to Micah. He pointed towards a spiral metal staircase that was only listing a little bit. "Can't keep Copper waiting. After you."

I hadn't been able to see it from the ground, but one of the offices had been rebuilt, with boards over the window and the door re-hung. Light peeked out under the doorway and as Micah opened the door, a wave of cool air greeted me.

Other than the lights and the air, this office wasn't in any better shape than the rest of the building. A skeletal desk had been pushed to the back corner, but that was the only furniture in the room. On the floor, surrounded by random bits of metal she was flattening with a mallet, sat the person who had to be Copper.

I'd seen pictures, videos, but I'd never met a Fyean up close. For the most part, they kept clear of Miroc, or any city with a strong Jansynian presence. I didn't know if there was a proper form of address or appropriate greeting, so I kept my mouth shut, waited for Micah to introduce me, and tried not to stare.

Copper was small. Not just short—although she couldn't have stood taller than four feet, if that. She was willowy, delicate, didn't look capable of the force with which she brought her hammer down on the metal sheet. She wore nothing more than a simple leather tunic and thick leather gloves. Her extra-jointed toes and elongated facial features made her look oddly stretched, like she'd been pulled out of taffy, and the waving pair of antennae that grew up from her hairline did nothing to dispel that image. Both her antennae and the sweeping points of her ears were topped with the burnished metal that was her namesake. It shone against her pale gray skin.

"Ash, meet Copper."

She yanked off a glove, and extended a hand to me without standing up. Her skin felt smooth and rubbery as we shook. Fyeans didn't have exoskeletons or wings and feathers, but they were still on the far side of the human-like scale. And like the birds and the boneheads, Fyeans had mostly kept to themselves before the Abandon broke the world.

I got right to the point. "What can Price & Breckenridge do for you?"

The slight nod of her head indicated approval for my directness. She held out her hand, inviting me to sit. Which I did, dropping down to a comfortable cross-legged position on the cool metal floor.

The hard look in Copper's orblike green eyes was at odds with her childlike stature. "Before we get into that, you need to know that you're only here because Micah vouched for you. I don't like this, bringing in outsiders. Your firm has a good reputation, and Micah swears that I can trust you."

She leaned forward, her voice low and intense. "You'll forgive me a blunt question, Mr. Drake, but how much is your integrity worth? To you or your firm? Because if your loyalty has a selling price, I need to know."

"Copper!" Micah was outraged on my behalf, but I understood exactly what she was asking—and why. Since she'd brought up the Jansynians, I understood a lot of things.

Trouble was, while I wasn't offended by her question, I wasn't sure I had an answer. "I haven't been with Price & Breckenridge long. I'd like to reassure you they can't be bought, but I don't know that. Not really." It was my turn to lean forward, matching her posture as I held her gaze. "But I can tell you that I know the Jansynians. I know what they have to offer and I'm not interested, and I don't see how Amelia would be either."

Copper picked up her mallet, but she didn't set back to work, only twisted her fists around the handle. "Yes, Micah told me about your knowledge of the Jansynians. It's why I agreed to this meeting. Why I'm willing to consider working with you people. But there's only so far I'm willing to take you at your word."

Copper bowed her head, closed her eyes, still clutching the mallet. Had she also been a priest? All I knew about Fyea's church was that their symbol had been a hammer. The moment stretched on until she seemed to reach some sort of decision and opened her clear green eyes.

"Somewhere in this warehouse there's a spy-bug hidden. Jansynian make. If you can find it and bring it back to me, you're hired."

What Copper wanted, she had no right to ask. She had no business expecting I could actually perform the task she'd set me to.

Except that Micah had undoubtedly told her everything.

Jansynians guarded their technology closer than they did their children. Your average joker on the street has maybe seen one of their hovercars or the sleek black energy guns their people carry in public, but *only* at a distance and never close enough to touch.

I was the exception to the rule because I'd dated Seana. She'd been not just a Jansynian, but a Jansynian security specialist. I got a crash course in the cutthroat dynamics of Jansynian competition. Seana belonged to Arisia, one of the smaller corporations here in the Crescent, but being small didn't make you any less of a threat to the bigger businesses.

Which meant people wanted to spy on her. Especially given the fact she was spending her time with an outsider. She had her own ways of dealing with threats, but she taught me what to look for, for the times she wasn't there. And because I'd been young and unable to resist showing off, I'd bragged to my friends about the secrets she'd shared.

It never got me into the trouble it probably should have. And now it was working in my favor. Too bad it took the end of the world to find a use for this skill.

Seven years ago, fresh off my breakup with Seana, I could have put on a show. Back when I was in practice, I could have stood in Copper's office, made a couple dramatic waves of my hand and not only located the spyware at a distance, but brought it winging back without ever having to break eye contact.

I wasn't that man anymore.

Look, magic is dangerous. It's change. It's chaos. We try to control it, confine it, limit it, but it's not like the laws of physics take a holiday just because we're wielding cosmic forces. And I was *really* out of practice. And in a piss-poor emotional state for the focus I would need to safely pull off any fancy effects. Other than a couple minor effects—like that push in the subway—I wasn't confident of anything. So I didn't try to show off. Didn't try to shortcut. I nodded acquiescence to Copper's request and eased my way back down the wobbly spiral staircase to the warehouse floor.

I can't deny a part of me was tempted to just keep walking. Right out the door.

What kept me here wasn't obligation. This wasn't about keeping my job or anything I did or didn't owe to Micah. Kaifail help me, I was curious. Which pissed me off something fierce. Curiosity was not a survival trait. Curiosity belonged to the Ash who spent his time chasing mysteries in antique documents and arguing the points of magic theory so specialized that even other priests of Dark Kaifail would roll their eyes and call me a geek.

Amelia had flinched at mention of the city council, and now something was going on that involved the Jansynians in the Crescent above, and my traitor brain *really* wanted to know how all this tied together.

I pulled my NetPad out of the wide pocket on the inside of my robe. It lit up, too bright in the gloom. I blinked and opened a simple drawing program. I hadn't touched it in months. Not since I'd tried to banish some cockroaches and accidentally exploded them. That had been when I recognized I wasn't fully in control of myself, and I hadn't dared touch the stuff since.

Now I had no choice. And, okay, it was kind of nice to be back to it.

Jansynian spy tech was practically magic in and of itself. Pinpoint lenses, flexible circuits, and a built-in camouflage made devices virtually invisible. They self-shielded so you couldn't find them by the power they ran on. And they broadcast on a wave that, so far, no outsider had been able to crack.

Not that anyone was trying very hard. Human companies that invested obvious time and talent into reverse engineering Jansynian tech met with bad ends.

I sketched a couple quick symbols. Focus. Clarity. Vision. A warm-up more than anything, but it helped me relax. A familiar calm descended. The only safe mindset in which to work.

It had been years since I cast this pattern, but the shape of it settled into my mind like an old friend. I cleared the NetPad screen and started a new drawing. An eye. Instead of a pupil, I drew the symbol for vision. I stared at it, locked my focus until everything around me faded away. I felt the familiar twist in my mind, the tingle of energy that meant the magic had snapped into place.

I slid my NetPad back into its pocket and wandered slowly through the warehouse. I didn't know what I was looking for, how strong the signal would be. Better to be careful than to try to impress Copper with my speed.

And there it was. A soft blue glow coming from one of the sagging metal shelves. Thankfully low enough I didn't have to worry about finding a safe way to climb. I felt around in what was roughly the center of the glow until my fingers slid over a slick spot beneath the shelf. I peeled off a thin, clear tab no bigger around than my thumb.

How did Copper get this in the first place? Fyeans had no magic. How had Copper found this and—I hoped—rendered it safe?

I took my prize back upstairs and dropped it in Copper's hand. "Nicely done, Drake," she said.

Micah winked at me. "What did I tell you, Copper? Ash is our guy."

But Copper still wasn't convinced. I could see it in her eyes. And I was tired. "Either you want Price & Breckenridge or you don't. Whichever it is, I'm done jumping through hoops.

"You have to understand." Micah's words were slow and cautious. "You *will* understand. This isn't a simple job. There are forces at work here—"

"Jansynians, yes, I got that. And I have to say, if you want us to follow one of them around or break into the Crescent, that isn't going to happen." I didn't even have to check with Amelia to know that was true.

"We don't need you to spy on them," Copper said with a sneer. "Who do you think reprogrammed their little bug? If I need information on the Jansynians, I can take care of that myself."

I took a deep breath, let it out. I would not yell at a client. Amelia would consider that unprofessional. "Then why am I here?"

"Because my sister is in danger. They're after her."

Which didn't answer my question, only brought up new ones. "Who's after her?"

"As to who—" Copper shook her head, her whole demeanor softer since mentioning her sister. "We haven't seen any directly. Just found the spy devices and—" she stopped, chewing at her lip, looked over at Micah who nodded encouragement. "They've made two attempts so far. An incendiary device and a bomb."

Two attempts. "And you found them before they went off?"

Copper rolled her eyes. "Of course we did. Just who do you think you're dealing with?"

I realized I had no idea. "So why come to us?"

"Because it's a distraction. And because, while we can probably keep ahead of them, all it takes is one mistake and," she mimed an explosion with her hands. "Better if we can make the attempts stop. Better if Spark doesn't have to worry."

I understood Copper's initial edginess better. I wouldn't expect a good mood out of anyone hunted by Jansynians. But I still didn't understand what I was doing here. "This sounds way outside P&B's area of expertise. If your sister needed a lawyer, maybe, but . . . " I trailed off at Copper's wide-eyed look of confusion.

"Just take the request back to your employer," she said, still looking at me oddly.

Obviously I'd missed something. Maybe a lot. "I'll do that, but Amelia's going to have questions." I assumed. "Like why are the Jansynians after your sister?"

CITY OF BURNING SHADOWS

She sighed. "I guess you'll have to know. There's a project—one they *think* they have ownership of. But really it belongs to my sister. And she won't let it go, won't let them just have it."

I hadn't met Copper's sister yet, but already I had a lot of respect for her. Even if I doubted her survival instincts. "Brave of her. Is it something big?"

"It's huge," Micah said, leaning forward in his eagerness. "It's everything. It's salvation."

"Salvation from what?"

Copper pointed up. "Salvation from everything, Mr. Drake. If my sister has the time and the resources, she'll be able to save the city."

Copper's bright green eyes held mine. "She'll be able to make it rain."

— 4 —

Shadows and Lies

Fyea was the goddess of creativity, of inspiration, of genius. As such, she was one of the few of the Thirteen who had a sizable following outside her own church. Even I'd prayed for her help a time or two, on projects where I'd hit an unsurpassable wall and I needed some jolt of insight to point me in the right direction. Did she help me? Hard to say. But I always found my way through the problems eventually.

Her best help, her real power, she saved for her own children. The things Fyeans could do with circuits and wires and chips were better than magic. So when Copper said her sister had found a way to make it rain, I believed her.

Trouble was, I couldn't see any way to help her. Even if P&B offered a wider range of services than I'd realized, the idea of trying to outmaneuver the Jansynians lay somewhere in between stupidity and suicide. I spent the whole train ride back worrying at the problem, but no matter how I twisted and turned the problem in my head, I couldn't see a way past the simple truth that with the Jansynians involved, we were completely over our heads.

Back at the office, I found Amelia in the library, balanced halfway up a ladder with three open books in her hands. The only person in, until I noticed the ginger tabby-cat that could only be Iris sprawled on a chair. They both looked up as I came through the door.

"So?" Amelia asked.

"So." I snagged an empty chair and resisted the urge to scratch Iris behind her fuzzy ears. "It's complicated."

"I'm not a fan of complicated." Pressing the books against her with one hand, she climbed down the ladder. "Tell me."

"Micah's boss is a Fyean, Copper, who wants to hire us to protect her sister, Spark." I stopped there, watching for Amelia's reaction.

Which was a simple nod. "Go on."

So that *was* something we did. But it certainly wasn't announced on the door. How did Copper and Micah know? And what other unadvertised services did we provide?

I pushed that thought to the back of my mind and went on with the information Copper had given me. "Copper's got a kid who runs errands. And spies for her. He'd been keeping an eye on the city council. He's seen Vivian there, and traced her back to us. Copper believes we share a common problem, and that problem comes out of the Corporate Crescent."

Iris shifted back to her human-looking self, talking before her body had fully formed. "Jansynians, Amelia! That would explain—"

Amelia lifted her hand, shushing Iris. "What else?" she asked me.

"Spark has a technology she's developed. Something the Jansynians are after. She tried to take it to the city council. It was after that—" I leaned forward. "Amelia, has Price & Breckenridge been investigating the death of the personal aide of one of the city councilors?"

"Copper knew about that?" Iris asked.

"Yeah. Copper thinks it was a threat from the Jansynians. She says after that, the councilor she'd been working with wouldn't talk to her any more about city support for Spark's work."

Amelia nodded. "We suspected it was a threat from someone. Iris had been following leads among Miroc's Children."

I knew about that group. Everyone in the city did. They were the most vocal groups of protesters demanding the city council release more of Miroc's stored water. They'd grown exponentially in the last few months, and I wasn't the only one who expected them to turn violent at any moment.

"What are they after?" Iris asked. "What's Spark got that they want?"

"She thinks she can make it rain."

Silence from both women. Amelia stood, thoughtful, and the moment stretched out. I could practically see the gears turning in her head.

So could Iris. "You can't be considering this."

"What are your thoughts, Ash?"

I'd told Micah I was done with crusades. But I guess that was just another lie. Kaifail would have been proud of me. "The logistics alone would be a nightmare. We couldn't do anything over the net. No computers. No conversations over wireless. Nothing. We'd have to be on constant alert for spy devices, and there's no guarantee that what Seana taught me seven years ago is still valid enough to catch everything. If they find us, they'll kill us. There won't be any room for error."

Iris was nodding along, but she wasn't going to like the rest of what I had to say. "On the other hand, it isn't like the Jansynians are a unified body. If we can figure out which corporation is hunting Spark, we might be able to reach out to their competition and level the playing field. They're smart, but they're predictable. Even inflexible. If we're quick on our feet, we might be able to stay ahead of them. So . . . we could do this. Maybe."

"Oh, well, if Ash says *maybe*, that's enough for me."

"Shush," Amelia said absently. She set the books she'd still been holding on a table and rested a hand on top of them, tapping her fingers as she thought. "If it were anyone but Fyeans claiming they could make it rain . . . "

"Oh come on." Iris's entire body flushed red, from skin to hair to clothes. An angry color, but I suspected that anger was driven by fear. Kaifail knew I couldn't deny the uneasiness in my own stomach. "Jansynians, Amelia."

Amelia went to her, took her hand. "If you want out of this one, I'll understand. But if there's even a chance we can get the water back, I can't ignore that."

Iris jerked her hand away and stormed from the room. "Iris—" I started, but Amelia cut me off.

"She'll be fine. She just needs time to get used to this." Amelia returned to her books, settling in for what looked like some serious research. History books, of all things. "Our first order of business is to get Spark someplace hidden. You'll work with Iris on the safehouse. We have a few that we use, scouted by field agents, in locations known *only* to the agents who work with them. I'll want you to do an initial inspection and then keep in close touch to make sure the house stays clean. Which means both you and Iris will know where it is, but you'll be the only two."

I nodded, swallowing against my nerves.

"You're going to be central to the security on this job. You up for it?"

I hoped so. I nodded again.

"I want Spark safe in our custody tonight. Once that's accomplished, we can figure out what to do about the people hunting her."

Amelia took her books and left me there, alone with my worries. I headed back towards my office.

There was one thing I could do while I waited for Iris to calm down and figure out the plan for tonight—one avenue of investigation I could start down without digging any deeper into Spark's past. One person I could contact who might be able to shed some light on this situation.

Someone I hadn't spoken to in seven years. Who had walked out of my life without a single look back. After all this time, you'd think I'd be over it. But in a lot of ways, it hurt worse now than it had seven years ago.

Seven years ago, the rest of my life had still been around to keep me distracted.

I pulled out my NetPad and tapped out the message to Seana. I went through several drafts before I had something I was comfortable with. I was asking a big favor. I was presuming on a relationship that didn't exist anymore. And sentimentalism wasn't a weakness that had ever been ascribed to Jansynians.

I settled on simple and honest.

Seana,

We need to talk. Can we meet? A friend is in danger and you may be able to help.

Ash

Turned out, I needn't have bothered. As soon as I sent the message, I got an error. SEANA ARISIA HAS NO ADDRESS IN THIS SYSTEM. PLEASE TRY AGAIN.

I did try again. Just to be sure. And got the same response.

Which gave me a whole new nest of worries. Where was she? What had happened? Had she left Miroc before everything collapsed? Had she—gods forbid—gotten caught in the riots somehow? Was she dead?

It was just one more loss on top of the rest. One more person I'd never see again. Factored on top of everything else, it was nothing.

I couldn't let myself get distracted. Not now. Not with what was undoubtedly a long night ahead of me.

All the same, it was a long time before I could move past this new shock and concentrate on the immediate problems at hand.

One nice thing about Iris—she never stayed grumpy for long. She never stayed anything for long. By the time we were ready to head out, she was back to her bouncy, colorful self.

Miroc woke up at sundown. Even before the Abandon, no one with any sense tried to do business under the sweltering afternoon sun. Twilight conjured the living city.

Such as it still was.

Green wasn't the only color my city had lost. Our man-made oasis in the middle of the desert had grown up around the intersection of three intercontinental tube lines and two overland trade roads. Despite our dangerous reputation—or perhaps, because of it—the streets of Miroc had thrived.

The transient traders had set the stage—giants in their rainbow finery; bird-folk and their vibrant displays; even the desert-trolls covered in rich, flowing earth-tones—each tent and stall flashier than the next, vying for the attention of the tourists.

And oh, the tourists. Gods bless them all. From the herds of the well-bred wealthy, clinging to the idea of safety in numbers, to the smaller packs of youths looking for danger and excitement. Be they human, Jansynian, or any other child of the Thirteen, downtown Miroc always brought the same look of awe to their faces.

Not that we had tourists anymore. After the disaster in Tala, tubes all over the world had shut down. Sure, people could fight their way through the desert on the overland routes, but why would they? Trade had dried up with the rains. Like everything else in this city, our world-renowned markets had crumbled in the heat and blown back into the desert.

This wasn't to say the streets were empty, just that the color and life had drained away. Desperate men and women, driven from their homes and storefronts by skyrocketing utility costs, hawked overpriced and dwindling goods to people who could no longer afford them. They called after Iris and me—our clothes were clean and neither of us looked water-starved—but even if that put us among the most privileged in the city, it didn't mean we had any money.

It was all such crap. "This is what the gods left us. These people, this city. What are any of them supposed to do?"

Iris didn't even blink at my comment out of nowhere. It was another nice thing about her. "This city is angry. The whole world is angry. It's just in some places, they have the hope of survival to distract them. Here, the only choices they have are ones that will just make them die faster."

And that was the problem, wasn't it? "Everyone sitting around and waiting for . . . what? For the gods to reappear as suddenly as they went away? For them to swoop back in and save us?"

"Any day now, I'm sure." Iris's voice was as rough with anger as my own. "Might as well wait for the desert sand to turn to water."

"We tried that, you know?"

Iris's eyebrows shot up and speckles of red and orange rippled over her skin. She still had some work to do before she could flawlessly pass as human. "You tried to turn the desert to water?"

"Before the worst of the riots. Before so many priests died. We thought—maybe if we all worked together. . . . "

Iris was a creature for whom magic was as natural as breathing, and even she was shocked by the idea. "Can you really—obviously you didn't—but could you have?"

"The scale was too enormous. The amount of water we would have needed to make a difference—the magnitude of the transformation. The definitions, the limitations—even if we could have worked out the math, created the right ritual, it would have taken far too many trained gifted to pull it off. By the time we had even an inkling of what we needed, well, it wasn't an option anymore. The temple leaders were dead and the rest of us were hiding."

"Humans," Iris grumbled. "You're all crazy. You, Amelia, all of you."

So she was still a little upset about the Jansynian business. "What choice do we have? We're stuck here. It's not like the rest of us can turn into birds and just fly away."

Iris sighed and her thick magenta hair paled and drooped. "And so I'm stuck here too. I can't leave her, Ash. Especially not to this."

Shifters weren't known for their long-term involvements. They weren't known for their long-term anything. And maybe if they'd met before the world collapsed, Iris's relationship with Amelia would have been an intense fling, burning bright for a time, then fading. But none of us were the people we used to be.

Unfortunately, I couldn't think of anything to say that would cheer Iris up. Nothing that wouldn't be a lie.

As night fell in earnest, the downtown streets became even more haggard looking. Shadows intruded in the gaps between buildings, in vacant windows and doorways. What had once been a prismatic sea of light was, like everything else, fractured and dying.

As we reached a corner that had managed to retain its working streetlights, Iris put a hand on my arm. "Wait here. One of Amelia's contacts lives right down that alley, but if he sees you with me, he'll spook."

I obediently planted myself next to a wall, under the light, and waited.

I didn't notice the man standing next to me until he spoke. "Tell me what brings a priest of Kaifail to this part of downtown."

That got my attention. I reached for my collar, but it was closed and in place. He couldn't have seen my tattoo. "Not a priest anymore, friend."

He wasn't a Jansynian. Human, but with skin that fair, he wasn't from around here. He was dressed all in black, expensively tailored, but death in the afternoon sun. "You avoid my question."

"Not sure that it's any of your business."

He smiled. Not charming, exactly, but something in it was trustworthy. "I *am* your friend, Joshua Drake. And I need to know."

Of course he was my friend. "We're scoping out a safehouse for a client. Jansynians are hunting her."

"Are they?" He leaned in closer. I couldn't look away from his deep blue eyes. "Have you seen these Jansynians? The ones who attacked your client?"

"No," I whispered, overwhelmed with disappointment I couldn't help this man. I wanted so badly to be of use.

"Ash!" Iris's voice.

I blinked and looked around. Iris was next to me, frowning. I'd been . . . how long had I been waiting? "What did you find out?" The question came out brusquer than I meant as I tried to cover the fact I'd drifted off.

"Who was that?" she asked, irritable again.

"Who was what?" I looked around.

She took me by the shoulders, pointed me towards the other side of the street. "Him!"

I still didn't know what she was talking about. "Iris, you're going to have to—"

She pointed, and only then did I pick out the man staring back at us. Human, but dressed all in black and pale—he wasn't from around here. Weird that I hadn't noticed him before; it wasn't like he blended with the crowd. "Who's that?" she asked again.

"How should I know?" Now I was getting irritated.

"It looked like you were talking to him," Iris said. "But, whatever. Let's go. The faster we get this night over with, the better."

As we headed out of the crowded downtown and into darker, less-travelled parts of the city, Iris shifted once more—this time, to an imposing, unkempt giantess. I envied the ease with which she did it, wishing I could learn the same trick.

If you want to be technical about it, magic is magic—whether it's Iris changing her shape or me doing what I do. The thing is, for Iris's people, it's something they're born with—part of who they are. Drinion wasn't just the god *of* magic—Drinion *was* magic. The very essence of change. And Iris's people are Drinion's children—or were, before it became dangerous to speak the names of the gods.

Kaifail stole the secrets of magic and passed them on to his children—us—but it's not in our blood the way it is for the shifters. If I were to try to do what Iris does. . . .

Matter destroyed still wants to become energy, and if you don't surround that act with the right controls and modifiers, you're going to get one ugly mother of a bang.

That's most of what those of us who have the aptitude for it learn in school. That's where the rituals help—codified limitations you don't have to hold in your mind. I couldn't wrap my head around the complexities of what Iris did every time she made herself different; I couldn't imagine what it must be like to be able to do that purely by instinct.

On the other hand, Iris couldn't do my kind of magic either. She simply didn't understand it. So it all balanced out. I guess. Except that her skills seemed a thousand times more practical and useful than mine.

Iris led us into one of the rougher parts of downtown. My heartbeat pounded and it got harder to breathe. Streetworn toughs, human and otherwise, lurked in the shadows and watched us as we passed. Either they weren't hungry for prey or Iris looked like more than they could handle. They left us alone. I kept a hand bundled in the fabric of my robe right at the neck, holding it closed. If Iris noticed, she didn't say anything.

Our luck held until we reached a particularly seedy looking apartment complex and Iris stopped. There was just enough ambient light for me to make out the splashes of graffiti on the walls of the building and the muzzle of a gun poking out through a gap in one of the boarded windows. Iris rippled and shrunk back down to my size, but with a different face than she'd worn when we left our building. Her whole body was lean, harder-looking than I was used to from Iris.

From the shadowed doorway, a man's voice called out, "Hey baby, you lookin' for some fun?"

"Shut up, Vik." Iris walked boldly up to the crumbling concrete porch. I followed, unable to look away from the gun pointed at us.

"Who's your friend?" Vik asked as he stepped into the light. Bald, burly, and carrying his own very large gun, Vik was not a man I wanted to be on the wrong side of.

"Viktor, this is Ash. Ash, Viktor. It's okay, Vik, he's with me."

Yet another surprise in a day full of them. I would never have imagined Iris knew people like this, much less worked with them. I smiled as best I could.

Vik's grin was predatory. "Your boy's nervous."

Iris stepped forward, somehow managing to loom over a man with twice her mass. "Stop screwing around. Ash needs to sweep the place."

"For what?" Vik slung his gun back over his shoulder and crossed his meaty arms. "Our security's been good enough for Price before. What, she thinks we're fucking up all of a sudden?"

"It's different this time. And I can explain. But only after Ash has done his thing."

Vik glared, but he stepped aside and let me through. I was glad Iris kept close. Especially as we moved through the hall and past a room with three more men like Vik.

Maybe I had been naive. It was no secret the influence the criminal element had in Miroc. The city's bad reputation was one hundred percent earned. Even back when we priests had real authority, this city was nothing like Tala, where the gods and the churches kept folks safe. Miroc was the place where dangerous people came to disappear, where criminal enterprises could count their money undisturbed, where back-alley deals didn't have to take place in back alleys.

The Ellsworths, the Ramiydhs, the Cuandos, the criminal families had as much influence over the city as the council did. So it shouldn't have been a surprise that to get things done, Amelia—via Iris—also worked through some questionable contacts. "Amelia trusts these people?" I whispered.

Iris turned to me and rippled through several different faces, settling back on the lean, hard visage these people knew. "Judging by appearances?"

Chastened, I said, "I just hope she knows what she's doing."

"Me too." By her flat look, I knew Iris was talking about me.

The apartment building wasn't large. Six two-bedroom units, all had seen better days. Four showed signs of occupation—by the men I'd seen here, I imagined. The fifth was storage. Guns and barrels of water and smaller bags of—I didn't want to know.

The sixth apartment was obviously our safehouse. It didn't have much in the way of furniture—a bed in each bedroom and a table with mismatched chairs in the front—but it was clean and secure-looking, with a new lock on the door and thick metal shutters over the windows.

I went over the whole building the same way I'd scanned the warehouse. The other men watched me as I moved through their space, but Iris's presence kept them from interrupting. I was as thorough as I could be. If this job went bad, it wasn't going to be because of me. It took an hour before I was willing to declare the complex safe.

Iris called all the men together—six of them including Vik—and explained the situation. They weren't any more thrilled at the mention of Jansynians than Iris had been.

"Amelia wants to move Spark in here tonight," Iris said over the grumbling. "Can you be ready?"

"Ready, sure, we're always ready," Vik answered. "And we know our business. But what kind of opposition are we looking at? We're not exactly specced to be holding off a full tactical team here. Especially one armed with Jansynian weaponry."

"Do your job right and it won't come to that. If they can't find you, they can't hit you."

That evoked more grumbling, but Vik said, "We'll do our part, so long as Price does hers."

Iris nodded and left without another word. I scurried to follow.

We had to go all the way back to the office to check in. Every tiny spark of communication in this city ran through the Jansynians' net. We couldn't take the risk they might be listening.

Amelia wasn't alone in her office. Josiah and Vivian—two more of P&B's "investigators"—waited with her. Both of them were visibly armed. I was starting to wonder if everyone in the firm was more than advertised. And were they thinking similar thoughts about me?

"Good, you're back," Amelia said to Iris and me. "I've been in contact with Micah and made the handoff arrangements."

She woke up the wall with a touch. It was set on a map of the city. "You'll be picking Spark up at the same location you went to this morning."

Josiah squinted at the spot Amelia pointed out. "Right under the Crescent? I thought we were trying to avoid Jansynian attention."

"Spark's already there," Amelia said, "and I trust our ability to move her safely better than I like the idea of her trying to get out on her own. Ash, since you're their point of contact, you'll be in the car with Josiah and Vivian. Iris will be in the air with an eye on the landscape."

Vivian stepped up to the screen, smoothly taking over. "Once we're certain we got away clean, we'll rendezvous with Iris *here*," she tapped a point on the map that was a couple neighborhoods away from the safehouse. "We'll ditch Ash and the client and then continue to drive around for a while, in case we missed any kind of tail. Ash and Iris will escort the client to the safehouse, tuck her in for the night, and we'll all celebrate a job well done."

"Any questions?" Amelia asked.

"Lots," I said.

Vivian took me by the arm. "We can talk in the car," she said. "Let's go get things moving."

The car was a hire and while it was necessary, I shuddered to think of what it cost. Not for the car itself, but the fuel. Given it had been four months since Miroc had received an outside delivery, driving had become prohibitively expensive. But what choice did we have? It wasn't like we could keep a Fyean hidden as we took the tube across town.

"This'll be easy," Vivian said as she settled into the huge back seat with me. Hire cars had to be spacious enough to accommodate the larger races. Anything short of a giant would be comfortable back here. Through the window, I saw Iris jump up and shift in the air. A falcon flew up into the night sky.

Josiah drove while Vivian talked. "Seriously, Ash, just relax. We've done this plenty of times before."

"Have we?"

Vivian grinned and elbowed me. "Welcome to the pro circuit."

I checked out the window, but if Iris was there, I couldn't spot her in the dark. "I'm not the only one uptight."

Vivian shrugged. As she talked, she pulled her two pistols from the harness she wore under her jacket and checked their load. "Iris'll settle down once we've got Spark to safety. That's when everything gets easier."

From where I sat, that was the point at which our real problems would begin. "It's not like we'll be sending them a memo that Spark's out of reach. They'll still be looking for her."

"Amelia's got plans," Josiah said.

Vivian patted my knee. "Focus on what's in front of you. Smooth handoff. Spark to the safehouse, and then we all get to go home. Worry about the rest when it happens."

She made it sound so easy, but as I leaned back in my seat and listened to Vivian explain the handoff process, I couldn't keep from staring out my window at the glowing dome of the Crescent growing larger and larger, like a monster waiting to swallow us.

—5—

Chased

Josiah turned off the car's lights as we reached the warehouse's street. He sat at the intersection longer than was necessary, letting our eyes adjust, then moved forward at a casual pace. As we got close, I noticed one of the side freight doors was open and a makeshift ramp had been set up. Josiah eased the car up and through the open door into blackness.

The door slammed shut behind us and sudden lights blinded us. I lifted my arm to shield my face, but Vivian tugged on my elbow. "Let them see you."

The lights faded to a reasonable level and I saw Micah in front of our car. Standing next to him, a lizard with a gun he was just lowering. I got out, followed by Josiah and Vivian.

Micah waved me over. Tonight, he was calm and polite, no trace of the anger that had sparked between us this morning. "Is everything in place? Are we good?"

If he could be businesslike, so could I. "We're ready if you are."

"Great. Vogg, I want you to meet Ash. Ash, this is—"

The lizard bowed, touching his clawed fingers to the horns atop his head. "I am Vogg Asad'Korel, Sentry of Miroc, Warrior of the Fourth Circle. It is an honor to serve you, Priest Ash of Kaifail."

"Just Ash is fine, really." I lifted my eyebrows at Micah.

"Vogg is Spark's bodyguard. He'll be coming with you."

I looked back at Vivian. This hadn't been in the plan, but she nodded. "Welcome aboard, Vogg. Let's get moving."

Micah and I went up to the office where Copper waited with a second Fyean who had to be Spark. They sat together on the floor, bickering as only sisters could over the wiring of a circuit board that lay between them. Copper still wore the plain leathers she'd had on earlier, but Spark was dressed in a long desert tunic of bright sunset hues and the wire wraps atop her antennae were a dark silvery metal.

After introducing us, Spark took her sister's hand. "You sure you won't come?"

"They're not after me." She leaned forward, pressed her forehead against Spark's. Their antennae brushed, then Copper pulled back and pushed her sister at me. "Keep her safe, Mr. Drake."

As we walked, I couldn't keep from stealing sideways glances at Spark. She caught me at it and smiled. "You're not used to being around my kind?"

"No," I admitted. "I've never been out of Miroc, and as far as I can tell, this isn't a popular city for you Fyeans to visit."

"It's true." Spark's huge eyes were a few shades lighter than her sister's, soft jade rather than brilliant emerald, and they glinted with a cheer at odds with Copper's stern demeanor. "Even Copper and I never meant to be here."

"What happened? If you can tell me."

"It's no secret." She sighed. "We were trying to get out of Tala. Took the tubes. This was just meant to be a stopover. As long as we were passing through—I had a couple friends at the university. Researchers I'd corresponded with over the years.

"Turns out, we were right to get out of Tala, but wrong to have delayed. We were still here when those *things* invaded and the tube system got shut down."

Shut down was putting it mildly. Every city and town with the resources to do it had collapsed any tunnel that led outside their boundaries. No one wanted the infestation that had destroyed the gods' own city to spread. That was when we'd lost our communication with the outside as well. The cables that connected us had been in those tunnels too.

"I'm sorry," I said.

"No need to apologize. Our story isn't any sadder than others, and better than most."

"Except for the part about the Jansynians hunting you," I pointed out.

"And you're going to fix that for us, so everything's fine," Spark answered cheerily.

We reached the car, where Vivian waited with the door held open. "Glad to have you with us, Spark. Step inside and we'll have you to your hidey-hole in a few."

Spark and I got in the back. Vogg entered last, carefully tucking his tail away from the door. Vivian joined Josiah in the front. Micah caught my eye and gave me a sincere "Good luck," as he closed us in.

The warehouse outer door opened. Josiah backed us out and we were on the street again. Step one accomplished. Now for the rest.

We had no choice but to drive under the Crescent to get back to our own side of town. I'll confess—every one of us in the car looked up and held our breath as we did so.

I couldn't bear the tense silence. "Why?" I asked Spark. "Why are they after you?"

"Because they are thieves," Vogg's deep voice rumbled.

Spark shook her head, making her antennae wave. "It's not like that. Not this time."

"This time?" Vivian turned around in her seat. "You've dealt with them before?"

Spark pursed her thin lips and looked away. "It's the way of things. It's how our lives have always been. The simple truth is there's no such thing as Jansynian innovation. They are as their god made them: brilliant, but lacking any true creativity. They hate my people for being the creators they can never be.

"And normally it doesn't matter." She addressed the words to Vogg, sincerity in her voice. "It *really* doesn't matter. There are more of them, and they're everywhere, and they have so much money and so many resources—it makes better sense for them to take our ideas and figure out how to distribute them. Manufacture, finance," Spark rolled her eyes. "Boring. There's not a one of my people who wants to spend their life worrying about those things. And it frees us up to move on to the next idea, which is never a hardship."

She twisted around in her seat to look at the glittering lights of the Crescent, now shrinking behind us. "Except this time, it wasn't a game. This time, we couldn't afford to wait the usual time it takes for things to go through the Jansynian research and development process."

Vogg crossed his arms, disapproving, which had the result of digging one of his elbow spikes into my ribs. It hurt. He didn't seem to notice. I squeezed a little closer to Spark. "Copper said you could make it rain."

That got Vivian and Josiah's attention. I guess Amelia hadn't filled them in on the details. Josiah looked around, although he quickly returned his focus to the road. Vivian straight-out stared. Spark squirmed under everyone's gaze. "I'd had the idea early, not long after we got stuck here. I'd worked out the math and drawn some designs. And at first, right after they stole it, I thought maybe it was for the best. It's not like Copper and I had the resources to build an orbital network."

"A what?" Vivian asked.

Spark brightened even more at the chance to talk about her idea. "It occurred to me—and I can't be the only one—but after the Abandon, well, there's all this sky. Sure, we couldn't do anything with it *before*, but Ouliria's gone. If she won't make it rain anymore, then she probably won't be swatting things out of the sky anymore either. There's a lot we could do from above that we could never manage from below. And one of those things . . . " she paused and flashed us a wide grin. "I think we could make it rain."

Vivian had turned all the way around, sitting on her knees in the front, although it was too dark to make out her face. "And they stole that from you. The way to make it rain?"

"Yes. And at first it was fine. They were working on it. It's not like you can hide tests when you have to launch them into space. It looked like they were moving forward as fast as I could hope. And why not? They're not as desperate as the rest of the city, but it isn't in their best interest to watch Miroc wither away to nothing.

"Except time passed and nothing happened. I knew they had the satellites up there, but they weren't moving forward anymore. I couldn't exactly ask them what happened, so Copper and I decided to go a different route. We took the plans for the system to the city council."

Vivian started at mention of the city council. In the dark, I almost didn't see it. And I had no idea what caused it. But I knew better than to ask in front of clients.

"That was when the trouble started," Spark continued. "When the Jansynians came after me. They must have found out, and didn't want the competition."

"We know they have spies on the city council," Vivian said. Which was news to me. Although hardly shocking.

Spark didn't seem surprised either. "I didn't think it would matter. They never used to attack us like that."

A lot of things in this world never used to happen. But now the referees were absent, the watchful parents who made sure all their children played nice.

Or mostly nice. History held plenty of conflict—from small territorial disputes to all-out wars, but while a number of those had resolved themselves naturally, just as many had ended with the direct intervention of one of the Thirteen. And numerous others had never begun because one church or another had simply forbidden it.

The Abandon had broken the world, and now who was going to save it? After people had risen up against the churches, after the madness and fear that led to the riots had spent, had any new leadership stepped in? Had anyone tried to rebuild?

Not here in Miroc. Maybe not anywhere. We were all still waiting, hoping we'd wake up one morning and everything would be back the way it had been.

Vivian had fallen silent and I looked up to see her staring out the back window, frowning. "Jo. . . . "

"Yeah, I know."

I craned my head around, but couldn't see anything wrong in the street behind us. "What's wrong?"

"We're being followed."

I heard the click of Vivian readying her gun. "What do you think?"

"They're faster and better armed than us." Josiah sounded remarkably calm. I twisted around in my seat and caught sight of the Jansynian hovercar skirting the shadows behind us. Stalking us, waiting for the moment to move in.

Vivian had also taken on a cool focus. "Around the next corner, slow down enough I can jump out. I'll get their attention, try to catch them in a crossfire."

"Is that a good idea?" I asked. She'd be exposed, vulnerable.

"Not really," Vivian said, "but our options are pretty much violence or violence. And better if they're shooting at me than the car."

It sounded like suicide to me, but what better solution could I offer? I'm not Iris. Complex magic on the fly is beyond me, too dangerous to contemplate. So what could I do that was simple?

"Vivian, wait. I've got a better plan."

I twisted around in my seat. "I need a good look at them, and we'll need to be going faster."

Josiah didn't hesitate. He yanked on the wheel and our tires screeched as the car spun. Josiah drove straight at the moving shadow, three blocks back, as the car picked up speed.

As we got closer, our headlights revealed four Jansynians, armed to the teeth, in a sleek black vehicle. The driver's startled eyes reflecting back the glare. I fixed the look of the hovercar in my mind as it banked in the air to follow us.

Now came the harder part. I closed my eyes and envisioned a link between the front of our car and theirs. The image had to be solid. It had to be sure. I had to focus on the reality I was trying to create, not the screeching tires or painful weight of armored lizard that kept falling into me as Josiah slalomed the car through the late-night city streets.

"Ash!" Vivian snapped. "If you're going to do something, do it."

I opened my eyes, grabbed at my bag, and pulled out my Net-Pad. I couldn't do this all in my head. I opened up the sketch program, but the motion of the car turned all my attempts to draw into jagged squiggles.

An explosion rang sharp outside the car. "Any time, Ash." Vivian pointed her own gun out the window. I could see now the Jansynians were shooting at us.

I slid down to the floor. Scrunched between Vogg's and Spark's legs with the NetPad pressed against the seat was as much stability as I could manage. I traced out the sigils I needed. Energy. Motion. Distance. Unity. Over and over in a rough circle. They weren't perfect, but they would have to do.

I blocked out the explosions. The jostling. The fear. In my mind, I retrieved the images of the two cars and to it I added this ring of symbols. I dropped the one over the other, and willed them to merge.

The effect was immediate. We stopped. Not a hard brake that threw us all forward, but an immediate absence of forward momentum. At the same time, the explosive crash behind us told me my pattern had worked just like I'd hoped. It was like we'd run head-on into their car, except we got to skip the part where our own vehicle became a smashed pile of flaming wreckage.

Josiah wasted no time getting the car moving again and we sped away from the crash.

After some time spent driving mazes through the city to make sure we had no further tails. I felt a little shaky once I didn't have to cling to the calm focus for magic, once I had time to think about what I'd just done.

We made it to the rendezvous point without further incident. Iris was on the ground, waiting. Spark and Vogg and I got out as quickly as possible, and I waved to Josiah as he sped the car away. We hastened to the safehouse.

Viktor stood outside, as before, and he nodded to Iris. "Everything's ready."

"Ash, would you take Spark and Vogg inside while I talk to Vik?" Iris asked.

I was happy to oblige. I didn't feel steady and my heart was still racing. I wasn't eager to look weak in front of the men with the guns.

Vogg paid close attention to all the building's occupants, but I couldn't read either approval or disapproval on his stoic face.

Only the occasional flutter of his ear-flaps communicated any emotion, but I had no idea what it was.

Spark's temporary living quarters had gained some dishes and blankets in the hours since I'd seen it, but it still couldn't pull off welcoming. She sat down at the table as Vogg took her bags into one bedroom and his one bag into the other.

Just to be safe, I did another check for listening devices or other Jansynian unpleasantness. The house was still secure. We'd done it.

I took the chair across the table from Spark, happy to have a quiet moment. Vogg joined us, kneeling next to the table, since we'd run out of chairs. Even so, his head was higher than Spark's. "So now we wait."

Spark rested her tiny hand over his large, armored one, but she addressed me. "Do you have a plan for what's next?"

Amelia hadn't given me any instructions on how much to tell Spark. I hoped I wasn't doing the wrong thing, being honest. "We haven't had a chance to discuss the next steps yet. I had a contact inside one of the Jansynian corporations, but I've lost touch with her and I'm not sure how to find her. Although I'm going to try. And I'm sure Amelia has plans for other routes of investigation. We're going to do our best to give them a better option than assassination."

I'd worried they might take my past involvements with Jansynians the wrong way. It wouldn't have been a bit unreasonable for them to be suspicious of anyone who had friends or former friends up in the Crescent.

Neither Spark nor Vogg looked upset by this information. Spark even smiled at me. "That would be extraordinary. Thank you. I told Copper she was wrong about you."

"Wrong? What did she say?"

Spark's voice was a mix of fondness and exasperation. "Copper, she thinks she knows everything. Just because she's older . . . " Spark sighed. "We had one of your people—a priest of Kaifail who would pass through my home town when I was a girl. A sweet old woman, full of stories. My mother always said you could trust Kaifail's priests with the children, but not with the blueprints, if you get what I'm saying."

"No," I answered honestly.

Spark waggled one overlong finger at me, in obvious imitation of her mother. "Storytellers and dreamers," she said, her voice low and serious. She smiled and was herself again. "Mother never trusted anyone who didn't work with their hands. And Copper takes after her."

"I'm not sure your mother was wrong," I conceded. "Once. But these days—"

Iris popped her head in the door. "C'mon, Ash. Time to go."

I stood. "Will you be okay?" I asked Spark.

"That's the hope, isn't it?" She smiled at me. "Stay safe, Ash. And thank you."

Kaifail was a wanderer. He loved this world and all the creatures in it. He travelled all over, always in disguise. As one of his own priests, as an old man in need, as a kid discovering freedom on the road. Always, he told stories.

There are innumerable tales of people who met Kaifail on a high mountain road, on a dark forest path, on a deserted city street. He would sit and talk, swap whatever tales they had to tell. Sometimes he would offer wisdom. Sometimes he would point them towards grand adventures. Other times he would strike his companions blind or deaf, or cripple them with some horrible disease. Kaifail always rewarded like with like, all based on how they treated him.

A great many priests were wanderers as well, bright and dark alike. Storytellers, healers, men and women questing for secrets in the farthest corners of the world. It made them easy targets when everything fell apart.

I had never understood that mindset. I liked having friends, family. A place that I knew and people that I loved. I'd spent months obsessing over the fact I'd lost all that, and maybe in doing so blinded myself to the fact I wasn't as alone as I thought. Working with Iris and Josiah and Vivian tonight, I felt a part of something. Something real. Something worthwhile.

Like I'd been wandering, lost, and was finally coming home again.

Iris walked with me to the tube station. "You did good," she said. "But now the hard part starts."

"See, that's what I thought. But Vivian was trying to convince me it's all smooth sailing from here."

She laughed. "Get some sleep. You earned it." With fluid ease, she changed back into a falcon and took off.

At this time of night, the tube station was near empty. I ran my card through the scanner, and sat down on one of the concrete benches alongside the track. Exhaustion hit me in a sudden wave. I closed my eyes and leaned my head back against the wall, wished I were already home and in bed.

"What did you find out?"

I opened my eyes. Sitting next to me on the bench, a man in a dark suit. His light skin marked him as a stranger to Miroc, and I'd certainly never seen him before.

Or had I? He almost looked familiar. Something poking at the back of my mind. "Excuse me?"

"Your client. Who is she?"

"How do you know—who are you?"

I meant to stand, to move away, but he touched my hand, saying. "It's all right, Joshua Drake, you can tell me."

Warmth spread through my skin from that point of contact. Of course I could talk to him. "Spark. That's who we're hiding. She's a daughter of Fyea, along with her son of Torin bodyguard."

He let go of my hand and crossed his arms, leaned back against the wall. "What could they want with her?"

"She doesn't know. It's not like most times when they steal an idea—"

His head whipped around to look at me. "Idea? What idea?"

"Something that could bring rain to the city." No question I was tired. I didn't feel any of the excitement this should have created. I didn't feel much of anything right now. "She said it's better they have it—that they have the resources to get it done and she doesn't. But it doesn't explain why they're suddenly trying to kill her."

"Who stole it?" he asked. "Which company?"

"We don't know." Now I thought about it, that was odd. "The car that chased us tonight—it didn't have any corporate markings. That's strange."

"Indeed. Enough to make one suspicious." Suspicious of what, he didn't say. A bright light washed across his face and he stood. "Your train is here."

The noise of it shook the ground. I jumped up, feeling that jolt of artificial energy follows an interrupted nap. I was more tired than I thought if I'd fallen asleep in the tube station at this time of night. My good luck I was alone, but I'd thought my survival instincts stronger.

After that lapse, I was extra careful getting on the train, walking halfway up the line to find a car that still had several people on it. I moved toward a bench in front of four chattering teenagers in fancy dress and reeking of alcohol. I knew they'd be getting off well before my stop, but the silent boneheads across from me were probably heading to my neighborhood.

The kids ignored me, but one of the boneheads swiveled his head around, following my progress with his eyeless, expressionless face. I couldn't tell if he was suspicious, curious, or trying to be friendly. Once I'd settled, he went back to staring—or whatever—straight ahead like his friend.

Just another night on the Miroc blue line.

— 6 —

Kidnapped

Water. Everything was about water.

Miroc was a planned city. Young, compared to Tala or most of the other big cities in the world. It grew up in a part of the desert unclaimed and untouched by any of the local tribes, became a trade hub, a crossroads, a haven for those who wanted away from the stricter, church-controlled cities and towns.

Water was a problem from the beginning, but a solvable one. Rain in the desert? A simple task for the Oulirians, the bird priests, back in the days when their goddess answered their calls. The Oulirians were proud, beholden to no one, but there are those born to every race who are motivated by greed.

The Miroc founders were men and women who wanted away from people looking over their shoulders, and they had the money to make that happen. But they weren't so short-sighted as to rely entirely on the fickle Oulirians. They constructed a reservoir— one of the greatest civil engineering projects the world had ever seen. A great dam just outside the city, a canyon in the desert hills expanded, a retractable metal dome larger even than the one over the Crescent, to keep the water from blowing away in the desert wind. Large enough that when it was full, it could provide for the city for years.

The trouble was, it had been years. Two since the Abandon,

since the last time rain fell on the city. The reservoir wasn't empty yet, but if we didn't get rain soon . . .

Spark's invention—if it could work—that was our hope. But someone had to make it work. Either the Jansynians or someone closer to home, it didn't matter. As long as someone made it rain again, we'd be okay.

Or so I believed.

I dragged into work late the next morning. After the day I'd put in yesterday, I figured Amelia owed me a couple extra hours of sleep. Blessedly, my night had been nightmare free.

I'd only just arrived at my office and set my bag down when the intercom came to life. "Ash," Amelia's voice crackled, "come see me."

I stopped in her doorway and stifled a yawn. Amelia had her back to me, standing at the touch-screen display on the back wall. On it, the map of Miroc I'd seen last night, only now sprinkled with red and yellow splotches. "What's that?" I asked.

"A different project." Amelia pressed her hand against the screen and it went dark. "Nothing you need to worry about right now."

As though curiosity could be sated with such assurances. But Amelia's whole being radiated impatience this morning. Not the time to argue. "So what *should* I be worried about?"

With a swipe of her finger, Amelia brought up a picture of the Crescent. "You did a good job last night. Vivian gave a full report. I'm impressed." She turned to face me. "But we've only just gotten started. We need Spark's invention up and running, and fast."

"How fast?" I asked the question despite being sure I wasn't going to like the answer.

"The council's kept this information secure, but it's only a matter of time before it gets out. At current rationing levels, Miroc has about another four months. Maybe less."

I thought of the reservoir, so closely guarded. Of the protesters—the Children of Miroc, especially—who were convinced the council was keeping vast stores of water hidden and out of reach of the people who needed it.

As if she read my mind, Amelia swiped the screen again to bring up a man's face. This one I recognized. "That's one of the Children of Miroc. I've seen him on the news."

"He's the other side of our problem. This is what Iris has been working on, but I'm afraid it's going to have bearing on your case as well."

She pulled up a collage of images, pointing to them as she talked. "This is the murder investigation Copper told you about, the one we've been working on. About a month ago, we were brought in to investigate. The aide of a prominent city council member was found dead in his home. Shot." She tapped the first picture she'd brought up, the leader of the protesters.

"Evidence pointed us to the Children of Miroc." She circled several news shots of masses of people in the street, obviously shouting. "You've seen their protests. We think they've been plotting worse."

The last picture was familiar to me. A publicity photo that had gone around several months ago. The city council, seated around a table, working hard to solve Miroc's problems. "Last night, an actual city councilor died."

I took a guess. "It was the councilor who'd been talking to Copper and Spark. The one whose aide was killed."

Amelia nodded approval. "This time, no obvious cause of death. But I don't believe it's a coincidence."

She swiped the screen blank, then sat on the edge of her desk, facing me. "We need to know precisely when Spark took her proposal to the council. We need to know every single person she and Copper talked to."

I thought I could see where this was going. "But it's the Jansynians who are after Spark. If you think the Children of Miroc are responsible for the council murders—"

Amelia shook her head, her disappointed expression silencing me. "Think harder. We've got a volatile group of angry people, growing by the day. We've got the council trying to hold the city together. But what if someone on the outside is trying to manipulate the situation, trying to prod them into outright violence against each other?"

The Jansynians had tried to kill Spark. They obviously weren't above assassination attempts. Planting evidence was certainly something they could and would do. The only question was: "Why? What do they gain if the city falls apart?"

"I don't know." Amelia crossed her arms, frowning, but this time, not at me. "But especially given what Spark said about the rain project suddenly not moving forward—it all looks suspicious."

Suspicious maybe, but it didn't make any sense. I opened my mouth to argue, but second thoughts held me back. What did I really know? Just because I'd been with Seana didn't mean I understood all Jansynians everywhere. And even if I couldn't see the profit in them trying to tear Miroc apart, that didn't mean it wasn't there.

"What do you need me to do?" I asked.

"Continue the investigation. Get answers to the questions I asked and anything else Spark and Copper know about the Jansynians."

Easy enough. Except for the fact I'd be trying to sneak around under the nose of the people who knew everything, saw everything, and last night had demonstrated a willingness to kill.

I called Micah. As soon as possible, we were going to have to figure out a safer way to get in touch with each other. I told him we needed to meet.

"No problem," he said. "Meet me in a couple hours, the same place as before."

"Is that safe? After last night?"

"We won't be staying." He hung up.

I found Iris in the library again, a ginger cat curled up on the rug. Her head lifted as I came into the room and she shifted back to person-shape, although her hair retained the cat's orange and white stripes. I held in my laugh.

"Amelia told me she was sending you back out." Her skin moved through several shades before settling into a deep-desert brown that actually worked with the orange. "You up for this?"

"Honestly? I have no idea. Any chance you could back me up?"

She stretched, still moving like a cat. "I can meet you over there in a bit. I've got a couple things of my own to take care of this morning."

"The city council thing?"

"Yeah. It's gotten complicated. Threats of . . . " She put a hand on my shoulder and smiled. "Nothing you need to worry about. You've got plenty to keep you busy."

On that, we were in total agreement.

With a couple hours to kill, I could check in on Spark at the safe-house and ask her my questions before I talked to her sister. It wasn't that I expected them to give me different stories. I just wanted to be thorough.

I walked out with Iris and turned to the tube station as she took to the air. I continued underground. I'd passed the ticket machines and video booths and was just about to the turnstile when I saw the first Jansynian face.

It wasn't like they blended in. Milk-white skin and silver-white hair made this woman seem to glow in the artificial underground light. I backed away from the line of people heading towards the platform, but she looked in my direction and I saw her lips move.

The mid-morning station wasn't so crowded I could easily get lost, but I made a go of it anyway. I pushed my way through a clump of people coming up from an arriving train and dodged down a hall towards the orange line. If I could get to that train—

No, another ghost-white face ahead of me. Were they on every platform, waiting? This guy was on alert and he spotted me as soon as I rounded the corner. So much for that escape.

"Ash Drake."

A voice behind me. I spun. A Jansynian stood right behind me. On the shoulder of his dark jacket was a logo I recognized— Desavris Intercontinental. They were the big fish in Miroc's Jansynian pond. Seana had always spoken of them with reverence. Desavris controlled the entry point into the Crescent, which meant every other corporation had to work through them or with them. And now, it seemed, they were after me.

As I hesitated, I caught sight of another white face approaching from the left. I looked back over my shoulder and spotted a third. Closing in. I was caught.

"Please come with us, Mr. Drake." His hands were empty, but I could see the outline of a gun under his jacket. Reassuring, in a way. If they wanted me dead, they could simply have shot me.

I appreciated they hadn't grabbed me, either. Jansynian security was nothing if not polite. "Where are we going?"

"Our director wishes to see you."

Which meant they wanted to take me into the Crescent. Kaifail knew if they meant for me to come out again. "I'm actually on my way to another appointment, but I'm happy to check my calendar for a more convenient—"

I stopped at the unmistakable prod of the nose of a gun being pressed into my back. The man at my front remained polite. "I'm afraid the timing is not negotiable."

I had no choice. "Then we'd better not keep the director waiting."

Outside, two hovercars waited in the street, engines humming. They weren't locked or secured in any fashion. Even in Miroc, no one dared steal from the Jansynians. I noted that these cars, like the one from last night, bore no logo. That thought did nothing to relax me. Nor did the six other Jansynians who came out of the station to join my escort. What sort of trouble did someone think I was going to cause that I needed nine armed guards to keep me in line?

I considered and then discarded the idea of trying to send a message to Amelia. So far, my captors hadn't seemed interested in searching me, but if I went for my wireless or my NetPad, they might confiscate either one. Better to sit tight for now.

The trip across the city was quick when we could skim over the top of the street traffic. We reached the receiving yard in no time. A sprawling, gated lot with security checkpoints and armed guards to sort invited guests from the riffraff.

I'd never been through these gates, past the checkpoints, up the lift. Even when Seana and I had been together, she always came to me. Bad enough the Jansynians had to allow some of Miroc's chaos to spill into their receiving area; if Seana had invited a human into their private haven, her career would have been over.

For all I knew, they were taking me to be tortured and killed, but I couldn't focus on that because this was so interesting. I was going up there, into the Jansynians' secret haven, and how many people got to say that? All these years I'd wondered, imagined, with nothing to go on but stories of questionable provenance and Seana's vague answers to my questions.

The gates opened for my escort and we zoomed through, dodging through the mass of freight being loaded and unloaded as it passed in one direction or another through the Crescent's single umbilical.

The lift itself was a marvel. A single tube that rose a hundred stories to connect the Crescent to the city below, encased in what looked like glass, but had to be something stronger to weather the occasional fire purges that swept through the Web. The lift was divided into a wide industrial platform and a smaller, furnished enclosure for people.

Three guards got out of the car with me, although not the same three who had captured me in the station. They escorted me onto the people side of the lift and we began to rise.

My escorts settled, keeping a careful eye on me, but obviously uninterested in the scenery outside. I was fascinated. As we moved up through the center of the Web, I couldn't look away from the strange world outside the Jansynian glass cage.

An entire community had taken root here, thriving in the protective shadow of the Crescent, and this was my first close look at it. The girders and wires that supported the city above offered the framework on which had grown platforms, tents, and bridges of plastic, canvas, and rope. As long as one wasn't afraid of heights, it was one of the safer places to be homeless in Miroc— close enough to the Crescent it made both criminals and law enforcement hesitate.

And even here, they clung to gods long gone. As we continued up, I caught glimpses of living spaces, suspended or wedged wherever possible, full of trinkets and reminders of better days. A group of lizards sat in a circle around a sword of Torin, passing bottles of water as they talked. A huddled cluster of human children sang beneath a rough replica of Fyea's hammer. And all around, woven into blankets, painted onto walls, carved into floors, Kaifail's doorway.

I stood at the inner wall of the lift, hands pressed against the glass, watching layer upon layer of habitation pass by. How many people here? How many who only a few years ago had jobs and lives? I couldn't blame them for being angry. I was angry too, at the gods who had fostered such dependence and then disappeared without a word.

As we neared the top, I stepped back from the wall. Not soon enough. Up here, under the Crescent's protective shadow, the Web had grown thick, but not so thick I couldn't pick out the familiar face in a cluster of men and women sitting around enjoying the shade. Micah had seen me, too. He jumped to his feet as I passed. The lift moved on, giving us no more than a glimpse of each other, but it was enough for me to see the fear in his eyes.

———————

Everything went weird once we reached the top. Weirder, I mean.

The doors slid open and the lift filled with cool air. I stepped off into a sterile gray reception area where a smiling young Jansynian gentleman waited for me. "Mr. Drake. Please follow me."

My guards followed, but at a distance. My new guide led me into a hallway and said, "This is your first visit to Desavris."

As though I were a guest, not a prisoner. As though they received guests regularly. "Yes," I answered cautiously. "I've never been to the Crescent."

"I do hope you'll find your stay enjoyable."

Was this a joke, some enigmatic piece of Jansynian humor?

I'd have to parse my guide later. If there was a later. Right now, I was overwhelmed with the strange experience of being surrounded by Jansynians. I'd never been in the middle of any large group of them before. I'd never gotten the full effect of their . . . I didn't even know the word.

All the races in the world, we've got our similarities and difference. By most measurements, the Jansynians are closer to human than any of the rest. They've got skin instead of scales or feathers, eyes in their heads, bodies that don't change from one thing to another. They're a little taller than us humans, a lot skinnier on average, but we could still shop in the same aisle of the clothing store if we wanted. Really, that's what made the rest of it so creepy. They could almost pass for human, if you squinted your eyes a little and didn't think about it too hard.

Except that they all looked alike.

Not exactly, I guess. If I looked really close—as close as I could pretend was polite—I could pick out maybe a shorter nose or fuller lips or some other tiny clue. But they were all the same height, the same androgynous build, the same pearly-white skin, and frosty-white hair and eyes the color of fresh ice cubes. It didn't help everyone up here dressed in the same black suits, so I was walking through the crowded halls feeling like some distorted photo negative with my dark skin, light clothing, and a body that didn't look like I'd been starving myself for the last six months.

Not a one of them was smiling, except my guide. He even made it look natural. How much had he had to practice?

We took another lift and came out into a fancier area, with cushy red carpeting and wood-paneled walls. Portraits lined the hall—serious, identical-looking men and women—but otherwise, my guide and my guards and I were alone. "Who are these people?" I asked, honestly curious.

"These are the current and former directors of Desavris Intercontinental. From today, back to the beginning, when Desavris was founded." I didn't miss the way he puffed up. "Desavris may be a young corporation, but our founders were some of the best minds in the world. We have the most holdings of any entity in Miroc, and we're third largest, worldwide." He caught himself and his smile slipped for a moment. "Second, I mean. Now."

He didn't elaborate; he didn't have to. "Now that Jansyn's church is gone."

He nodded. "Most of their research and for-profit branches were swallowed by various corporations. We were fortunate to acquire many of their best and brightest."

The guards had stopped back at the lift, and my guide led me to a door halfway down the hall. "Through here, Mr. Drake. The director is waiting."

I took a deep breath, steeled myself for whatever interrogation waited on the other side of that door. But I underestimated the universe's recent glee for turning my world inside out.

No team of torturers, no squad of toughs, no men with guns greeted me as I crossed the threshold. All the same, my hands went cold and I forgot how to breathe. Across the spacious office, behind an imposing desk, a woman waited.

Not *a* woman. *My* woman.

The director.

Seana.

—7—

Interrogated

In all our years together, I had never seen Seana in her native environment, but I had to say it suited her. As I looked around her office—anywhere but at her—I was impressed. The walls behind her and to either side were covered with monitors, all showing some different area of what I assumed was this building. To one side of her sprawling, glossy black desk, sat a computer far sexier than anything I could afford. Spread across the other side, an array of handheld gadgets ranging from the easily identifiable—touch-screen wirelesses and memory sticks—to the arcane—shiny black boxes with no obvious inputs and slim, flat arrays of blinking lights. No lack of toys for a director of the second-largest Jansynian corporation in the world.

And Seana—I couldn't keep my eyes away forever—she hadn't changed. Not at all. What had been wrong with me that I thought all Jansynians looked alike? I knew—how well I knew—the precise curve of her cheek, the arc of her eyes, the line of her jaw. The face I'd scrutinized with all the precise attention I'd given to any of my professional studies.

I lingered in the doorway; she stood behind her desk. I didn't know what to say, how to begin. Captive to captor, and seven years apart to make us strangers.

She broke the silence, alleviating my growing fear I'd stand here gaping like an idiot until the end of time. "Come in, Ash. Sit down."

I stepped in, heard the door swing shut behind me, and took the offered seat, the whole time dredging through my stuttering brain for appropriate small talk. Something charming and breezy, the sort of opening line I'd heard Amelia use any number of times to show she was in control of the situation. "Seana why—how—what am I doing here?" No, that wasn't it.

Seana's right eyebrow twitched; the left corner of her mouth wrinkled. Tiny signals I could still read. Hinted expressions that spoke volumes. Even if her voice held none of the impatience I saw. "You requested this meeting."

Something broke inside me. "And this—*this*—is how you respond? Armed guards to kidnap me out of the tube station? Dragging me up here against my will? I didn't even know the message got through! I thought—" Even as my brain slid into emotional overload, I knew better than to finish that sentence. If I confessed to expectations of rough interrogations, it would only lead to questions of why.

Seana bore my outburst with her usual stoicism. "I'm a busy woman. I don't have leisure to negotiate chats over coffee anymore. I told my people to bring you here and they did."

But I wasn't done. The words boiled up, burned in my chest. "Never a call to see how I was doing. After the Abandon, after the riots, after everything. Like you didn't even care if I was still alive."

"I knew you were alive." Seana brushed one pale finger across her dark monitor and it came awake, showing a picture of me snagged from some ID or another. "Of course I knew."

Flashing across the screen was, as far as I could tell, every bit of information on me that had ever been recorded. Starting with the official city copy of my birth certificate. My parents' death certificates. Public school records, with the accompanying notes of concern regarding my early experiments with magic. The rejected scholarship application that had killed my chances at university and left me with only one career choice if I wanted to pursue my one real aptitude.

Had Seana gathered all this back when we'd been together?

Scrolling forward, the more recent stuff. News articles about the post-Abandon riots. A video of Kaifail's church burning. My apartment complex burning. My hospital admission form and the attached release, dated six months later. "Stop it! Just, stop. Enough, okay?"

"I'm sorry," she said. I believed she meant it, but I couldn't tell what, of all her sins, she was sorry for. Sorry for sending men with guns to fetch me like some criminal, sorry for leaving me to my fate during the Abandon, sorry for the reminder of all that had happened, or even sorry for leaving me in the first place?

My one consolation was that she didn't seem any more comfortable than I was. For all her talk of being busy, she certainly wasn't pushing along to business.

"I'm sorry," she said again. "I thought this would be easier. I thought. . . ." She shook her head. "It doesn't matter. Please, Ash, sit. We need to talk."

I sat, reminded myself I'd contacted her for a reason.

"In truth, your message came at a fortuitous time. I have a problem, and you may possess the skill set to help me."

I fought down a bitter laugh. Seana wanted my help. "Tell me something. Would you have gotten in touch with me if you didn't need me to do something for you?"

She shrugged. "I'm not good with hypotheticals."

That familiar bluntness—Seana had never been one to lie to spare my feelings—it drained away some of my anger. "What is it you want?"

She didn't answer immediately, only watched me from across her desk. Silence stretched between us. Familiar, comforting. Reminding me of evenings together in my tiny apartment, Seana on one side of the couch working on her computer, me on the other side working on mine. We'd never needed chatter or hand-holding or any other sort of artificial reassurance of each other's presence. Our intimacy had thrived in the quiet times between the demands of our two worlds.

She broke the moment, angled away from me to face her computer. She tapped her screen again and my life history disappeared, replaced by one of the camera feeds from the wall. I saw a workroom full of computers and circuit boards with a number of Jansynians who had layered white coats over their dark suits. She pointed at a man hunched in deep concentration over a keyboard. "My husband, Eddis."

My stomach lurched. I wasn't ready for that. "Since when?"

She kept her eyes on the screen, wouldn't look at me. "Five years." Her lips tightened and twisted. "He was a priest." Her eyes flickered to meet mine, acknowledging the irony. "Jansyn's, of course. But he left during an administration change. He didn't care for the new Favored Son."

"Before the Abandon."

She nodded. "We both came to the company at the same time. Desavris had attempted a takeover of Arisia. I uncovered their maneuvers and obstructed their efforts. So they hired me. As we were both newcomers, it made sense to pool our resources, present a united political front, and establish the sort of personal stability that reflects well on the company."

Of course, the company. "First in your thoughts, last in your thoughts, always in your thoughts." Words I'd heard her say so often.

"Yes. You understand."

I had understood. That loyalty, I'd found it beautiful. Even when it had taken her away from me. "So what about him?"

Once more, she touched the screen, then balled her fingers into a fist and dropped her hand to her lap. "We've both done well here. I'm director of security now, and Eddis is project manager of what may be the most important research Desavris has ever done. And while one can never be certain, our best intelligence reports that none of our competitors are anywhere close. This technology is revolutionary—critical not only to Miroc's future, but the world's."

She hesitated. The next words she spoke were slow and deliberate. "We have a chance to save Miroc. The research is solid. Eddis believes we can bring water back to the city."

I jerked forward in my seat. I couldn't help myself. "How?"

Seana shook her head and leaned back in her chair. "I don't understand the technology well enough to explain it. It ties in to the space program we started after the Abandon—after Ouliria wasn't around anymore to knock things out of the sky. We have satellites. A prototype in the air, as of two weeks ago. It should have worked. It should have brought rain. It didn't."

Rain to Miroc. Spark's technology. And Seana's company was the one that stole it. So much for calm and comfortable. "I don't see what I have to do with this." Was I speaking too loud? Too fast? I had to breathe, to relax again, or Seana—who knew me every bit as well as I knew her—would know something was wrong.

Seana frowned, with that little line between her eyebrows that had always meant I was missing something she thought obvious. "The technology should have worked. We're not making guesses and throwing them up into the sky. We know exactly what should happen and what shouldn't. This was—there have been problems."

I stared at the video feed of the lab, tried to look intent on the men and women in pristine white suits sitting at pristine gray desks, hard at work on the computers before them. "What sorts of problems are we talking about?"

"Minor accidents. Failures in models that had previously worked. Those were the most obvious issues."

I risked a question. "When did this start?"

"About a month ago."

About the same time Spark took her plans to the city council. But what did that mean? What could it mean? Could another company's spies have learned about it then? "Could it be sabotage?" I wondered aloud.

"Ash." Seana's sharp voice forced me to look at her. "Focus, please." She changed the camera angle so it no longer pointed at Eddis. "Sabotage is not a casual word. The security on this project is immense, and I've gone over every detail. There's not a single hole. Unless. . . . "

I held my breath. If she knew about Spark and Copper— Copper had already shown the ability to poke holes in Jansynian security. If Seana was suspicious . . .

She finished her sentence. "Unless we are betrayed from the inside."

And I could breathe again. "Inside? You think one of your own people?"

Seana rested her hands on the desk. Her fingers laced together. It wasn't like her knuckles could get any whiter, but I could see her fingertips digging into the back of her hands. I'd never seen her this distraught. "It is impossible to believe. We are Desavris. But I believe the data has been altered. Is being altered. Only a few have that level of access."

"And one of those people is your husband." Seana looked down and away and I revised my statement. "Not just one of— you think he's the one."

"I cannot find any evidence that Eddis is involved in this disruption, but I am aware my judgment may be compromised."

She took a deep breath. "If he's betrayed Desavris—if I misjudged the character of my husband so fundamentally—then I don't deserve my position. I wouldn't deserve any position here."

I began to understand. "But you just said, you married him when you were both new here. You hardly knew each other. Maybe some other company made an offer—or a threat—I don't know, he might have reasons—"

She cut me off with a wave of her hand. "No. That isn't how we do things. We aren't savages." And by savages, she meant humans.

"First, last, and always, Ash. If Eddis were to betray that trust—for him to turn against his family—no other company would pay for information obtained in such a fashion. He'd never work again. He'd be throwing away his future. It would be psychosis. For me not to have seen it. . . . "

"Okay," I said. I couldn't take the pain in her voice. So despite the fact I still had no idea what I was agreeing to, I said, "I'll help."

She reached into a drawer and retrieved a sleek, black data stick. She slid it across the desk and I slapped my hand down to catch it. "What you have there are all the records and files associated with this project. Logs, technical files, communications, video surveillance—everything. I shouldn't have to tell you how important it is that information never leave your person."

I turned the stick over between my fingers. What would this data stick be worth to Copper, to Spark? And Seana trusted me with it. "You think something in here's been messed with?"

"I've run every test, used every measure at my disposal. And believe me, Ash, Desavris wouldn't be in the position it holds if we didn't use the best security algorithms that exist. If anything on that stick has been doctored, they didn't leave a pixel—not even an electron out of place."

Now I understood. "You want me to use magic." I closed my hand around the data stick, felt its smooth weight against my palm. I couldn't deny the thrill I got at the idea. All this time lately being a mediocre secretary and a reluctant investigator—it would be nice to do something I was good at. Something I could sink my brain into.

And there were other reasons to help. "You're going to owe me."

She was all business again. "Yes, of course. The message you sent. A friend who needed help? What was it you needed?"

I squeezed the data stick. "We can talk about it after I'm done." Whatever I found, I hoped it would be enough leverage to buy off the assassins chasing Spark. And maybe even get Seana's help tracking down any plots against Miroc. The trick, of course, would be finding a way to ask Seana for that without her thinking I'd betrayed her.

That was going to be the trick with everyone.

Kaifail stands at the center of the Thirteen. The gods to his right live at odds with the gods to his left. Conflict in the heavens spills down to the world and we, their children, are driven to walk in our parents' footsteps. Giants and lizards make war when their father-gods argue. Birds hunt boneheads. It's not as though our world was at peace before the Abandon.

As Kaifail served as mediator for the rest of the Thirteen, so he taught his priests to do the same. Another Bright God specialty, of course, but even we priests of the Dark God who spent most of our days lurking in libraries and arcane laboratories received some amount of training. To the outside world, a priest of Kaifail was a priest of Kaifail and it wouldn't do to embarrass the church if someone came to us in need.

Today I was the person in need. If Micah told Copper what he'd seen—and I had to assume he would—she wasn't going to take it well. It wasn't like I could tell her the truth. If Copper knew I was now working for Seana, that Seana trusted me enough to simply hand me a copy of the information that had put Spark's life at so much jeopardy, what would she think? What could she think?

Seana's guards escorted me back to the base of the lift and asked if I needed them to take me anywhere. They didn't question when I said I would walk. "Talk to the officer at the gate," one of them said. "You'll need a security badge for when you return."

The checkpoint agent expected me. She invited me inside her

cramped booth filled with viewscreens and computers. I stood in the corner under the uncomfortable scrutiny of guards watching through the windows. "The director had a sample of your DNA to provide," she said without inflection. A printer next to her came to life and spit out a thumbprint-sized disc. On one side, tiny metal dots connected to inner circuitry I could just make out through the semi-transparent plastic.

"Wear this against your skin," was the only instruction she offered as she handed the disc to me.

When my fingertip touched the metal side, the disc lit up and then went dark. It stuck to the end of my finger; I had to pry it off. "Thanks." I dropped it into a small pocket inside my shirt. No way was I wearing this thing to go meet with Copper.

Back out on the street, once I'd made it a couple blocks from the Jansynian compound, I ducked around to the shadowy side of a building and sat down against its wall. It wasn't the best spot—the alley smelled of baking metal and I had to pull my hood up against blowing sand—but it was out of sight of the Crescent and that's what mattered. I slid the data stick into the hidden pocket alongside the security disc. There they would both be safe from getting lost or stolen or accidentally discovered.

Just to be safe, I summoned the security pattern and worked the magic to make sure neither of Seana's presents were broadcasting anything back to Desavris. Not only didn't I want Seana's people following me, but Copper seemed to have some way of picking out Jansynian spy devices, and wouldn't that look suspicious if she found one on me? Both the data stick and security disc lay dormant. Good.

It felt like this morning had lasted a lifetime already, but when I checked the time, I was still on track for my meeting with Micah. Assuming he showed up at all. I hadn't seen him on my trip back down the lift, so for all he knew, I was still a prisoner.

The warehouse was easy walking distance, even as the late-morning sun set the street temperatures to broil. I'll admit I was distracted, my brain volleying back and forth between the magic Seana wanted and thoughts on Seana herself.

Stupid—I'd lived in Miroc all my life and I should have known better. Even in bright sunlight, even on an empty-looking street, I should have been paying attention to my surroundings.

I heard the click of the gun readying above my head. I squinted up to see Copper on the edge of a nearby roof, a serious-caliber weapon pointed in my direction. "Micah says I should hear what you have to say. Micah says I should trust you."

Her arm straightened. "But given the state of things, if the Jansynians decided to let you live, I'm pretty sure that means I have to kill you."

— 8 —

Plans within Plans

I heard all three sounds at once. The scream, the screech, the explosive release of a three-burst round. I had trouble connecting those with the sight of a dark object streaking towards Copper from above, of Copper bringing the gun around, but not fast enough to stop Iris from ramming into her. Iris, shifting as she dove, from falcon to tiger. She landed atop Copper and knocked the gun away with one swat of a massive paw.

Another shift and Iris was Iris again, sitting with a knee on Copper's chest. "Ash! Are you okay?"

I had to look at myself to be sure. I still stood. No blood I could see. "I think so."

"Good. Now what the hell?" Iris stood and pulled Copper up with her. Twice the Fyean's size, Iris had no trouble overpowering her.

"Don't hurt her." I spotted a fire escape I could use to get up there. "I can explain."

"He betrayed us!" Copper struggled against Iris as I climbed. "The Jansynians let him go!"

Iris pulled Copper's wrists behind her back, held her still. "What Jansynians?"

I pulled myself up over the edge of the roof. "They grabbed me in the tube station. Took me up to the Crescent. I spoke with

87

Director Seana Desavris."

Iris's eyes widened and a wave of white rippled through her hair. She was as surprised to hear Seana's name as I'd been to see her. "Listen to me, Copper. *Listen to me.* We have to talk to them. To protect your sister, we have to find out who's after your sister, and this is the best way to do it. I swear, I didn't tell her anything about you or Spark."

Copper had stopped squirming. A cold look passed through her eyes, quickly hidden behind a considering squint. "You talked to Desavris," she said carefully.

"They're the ones who have Spark's tech." I kept my voice even, but unapologetic. "What I don't know yet is if they're the ones trying to kill you."

Copper looked calmer now, but her eyes kept flicking over towards the gun that lay out of reach. I was glad Iris still had a grip on her. "What did they offer you? What's the going rate on betrayal these days?"

"They didn't offer me anything. Have you ever actually talked to a Jansynian? They'd never ask me to betray my employer, and wouldn't want to work with me if I were the sort of person who would."

"So they just brought you—a human—up into the Crescent, where nobody goes, all for a little chat? Forgive me if I find that hard to believe."

She had a point, but it was the truth, so it was what I had to work with. "Remember what you said the very first time we met—that you were willing to work with us because of my past experience? This is why you came to us. Because I know about Jansynians. Because I *know* Jansynians."

Outside of Copper's view, Iris raised an eyebrow. And, okay, maybe I was stretching the narrative a little. Having contacts among the Jansynians was one thing. Getting invited into the Crescent . . .

"We're all on the same side," Iris said and let Copper go. I had to trust she knew what she was doing.

"Are we?" Copper looked at each of us. Looked at her gun, but she didn't move toward it. "Micah's waiting in the warehouse. I'm going to go get him and bring him back here. Don't follow me." At Iris. "I want to talk to him. Alone."

"We'll wait."

Iris stood at the very edge of the roof and watched Copper go. Once Copper was safely out of sight, she brought me the gun. "Keep this."

"What should I do with it?"

"It's a gun, Ash. What do you think?" She sat down cross-legged on the tiles that lined the rooftop. It couldn't have been comfortable, given the heat I could feel radiating up just standing here. "So what really happened?"

I slid the pistol into my bag. "Seems like she got my message after all. And the timing was *fortuitous*." My voice twisted on the last word and Iris squinted one eye open at me.

"Correct me if I'm wrong, but in the three years you were actually sleeping together, she never once invited you upstairs."

"That's right. Maybe it's different now she's a director. Maybe it's because—" Reflexively, I pressed a hand against my pocket to double check the data stick was still there. "She asked for my help. Which is probably a sign of desperation right there. But probably safer for her to bring me up there where she knew we could talk without anyone spying. Even if my presence raises some perfect white eyebrows."

Iris leaned back, basking in the warmth. Shifters. "But you know she has Spark's technology?"

"Yeah, Desavris has it, but they're having trouble with it. Seana thinks sabotage."

Iris jumped to the same conclusion I had. "You think it's a Jansynian conflict? Sabotaging Desavris while they try to whip the people of Miroc into a frenzy?"

"It occurred to me. But Seana thinks it's an inside job."

"What does she expect you to do about it?"

"Magic. She expects me to do what I do." I glanced back at the street, but there was still no sign of Copper and Micah. "If I help her, she may help us."

It wasn't going to be easy, though. "This magic she needs, I haven't done anything like it since before the Abandon. I'm going to need supplies and a real workroom."

Iris nodded. She knew what I meant. She knew where I meant. "I better go with you. I don't trust you to stay out of trouble on your own. We'll go tonight, after dark."

That settled, we had nothing left to do but wait.

Seana and I first met because one of Arisia's directors loved the theater.

As I came to understand, he was a bit of an eccentric. He liked to watch non-Jansynians going about their lives and entertainments. Not unlike going to the zoo. I never met him face-to-face, so I don't know if he was as unpleasant a person as he sounded.

But I did meet Seana as she and her security team scouted Kaifail's temple in preparation for his attendance.

I drew short straw that week, so I'd been assigned to assist her and her team, to show them anything they wanted to see and keep them from getting lost on our sprawling campus. Four Jansynians in sleek black suits, taciturn and superior and—I was certain—quietly judging me. Because I wasn't one of them. Because I was different. I knew enough about them back then to understand that, in their eyes, different was one of the greatest sins I could commit.

I hated it. Not just because they weren't any fun to be around, but because I had research of my own sitting neglected while I played babysitter. I wanted it over with. I wanted them to go home.

Until Seana started asking me questions. Not just questions about how many doors there were into the theater and how many people we expected opening night, but questions about the art on the walls, the stories behind the topiaries in the gardens and the mosaics in the narthex.

Then she asked if she could see the library. Of course I was happy to show it to her. Her companions were impatient. What could Kaifail possibly have here that Jansyn hadn't already collected, cataloged, processed? Seana sent them back to the Crescent and I escorted her alone on what I would later think of as our first date.

Seana was a sensualist at heart. As I walked her through Dark Kaifail's cathedral, she traced her fingertips down leather bindings, inhaled the scents of old paper and ink. She marveled at the research room in the archive, and listened so attentively I rambled at length about my job.

We went for coffee and it was my turn to listen. She talked about Arisia, about the Crescent, what it was like to be born into a life where you knew there would always be a place for you, always someone to care for you—even if that someone was a company. No, not a company, she explained—a family.

Two nights later, she came to my house. In her hand was a bottle of wine, because she understood that was how humans pursued romance. I didn't turn her away then, or any night that came after.

She was intense. Brilliant and interested in everything, and deeply passionate, even if she expressed that passion differently from any person I'd ever known.

I loved her. She loved me.

For three years, I believed that was enough.

When Micah and Copper arrived, neither looked pleased with the other. "What happened?" Micah asked as soon as he was up on the roof. "Are you all right?"

"Iris got to Copper before she could shoot me."

"Before she could—what?" Micah rounded on Copper who'd just stepped off the ladder. "You tried to shoot him?"

Copper rolled her eyes. "I didn't plan on shooting him. I just had the gun out so he knew I was serious."

Which was a lie. Or maybe, now she'd had a chance to calm down, Copper believed that. Either way, it wasn't worth arguing about. "It doesn't matter. Everyone's fine."

Micah still looked uneasy but didn't argue with me. "We should get out of the sun, at any rate. Let's move this upstairs."

"Fine," Copper said. "Might as well show them where we're hiding. Not like that's a secret anymore, since he saw you from the lift. And then next we can send engraved invitations to the Jansynians." She gave me one more black look, then waved for us all to follow.

From the rooftop, we crossed a rickety-looking plank bridge to another access ladder that ran up a girder. That terminated at a locked electrical box, but a rope web had been woven among the thick wires that led out from the box. Copper made it look easy, finding purchase on the rope with her overlong fingers and toes. Iris tugged on one of the ropes, then shifted to become a monkey and scrambled up behind Copper.

"It's more solid than it looks," Micah assured me.

Good thing I wasn't afraid of heights. Even so, I didn't look down as I climbed.

From the top of the rope-ladder, we stepped onto a walkway that led to a part of the Web like I'd seen around the lift. Platforms and hanging tents spread around us to form a city that was almost solid.

Above us, the Crescent offered shade from the punishing noon-day sun, but there was no escape—ever—from the withering desert heat. Even a couple hundred feet up, as I worked to catch my breath after the climb, I sucked in nothing but hot, dry air.

I'd lost sight of Copper. She hadn't waited. "I'm sorry." Micah wasn't at all winded. "She's been on edge all morning. Even before this business with you and Desavris."

"Any particular reason?" I alternately flexed and squeezed my hands, trying to work out the stiffness the climb had put into them.

"One of the kids who runs errands for us—he died this morning."

"I'm sorry," I said automatically. "Was it the Jansynians?"

Micah shook his head. "There wasn't any sign of violence. He just collapsed while he was giving Copper a message. Although that raises its own issues—poison or sickness—serious problems if that's what killed him."

I found the timing suspicious. On the same night we moved Spark into hiding, a kid working with Copper died. "No idea how it happened?"

"She didn't want to talk about it, and I can't blame her." He added, "I wouldn't bring it up." As though I were looking for more ways to agitate the woman who tried to kill me less than an hour ago.

People called out to Micah as we passed through a maze of platforms and walkways. Most of them were human, and a surprising number were foreign. I saw skin both lighter and darker than my own, heard lilts and drawls and close-cropped consonants. I thought of university students, of tourists, of businesspeople—all the different ways people could have become trapped here when the intercontinental tubes shut down. Even assuming they had homes to go back to.

Hard as it was for those of us who had been in the middle of it to accept, Miroc had been spared the worst of the post-Abandon violence. After the Favored Children had been assassinated— after the world saw the gods no longer protected their own— all the lost and frightened people had turned against the priests. Miroc, as one of the few places in the world that hadn't been born around or led by one of the churches, had come through relatively unscathed. Sure, there had been riots and fires and— things I didn't want to think about—but our city leaders were no strangers to violence and had kept it contained while it ran its course.

I didn't know for certain what happened elsewhere in the world. But I couldn't imagine anything good. The mere fact that no one had ever come to our rescue, what did that say?

But that was too huge a problem to contemplate. Even Miroc's dwindling water supply and growing desperation were too overwhelming for me. Manageable problems like keeping Spark safely hidden and helping Seana find her saboteur—they were more than enough to keep me busy.

Micah led me across and up and back and down and up again, until I had no idea which way was forward or back. I did know when we crossed into a different—what, neighborhood? Territory? Something had changed, no question.

First of all, there was electricity. Cables ran all about, connecting tents and shacks in a complicated snare, with dormant lights hanging down throughout. All around, I saw people working. Children sat on the edges of platforms, their feet dangling into nothingness, wrapping wires around various hunks of metal. I saw a man with a soldering iron, bent over a circuit board on a table that was little more than three rough boards hammered together. Two women sweated at a forge that had been welded onto one of the cross-girders. Scattered in among them, above them, below them, more armed men and women that I had seen all together in a long time.

"What is this, Copper's army?"

"Nothing so organized." Micah waved to people as we passed, smiling back at the friendly greetings, his actor facade plastered on his face. "Copper and Spark—they've helped these people. Especially Copper. I swear, Ash, you're not seeing her at her best."

In the center of it all, a large wooden dome with mismatched glass windows and an actual door. Micah took me inside to a cluttered mess of electrical and mechanical junk in various states of disassembly—or rebuild. It was hard to tell.

Copper and Iris waited, glowering at each other. Micah still wore his fake smile. And I resigned myself to a long afternoon.

There weren't any chairs in here, and the two cots in the corner were full of mechanical odds and ends. I sat on the floor, next to Iris, while Micah found a stable pile of boxes and Copper squatted on a heavy-looking engine block. "So now Spark is safe—"

Copper cut me off. "Is she?"

"Of course she is," Iris snapped back. "We took care of that last night."

Under the Crescent's shadow, only dim illumination made it through the windows, but Copper hadn't turned on any of the electric lights. Even in the gloom, I could see her glowering at me. "I want to see her."

I tried to focus on the fact it was her sister in danger, on the insurmountable resources of the Jansynians, on Copper's precarious position, and not on the fact she'd tried to kill me. "Right now, Iris and I are the only two people who know where Spark is being kept. You have to see how it doesn't help her if we share that information with anyone."

"We talked about this." Micah leaned forward, his voice soothing. "You're just upset. And maybe that's what they want." He glanced up. Even if the ceiling blocked it, the Crescent still loomed over our heads. "If they do know Ash was working with us, they may have grabbed him just to prompt this sort of panic—to maybe give them another chance to follow you to Spark."

I continued where Micah left off. "It's not my decision, anyway. I'd have to clear that with Amelia and I know she's not going to jeopardize the safety of her client, no matter how much you want to see Spark. You hired us to do a job. Let us do it."

Copper considered, staring at me. I wished I could read her expression, decipher her alien face. "Very well," she said, her voice soft. "Let's move on. For now."

"Right."

But before I could frame the first of my questions, Micah jumped up and went over to a desk I hadn't noticed, buried beneath bundles of canvas and wire. He rummaged around and pulled out a crumpled mass of paper.

"Vogg and Copper put this together." He spread the paper out on the floor. Iris and I both leaned in, straining to see in the inadequate light. Copper didn't offer to turn any on for us. Petty.

"It's a map?" Iris asked. She traced her finger along lines and symbols without seeming to make any more sense of it than I could.

"Oh yes." Micah held it flat and grinned.

I had no idea what I was looking at. Several thin sheets were stacked together so I could see different layers of drawings of tubes and lines and squares and arrows. I looked over at Iris who shrugged back at me.

"Oh for Fyea's sake." Copper came down off her perch and squeezed in between us. "There," she pointed at one of the squares. "That's an access panel. Here," she pulled up one of the sheets, traced along a curving tube, "a maintenance hallway. At this point," she peeled back another sheet, pointed to another square marked with an arrow, "only one thickness of wall separates the hall from another corridor that's *past* the security checkpoint."

Iris and I still didn't get it. Copper slapped the paper. "Don't you see? It's the Crescent. It's the way in."

— 9 —

No Action without Reaction

Micah did most of the talking. Copper still seemed hostile to the idea of sharing any of this with us. Micah was excited enough for both of them. "It's something that's never been done before. Imagine the story it will make."

"It's not a bad plan," Iris said thoughtfully, staring at the blueprints. "A small, tight group, well-armed and well-informed."

Encouraged, Micah went on. "Copper can build jammers to block their passive security. Then it's just a matter of—"

"No."

Both of them turned, looked at me like they'd forgotten I was there. "The Crescent's security isn't just a matter of sensors and checkpoints," I said. "They've got layers of plans and redundancies created specifically so no one from the outside can predict them. The things Seana used to tell me about—and that was all before the world went to hell. You think, now they're the only people left with real resources, their security isn't going to be even tighter?

"Plus, they're all Jansynians up there. And we're not. So the first time any of Copper's people get spotted by anyone, it's over. No one's going to think for a second they belong."

"Copper knows what she's doing," Micah said, looking to her for help, but Copper just sat staring. Still sulking? Micah pushed on, but with less confidence. "We've got breakdowns and schematics—"

"You may know the tech, but that doesn't make you an expert on Jansynian security. None of us are. I'm the closest we've got, and I'm saying it isn't possible."

Copper snorted. "Not an expert. Just someone who used to date a girl who liked to pillow-talk."

Micah spread his hands, a pleading gesture at Copper. "What's wrong? Yesterday you were five kinds of excited about this."

Copper looked at me, her eyes narrowed. Suspicious. A clear answer.

Micah folded the plans back up. "Maybe we should drop this. Until everyone's calmed down."

"Maybe." Copper stood, brushed off her knees. "For now, I've got a circuit board that needs rewiring and tools to forge."

I knew a dismissal when I heard one. I hadn't gotten to ask any of Amelia's questions, but Copper didn't seem in a mood to answer. "We can talk again tomorrow." After I'd helped Seana. After I'd earned a Jansynian favor. When I'd be able to prove it wasn't so horrible that I was working with them.

Micah, Iris, and I left Copper alone. We gathered at the edge of her platform. I leaned against the railing, took in the dizzying view. From here, there were enough shelters and platforms and walkways between us and the lift I couldn't see any hint of it. I could almost pretend we were in our own world. "So what's the next step?"

"I should go fill Amelia in." Iris climbed over the rail. "I'll see you tonight." She stepped over the edge, shifting as she fell until falcon-Iris snapped out her wings and sped back towards downtown.

Micah watched with open admiration. "Wouldn't that be a handy trick to know?"

"No kidding."

"Look," he said, "I don't know what's gotten into Copper. But she isn't usually like this."

I could understand. "Her sister's in danger. The Jansynians are scary. And it's the end of the world. None of us are exactly at our best right now."

Micah laughed. He'd always been like that, quick to laugh, quick to find joy in things. I was amazed he could still be that man.

And I realized that somewhere along the line, without even noticing, I'd stopped being mad at him.

Micah moved up next to me, leaned onto the railing so that he rested on folded elbows. "Do you believe that?" he asked. "That it's the end of the world?"

"What else could it be? Since the Abandon—"

He laughed again. "Oh, come on, Ash. Don't tell me you've bought into that."

"Bought into what?" I might not be angry, but that laugh had been annoying. Like he knew something I didn't. "What else would you call it?"

He must have heard it in my voice, because he leaned in, bumped our shoulders together. "Sorry, I didn't mean anything. I was surprised, is all. One thing when all the news started talking about the Abandon. I get that. They needed some flashy word, some way to talk about the story. But you're a priest. You really think the gods would just run off and leave us?"

"They're not here anymore." I swept my hand out, the whole city before us. "People are dying. The whole world is dying. What else can we think?"

"That there are reasons," Micah said softly. "That the universe makes sense."

I shook my head, although I couldn't have told you what I was denying. "How else would you explain it? What else would you call it?"

"I don't know," he answered calmly. "That answer's going to take wiser folk than me. But I don't believe they'd just leave us here without warning or explanation. I don't believe any of the Thirteen were that cruel."

I had nothing to say to that, nothing that wouldn't be me lashing out at Micah who'd done nothing to deserve it. Maybe he had faith, but I couldn't move past the evidence of the world before my eyes. If the gods weren't here anymore, how could that be for any reason except they no longer wanted to be?

We stood together in silence. If nothing else good came out of this business—if we couldn't save Spark or Miroc or anyone, I was at least grateful to have found Micah again. For however long we had left, it was good to be with my friend.

"I should go," I finally said. If I was going to do serious magic tonight, I needed time to prepare. To remind myself what I was doing.

"Come back tomorrow," he said. "I'll talk Copper around."

I had to be honest. "It's still a bad plan. Breaking into the Crescent—it'll be a disaster."

Micah put a hand on my shoulder, his voice both earnest and desperate. "Bring us something better. Find us a way out."

"I promise."

He nodded and let me go, even if he knew as well as I did it was a lie. The gods were gone now.

We'd run out of miracles.

— 10 —

Storyteller and Dreamers

No one with any sense went into the temple district anymore. The burned-out ruins had become home to the worst kinds of criminals. Desperate, angry, and independent—not the sort you want to run into in the dark.

This wasn't my first time sneaking into Kaifail's lost territory, but that didn't mean I felt confident as Iris and I slipped from shadow to shadow moving towards the city's rotten core.

Leftover light from the still-living parts of Miroc outlined the skeletal remains of the once magnificent complex. The buildings that made up Kaifail's church had spread across four city blocks, with the two largest being the great theater in the front and the library in the back. We were here for the latter.

Iris and I stopped across the street from the theater. We took one last look around, as though we'd be able to spot anyone lurking in the darkness behind us. At least no one would follow us once we made it onto church grounds.

Iris waved me across the last open patch we had to cross before the edge of the ruins. "Your house, you lead." She hated this part as much as I did.

Faking a boldness I didn't feel, I stepped forward into the ruins.

No matter how many times I'd been through it, I wasn't prepared for the ward. What started with a buzzing in my spine spread through me as a fever chill. As I crossed an invisible boundary buried in the long-dead grass, the world spun around me.

Behind me, I heard Iris gag. Her discomfort more than my own pushed me forward.

As we picked our way through the charred and sooty mess that had been the narthex and visitor's center, I struggled against the dizziness and nausea of the warding pattern. This was magic beyond my comprehension, and while I recognized how important it was to protect our space and our secrets, I hated that I was as vulnerable to it as any trespasser.

The inner courtyard—desiccated and rocky, but still recognizable—marked the boundary of the outer ward. I made it there just in time to keep from losing the meager dinner I'd scrounged from the office fridge. As soon as Iris crossed out of the trouble zone, she dropped to her knees, gasping for air.

I waited. It always hit her harder, but she would recover faster than I. The cost and benefit of being less-than-solid in a metaphysical sense. A shudder rippled through her, then she got to her feet. "Let's go."

Dark Kaifail's sanctum had been skeletonized by the fires, but it was more stable than it appeared. Decay and rot were siphoned off by more magic. Amazing the greatness desperation had driven us to. Before the Abandon, we were far too bickery to have ever worked together on magic of this scale. I picked my way through fallen timbers and scorched granite, trying not to leave tracks in the soot.

At the staircase down, I took Iris's hand. This was the last and most serious layer of protective magic. Nothing harmful or painful. A simple and powerful misdirection. To those who didn't bear Kaifail's mark, these stairs didn't exist. She closed her eyes and let me drag her down. Her entire body was tense. Even though she'd been here before—even though she knew the stairs existed and led to very real rooms below—she had to fight against the evidence of her senses and a conviction that I was dragging her into the floor.

Powerful magic indeed.

Fortunately, this magic had a boundary as well, and I was able to let go once we'd stepped through the archway at the bottom. "You okay?"

"I'll live." There was still just enough ambient light from the city I could make out her yawn. "Let's get moving. I don't want to spend another whole night in the field."

Only one room in the basement remained intact, and it was worth every bit of the magic that had gone into its protection. Too bad I was the only priest still alive who got to use it.

Once we were inside with the door closed behind us, I pulled out a couple mini-lamps and hung them off hooks in the walls. I unpacked the equipment I'd brought, as Iris prowled all about, looking for entertainment.

Before the Abandon, this workroom had been a hub of activity. Archivists like myself, historians, mathematicians, and mystics alike had used this space for the trickiest of magic, taking advantage of generations of rituals that had been carved into the floor. Now the spacious room was a crowded mess of what books and artifacts and miscellaneous treasures we'd managed to rescue.

Iris had no interest in the books and only passing curiosity for the arcane paraphernalia. "Here, help me with this," I called over to her. "The faster I get set up, the faster I can be done."

She helped me shove aside books and papers and bags of who-knew-what to clear the circle I needed. Then she stepped back to watch as I pulled out some chalk and started carefully adding to the sigils that were already carved into the floor. It was finicky work that required the whole of my concentration.

"You humans." Iris stepped up onto an overturned dresser as I had to extend my sigils to where she'd been standing. "You treat magic like it's a chore." She dropped her voice into an eerily accurate copy of my own. "Oh no, laundry day again. This pattern isn't clean enough. Better add more starch."

I refused to take the bait. This time. "There's a chest-of-drawers with candles in the back. You want to bring me a few?"

I focused on my ritual edits; even if I'd done them hundreds of times before, careless mistakes could be disastrous. So far, I was laying standard designs; I hadn't started trying to work in the changes I would need to adjust for the new media. By the time I was done, I realized Iris still hadn't returned with the candles. I sighed and went to look for her.

Iris had made it to the candles and even had some in her hand, but I found her sitting on a pile of atlases, staring at the mural that covered the back wall. "You have the attention span of a goldfish."

Iris rolled her eyes. She held out the candles without looking at me. "I never noticed this before."

The mural spread out at least thirty feet along the wall. This had been just another workroom in the vast temple, and I remembered when this mural had been painted, but I'd never given it much thought. It was only one of many great artistic works throughout the Dark God's sanctuary.

Now I gave it a serious look, and it was easy to tell why it had grabbed Iris's attention. It was quite something. Just because we priests of the Dark God weren't as prone to theatrics as our Bright God compatriots didn't mean we lacked a sense of story. Whoever had painted this mural had been both gifted and faithful.

Kaifail was at the center, naturally. Vibrant and alive, taller than the rest, laughing. I recognized the face he wore. The mural's artist had used our now-dead Favored Son as his model for the god. For all the gods, I assumed, he'd used their Favored Children.

Not that I'd ever seen most of them. But Jansyn, just to the right and a little behind his brother, had a face that echoed every one I'd seen in the Crescent. Settled in the grass in front of Kaifail, Fyea could have been another sister to Copper and Spark. All the gods looked happy, or at least content. A far more harmonious tableau than they ever managed in reality.

Her entire body radiating sadness, Iris crept up to the far left of the mural. Her Favored Child wasn't present like the rest— how could one paint a creature who had no real shape? She reached out to touch the radiant sphere of energy that was the artist's rendition of Iris's creator. Drinion didn't answer, of course. I had to look away from the naked loss on Iris's face. We didn't talk about the gods, she and I. Not about our lives as priests or what their disappearance had meant. And almost nothing remained in the city to remind us of them in day-to-day life.

"Micah said—earlier, he and I were talking. He doesn't believe in the Abandon. He doesn't believe they just left us."

"Does it matter?" Iris asked in a defeated voice. "They're gone. Knowing why, it won't bring them back."

I hated that she sounded like that. I walked along the wall in the opposite direction, tried to give her some privacy. The other end of the mural, on the far side from Drinion, was a human-looking man, shrouded in shadow. His skin was pale, his eyes deep blue, and for some reason, he looked familiar. It must have been the late hour, the stress of the last few days, the fact I'd passed this mural a hundred times back when the church had been alive, because I knew I'd never met the Silent One's Favored Son.

But I was stalling. I had work to do.

Candles in hand, I fetched the data stick and my NetPad, along with the small portable generator I needed to power it. Now came the tricky part. If this had been a physical book or papers, I would have known exactly what to do. As it was, I would have to improvise.

But this was my job, and dammit, I'd been good at it. One of

Kaifail's archivists, I'd spent my time analyzing documents, digging out the truth of their authenticity. Anyone could trace history and provenance, but with magic, we could reach into the reality of the object itself and determine if any changes had been made at any point over the course of its life.

And oh, but I couldn't deny this felt good. I missed the careful, crunchy precision magic demanded, drilling down layer after layer to detangle the complex strings of reality. I loved the problem. I loved the working through it. For me, the real high was not finding the solution, but the moment of inevitability when I first realized the solution could be found, and that I was the one who could find it.

The data stick held one folder. Within that, a mix of videos and documents. On the surface, nothing looked wrong, but anything so simple as a modification date out of place, Seana would have found. I needed to go deeper.

Even the best forgeries left traces. A lesson from day one of my training. No secret was so well hidden it couldn't be found. The trick was learning not just where to look, but how to look. How to see. That was where the magic came in.

But how? Working with a book, a physical page, I would have sensory clues. Rough edges, tiny smudges, even a change of ink texture. The physical cues guided my focus, helped me zoom in on potential problems. Without those, it came down to a matter of examining the files word by word, sentence by sentence, in a process that could take weeks or months. We didn't have that kind of time.

I opened a couple of the documents. Technical specs and a paper on the weather science. All of it over my head. But again, if the problem had been something a subject-matter expert could find, Seana wouldn't need me.

I moved the NetPad to the center of my work circle, arranged and lit the candles, read through the weather paper. Harder to focus when I didn't understand what I was reading, but not impossible. I read it a second time. Locked my eyes on the screen and let my peripheral vision blur. As I sunk into a meditative state, the glow of the candles grew and everything outside the circle faded to shadow, lost behind the wall of light.

I read through a third time. This time, I hardly saw the words on the screen. I read their shape, their pattern, their rhythm. Compared it to the words I had absorbed on my first two readings. Nothing caught; nothing triggered. I got to the end of the document with no sense of anything that didn't belong.

Which meant either the papers hadn't been altered, or they were going to require a detailed approach. Time to look at the videos.

I had to admire Seana's meticulousness. She'd given me a folder full of video files, organized by camera, time-stamped, with lists of every person who came into the camera's field. Trouble was, everything was so well ordered I could easily calculate the days—no, weeks of footage.

Overwhelmed, I stood, and the world snapped back into focus. Iris had wandered back over and had stretched out on the floor just outside my circle. I sighed. "This is hopeless. I don't even know how to start."

"My problem," I said to Iris as I dragged the cursor across random files, "is I've got too many variables. The first unknown is *if* any of these files have been tampered with. The second question is whether my usual approach will work in this different medium. So if I look at a file—really look at a file—and don't find anything, is that because there's nothing to find or because I'm not using the right method to find it?"

Iris stared up at the ceiling, arms crossed over her face. "How should I know?"

"Will an electronic medium even retain traces of change?"

"Oh god." Iris knocked her head against the floor. "We're going to be here forever."

"If I could just—"

Iris's body melted until she was once again the orange cat. She gave an imperious meow and curled into a ball. So much for help from Iris.

At least I had a place to start: Seana's suspicions of her husband. I had to admit, I wanted him to be guilty. It wasn't like he'd taken her from me—our separation had been much more complicated and came long before he'd entered the picture—but he stood for everything that had come between us. Jansynian blood and Jansynian politics and Jansynian business—first, last, and always.

Skimming through the lists of names attached to each camera's recordings, only three of the five cameras listed him regularly, and after a quick glance at footage from each, I was able to narrow my target to one—the camera focused directly on his work area—rather than the two that covered areas he just moved through a lot.

I had one more data point. I knew that sabotage, if it had occurred, happened before the first satellite test failed. So that narrowed my field further.

I went back to the documents folder. Separated out everything that had Eddis's name on it. Here, again, I was able to winnow things down, separating out papers, reports, and specs he had authored from those he simply approved.

I opened the versioning log, and here was where I started to see a pattern. Eddis was a man of routine. Most Jansynians were, as far as I could tell, but Eddis raised anal retentive to an art form. Each day, he apportioned his time—down to the minute—in the exact same way. If he was reviewing code for the higher-level satellite functions at ten a.m. on the first day of the week, he was doing the same thing at the same time in the middle of the week, at the end of the week, at the end of the month. Once I had all the files arranged by what aspect of the project they belonged to, I could see the history of Eddis's life writ large across the check-out and update log. Day after day after day.

Except for one.

I double-checked the log, counted through the versioning history, made sure I really was seeing what I thought. One evening— one single instance over the course of three months, where he kept a file checked out an hour longer than usual. Had he just had extra trouble with it that day? Had he been interrupted? What had happened?

Time to go back to the video.

I found the footage for the evening in question, started it running twenty minutes before the usual time he would have checked the document back in . . .

And spent the next hour staring at Eddis's back, hunched over the computer terminal. Nothing I could see—no reason he should have changed his behavior, no interruption that should have broken his pattern. Everything exactly the same.

At least, as far as the video showed. "Gotcha," I whispered.

Kitty-Iris raised her head, tilted it to one side, her ears pricked forward. A clear question—was I done?

"Sorry. Just getting started." But now I knew where to start. One variable solved. Now all I needed was the magic.

Something happened to Eddis that kept him from sticking to his pattern. Of that much, I was certain. I was also sure Seana had found this same inconsistency. She probably ran this bit of video through whichever tests she had. Which meant the shenanigans, if they existed, were buried deep.

I selected a fifteen-minute segment before what should have been the check-in time and set it to run on a loop. As before, when I'd been reading the file, I let myself sink into it, locked my eyes on the screen and let the rest of the world fade away. Over and over, I watched him sitting there, typing on his computer. Now reaching for his drink. Now tapping on the desk. Now scratching at his neck.

I turned up the audio and closed my eyes. Heard the steady hums of computers and fans. The whisper-sigh of the air conditioning kicking in. The soft clicks of Eddis's keyboard.

I opened my eyes again and measured my breathing against his. In and out. In and out. Sigh. Shift. Rustle. Until I knew every rhythm of his body. Confident I would recognize the slightest variation, catch the smallest glitch, I backed up a full hour and settled in to watch.

Except . . . I didn't see anything. Even in my heightened, meditative awareness, I couldn't find a single breath out of place. No twitch in posture, no break in typing, nothing. Whoever had modified this tape was better than good. Whoever fixed this video was a master.

The other option was I had simply picked wrong, but I wasn't ready to consider that. Not yet.

Once more, I backed it up. This time, only half an hour. If finesse wasn't going to find me the weak point, I'd have to do this the slow way. I closed my eyes, lay a hand over the screen, and clicked forward frame by frame.

I had no idea if this approach would work. It usually required direct, physical contact for me to sense the magic, sense the change in whatever I analyzed. Was the video too many levels removed from the physical computer for me to get any sense of it?

Could I get further inside? The screen beneath my fingertips was glass. Under that, the video, projected by lights. Images defined by electrical pulses. Those pulses triggered by . . .

I had no idea. So much for that train of thought.

I needed to listen for the change—the change I knew had to be there. But it was well hidden. I no longer believed this could simply be sophisticated video editing. No technological solution could have buried the threads of the change this deep. Was Seana not the only person at Desavris hiring people who could do magic?

Oh but there! There it was. The tiniest jolt beneath my fingers. A twist of energy that didn't belong. The slightest echo against reality. The circle around me caught the breath of energy and amplified it, drew it through the lines, and the candles around me flared. Yes, I'd found it.

I clung to that tendril of change, fed energy back into it, traced it to its heart. Now I had a lever. A wedge to press in between the video I'd seen and the real video that lurked beneath. Data could be erased, changed, altered, but the universe forgot nothing. No pattern, once created, ever disappeared. All I had to do was trace the line of change, follow it back, strip it away.

Like a loose thread in a sweater, once I'd found that one little piece sticking out, the rest unravelled. All it took was one good tug. I opened my eyes again, double-checked I hadn't shifted in the circle.

And pulled.

As before, I saw Eddis at his computer, typing away. But I was so attuned to his rhythms, his mannerisms, the difference this time was obvious. He kept shifting his weight, fiddling with his jacket, and once he even glanced back over his shoulder. The man was nervous. More than that. Afraid?

Afraid of what? I had to wait and watch. Now I'd sunk into the magic, the scene had to roll along at its own pace. I was a passenger on this trip.

Except—why could nothing about this go smoothly? The scene wavered and blurred as the magic tried to slip away from me. I pushed back, worked to keep my concentration. This had never happened before. Once I was in, I should be in.

I didn't even know how to fight it, except through focus and resolve. But that was the spinning-plate approach to magic, where the more I thought about it, the harder it became. All I could do was force my mind clear and bend all my will to watching Eddis fidget.

He looked over his shoulder again, back into the workroom. "Hello?" he called out. "Is someone there?"

I couldn't pick up on whatever had him jumpy. I didn't hear footsteps or breathing or any other noises that would suggest someone else in the lab. Paranoia? Unsurprising if he were about to commit some act so heinous he had to cover it up with magic.

The thought excited me and again the vision rippled. I took a deep breath, calmed myself, sunk deeper in until I'd lost all track of my own body. All I knew was Eddis Desavris and his sterile workroom in the heart of the Crescent.

When the shadows started to move, I thought it was some trick of the magic. Another waver in the vision, or an artifact of the dark, shadowy room in which my body sat. Only when Eddis started staring at the same murky corners, the tenebrous caves under tables and desks, did I realize he saw the same thing I did. The shadows in here were changing, reaching, spreading. Although the light hadn't changed, the darkness grew.

I pushed further into the vision, anchoring myself in a web of magic. I closed in on the time Eddis should have finished with this work; something was about to happen. I knew it.

But knowing it was coming wasn't the same as being ready.

Eddis turned back to his computer; his typing picked up speed. Trying to finish quickly and leave. He didn't see the shadows flow out from their homes. Didn't see them pool on the floor behind him. Didn't see them rise up into a form that wouldn't quite resolve. A twisting shape of claws and wings and teeth, all made of darkness. He didn't see the thing swoop down on him from behind. Didn't have warning. Didn't know what was about to happen.

The shadows wrapped around him, dragged him backwards off his chair. He tried to scream—I saw his mouth open—but a stream of darkness rushed into the open orifice and he made no sound. He thrashed on the ground. No more than a few seconds, but it seemed an eternity. And all I could do was watch.

I wished to Kaifail I hadn't.

For a long time he lay still, covered by the shadow. He'd stopped breathing. No question in my mind he was dead. When the shadow around him started to diminish, I thought it was fading away as inexplicably as it had arrived.

Until I realized, it wasn't fading away. It was flowing into Eddis. Seeping in through his mouth, his nose, his eyes. Soaking into his body. Until it was gone.

I thought I'd seen the worst of it.

And then Eddis blinked.

And looked at me.

I jerked awake, jumped to my feet, opening my eyes to chaos. Roaring columns of flames surrounded me—the candles gone wild.

"Ash!" Human again, Iris paced back and forth outside the circle.

"I'm fine. Stay back."

The circle was a mess. My NetPad was a melted puddle of plastic and circuits. The inset patterns had done their work—they'd shunted the magic backlash away from me—but they hadn't survived the experience. The whole working circle had scorched and cracked.

The fire guttered and died, leaving a ring of smeary black wax. I stepped out of the circle, next to Iris, and surveyed the damage.

"What happened?" Iris pulled at my sleeve, brushed my hand. Brief, fluttery touches of concern.

"I saw him die. Gods, Iris, I saw Eddis die."

"Seana's husband? But he's still—" She broke off, concern drawing her brows together.

We were out of our depth and I knew it. But one thing I had to do—and fast—was warn Seana of the monster in her house.

I pulled out my wireless. She answered immediately. "Ash, where are you?"

I couldn't think of a good way to break the news, so I settled for fast. "Eddis is dead."

Silence on her end. Then, "How did you know?"

"Wait, what?" Too much happening too fast for my brain to parse her question. "Say that again?"

Seana's voice was calm, without a trace of upset. Even knowing this was the Jansynian way, I found it chilling as she explained what happened. "We were sharing a late dinner in our apartment. Nothing unusual. When he started to convulse, then fell over. Before the paramedics could get here, he was dead."

"When? How long ago?"

"Minutes," she said.

I had to stay calm, had to think. The shadow-creature that had been inside Eddis—had my magic driven it off somehow? Was it still—"Seana, listen to me. You're in danger. There's a thing . . . a monster . . ." How could I explain it? "Stay in a well-lit area. Wait for me. I'm on my way."

I hung up. Iris was watching. I'd left the workroom an awful mess, but I wasn't going to take the time to clean it up. I did take a careful step back into the circle to grab the data stick. The plastic had melted away, but the information might still be retrievable. "Let's get out of here."

I wished the wards could tell the difference between people coming and going, but exiting the grounds was just as nausea-inducing as entering. More, given I'd spent the last few hours sensitizing myself to magic. The vertigo was intense. I had to stop and rest several times, leaning over with my hands on my knees to support me. I kept my feet most of the way, managed not to collapse until I reached the edge of the grounds. Iris stood over me as I fell to my knees, gasping, hoping if I breathed deep enough the world would stop spinning.

Which meant she was paying attention to me and I was paying attention to the withered husks of grass between my fingers and neither of us noticed the shadowy figures moving in to circle us.

Until one of them spoke. "Told ya, boss. Told ya I saw scavengers in your territory."

Because the night wasn't already bad enough. Without lifting my head I glanced around, counted seven sets of feet. Four pairs were human, clad in frayed sandals and a pair of boots. Two sets belonged to lizards—clawed, armored, and muscular. And the last pair, also clawed, but delicate, arching, and feathered.

One of the men had spoken, but it was the bird our would-be-brigands looked to. Iris's leg, pressed against my shoulder, tensed. I raised my head, but didn't try to stand. Not yet. "We're not scavengers."

The Oulirian looked down at me, feathered arms folded across its barrel chest. Her? His? In the dark, I couldn't make out the colors of the beads and ribbons woven through its wings that would tell me its gender. To guess wrong would be dangerous.

I didn't like the fact the bird was in charge of four burly men and two burlier lizards. And that of all of them, the bird was the only one unarmed. This was obviously a gang that valued strength, but Oulirians weren't strong. Mostly feathers and hollow bones in the shape of a man. Either of the two lizards should have been able to break this bird in half. Which meant it brought something else

117

to the table. Something the rest of them didn't have.

Like me, like Iris, the Oulirian was gifted.

"What did you take?" The Oulirian asked in its strange warbling voice. They didn't have beaks—not exactly—but the sharp ridges around their lips weren't flexible and didn't move as they talked. The words came from deep in its throat, while its mouth stayed eerily still.

"Nothing," Iris snapped. I lay my hand on her calf, trying to calm her. We had to stay calm. Couldn't afford to panic. Not now. Not now.

"You were in there an awful long time for nothing," said the man to the bird's right. The same who had spoken before.

The Oulirian waved a graceful, clawed hand, silencing its man. At the same time, I felt the hairs all over my body standing up. Gods, this was bad.

"Easy this will be." It raised its hand and the air around me sparked. Motes of electricity danced and streaked to surround its hand, combining into crackling bolts of energy. "Share." A bolt of lightning shot out from its fist, shattering one of the stones within Kaifail's courtyard. "Or suffer."

"Share what?" I tried to sound annoyed, rather than terrified. "There's nothing in there. Nothing of value."

"Then why all the magic?" That from one of the lizards. "Why all the work to protect something that's got no value?"

"On your feet." The Oulirian punctuated the order with another bolt of lightning—this time, close enough I could smell the singed air.

Iris grabbed my arm to help, and in doing so, pulled my shirt askew. In the dark, it shouldn't have mattered. Turned out the bird could see far better than I could. "Priest!" it shrieked. Wind swirled around us as it spread its wings and launched into the air. "Kill them! Kill them both!"

That was enough for Iris. Faster than a blink, the woman beside me was gone, replaced by a towering, snarling bear.

"Shifter!" the Oulirian hissed.

One of the men was in reach of Iris and took a blow to the head that sent him flying. When he hit the ground, he didn't move again. But that trick would only work once. The other five all stepped back. The lizards had their swords out, and while bear-Iris had the advantage of height when she reared up, they had mass. And the horns and plates that protected their bodies.

The men all had guns, and we had about half a second before they remembered to use them. And I couldn't forget the Oulirian up above us, whipping the air into a storm of dust, with lightning at its beck and call. The only thing our side had going for it was the fact they were all looking at Iris right now. Ignoring me.

I grabbed for the first idea that popped into my head—the same patterns I'd used last night against the Jansynians. Only quicker and dirtier. The Oulirian flapping around in the air above our heads, generating all kinds of kinetic energy, while his guys on the ground were taking aim at Iris. A link between them established in my mind set the men swearing and dodging invisible blows. It caused trouble for the Oulirian, too, as it had to work harder to keep the sky. Beating its wings faster and harder. Increasing the assault on the men.

The Oulirian knew exactly what I was doing. "Kill the priest!" it screeched.

One of the lizards came at me, but Iris grabbed him by the shoulders, digging her claws into the cracks between shoulder and back plates. He pushed back, drove an elbow-spike into her flank and she roared at the sudden pain of it. In the darkness, I couldn't see if he'd drawn blood. He flipped his sword around in his other hand to run her through, but she shoved him away.

I didn't waste any of the time she'd bought me. I dug my finger into the dead husks of grass, into the sandy dirt beneath, and turned a circle around myself. The rough circle became the physical anchor of a different twist to the magic I'd already done. A barrier that would turn kinetic motion aside. Just in time as the second lizard rushed at me, sword forward. My barrier flung him sideways. Same for the bullets that crashed in my direction from the men, now free of my original pattern.

They learned fast, these guys, and shifted their aim to Iris. She roared again as they pelted her with gunfire.

I'd run out of clever ideas. We were pretty much fucked.

— 11 —

Secrets

Rescue arrived in an unexpected form.

Gunfire added to gunfire and I didn't know it came from out-side until I saw one of our attackers yell and clutch his shoulder. Then another did the same.

The Oulirian spun in the air, casting about for the new threat. I couldn't see anyone or anything in the shadowy street, and I didn't want to waste time looking.

Iris pounced on one of the lizards. His sword impaled her shoulder, but the inertia of her jump was enough to knock him to the pavement. She brought one massive paw down against his head and he went limp.

This was too much for the thugs. The bird shot straight up and was quickly out of sight. With their leader fled, the rest lost heart. The four who could still run, did.

Iris shifted back to herself. I could see blood all down her chest, dripping down her leg, but in the dark, I couldn't tell how badly she was hurt. "Iris, are you—"

"Shh." She stood at alert, head cocked, her gaze darting up and down the street. "Who's there?" she called out.

The man who stepped from the shadows was too pale to have been from Miroc. But he looked familiar and, after a moment's thought, I knew why. I'd seen his face on the mural mere hours ago. "Iris, be careful."

The man—the Favored Son—looked over at me with a little smile. "I just saved your life, Joshua Drake. You have nothing to fear from me."

I dredged his name from the back corner of my mind. Syed. From the list I'd memorized in primary school. Every kid had to learn the names of all the Favored Children. The same face on the mural, because Syed had been Favored Son of the Silent One at the time that had been painted. He'd been Favored Son of the Silent One when I was a kid. As far as I knew, he'd been Favored Son of the Silent One since the first ape learned to walk upright.

The only problem was, all the Favored Children were dead. What horrible compounded nightmare were we living in that this man was still alive? That alone of all the Favored Children, he'd escaped assassination?

And what was he doing here, on the streets of Miroc in the middle of the night?

Iris looked back and forth between us, dazed. As I stepped closer, I could see her hands shaking. How bad was she hurt? "Ash," her voice wavered on the word, "do you know this man?"

"Don't you recognize him?" He'd been down at the far end of the mural, away from her god. Maybe Iris hadn't seen.

Syed looked at her, shook his head with only the barest motion. Iris looked away and limped over towards one of the unconscious men still lying in the street. "Should we do something about these bodies?"

I didn't like the floaty sound of her voice. "I think they can wait."

Syed spoke again. "Leave her be, Joshua. She's forgotten us for now."

"What?" I backed away as he approached me. For no reason I could say, I panicked at the thought of him touching me. "What did you do to her?"

"Nothing that will hurt her. We need to talk, you and I. I need to know what you did inside the temple."

"Undo . . . whatever." I waved towards Iris. "I'm not telling you anything until you make her better."

He sighed. "You insist on making this difficult."

A dizzy grayness washed over my mind. I backed another step away. "Stop it." My fists clenched as I fought for focus. Just like inside, when I'd been trying to see through the altered video, only Syed made the whole world slippery. My thoughts tried to skip away in different directions, but I kept my eyes locked on him and my mind clear. I concentrated, pushed deeper, anchored myself in my body on this street in this moment.

That was when I saw it. The darkness behind his eyes. The shadow that moved over his face.

The shadow assassin that had been in Eddis was here. Standing before me. Was in Syed. No, it *was* Syed.

"Iris!" I imbued her name with the same focus, a sense of *her*. It worked. She turned towards me, blinking and confused.

"Ash? Are you here?"

Syed was gone. I hadn't seen him slip away, wasn't sure when it had happened. But I remembered he'd been here. And any moment he could return. "Come on. We have to go. We have to go now."

She continued to stand there, shaking all over. How much blood had she lost? Or was this some lingering affect of whatever Syed had done. "Iris?"

She dropped to her knees, tried to stand again, then collapsed completely. "Iris!" I shook her shoulders. My hands came away slick with blood, but she didn't stir. I was alone on the night-black streets of Miroc with an unconscious friend, and somewhere out in the shadows, the monster that stalked us.

No way could I drag Iris back into the church. I wasn't even sure if, in her condition, bringing her back through the ward would be safe. Trying to watch every direction at once, I fumbled for my wireless and dialed Amelia.

Kaifail was smiling. Amelia answered on the first beep. I didn't wait for her hello. "We're in trouble. Iris is hurt. We got attacked coming out of the church."

Her voice was calm as she cut straight to the pertinent questions. "Where are you? Are you in danger?"

"On the street right in front of the theater. Probably."

"Vivian's on her way. If you have to move, call me back." The line went dead.

I stayed crouched next to Iris. All around, the street was quiet, but I couldn't trust that we were alone. From now on, I was going to start packing a flashlight.

Belatedly, I remembered Copper's gun, buried in my bag. In easier reach was one of the pistols dropped by our attackers. They hadn't stopped to collect their things before they fled. I fumbled the closest one into a comfortable grip and pointed it forward, out into the darkness. I could only hope I looked like I knew what I was doing.

Was Syed still out there, lurking in the shadows? Had he sent that thing inside him back out into the night? Would I see it coming? Every strip of darkness was suspicious. In the corner of my eye, every shadow seemed to be moving.

Every breath of warm air that blew across my face made me startle. Just the breeze—probably. The sounds of distant traffic that had been too faint to notice during the fight now pounded against my ears—did it cover breathing, the low scrape of stealthy footsteps?

I didn't know how long I sat there, struggling to stay calm against the certainty that any moment some deeper darkness would fall over my eyes and that would be the end. Every second stretched and warped into an eternity. If the heat death of the universe arrived before Vivian, I would not have been surprised.

The world didn't end and my brain wasn't eaten. Screeching tires and engine noise, followed by a wash of headlights announced my salvation. Vivian drove up in a cloud of dust and sand and I'd never been happier to see anyone.

Vivian pulled around next to Iris and me. In the glare of light, I could see the mess we made. So much blood. Was all of it Iris's? How much could a body lose? She was still breathing, but other than that, I had no idea what shape she was in.

Vivian came out of the car, gun drawn. "Are you hurt?" she asked, looking all around.

"Not me, but Iris needs help."

"In the car. Now. Amelia's calling a doctor."

Between the two of us, we got Iris into the back seat without slinging her around too much. I got in with her, rested her head on my lap, and took hold of her shoulders. We left the bodies of our attackers lying in the alley.

"Hold on, Iris." She probably couldn't hear me, but I didn't know what else to do as Vivian wound us through the Miroc streets.

But not downtown. Vivian sped up a ramp onto an elevated road that led to a side of Miroc I'd never visited. That I'd never been invited to. "Where are we going?"

Vivian kept her eyes on the road. "Amelia's place."

We passed withered husks of parks and half-empty shopping centers. Boarded-up cafes and broken-down ball courts. But for all that, the signs of decay were less here than in the rest of the city, and as we moved into the residential area, they all but disappeared.

Our road dropped back down to ground level and we approached a tall iron gate across the road. Vivian pulled a card out of a driver-side compartment and showed it to the man who sat in a booth outside the gate. He scanned it with his wireless, nodded, and the gates swung open. As we drove through, I saw the armed men milling about on the inside.

Not much further, Vivian drove onto a driveway that serpentined through a long-dead lawn. At the end was a compact but elegant two-story house with several other cars in the circle drive in front of the door and what looked like every single light on.

Good. I wasn't eager to stand around in the dark right now.

Half a dozen men came out of the house, all armed. Three spread around the car, watching out into the night. The other three opened the back door and carefully removed Iris. They carried her inside. Vivian and I followed.

Amelia waited just inside the door. I'd never seen her outside the office before, and she looked strange in a robe that had been thrown on over pajamas. Where another woman might have been diminished, receiving visitors in her nightclothes, Amelia was as cool and in-charge as ever. "Ash." She looked me up and down, her eyes catching on the blood smeared on my clothes. "Are you all right?"

That was a more complicated question than she knew. "I'm not shot."

"Good. There's a bathroom down the hall. Go clean up. I'll have someone dig up something fresh for you to wear."

I tried not to gawk on my way to the bathroom. Amelia was my boss, and I'd never looked beyond that to wonder who she was or where she came from. But this house—I knew P&B did well, but did it generate the sort of money to afford this house and all this security?

I passed a lavish sitting room, complete with crystal chandelier and hand-woven silk rugs I suspected were real, not the cheap knock-offs they hawked downtown to tourists. The dining room had an ornate table of real wood—expensive to import, here in the desert—and shelves full of silver and porcelain behind the glass doors of the cabinet. And it wasn't just the big things. Little touches, all over—a vase that matched the curtains, or an arrangement of silk flowers on the table—it all bespoke the kind of artistry and taste that could only be achieved with money.

Just who was it I worked for?

Even the bathroom was well appointed, with crystal knobs on the faucets and a gilded mirror over the sink. A delicate ceramic vase stood empty on the counter—how long had it been since it had held flowers?

I stripped out of my bloody clothes and ran a small amount of water into the sink, trying not to abuse Amelia's hospitality. I did claim one of the soft, embroidered washcloths from the rack that may or may not have been decorative. It felt good to scrub away the dirt. The cool water against my skin, the quiet isolation—for a few minutes, I could forget the strange horrors of the last few hours.

But only for those few minutes. "Ash!" Vivian pounded on the door, then opened it wide enough to shove fresh clothes through the gap. "Hurry up. Amelia wants to know what happened."

Sadly, I'd been there, and I wanted to know the exact same thing.

Vivian waited for me outside the bathroom. I followed her to a more casual sitting room, where a tray of sandwiches and a pitcher of tea had been set out. "Amelia thought you might be hungry."

Now I was staring at food, I was famished. "Where is she?"

"Said she had to talk to the security guys." Vivian went straight over and grabbed herself a sandwich from the pile.

I followed suit. The first bite was cold and delicious—a blend of meat and cheese, some flavors I didn't recognize, but I wasn't going to complain. "Those guys—do they work for P&B?"

Vivian shook her head. She talked around a mouthful of food. "Never seen them before. Don't know where they came from, but Amelia seems to trust them all right."

I finished one sandwich and had started on the next when Amelia joined us. "Iris will be fine," she announced, taking one of the thick, cushy chairs. "I just spoke with the doctor. He was able to remove the bullets, and with the foreign matter out of her body, her own instincts will take care of the rest."

"How soon before she's up?" Vivian asked. Without being asked, she poured a glass of tea and took it to Amelia.

Who nodded her thanks. "She'll be recovered in a day or two, I would imagine."

"Remarkable," Vivian said.

"That she is. Thank you, Vivian. You've been a great help tonight, but I shouldn't need you any further."

Vivian closed the glass-paned doors as she left, giving Amelia and me privacy. "What happened," Amelia asked, concern softening her voice. "Did something go wrong with the magic?"

"That's . . . complicated." I recounted, as best I could, what I'd seen in the pattern. I described the shadow-creature that had eaten Eddis with as much detail as I could, but Amelia's blank look told me she didn't have any better idea than I did what the thing might be.

"So this thing, this creature, has been living in the Jansynian's skin. That's how the project got sabotaged. I'm sure of it. But then it gets more complicated."

Her eyebrows drew together. "What else did you see?"

"Not there, not with the magic. Although—I have to say—something wasn't exactly right with that either." I flailed for the right words. "Like the pattern was fighting me. Or something was fighting the pattern. I don't know that it matters, but I don't know that it doesn't."

She nodded, sipped her tea. "But there was more?"

I recounted my call to Seana as close to word-for-word as I could manage, along with my own thoughts on the timing of Eddis's death. His second death. "I knew I needed to explain to Seana—to warn her. I still do. But when we came out, we got jumped by a street gang. Thieves. They freaked out when they saw I was a priest. That's how Iris got hurt." Amelia's lips tightened and I hurried on. "I don't know what we would have done, except that we got rescued."

"By whom?"

There was nothing to do but say it. "It was one of the Favored Children."

"The Favored Children are all dead," Amelia responded automatically.

"That's what I thought, too, but—" I stopped. Was Syed even alive?

Once again, I tried to remember every little detail to describe the encounter to Amelia. I hoped she'd notice some connection, some clue I had missed, but all she came up with was the same question I'd asked myself. "If this thing—Syed—made Iris forget it was there, why couldn't it do the same to you?"

"I don't know."

Amelia stood up and went to the window, looking out over landscaping that had lost its war with the desert. Floodlights still lit the grounds. My opinion—they could stay on all night. Amelia leaned her forearm against the window, tapped her fingers against the glass. "This is getting esoteric. Outside my realm of expertise." She thought a moment longer. "What do you know about the Silent One?"

Time for another sandwich. Not that imparting the sum total of my knowledge was going to take long. "He's the god of secrets.

No one knows much of anything about him. I can tell you he's one of the few gods who never created children to follow him. Syed was his Favored Son, but Syed's human." Or so I'd been taught.

"There are stories, sure. Fairy tales to frighten kids. But there're stories about all the gods. The only facts I know are that the Silent One had his temple in Tala like the rest of the Thirteen, where Syed has been his Favored Son for as long as people kept records. He didn't have any other followers or any other temples. As far as we knew, he just minded his own business."

Amelia said aloud the thought that had been lurking in the back of my mind. "That would make him unique among the gods."

The god of secrets. "So that's all of what I know. As to what I believe. . . . "

I hadn't seen more than a glimpse of Eddis in the vision, after the shadow creature had taken him. How much could I trust of that one brief impression? "The shadow came from Syed. I'm almost positive. It belonged with him, seemed more part of him than it did with Eddis."

"Which would bring us to the question of, what does he want with Desavris?"

"Maybe exactly what he's gotten. Maybe he wanted to destroy the weather project."

Amelia turned to look at me. "Then I have to wonder, does he know about Spark?"

Something tugged at the back of my mind. A memory? A suspicion? I couldn't grab it. "I think it's too dangerous to assume otherwise."

"I agree." Amelia set her glass down on the windowsill. "This technology—we can't let him destroy it. It's a matter of survival. I think it's time to bring in more help."

"There's more help?" I asked.

"For this, I think yes. But it will take some time for me to get the right message through to the right people. I don't want to draw attention. In the meanwhile, you need to check in with Director Seana. Warn her she could still be in danger."

That was one way to put it. "I'll do that right now."

After everything else I'd done tonight, tossing off the pattern to make sure my handset was still secure seemed a trivial thing. I dialed Seana.

She answered immediately. "Ash! Where are you?"

I looked over at Amelia, who nodded. "I'm at my boss's house. There's been—I got attacked. But I'm heading your way now."

"I'm sending someone to get you. Stay there." The line went dead.

I slid the handset into my pocket, along with Seana's data stick. I fished the Desavris security tab out of my bag and stuck it just below my collar bone, where it wouldn't be obvious but was still easy to access. The rest of the bag—including my growing collection of guns—I left on Amelia's floor. "What should I do after I've talked to Seana?"

"Take your time with her. She's another ally it wouldn't hurt to cultivate. Find out how far behind they are with their rain machine with Eddis removed from the picture. Get back here when you're done. Hopefully by then, I'll have progress of my own to report."

"Good luck." I was pretty sure we all were going to need it.

— 12 —

Dinner for Two

This time, the Jansynian security folks were much more polite. They held the hovercar door for me and, after a cursory scan at the security checkpoint, even invited me to enjoy my visit.

Riding up the lift, looking out into the Web, I didn't see anyone I knew. I wasn't surprised, as close as we were coming on towards morning. All reasonable people were asleep. I certainly wished I were.

Even the Desavris halls were empty of everyone but me and my escort. Which surprised me. With Eddis's sudden death, I expected more chaos—security people rushing about, or medical or something. But I'd never understood how Jansynians worked.

Again, I was escorted to Seana's office. She was at her desk. She looked up as I entered the room. Despite all that had happened, she showed none of the signs of agitation that had been there in our last meeting. Seana in a crisis was Seana at her best. She skipped over a greeting and went straight to, "Tell me what you know."

So much for small talk. "You're in danger. More than you realize. Eddis was the saboteur, but Eddis wasn't Eddis."

"Eddis is dead. He's no longer a threat."

Her words were cold. Her eyes hard. Too late I realized how this would sound to her—the accusation it seemed I was leveling.

Her husband had betrayed her. Worse, had betrayed the company. Except her husband hadn't been her husband. And if the power the shadow-creature had could alter the surveillance footage, if Syed could make Iris forget his presence right in front of her, who knew what sort of misdirections this creature had been using to keep Seana and the rest of Desavris from seeing it?

"Eddis is dead, but the monster inside him is still out there."

Seana raised an eyebrow and gestured for me to sit down. "You're going to have to explain."

I didn't try to sugar-coat. I knew this woman far too well to give her anything but the truth straight-up. I told her about my discovery with the research, the struggle I had getting the pattern to work, the vision, and the way the magic had exploded at the end.

Whatever she was thinking, feeling, I couldn't read it in her face. She got up from her desk, walked around to stand next to my chair. She looked down at me. "Truly, you saw this thing?" Her hand twitched, like she wanted to reach for me. My own hands felt weighted down by the gulf of years since we'd last touched.

"There's more."

She stepped back, putting a more professional distance between us. "What more?"

I told her about Syed. What he'd done to Iris. What he'd tried to do to me. "I resisted him, this time. But he's tied to this. Whatever magic killed Eddis, I would bet money Syed is behind it."

"And he's here, in Miroc?" Seana took another step back. It seemed even Jansynians told horror stories about the Silent One.

"Yeah. I don't know what he knows, but I have to assume it's a lot."

"And you resisted his power." Seana went back to her chair. I could tell all this had shaken her. She sat down and folded her hands before her on the desk. She sat, silent and still for several minutes. I let her think.

Finally, she looked at me again. "Tell me your analysis of the situation."

It sent a thread of warmth through me, that she would ask my opinion. "Everything ties back to Eddis's project. I don't know why Syed would want it stopped, but that's about the only conclusion I can draw."

"He may have succeeded." Seana leaned back in her chair. I'd never seen her so tired. "With Eddis dead, the research tampered with—I don't know if we'll be able to recover."

I fished the data stick out of my pocket. "Not all lost. I don't think. I was able to pinpoint the files that got changed. At least, the timing of when Eddis was . . . taken. Could the rest of your team work forward from there?"

I slid it across the desk, and she caught it. "It's possible."

That was some relief, I supposed, that we might still be able to save Miroc. Nonetheless, I'd be sleeping with my lights on tonight. If I could sleep at all.

Seana flipped the data stick through her fingers, staring at it. "I must admit," she said without looking up, "when Eddis died, my first concern was for you."

The confession made my stomach lurch. Especially coming on top of everything else I'd been through today. "What?"

She stood, still not meeting my eyes. "In all this, I never did get dinner. Although now it's closer to breakfast-time. Either way, would you care to join me? For food? In my apartment?"

I blurted out the first thing that came into my head. "Where he died?"

"It's been cleaned."

It was such a Seana thing to say. And I'd never been able to say no to her. "Sure, let's go."

135

When we'd been together, Seana had always come to my place. I'd tried to imagine what her own living space might look like, but had only managed an image of a better-organized, fancier-furnished version of my own home.

Turns out, it was nothing like that. Or like anyplace I'd ever seen. Amelia's house had been fancy, but in a perfectly normal way. Seana's home was something else.

At first, I thought we'd somehow gone outside. Except that even when the bird priests had summoned all the rain Miroc could absorb, it had never looked like this. The walls, the ceiling, even half the floor were covered with plants. Seana lived in a garden.

And it was beautiful. Flowers I'd never seen before created living artwork along the walls and between the furniture. Here and there, fruits and vegetables peeked out from clusters of greenery. Even the lights had been embedded within the plants, giving the room's illumination a soft, green feel.

Seana pushed aside a curtain of tangy-scented vines covered in waxy white flowers to reveal a closet into which she kicked her shoes. She wandered through a sunken living-room, brushing her hand along a soft-looking hedge of ferns that defined the space. Ahead of her, stairs led up to an open second floor, where I could see a bedroom and into a bath area with the most decadently huge tub I'd ever seen, but Seana turned the other direction, towards the kitchen. "Are you coming?" she asked over her shoulder.

I hesitated in the doorway, struggling against this reminder of the gulf between us. "Are you sure about this? Sure I should be here? Couldn't it hurt your reputation?"

Seana waved the question away. "I'm the director of security for Desavris Intercontinental. This is the job I needed a pristine reputation to get. And now I have it."

Conscious of the dirt—and possibly worse—on my boots, I pulled them off and dropped them next to Seana's shoes before I came all the way into her home. "This is amazing." I dug my fingers carefully through the solid layer of foliage to find the wall beneath them, discovered a rough, porous surface. The plants grew out from it.

I turned to catch Seana watching me, her face unreadable. "To be honest, I've never done much with it. Many people make their homes into a hobby. Intricate designs, living sculptures. Eddis and I never had the time."

"Does everyone have homes like this? With the plants and all?"

That earned me an affectionate smile. "With the plants, yes. Look around you, Ash. The Crescent is a city in the sky. Below us is the desert. Where else would we grow anything?"

I followed her into the small, sleek kitchen. In here, close at hand were a greater density of fruits and vegetables and greens, all carefully trimmed back from work surfaces. A flat stovetop and oven sat in the center of a u-shaped arrangement of countertop, with a sink off to one side. Along the counter were various smaller appliances, but I saw no storage anywhere. No cabinets, no pantry, not even a refrigerator.

Seana woke up a touchpad on the wall. Her fingers tapped through menus faster than I could read them. A panel slid open next to me and a pot presented itself. "Fill that with water, please." She typed some more and a different door opened, this time revealing a wrapped bundle of dry pasta and a bowl of olive oil, by the smell.

I wanted to ask how all this worked, how the system was set up, whether everyone in the Crescent lived like this. But maybe this wasn't the time. So I pushed aside the questions I wanted to ask and brought up the only subject that mattered. "How long do you think it will take, now, to get the weather satellite working?"

"I'm not a scientist." Seana requested a knife and cutting board from the magic panel and started chopping vegetables after setting the water on the stove to boil.

Right then, I knew what I should have done. If I'd copied the data stick before returning it, I could have shown it to Spark. It had all been her brainchild to begin with. Surely she'd be able to figure out what Eddis had broken and fix it.

Just how far could I trust Seana? How much was I willing to gamble on remembered affection and a woman who may have changed in the last seven years. If I made the wrong choice, Spark would suffer far more than I.

At some point, I was going to have to bring up Spark if I wanted Seana to make the assassins stop. But I didn't want to shatter the regrowing intimacy between us.

Seana ordered up more utensils and some spices in order to cook the vegetables. "You're being quiet."

"It's been a long day." My evasion was also truth. Parked on a stool in the peaceful safety of Seana's home, body and mind were starting to feel the effects of all the excitement.

Her gaze held steady. I couldn't tell what she was thinking or what she'd seen on my face. "No question the city has become dangerous." She returned her attention to the food. "And it will only get worse."

No question about it, if we didn't get water soon. "Miroc was always dangerous."

"Not like this."

The food she stirred was starting to smell very good. Tangy and sharp and fresh. I couldn't remember the last time I'd been able to afford anything fresh. Even after the sandwiches at Amelia's, my stomach rumbled. "There's nothing I can do about Miroc, except help make sure this rain gadget gets up and running. It's not like there's anywhere else I can go."

"But there is." Her voice was soft. Her words, hesitant. "Here."

Seven years ago, she'd walked out my life with no tears, no apology, only the reminder that she'd told me from day one her career came first. Her duty to her employer came first. "You left me, remember?"

"I did what I had to do then." Even now, she didn't apologize. "This is what I'm free to do now. I've missed you, Ash. And you are," a little smile broke free, "useful."

This was too much to think about right now. "I owe a lot to Amelia. I couldn't leave Price & Breckenridge."

"I would never ask you to. I can't believe you'd think I'd ask you to abandon your employer. All I'm saying is, this could be the home you return back to."

Way too much. Maybe for her as well. She turned away to summon a colander and busied herself setting the food out on plates.

It tasted amazing. We sat across from each other at the counter, both of us hyper-focused on the act of chasing the pasta and veggies onto forks. This food, the casual way she'd had me draw the water, the utter luxury of our surroundings, I couldn't deny the temptation of it.

I'd loved Seana. I still loved Seana. And when she looked up at me, her ice-gray eyes intense and said, "Stay the night. What's left of it," that was too much.

"Sure," I answered. Like she'd asked if I wanted any salt.

Seana nodded and returned to eating.

After the Abandon, after the riots, I lost myself. My mind went to sleep when my body was broken, and it never woke all the way back up. I'd been moving through a hazy world, half-aware and numb and I hadn't known it at all until now, this moment, as I followed Seana up her stairs and realized just how much I wanted her.

Not just her, if I was to be honest with myself. I wanted the world as it was back when we'd been together. I wanted my life as it had been. But that, I couldn't have. The Thirteen had found new and better toys somewhere else in the universe and had left us crying in the sand on our dying world.

I would never have the rest, but at this moment, I could have her. And in the cool, quiet air of the Crescent, where flowers still grew and water still flowed, I could forget about the city below.

At the top of the stairs, I grabbed Seana's wrist and pulled her to me. She allowed me a brief kiss, her lips cool and familiar against mine, then twisted out of my arms. "Come along, Ash."

I came along. To the bedroom, where Seana pulled off her jacket and lay it over the arm of a chair, then began unbuttoning her shirt, as efficient in this as she was with everything else in her life.

I remembered. I remembered how I could make her shiver with a touch along her spine where her shirt joined her jacket. I remembered the fit of her arms around my shoulders as I scooped her up and carried her to the bed. I remembered the feel of her lean body against mine.

We humans were the first race, and when it came to sex, we served as the blueprint when the other gods created the rest. It was something I'd worried about, our first time. Just how alien were the Jansynians? Turned out, in bed, not very. Not physically, at least.

Seana made love like she did everything else—she offered no quarter, accepted nothing short of perfection. We rolled back and forth, a mostly good-natured struggle for who got to be on top. This time, I surrendered. I just wanted—

I wanted to forget. I wanted to lose myself. I wanted to find myself.

I wanted to close my eyes and to open them again on a world that wasn't broken. I wanted to be that young man, seven years ago, whose biggest worries were his quarterly performance review and whether or not his workaholic girlfriend was going to take the weekend off.

That young man who had lived with his head in the sand. No different from the countless citizens of Miroc who trudged through their days, clinging to every familiar habit they could, waiting for the Thirteen to miraculously return.

Seana's hand stroked my cheek, and I opened my eyes. Her finger moved down, traced the lines of my scars. I'd never seen such a tender look on her face.

The moment passed as waves of pleasure engulfed us both.

After, we lay alongside each other, our only point of contact her hand resting on my chest. It felt possessive, much more familiar than the earlier open affection.

So easy to lose myself like this. To take Seana up on her offer, to give in to the security and comfort she offered. How much did Seana know about the city from which she offered rescue? "Amelia says Miroc doesn't have much time left."

"No, it doesn't." Seana spoke with calm. "We are aware of the situation below."

"What do you think will happen?"

Seana leaned up on her elbows, serious now. "If the satellite can't be fixed? I expect word will get out. The city council can't keep the water shortage secret forever. At which point you'll see chaos. Rioting, looting, burning—worse than after the Abandon, I would imagine. The city will tear itself apart. And then it will die."

Her face softened to something like regret. "It's a terrible thing, but it isn't just happening in Miroc. I can tell you that, Ash—it's all over the world. Miroc may be the worst. It was never a natural city. Elsewhere—the whole world. . . . " She sighed. "No one has the resources to save it."

Seana herself was just another of the people waiting. I shouldn't have been surprised. I took her hand, kissed her fingers. "Bring us the rain. Buy us some time."

"Time. Of course." Her eyes had gone unreadable again. She lay back down, but continued to watch me. The sun would be coming up soon, but she didn't seem at all sleepy.

"Do you miss them?" she asked. My confusion must have shown. "The gods," she clarified. "You were a priest. It must be . . . lonely?"

She'd never before wanted to know about my relationship with Kaifail. A little talk about the end of the world, and suddenly everyone discovers a spiritual side, I suppose. "I never had that kind of relationship with Kaifail. None of us did. He didn't involve himself with us."

The party line. So easy to say. And such bullshit. "We dealt with the Abandon fine because we didn't lose anything. And that was for the best, really. I knew priests from the other churches. Churches where their god took an active interest." I thought of Iris at the mural. "They were lost when the Abandon happened. Heartbroken. I can't imagine what it was like."

I squeezed her hand, not for her comfort, but my own. I stared up at the ceiling as the resentment I was always fighting to greater or lesser success bubbled up inside me. "I guess I did feel . . . all this time, we felt so independent, so proud of ourselves. We didn't need Kaifail holding our hand, whispering in our ear. We were grown-ups.

"But all along, we—all of us—assumed that if we *did* need him, if something truly awful happened, that he'd be there. That he'd help us. That if things ever got really terrible, that he'd save us."

Seana pulled her hand free, ran a finger down my cheek. "Maybe he wanted to. Something I've always regretted—what I never said to you. I promised myself if we ever crossed paths again—" She looked away, and then got up out of bed. Another touchpad, another panel, and she had a fresh stack of clothes. "I have work I need to get to. Stay and sleep, if you like."

Just like old times. I didn't know if this was true of all Jansynians, but Seana could and would go days without sleep once her mind was fixated on an important project. I envied that. "I think I will grab a nap before I head out."

She nodded. She hadn't once looked at me since she'd gotten out of bed. "Come back tonight, if you can. If your business allows it." She didn't wait for my answer, heading out of the room still half-dressed.

I could have called after her. It wasn't like there were walls between us. But I respected her need for escape. And, to be honest, I was exhausted.

I dug my wireless out of my pants and set the alarm for two hours from now. All it took was to close my eyes and I was asleep.

— 13 —

City on Fire

Exhausted as I was, I didn't sleep well. Strange, restless dreams chased me. Seana and Micah hunted by Syed, who was both man and shadow all at once. I tried to help them, tried to save them, but we were out in the desert and I couldn't breathe it was so hot and I wanted water—so badly wanted water.

I woke up sweaty and disoriented, clawing at my handset a long while before I could figure out how to stop the noise coming from it. Slowly, I remembered where I was and how I got here.

I went into the bathroom, and splashed water on my face. Then found myself staring at the sleek black shower stall. As long as I was here, how could I resist? Showers were a luxury I hadn't known in a long time, since they drove my water bill higher than my monthly salary.

The touchpad in the shower took me a minute to figure out, but after that I was rewarded with the magnificent wonder of warm water all over my skin. Talk about reminders of a better time. This was pure, sensual bliss.

It woke me up better than the alarm had and relaxed me enough my brain kicked into gear. I would have loved another few hours of sleep, but there was too much to do, too much to think about.

The world was getting worse, not better. And maybe—just

maybe—I could stop that. Not the ineffective fumblings that got me sent to the hospital last time, but real, substantive change for the better. All the pieces lay in front of me if I could get my head out of my ass long enough to figure out how to put them together.

I stepped out of the shower, refreshed and ready, when my wireless chimed—Amelia calling. As I reached for it on the bed-side table, I noticed what else lay beside it.

The data stick. With all the information about the satellite project. Seana must have laid it here last night when she un-dressed. I grabbed it and slipped it in my pocket as I answered Amelia's call.

"Are you watching the news feed?" Amelia asked in a flat voice without so much as a hello.

"Hold on." I fumbled at the screen embedded in Seana's wall across from the bed. It responded to my touch, and I dug through menus until I found what I was looking for.

Once I would have had to ask Amelia which feed she meant. These days, the only news we got—and the only news that mattered—was the city channel. I touched that option and Seana's screen filled with images of thick, black smoke.

The camera pulled back and a reporter's voice identified the scene. "The library at Dorian University is the latest target in the series of attacks that have shattered the morning quiet."

The room suddenly felt colder. I couldn't catch my breath. "What is this?"

Amelia's voice in my ear drowned out the reporter's litany of the damages. "Terrorists. Connected to the protesters I told you about before. They want the city to open up the reservoir and re-lease the last of Miroc's water reserves."

On the screen, a map flashed up of all the attacks that had hap-pened this morning. It looked familiar, but it took my stunned mind several seconds to figure out why. This same pattern—I'd seen it in Amelia's office just yesterday—the work for another client. "You knew about this!"

"We knew it was coming; we just didn't know how soon."

For the second time in as many days, I was reminded just how little I actually knew about my employer. "Who's *we*?"

Amelia ignored the question. "Listen to me. This highlights the urgency of getting that Desavris satellite to work. Tell me where you are with Seana."

"I don't think Seana's the person I need to talk to." I didn't say any more. I couldn't. Not here. Even if the wireless wasn't being monitored, I couldn't assume a lack of surveillance just because I was in the director's own suite.

Fortunately, Amelia knew what she was doing. Probably even better than I did. She didn't ask what I planned to do. Although honestly, she probably didn't need to. "Make it your priority," she said.

Image after image of devastation flashed by on the screen. Dorian library. The southside market. A public school. The martial academy. A shipping depot not far from the Crescent. Fire and rubble, but it didn't look like any casualties were being reported. In fact, all these were building that had pretty much fallen to neglect as the city struggled to survive. "This was a warning shot, wasn't it."

"Very good, Ash."

Another live shot of the still-burning library. I'd spent quite a lot of time there in the old days, but after the destruction of the churches, my sense of outrage had gone numb. "So what's next?"

Amelia didn't answer immediately and I reached up to turn off the news feed as the scene shifted to the reporter talking with people on the streets. I didn't need to hear witness accounts. I'd witnessed plenty first hand.

"You just focus on your job." Amelia's words came out clear in the suddenly silent room. "Let me worry about mine."

A dismissal. Except I had one more question. "How's Iris doing?"

That evoked a smile I could hear. "She's up and talking. Annoyed I'm making her stay in bed. I don't imagine I'll be able to keep her off her feet long."

Relief went a long way to easing the tension the attacks on the city had evoked. "Say hi for me."

"Say hi yourself. I want you back here to report this afternoon."

She hung up on my affirmative.

Miroc was on fire. As I rode the lift down from the safety of Desavris, I had a clear view of smoke rising from five still-burning buildings and a number of smudgy dark clouds that marked fires recently extinguished. I waited to feel the panic, the suffocating chill I'd woken to for months after the riots that had hospitalized me. But time, it seemed, truly did bring healing, and a different emotion was rising within me. A clear, hot anger.

Terrorists, Amelia had said. And what better weapon than fire to bring terror to a city with no water?

I fished the security disc out of my bag and pressed it against my collarbone, where it would be easy to conceal under clothes. Unnecessary, as it turned out. The Jansynian man at the security checkpoint greeted me without scanning it. "Mr. Drake."

Probably not a lot of humans going in and out on Seana's say-so. "I need to borrow a vehicle."

"How large?" he asked without arguing.

I fought to hide my surprise. This had been a gamble. I'd expected to have to throw Seana's name around and pray she didn't mind. But this was the Crescent, after all. The weight of Seana's authority was unspoken and assumed. It would have been graceless to force me to say it.

"I'd prefer something small and mobile. The streets today are going to be—"

"Yes," he cut me off. "Wait here, please."

Minutes later, a woman on a sleek black cycle pulled up alongside the checkpoint. She slid a tiny card out from its handlebars, which the guard inside ran through his computer, then handed to me. "It's keyed to your security disc and fully charged. It should suit your needs."

"Thanks." The woman hovered as I slid the card back into the cycle's control panel and swung my leg over. As I settled in the seat, the engine came to life—a soft, humming vibration I could feel all through my body. I looked around for anything resembling an accelerator.

"It responds to your body-weight," the woman said. "Lean forward to accelerate. Back to slow. It's sensitive, so don't overdo. The cycle will correct itself in emergency situations."

I lifted my heels to the footrests and felt the cycle find its balance without my help. I took hold of the handgrips and leaned in. The bike zoomed forward towards the security fence. I pulled back. It screeched to a stop just short of collision.

I glanced back at the Jansynian woman, but she retained that perfect expressionlessness of which the Jansynians were so adept. The real question was, what would Seana hear about this?

I aimed myself at the gate and leaned forward again. Sensitive was an understatement. It was like the bike could read my mind. If I wanted to go slow, just thinking about forward gave the cycle enough cues to move. And if I really hunched down, we moved so fast it was almost like flying.

I could get used to this.

I raced through empty streets of blowing sand, until I'd gotten well out of range of any visual surveillance from the Crescent. I pulled over to the half-buried sidewalk, wished for some shade from the mid-morning sun, but miracles were out of the question these days.

I'd done the magic enough in the past couple days that the pattern to detect Jansynian spy tech came solid and energized to my mind with only a moment's thought. Lucky thing, too, because today I actually found some.

Locators on the bike were no surprise. There were all sorts of legitimate, even helpful reasons for it to stay in contact with the computers back at Desavris. For my purposes, however, that wasn't going to work.

The whole circuit board in the handlebars glowed blue, sending little tendrils of energy up into the air. This was going to take some delicate work if I still wanted the cycle to function once I was done. Taking one more quick look around to make sure I was alone on the street, I closed my eyes and focused on the pattern.

Magic is a slippery, finicky thing. We create patterns to help our minds lock magic into a shape we can control. The broad strokes, common controls and limitations, had standard symbols that everyone used so that places like the workroom in Kaifail's temple could exist. But this was magic I'd figured out for myself, based on Seana's explanations, and the pattern in my mind was an almost random series of numbers and shapes—suggestive of an order, but nothing that would make sense to anyone else who happened to see it. It was all metaphor, short-cuts and mnemonics to trick our brains into doing the things that came so naturally to Iris and her people.

But it worked. I concentrated on the imaginary images, muttered nonsense syllables that seemed to fit the rhythm. When I opened my eyes again, the fuzzy blue glow had sharpened, shrank. I stared, willing my vision to sharpen with the magic, until I could identify the tiny bridges on the chip that were sending out the signals I wanted to stop.

Three different locations. I leaned in, saw the blue lines reach up from one to strain in the direction of my collar. Searching for my identification. That one had to stay. The other two . . .

Another layer of control in my mind to limit the power to just those two circuits. And then a jolt, a flare, drawn from the energy of the bike itself. Just a touch—I hardly dared think about it. But I caught a tiny whiff of ozone and the blue glow faded away.

As satisfied as I could be that no one could follow, I set off for downtown and a looping, evasive ride to Spark's safehouse.

— 14 —

Promises and Threats

As I pulled up to the building, Vik was out on the front steps, smoking a cigarette and watching the plume of black smoke clearly visible from the nearest of the fires. All business this morning, he didn't give me any trouble. Just nodded. "Ash."

"Vik." I tried to gauge the distance of the fire. "You think that's going to be a problem?"

He shook his head. "Saw some bird priests flying in that direction. They should be able to keep it contained." Still, he didn't move except to give me space to climb the steps, and his attention never left the smoke.

The Oulirians had their own kind of power. The gifted ones— like the priests, like our attacker last night—had a relationship with the physical world that gave them power over air and flame. When their goddess had still been around, their power had been greater—thus the plentiful rains for our desert city—but even diminished, they should be able to keep a fire from spreading. Except there wouldn't be near enough of them to protect all of Miroc if the terrorists got ambitious.

I knocked on the door to Spark's apartment. Vogg's armored bulk answered the door. "Priest Ash of Kaifail." He sounded surprised. "Is there trouble?"

The answer, of course, was yes. "I need to talk to Spark."

He stepped aside, once again touching his fingers to his horns in what I guessed to be a gesture of respect. With Vogg out of the way, I could see Spark at the kitchen table, an array of computer bits and less identifiable tangles of wires and circuits. "Hi Ash," she greeted me brightly. "You here to keep me company?"

"I brought you a present." I dug the melted data stick out of my bag and slid it across the table at her.

Spark's long, nimble fingers dug an ancient-looking NetPad out from under a pile of other parts. She slotted in the data stick then exclaimed, "My research!"

"That's everything the Jansynians have done. All the information on their project. And somewhere in there, something is broken. The researcher they had working on this is dead." I saw no need to go in to details. "I don't know how long it will take them to sort out what went wrong. Maybe too long."

She sobered, looking up at me with her huge, clear eyes. "I saw on the news this morning. It's getting bad out there."

"It's been bad for a long time," Vogg said. His eyes found mine. "I was still with the city police during the riots, after the Abandon. There was no honor in what happened." He turned back to Spark. "The sickness has lived in this city a long time. It will be all that's left when everything else is burned away."

Spark shook her head, smiling. "People will surprise you if you give them a chance. Have faith, Vogg."

Faith in what, I wondered? "Everything will calm down if you can fix the satellite and make it rain."

"I should be able to. Once I sort through their schematics. How should I get in touch?"

"You shouldn't." I didn't want even a secure call from Spark coming in while I was up in the Crescent. "I'll check in again tomorrow morning."

Spark focused her attention back on the files. I'd lost her attention for now. Which was fine. I left her to her work.

Vogg walked me out. "I'm glad you brought this. Not just for the city. This project was dear to her, more than she would admit. It wounded her to lose it. Even more when the Jansynians couldn't bring it to fruition."

Vik was still outside, watching the thinning smoke. He moved a polite distance away and pretended to ignore us. "How long have you known Spark?" I asked the hulking lizard.

"When I left the police, Copper found me. The city wasn't yet desperate, but Copper is smart. She saw how the wind would blow. And she knew the importance of Spark's idea."

His massive, claw-tipped hands gripped the bare wooden railing that bordered the apartment building's tiny porch. "I must confess, there have been times I've questioned—I'm not certain I believe this city worth saving." He, too, looked up at the pillar of smoke, avoiding my eyes. "I was there when your temple burned. I stood aside as I was ordered. We—the police—we stood aside to let the rabid crowd have its way."

Destroying the temples had been the final act of the maddened populous. The violence against priests had started weeks earlier, and I'd been caught up in it—brought down by it—long before the temple fell. "I was in the hospital when it happened. Unconscious."

"It was shameful." Vogg didn't specify if he was talking about the rioters' actions or his own.

"They were terrified." My own hands clenched at the memory. "They still are." Now, as it had then, the air smelled of burning. My pulse spiked in response. "They're desperate and their gods have abandoned them."

At least the terrorists were taking action. Horrible, dangerous action, but it was something. "We've all been wandering, waiting for something to happen. Waiting for rescue." Waiting for the gods to come back. "If Spark's device works—if we can take that step towards saving ourselves—maybe then everyone can go back to living forwards. Maybe we'll be able to rebuild."

"You have more faith than I, Priest Ash of Kaifail."

Faith? I tasted the word. Found it bitter. "Keep safe, Vogg. I'll see you in the morning."

He stayed out on the porch to watch as I swung onto my Jansynian cycle and zoomed away.

I aimed for home. I wanted a change of clothes and maybe another quick nap. Sooner or later, I was going to need a real night's sleep, but for now, the couple hours I'd grabbed here and there were enough to keep me going.

My apartment complex was a lot like Spark's safehouse. The main floor boasted five more units like mine, with the second and third floor holding the more generous one- and two-bedroom spaces. The neighborhood sat on the far edge of Miroc—a short evening stroll could take me past the city limits and into the desert—but it was cheap and relatively safe.

I was the only human who lived in my building. Safer that way. While I kept to myself, the boneheads and lizards who shared walls with me were less likely to freak out about my status as a former priest than other races might have been—my own included. Most lizards were like Vogg or the two on the train the other day—respectful, if not always friendly. And boneheads, well, I'd never seen one of them freak out about anything.

Speaking of, one of my neighbors was out in front of my building as I pulled up, toiling away in the small, decorative cactus garden he'd managed to keep alive through the drought. He stood as I pulled up, turned his head in my direction.

I don't say he looked at me, because he didn't. Boneheads—the race formerly known as Lorath's Children—had no eyes. If Jansynians were the race the most like humans, the Lorathians were strong contenders for the title of least.

Their overall shape was similar—two legs, two arms, and a head—but there any resemblance ended. They had skin of a sort—pale and desiccated and so thin you could see the clear lines of their blood vessels underneath—but that skin was mostly covered by the knobby chitinous exoskeleton that supported their bodies. Sure, the lizards had armor plates over most of their bodies, but they still had bones on the inside. Not the Children of Lorath.

Also, did I mention they had no eyes? The entire top half of their head—from their inset nostrils up—was a ridged dome of bone-matter. They moved through the world with the use of a finely honed psychic sense that every one of them seemed to have in equal measure. Most races, some were more gifted than others. The boneheads were more like Iris's people, where every single one of them shared that same ability.

"Drake," he said in a low, grinding voice. They always sounded rusty when they talked—something they didn't do very often with me, and never among themselves.

I didn't know his name, or even if he had a name. I didn't even know if he was actually a *he*. "Hi. I don't think we've met."

"Strangers here. In your space. This morning. Searching."

A cold chill washed over me. Had Syed tracked me down? "Human strangers?"

"No. Your minds are empty spaces. Quiet. The minds in your home were of Jansyn."

A relief—sort of. Had they been Seana's people? When she and I had been together before, I'd suffered through a number of random security sweeps. If she considered us back together, she would have sent her people over here for an inspection without a second thought. A good thing I hadn't left any information about Spark in the apartment. "Thanks, but they were friends. I think."

Without any sort of acknowledgement or dismissing gesture, he bent back down to the garden. In the whole conversation, he'd made no expressive or communicative gestures at all. A little creepy. But I had bigger concerns right now than interracial cultural divides.

"Thanks," I repeated, hoping I hadn't offended him in some incomprehensible way. I went inside.

The inside hallway was dark. Some neighborhood kid stealing lightbulbs again. Our building was easy prey—the boneheads didn't notice one way or the other, and the lizards—like me— kept odd hours. Nothing more sinister occurred to me.

Until I opened my door and reached for the light switch and nothing happened. And remembered the shadow that had attacked Eddis. And the way Iris had forgotten Syed the moment he'd told her to. What made me think my Lorathian friend outside would be any different?

But this wasn't a dark, empty street. This was my home. "Light!" I called out in a strong, clear voice. I'd enchanted the sconces months ago, during a time I wasn't sure I'd be able to pay the electricity bill.

My apartment lit up to reveal—yes—Syed standing in wait.

He stood at the wall, looking over the pictures I'd taped to the bare plaster. Reminders of better days.

"Joshua Drake," he said, and my mind started to swim in that unhealthy way. But by now I was used to his tricks. I focused, pushed, and anchored in a way that was becoming reflex.

"None of that." I didn't move any closer, but neither did I back away. "What are you doing here?"

"Where is the Fyean?" he countered. "Where is Spark?"

"What do you want with her?"

"I don't care about her," Syed snapped. "It's the people who are after her I want."

The Jansynians. "Why?"

His eyes narrowed and the shadow swam inside them. Once again my mind tried to go gray. I fought it back, and asked through clenched teeth, "Why are you trying to stop the satellite project? Why don't you want them to bring rain to Miroc?"

He took a step towards me. "How do you do that? How can you push me away?"

Even if I knew the answer, I wasn't about to tell him and lose whatever edge I had. "If you won't answer my questions, I don't see why I should answer yours."

"Enough of this." His eyes went black, and then every light in the room snuffed out.

The darkness wasn't natural. I couldn't see the glowing clock on the oven, the blinking red of my NetPad's charging station. Only blackness. And somewhere in that blackness, Syed and his murderous shadow.

I fled.

The hall was just as dark, but sunlight greeted me—blinded me—when I opened the outside door. I stumbled forward, ran for the bike, didn't turn around. I didn't know what he could do. The shadow that had killed Eddis, the shadow I'd seen swimming behind Syed's eyes, I didn't know if it could survive in the sunlight or if it needed darkness to kill. To possess. I had no plans to linger and find out.

I dared a glance in the rearview mirror as I leaned in hard to speed away. No sign of Syed. He hadn't followed me out into the street. At least, not that I could see.

That thought sent a shudder through me.

We'd believed all the Favored Children dead—assassinated when their gods went missing. I never thought I'd be this upset to find out one had survived.

If Syed was after me—if he was after Seana—if he was trying to stop the rain and Miroc's salvation, I needed to find out everything I could about him and what he could do. And fast. Trouble was, how did you find things out about the Favored Son of the god of secrets?

159

I turned toward the road that would lead me to Amelia's part of town and hoped she'd have an answer.

A strange man answered Amelia's door. "Miss Price is in a meeting," he said. "She said you might make use of her office."

I followed the butler-housekeeper-security-guard-whatever to an office as lush as the parlor I'd been in last night. And I wasn't alone. "Iris!"

She looked good, back to her normal self with no sign of injury. But that was her nature, after all. If she was still hurting on the inside, it didn't show as she stood to greet me with a bright smile. "About time you got here. I'm bored to tears waiting for Amelia to get done."

I went over to Amelia's desk—a burnished monstrosity of imported hardwood. I had to assume the invitation to use her office included access to her computer. "Who's she meeting with?"

"Big-wigs. The city council. Her father."

"Her father?"

Iris hopped up on the desk—there was plenty of room—and sat down cross-legged next to the computer monitor. "I swear, Ash, even I know this shit. Her father—Lucien Ellsworth."

It was true I didn't pay much attention to politics—and had paid even less back before the Abandon—but even I had heard of Lucien Ellsworth. "Amelia's an Ellsworth?"

Iris must have heard the horror in my voice. "And that's why she goes by her mother's family name."

Now it made sense. Amelia's money, her connection to the city council—all her connections. "What are they talking about in there?"

"The bombs is my guess."

After my encounter with Syed, I'd almost forgotten. Too many things happening. Danger coming at us from all sides. And all of it might go away if we could just make it rain.

"I've had my own exciting morning." I filled Iris in on my encounters with Syed, both the attack in my apartment this morning and what she'd missed while she was zoned out by his manipulations last night.

As I talked, she got more and more fidgety. First, fingers drumming on her knees, then feet twitching, until her skin itself began to ripple. Once I finished, she shook her head hard, a fervent denial. "He's supposed to be dead. All the Favored Children are dead."

I shrugged. "Secrecy is the very nature of the Silent One. Maybe he was able to hide."

Iris shook her head again. "Not secrets, Ash. Well, yes, secrets. But that's the effect, not the cause."

She jumped up, started to pace. As she moved, her body morphed—tall, short, skinny, wide, dark, light, human . . . not. Like her entire self had lost focus. "Iris, what—"

"You Kaifail priests, you think you're so smart. With your books and your words and your talking. But he kept secrets from you. From all of you. From Kaifail and Jansyn and Lorath and all the rest. Only we know. Because of what we are, we had to know."

She stopped and faced me. Black shapes moved across her skin. The suggestion of shadows. "You humans, you can't understand. Kaifail's experiment—you became what you were, grew and evolved in the world for his entertainment. You aren't reflections, limited by the imagination of your creator." Her body had become a fluid thing, pulsing with her agitation.

"I don't understand," I said as calm as I could. "What does this have to do with Syed?"

"He's the nightmare we are raised to." She raised her hand. Her fingers fused, separated, became bird claws, then lizard, shimmering with a rainbow of color. "This is what I am. This is what all my people are."

"Magic."

"Change," she corrected. "Magic is what your people use to touch it, but change is what we *are*."

I thought of the mural, of Iris's creator Drinion on one side and the Silent One on the other. "The Silent One is against change."

"He's the opposite of change. He's stasis. The Silent One keeps secrets because information that isn't free can't change things.

"Syed is a shadow in the dark. A whisper in the silence. He's the horror my people learn as children. His voice can hypnotize. His touch can kill. He can be anywhere, in anyone, looking out through their eyes and speaking with their voice and no one can tell the difference."

"I can," I said.

Iris rippled back into a subdued version of her usual shape. "If he learns you can see his secrets, he'll kill you."

I was pretty sure that ship had sailed. "He's after the rain project."

"Of course he is. If Spark and the Jansynian's succeed, it changes everything."

I pushed a hand back through my hair. "Hasn't he realized his god is gone? He's fighting a lost cause."

"He is the Silent One's voice, the Silent One's face, its only creation. He's not going to just move on."

Which left us limited options. "Can he be killed?"

Iris shrugged and came back to sit at Amelia's desk. "When the gods were still here, I'm not sure anyone ever had the guts to try."

Desperate times. "You—other shifters—you fear him because he's the antithesis of what you are. But doesn't that go both ways? Couldn't you be just as much a threat to him? More specifically, couldn't magic be a threat?"

Iris sat thoughtful. When she spoke, her words came slow, considered. "Whatever you did to see Eddis, it's broken his hold on you somehow. Maybe if you could figure out how and why . . ."

Any weapon we could find would be welcome, but if I was going to go hunting ancient monsters, I wanted something more certain. "Surely someone knows something about him. Your people tell stories—could there be facts buried in the heart of them? Records some other race has? If he's been around forever, this can't be the first time he's made a mistake."

"This may be the first time he hasn't had the Silent One assisting his secrecy."

It was all overwhelming to think about, but what else could we do? We couldn't ignore him. We couldn't leave him to find and kill Spark or the rest of the research team. Or Seana.

At least I knew a place to start. "I need to go back to Desavris. We know he was there, as Eddis. I'm pretty sure he was there for a while. If there's any place I can get a feel for what he's doing and maybe figure out a way to fight him, it's there."

"Will they let you?"

Iris's question was a good one. Syed wasn't the only creature in the world who valued secrets. But Seana was invested in success, and I had to hope she trusted me enough to let me do this. "All I can do is ask."

"I'll let Amelia know." Iris laid a hand on my shoulder. "Be careful."

"You too."

— 15 —

Safety in Numbers

The hardest thing was not giving in to the horror. So easy to think about what Syed could do to any of us. While I was at Desavris, he could sneak into Amelia's house. While I was at Amelia's house, he could sneak back into Desavris. I felt relatively safe on my own, riding along city streets under the blazing mid-afternoon sun, but I couldn't shake the nagging fear that he was around, just beyond the corner of my vision. Lurking. Waiting. Watching.

I didn't know how he'd gotten into Desavris the first time. Did he need to be there physically to send his shadow to kill and possess? I'd seen the shadow still in his eyes, which meant we were safe for now. I hoped. I had to believe that. Madness to think otherwise.

As I pulled back into the Crescent's receiving yard, I realized I had no idea how to contact Seana, besides going back to her apartment and waiting for her. I went to the security booth—wondered if they were getting tired of me and my random requests. "I need to speak with Director Seana. How might I go about that?"

A different man in the booth from this morning. At least, I thought so. I still hadn't developed much eye for the barely perceptible differences between one Jansynian face and another. "I will pass along your request," he said without inflection.

Which led to my next, probably strange question. "What am I allowed—what permissions do I have?"

No smile, no frown. Nothing. "Your current access level allows travel through security one and security three corridors. Residential and commercial areas of Desavris are permitted. You have key-clearance to Director Seana's living suite, as well as access to her credit line."

That sent a thrill of warmth through me. An open invitation to her apartment—she couldn't have sent a clearer signal that she was serious about rekindling our relationship. "How will I know which corridors are safe?"

"Your security chip will vibrate, alerting you if you try to go anywhere you are not permitted. The armed guards moving to intercept you will also be informative."

It almost sounded like he was making a joke. Even if his face and voice were still as bland as before. Jansynians had the market cornered on dry wit.

Still, I'd do my best to avoid taking chances. "Thanks."

On my ride up the lift, I stared out into the Web. Were Copper and Micah still planning their assault? I'd have to check back in with them soon. So many balls to juggle. But I still held out hope I could persuade Seana to call off the hunters once Spark figured out how to get the satellite working again, eliminating the need for Copper's ill-considered attack. The timing was the tricky part, but there was definitely a clear path out of this mess where no one had to get hurt. At least, there was if I could keep Syed from getting in the way.

Seana's assistant waited for me at the top of the lift. I recognized his smile. "Mr. Drake, the director will see you now."

No one could complain about Jansynian efficiency. I followed him through the familiar hallways to Seana's office. "What level corridor is this?" I asked him as we walked.

"Security seven. I would not suggest trying to navigate this visit on your own."

Good safety tip.

Seana was at her desk, watching video images on her computer. I sat down across from her as her assistant left us alone. "What is it you need, Ash?"

Feeling more than a little paranoid as I did so, I called up a spark of magic and focused it through everything I knew about Seana—everything she was, everything she meant to me. Her eyes remained clear, empty of any shadow. Relief mingled with guilt as I answered her question. "Information. Hard-to-find information. About the Silent One."

"Information is accessible, certainly."

She was all business today. That was fine. I was here to work. "I was ambushed in my apartment this morning. Syed again. I don't think he's going to leave me alone. I think he's hunting me."

That got a response. Seana looked up from her computer for the first time since I'd stepped through the door. "Are you all right?"

"A little shaken. No worse. But—"

"I want you to have a bodyguard."

"No," I said—too quickly. I could see the hurt on her face.

"That man is dangerous. You're a librarian, not a soldier. I can't have you getting hurt when I could have done something to prevent it."

I thought about the gun in my bag, of the thugs who jumped us outside Kaifail's temple, of the car chase that had ended in an explosion. No, I wasn't a soldier, but my resume had definitely expanded past librarian. "I'll be careful. I promise. But I've seen this guy in action. A bodyguard might be more of a danger than a help, if Syed can take over his mind like he did Iris."

Seana drummed her fingers on the desk—a surprisingly fidgety gesture. This had her worked up. I was touched.

I tried a different approach. "It's my job. I have to protect the secrets of Amelia's clients."

She flattened her palm against the desk and closed her eyes for the briefest moment. Then her perfect, bland Jansynian expression returned. "I understand. I cannot with any conscience ask you to endanger your employer's secrets."

Which didn't put me in the best position for my next request. "You're right that Syed's dangerous. And I have an idea of where I could start looking to track him down."

She said nothing, waiting for me to continue.

"The lab where Eddis worked—where he was taken. If I could get in there—"

She shook her head with sharp finality. "I'm sorry, Ash. I, too, must protect my employer's secrets."

How could I argue after I'd just made that same plea? "I understand. I just wish I had an idea where else to start. He's out there, somewhere, and if he got in here once, he could do it again."

"Since you discovered Eddis's . . . situation, I have taken additional security precautions."

I held back my question of what those were. If she could tell me, she would. But we walked a delicate line. Our goals were the same here, but I wasn't an employee of Desavris. During the years of our relationship before, I'd learned all the hard boundaries of what that meant. I could respect them now. Especially when I had my own secrets to protect.

Her fingers started tapping again. "You are correct, however, that he presents a threat. If we could find a way to neutralize him . . . " She paused, considering. "You do seem uniquely suited to that task. However you came by this ability you have, you may be the best weapon, the only weapon . . . "

She fell silent. I waited. Finally, she said, "I don't know all the resources you have at your disposal." She spoke slowly, carefully. "And I will not ask. But I can tell you what I know about this creature and hopefully you can find a use for the knowledge.

"He is ancient, but his body is human, and vulnerable. Although less so than yours. He does not require sleep or food or even to breathe. But you must destroy his body first if you are to kill him."

How did she know this? I marveled at the information resources Seana had at her disposal. In Kaifail's church, we had informational archives that coordinated thousands of years of research and study, but it couldn't hold a candle to what the Jansynians knew. The idea that they had teased these secrets about the Silent One's Favored—it was truly remarkable.

"Once his body is dead, he has only his spirit—the shadow creature you saw. That is what you must destroy."

"How?"

Her lips formed a thin smile. "That is the question, isn't it?"

"Magic," I said, because that was the answer. Magic had helped me break through the web of secrets Syed had woven around Eddis. Magic helped me fight against his attempts to control his mind. And as Iris had explained, magic was his opposition at his very core.

Seana nodded. "Magic is a tool I don't understand, but from what I've seen, if there's a power that can unmake Syed, magic is the top contender."

And for magic, I did have resources. "Thanks. That gives me someplace to start."

We stood together. She came around the desk and reached up to touch my cheek. "Will I see you tonight?"

"If I can, yes."

She nodded. She understood. Work came first. "Don't get killed."

———

If magic was to be my best weapon against Syed, then I wanted all of it I could get my hands on. Iris and I were a start, but Iris's power was inwardly focused and limited to what she could intuit. She wasn't going to be learning new tricks. I needed someone else like me—someone human and gifted. How lucky for me I knew exactly where to find that person.

I'd wanted to check in on Micah and Copper anyway. This gave me the perfect excuse.

In the old days, there'd been a lot of rivalry between Kaifail's bright priests and his dark priests. Friendly, mostly, but my fellow priests of the Dark Kaifail would have laughed at me for going to a bright priest for help with magic. We were the scholars, the mystics, the experts. They were poets and actors and dilettantes.

The divide was artificial. We all worshipped the same god— although sometimes outsiders had trouble understanding that. Kaifail was simply complicated, and it took a two-sided priest-hood to address all his aspects. But human nature is what it is, and division breeds competition, which breeds separation and resentment and . . . well, you get the idea.

It all seems dumb in retrospect. But how could we have realized the sheltered, privileged lives we led under the shadows of our creator? The gods had always been there. We had no reason to believe it possible they ever wouldn't be. Not until the day we called and they didn't answer.

Micah was happy to see me. Copper was not. "You're still working for the Jansynians!" She yelled the accusation over the sound of her power-saw cutting through metal. "People see you going in and out of the Crescent."

"I work for Price & Breckenridge," I yelled back, "who you hired to keep your sister safe. If I'm working with the Jansynians it's to that end."

Copper didn't just roll her eyes; she rolled her whole head. "If you're too stupid to realize Jansynians are using you for their own ends, I don't know what to say."

Micah was helping Copper with some unfathomable construction project. Right now it resembled a bird's nest of welded pipes and metal spikes. I didn't even want to know. "So far I've gotten more help from the Jansynians than you've been able to offer."

"Both of you need to take a deep breath," Micah said, his voice strained from supporting the heavy pipes as Copper worked. Even stripped down to nothing but a loose pair of pants, he was covered in sweat. "Ash, it's nice to see you and all, but I assume you came here for a reason other than to argue about our neighbors upstairs."

It was true. "I need your help with something. Something to do with keeping Spark safe," I added quickly at Copper's dark look.

"Anything, of course." Micah's smile was genuine. It warmed me, relaxed me. Something I'd forgotten in the months I'd been hiding from the world—from myself: how nice it was to have friends.

Too bad I had to drag him into this business. "It turns out, the biggest threat to Spark isn't the Jansynians."

"What are you talking about?" Copper snapped.

By now, I was getting good at laying out what I knew about Syed and the threat he represented. Especially as people like Iris and Seana were able to fill in bits of information that were beginning to all fit together in my mind. Copper glared the whole time I talked, her frown so tight I was amazed her face muscles didn't cramp.

Micah listened like—well, like a priest. This was something new and interesting, and even the danger couldn't dampen the excitement on his face. Of course, he hadn't faced Syed yet. It was hard to communicate the visceral terror of seeing the strange, shadowy monster moving inside a person who looked otherwise normal.

"This is incredible," he said. "All of it."

"And your Jansynian woman told you how to kill this . . . this thing." Copper sounded, of all things, angry.

"She told me what she knows." I shrugged. "Obviously no one has any hard data, since he's still alive and walking around, but based on my own experiences, I think her theory is sound."

Copper finally waved Micah back. He took a deep breath, blew it out slowly as he wiped his arm across his forehead. "This is all . . . I can't even imagine what we're in the middle of. And you know I'll do anything I can."

"But?" I asked. I could hear it in his voice.

He touched the tattoo on his shoulder—the one both like to and yet different from my own. "Bright God, remember? I never learned any of the fancy, theoretical magic you can do. Everything I know is lights and sound effects—stage dressing."

"I think it doesn't matter." I hoped. Gods, I hoped. But we were running without a textbook. "It's not so much what you do as the power behind it."

Copper slammed her gloved fist down on the metal mass. "This is stupid. You're just going to get yourselves killed. And then where will my sister be?"

"He'll find her." This, I knew for sure. "If we don't stop him, he'll find a way to get to her. I've been lucky this far. But he's—he's like something out of a nightmare. I won't stand by and let this monster hunt my friends."

Copper rolled her eyes again. "I can't believe Seana would—" She threw up her hands. "Fine. Fine! But I'm coming with you."

"No." Bad enough I was dragging Iris and Micah into this. I didn't need another person's safety to manage. "You don't have magic. You have no protection against him at all."

"Oh, so you're the expert now?"

I understood her frustration. I would probably have felt the same in her position. "Sorry, Copper, but no civilians tonight."

That, it seemed, was one insult too many. Her eyes went cold as she glared at me. "Fine. But whatever happens tonight, it's on you. It's what you wanted."

I hardly needed her to tell me that. "Come on, Micah. Let's go talk strategy."

"No!" Copper banged her fist again. "Take him later if you have to, but he's going to stay here and help me finish this. No one else in this damn community has steady hands."

Micah shrugged and gave me a *what can you do* look. He didn't want to rock the boat any further.

It was fine. I could deal with that. It wasn't like Micah was going to be able to offer much help planning a street-ambush. "Meet me at Price & Breckenridge when you can get away. But make sure it's before sunset."

He looked at Copper. She waved dismissive approval. Good enough.

I got out.

— 16 —

Something to be Remembered For

Amelia's house had emptied by the time I got back. The herd of vehicles that had been parked here while Amelia was having her meeting was gone. I pulled my cycle into the driveway and sat for a few minutes, soaking up the quiet. So much had happened so quickly, and now I was gearing up for a confrontation with a nightmare out of legend. Nothing about this was good. Nothing about this was going to be easy.

At the door I was met by the same man as last night. I used the same magic on him as I had on Seana. Even if I didn't know him well, I could focus on *human* well enough. He was clean.

He let me in and directed me to the sitting room where I'd met with Amelia last night. I went straight there, but stopped short two steps through the door. Amelia was in there all right, on the long couch, with a book in her hand. Iris had stretched out on the couch next to her, her head in Amelia's lap. Amelia stroked Iris's hair—today a deep, contented blue—as she read.

The scene was tranquil, intimate. I couldn't bear to interrupt.

Too late. Amelia lowered her book, but the smile she gave me was warm. "It's all right, Ash. Come in."

Iris opened one eye, narrowed it at me, then closed it again. *She* obviously wasn't happy I was interrupting their quiet time. But Amelia was the boss.

"I have the beginnings of a plan," I said as I claimed an over-stuffed chair across the rug from them. Again I summoned the magic to make sure Amelia was still Amelia, that Iris was still Iris. Even if Iris had her eyes closed, I was certain—fairly certain—I'd feel the shadow within her. I saw nothing strange, felt nothing strange. Maybe it was silly to do this to everyone, but I was still rattled by Syed in my house.

And he could be anywhere.

Amelia set her book down, nudged at Iris with her leg. "Time to wake up, love."

Iris sat up, giving me a full-on glare. "Sure, because Ash's plans so far have gone so well."

I looked down, away from both her and Amelia. I was going to be asking Iris to go into danger again and I didn't even know if she was fully recovered from being shot.

It must have shown on my face. "Ash, look at me," Amelia said.

I looked up. She took Iris's hand. "Iris getting injured wasn't your fault. This is a dangerous business. People are going to get hurt. You can't let that stop you from doing what needs to be done."

It was a sentiment Seana would have agreed with. That didn't make it easier to swallow. "It's going to be dangerous. More than anything we've done yet. I'm working on guesswork and rumors and second-hand data. But I don't think we have a choice. We have to hunt Syed."

Iris flinched as I said his name. Amelia leaned back against the couch, crossed her arms. "I don't necessarily disagree with you, but I'd like to hear how you got there."

"We need water. Our best hope for that right now is the De-savris satellite. But for that to work, we need either one of their scientists to fix what Syed broke or for Spark to figure out where the problem is. And we also need Copper not to disrupt things in a misguided attempt to help her sister." I ticked off the points on my fingers as I made them. "We can't help Seana's scientists.

CITY OF BURNING SHADOWS

We can't help Spark fix the design. Copper isn't going to move tonight. What we can do—what I hope we can do—is find Syed and neutralize him."

"Kill him," Amelia corrected.

Hard to face that. Hard to wrap my mind around that cold purpose. I'd never killed anyone. I leaned forward, buried my face in my hands. I'd been a librarian, dammit. "Yes," I muttered into my palms. "Kill him."

"He killed Eddis Desavris," Amelia said in a soft, chill voice. "Destroyed research that could save millions of lives. He's followed you, broke into your home, tried to erase your thoughts, and would have left Iris bleeding to death in the street if you hadn't chased him away with magic. Yes, Ash, you're going to kill him."

Iris pressed her shoulder against Amelia. Amelia patted her knee and asked, "Do you think you can?"

"Magic works against him. I know that much. I know I have to destroy his body, and then the shadow-thing inside. I also know he's an ancient monster who's existed in stories as long as humanity's been telling them."

"But he's alone now," Iris said, an edge to her voice. "Just like the rest of us. His father can't protect him anymore."

Amelia nodded. "When?"

"Tonight. Micah's meeting Iris and me at P&B. Then we hunt."

———————

At Amelia's suggestion, I went to the kitchen to make myself some dinner. I suspected she wanted alone-time with Iris, before Iris and I went hunting legends. Syed could kill us tonight. Or worse. I didn't want to think about the worse.

I took advantage of Amelia's well-stocked fridge and built a sandwich as thick as my arm. Not just meat and cheese, but lettuce and cucumbers and tomatoes that I hadn't been able to afford since I got out of the hospital.

If Spark's technology worked—if Seana and Amelia and I could pull this off—everyone could have these things again. Miroc could come back to life. Not because the gods had deigned to return their gifts to us, but because we, their children, had found a solution. Because we stepped up and reshaped the world in our own damn image.

Survival wasn't just a dream. It was in our reach.

Before I'd finished, Amelia joined me at the kitchen counter. She pulled up a stool and sat beside me, snagging a couple pretzels out of the bag I'd found in her pantry. "I wanted to say thank you," she said. "I know the past few days I've asked a lot."

"I'm the one who should say that." I pushed the bag towards her so she'd have easier access. "You took me in when you had no real reason to save me. You've been patient. You've been understanding."

"And now I'm turning you into a killer, sending you out after a monster that may or may not be able to die."

I shrugged. "At least my final days won't be boring."

Amelia laughed softly at that. "Boring wouldn't be so terrible. At least for a little while."

"Is that what you want?" I was honestly curious. I had no better idea now than I did when we met of what made Amelia Price tick.

She went to the fridge, poured herself a glass of tea, considering the question. "No," she finally said. "I could have had that. Barring the Abandon, I mean. I could have stayed home, lived a life of quiet luxury. I certainly didn't have to help Jonathan start up Price & Breckenridge."

Ice cubes clinked as she swirled her glass, thoughtful. "It seems so pedestrian, but I really do want to leave my mark on the world.

I want to accomplish something I'll be remembered for."

"If we make this satellite thing happen, that's a pretty good start," I said.

"Indeed." She poured me a glass, slid it over. "What about you, Ash? What do you want more than anything?"

A year ago, my easy answer would have been that I wanted the world back the way it had been. I wanted my quiet life in the temple. I wanted the certainty of the gods and the status quo as it had been for thousands of years.

In the last few days, that answer had changed. "I want this. I want to see things happen. I want to help the world change. I want to live surrounded by the people I care about, and I want to live in the world as I choose it, not as it's handed to me by the gods. By anyone."

Amelia smiled at that. "A good answer."

She leaned back against the counter, looked out the kitchen window. Far away, on the other side of the city, the Crescent shimmered like a mirage. "Your Jansynian woman—Seana. Do you think you'll go back to her? For real, I mean. After we've settled this business with Spark and the satellite."

I wanted to. Kaifail knew I wanted to. But even after last night, there was still so much distance between us. Arguments and decisions and things that had gone wrong before. "I don't know."

"You love her?" Amelia asked, like it was the simplest question in the world.

In truth, it was. "Yes."

"My advice to you—never waste a moment of that."

This from the woman in love with a shifter. Even if Iris didn't lead a dangerous life, it wasn't as though her people were known for their long-term commitments to anything. "I'll try to keep that in mind."

She nodded and her soft look fell away. All business, Amelia straightened up and looked me over. "Check in tonight—as often

179

as you can. I don't care how late things go. Keep me informed. I'll have Vivian and Josiah on standby if you need them."

"Thanks." I stood up. "Wish me luck."

Amelia shook her head. "No wishes. The gods are gone, like you said. It's time we make our own luck."

— 17 —

A Shot in the Dark

Kaifail was a lecher. Other gods settled down, romantically speaking. Jansyn and Zifla were soulmates—or whatever you called it when the gods were involved. Torin had his consort. Ouliria had hers.

Kaifail seduced mortal women and goddesses alike. He convinced Robain she was his one-and-only. His affairs with each of the Twins drove a wedge between them. And there are so many stories—more than I can count—of the mortal women he beguiled and then abandoned.

Humanity was Kaifail's great delight, or so he claimed. Of all the sentient races, we were the only one that wasn't created. We evolved on our own terms, under Kaifail's watchful eye, and he always said he couldn't be prouder. And yet, one of the fundamental principles that separated us from the animals, one of the greatest gifts of our humanity was the ability to love. To empathize. To care.

Ironic. And sad. Was he ever jealous? Our great, wondrous god who, no matter how he tried, could never invoke those qualities in himself.

The office building was dark as I pulled up in front of it. No one working late tonight. Except us.

Iris landed next to me, changing from falcon to human as she did so. As I turned off my bike, Micah emerged from the shadows along the side of the building. "About time you got here. You said be here before sunset." His voice quavered on the last word.

Nerves. I felt the same way. "I'm sorry. Couldn't be helped. Let's get inside."

The lobby was empty, so we didn't bother to go all the way up to the P&B offices. I did give the room a magical sweep for any Jansynian listening devices, and checked both Micah's and Iris's eyes again for shadows. Gods, I wanted this to be over with. I wanted to be done with having to watch over my shoulder every second, with having to worry every moment if my friends might be possessed.

"How's Copper doing?" I asked as I worked.

"Still in a snit." Micah watched me circle the room, his eyes curious beneath the ivory hood of his robe. "You probably shouldn't try to talk to her for a while."

"Is Copper ever not in a snit?" Iris asked. She'd hopped up onto the security desk, where she now sat, swinging her legs.

Micah snorted. But he didn't answer.

After two times around the lobby, I was satisfied we were safe. "We can talk." I fished the automatic pistol I'd taken from Copper out of my bag and handed it to Micah. "Take this."

He took it without hesitation, checked the load, checked the safety, then stuck it in his belt beneath his outer robe. When this was over, when we had time to talk, I was going to have to hear the story of what Micah had been doing since the riots. He'd obviously picked up a few new skills.

"So I've got the gist of the plan," he said. "Flashy lights from me. Iris kills the body. You magic away the shadow-monster. But what I don't know is how you intend to find Syed."

This was why Iris and I had gotten here so late. "I know where he is."

Micah tilted his head, stared at me with honest amazement. "Are you telling me you've managed to unearth the hiding place of the Favored Son of the Lord of Secrets? How is that even possible?"

"Turns out I'm getting really good at finding new uses for my skills as an archivist."

The magic had been complicated, but no more so than the work I'd done with the Desavris files. I probably couldn't have figured it out if I hadn't already experienced the deceptions surrounding Eddis's death and if I hadn't met Syed twice now and felt the touch of his power. "I had to go back to the temple. There's that excellent painting of him there—I was able to use it as a focus. I knew he was in my home this morning, so I was able to work through a city map and track the trail of his presence. He's over near the Crescent."

"Near the Web," Micah said.

"Still looking for Spark?" Iris looked between us. "Or after the Jansynians?"

"It shouldn't matter much longer." I took a deep, steadying breath. "Are we ready for this?"

"Better be," Iris said. Micah flashed me a tight smile. And there was nothing left but to head out into the night.

The night's clear sky meant no reflection of the city lights, which left the warehouse district near pitch-black. Micah rode behind me on the Jansynian bike, his hands locked against my hips and tension radiating from his entire body. Iris was above us, invisible in the darkness. In the distance, up in the sky, the Crescent glowed like some untouchable alien world, but its light didn't reach down to the streets we travelled.

I turned the bike's lights off as soon as we were out of the downtown, but even so, I parked several blocks away from where

I'd sensed Syed. I didn't want to give him any more warning than I had to. As we climbed off, Micah pulled his gun and held it at the ready.

I considered pulling out the second gun that rested at the bottom of my bag. But really, what would I do with it? At best, I could use it as a threat, but I wasn't sure I could—or should—pull the trigger with no idea of what I was doing. I'd have to leave that to Micah and hope he had the experience his casual handling of the weapon implied.

"Can you sense him?" Micah whispered.

"No. Not unless I drop into a trance." Which I didn't want to do, not here out in the open. "But as far as I can tell, he's after me just as much as I'm after him."

Micah was no more than a shape in the darkness, but I saw the motion of his nod.

I stood still, letting my eyes adjust, listening to the distant sounds of the city. If anything moved around us, I couldn't see it. Couldn't hear it. I tried not to think too much about shadows moving at the edge of my vision. If I let my imagination take over, started jumping at figments, we'd be lost.

I aimed us towards the warehouse where I had first met with Micah and Copper. If Syed was following our trail, that was where he'd be. If not, my plan was to cast around among the warehouses, check the entries up to the Web, and then if we still hadn't found him, only then would I turn back to the magic.

Our footsteps scuffled along the sand-covered sidewalks. Micah's breathing, my own, seemed impossibly loud. Was there any way Syed wouldn't see us coming? Was there any way he wasn't lying in ambush, hidden in his native darkness, stalking us with that part of him that had driven Eddis to the ground, filled his nose and mouth and eyes, sucked out his life and replaced it with—

"Ash," Micah hissed.

I bit back a scream, spun around to see him pointing ahead.

I followed the direction of his finger, saw an abandoned warehouse that looked like every other abandoned warehouse. Edged by dunes of sand and with its freight doors a broken pile before a gaping black hole. "He's there," Micah said.

"Are you sure?"

Micah nodded, biting at his lower lip. I wished I could see his face better. I'd find it a comfort to know he was just as terrified as me.

What had he seen? If Syed was really in there, we didn't have time to discuss it. "Stay close," I breathed.

That black, looming maw terrified me, but we had no choice. I took another breath, tried as best I could to steady myself. Magic was tricky under the best of circumstances. If I panicked, I'd never be able to pull this off.

I waved Micah to follow and ran across the street, jumped up onto the concrete ledge of the receiving dock. I could hear Micah behind me. Nothing in front of me. We needed to see. Needed to see now. "Light, Micah. Do it!"

Nothing happened. I spun around to see Micah with his gun pointed into the blackness. Bright flashes and deafening retorts as he fired into the warehouse in front of us. I dove to the ground. "Micah!"

From the darkness, a deep, mocking laugh. "Do you know who your friends are, Joshua Drake?"

A shadow streaked past me with a screech. Iris. I heard her impact with more force than one little falcon could manage. She must have transformed as she dove. My head swam as I felt Syed push against my mind, against her mind. Trying to distract us and escape.

I pushed back with all my will. Focused on the core of me, of Iris, of Micah. Syed wasn't going to take us, not like that.

Except that Micah . . . wasn't Micah.

I focused the power, felt it move through me as I willed our essences against Syed's confusion. It was the same way I'd brought

Iris back to herself when Syed had attacked us outside the church. Only this time, when I focused on Micah, I felt no echoing resonance.

This time, I saw the shadow in his eyes.

I smelled blood. Syed's? Iris's? Heard the sounds of struggle. I had to—

Had to—

Micah was dead. For how long? Had Syed taken him while we'd been walking the street?

If Syed was inside him, why had Micah shot at Syed?

Iris gave off a roar of pain. Micah aimed his gun once more. Fired.

Iris shrieked.

"Micah's one of them!" I yelled at Iris.

He turned, leveled the gun at me. "Do what you came here to do, Ash," he said. "Kill Syed."

I remembered, in that weird, floating, dissociative way that meant I was slipping into real panic, that just last night I'd been thinking I needed to start carrying a flashlight.

"I've lost him!" Iris yelled. Meaning Syed. Real words, which meant she was no longer an animal.

"Useless," Micah snarled, and shot once more into the darkness. How many rounds did he have left? Even if I'd been counting, I wouldn't know. "He's there!" Micah yelled, pointing.

I couldn't see. Couldn't think. Syed was there, but Micah—Micah—Micah had a shadow inside him. And was still trying to kill Syed. Another shadow? A different shadow?

The shadow inside Micah had killed my friend.

That I knew. That one thing I knew. None of the rest made sense right now, but Micah . . .

"Who are you?" I demanded, taking a step closer to the creature that had been my friend.

The gun swung back in my direction. "Do not overestimate your value, Ash. The only reason you still live is because you've

186

proven yourself capable of fighting Syed. If you can't—or won't—then we have better uses for your body and your mind."

We. Gods. Syed *wasn't* the only one. What did that—all this time—

A shadowy bulk hurled itself at Micah, knocked him to the floor. His gun spun away into the darkness. Iris as a great cat leapt back off. Micah scrambled to his knees.

Iris was liquid motion beside me, human again. "Don't let it touch you," she gasped, and then her body grew and changed as she moved back out of my sight.

Not out of Micah's. I could make out enough detail to watch his face turn as he tracked her movement.

Where was Syed?

Too dark. Too fast. Too much. "Iris!" I yelled, and ran for the door.

Micah launched himself at me, snagged my pants leg, and yanked. I fell. Pain shot through my arm, my chest, my shoulder as I slammed into the concrete floor.

Micah—no, not Micah anymore—was strong. His hand around my ankle, dragging me back, solid as stone. He grabbed my arms, my shoulders, held me down. "One last chance," he whispered, cold as death. "Whose side, Ash? Will you stop this pointless struggling and help me kill the real monster?"

My eyes could barely resolve the features of his face, but I could clearly see the shadow in his eyes. Writhing, twisting. Laughing.

"Ash!"

The scraping sound of something sliding across the concrete. An object struck my side.

The gun.

If I hesitated, if I stopped to think, I'd die.

I grabbed the gun. Raised it. Fired.

The force of it drove my arm back into the floor, shocking pain as my elbow struck concrete. Micah fell back, the right side of his head a fractured mess.

And I knew—I knew—the danger had just gotten worse.

I had to shut out the panic, the pain, the sound of Iris calling my name. Too dark, I couldn't see what was happening with Micah's body. I couldn't see if a shadow was oozing its way out into the greater darkness. Coming for me. Coming for Iris.

"Iris, get out!" I yelled. I heard her scramble, heard the rustle of wings.

Which just left me. And the monster.

I called on the magic. Magic could protect me. Somehow. How?

Magic was the opposition to their power. I knew that, but did I understand it? Could I use it that way? Without shape, without purpose? Just pure, raw change through my body like a force. Would it drive the monster back? Would it kill me?

Kaifail help me. The prayer was reflexive, unconsidered, but I didn't have time to be angry at myself. And honestly, if Kaifail did happen just this once to be listening, I wouldn't reject any assistance he was able to give.

A chill ran up my body; the air around me had dropped fifty degrees in a heartbeat. A burning cold touched my hand, my cheek. I opened my mouth to scream, but icy cold filled my lungs, robbed me of breath.

I fought back with a searing core of magic. I fought back with the power of who I was. I pushed back against the cold, the silence, the dizzying darkness. I fought for my life, and for the lives of those depending on me.

Magic, pure magic, the raw primal chaos of it ripped through me. It drove back the cold, but left scorched agony in its wake. I tried to scream but still couldn't breathe. I'd driven out the monster, but now the undisciplined fire of my own power was going to burn me away to nothing.

— 18 —

The Heart of Magic

I wanted to live. I very badly wanted to live.

I fought back against the magic the same way I fought the power of the shadows.

First my name, an easy thing. Even in the center of this pain, in the center of the pure, unbridled chaos, I could remember that. *Ash, I am Ash.*

But that was only the beginning. I had to remember myself, define myself, fight back against dissolution by force of will, by utter conviction that I would continue to be. That I would continue as myself.

Ash the priest. A broken, angry priest who still fell back on prayers for help in moments of desperation.

Ash the friend, who dragged Micah and Iris into danger he didn't understand, who got Micah killed and Iris—I could only hope Iris got away.

Ash the lover. Everything I'd wanted to say to Seana when she left me before. Everything I'd never get to say if I never walked out of this warehouse.

I clung to thoughts of Seana. Of Amelia. Of Spark. My anchors, the people depending on me, my connections to this world.

It was enough.

I gasped my first breath in what felt like hours. I opened my eyes on a room just as dark as it had been when Micah had attacked. Was the shadow still here, invisible? I scrambled to my feet, shocked at how well my body still worked. Even the parts of me I'd been certain were bruised or broken moved with painless ease.

All to the good. I ran out into the street. Was the creature near? Would I see it? Feel it?

The chill breeze out of the desert made me startle and spin. Shadowy movement in a derelict truck could have been a trick of my eyes or something more sinister. I stumbled over a ridge of sand, almost fell. There'd been two of the creatures—one in Syed and one in Micah. If there were two, could there be more? A dozen, a hundred, a thousand? Was the night air full of shadows, invisible and unknown as they—

With an effort of will, I dragged my thoughts back in line. Working myself into a terrified frenzy wouldn't do anyone any good. I forced myself to slow down, to listen, to watch. To try to calm down, even if I couldn't see what lingered in the darkness or hear over the terrified pounding of my heart.

I still had the gun in my hand. The gun I'd used to shoot my friend. I wanted to throw it away, except I didn't dare. I dropped it in a pocket in my robe and zipped the pocket closed.

I made it back to the bike. Where, if the creature was smart, it would be waiting. Walking up to the bike, throwing one leg over it and turning my back on whatever floated in the darkness behind was the hardest thing I'd ever done.

The lights came on. The engine woke. I leaned forward and raced away as fast as I could make it go.

I couldn't make it back to Amelia's. A drive across Miroc in the dark—my nerves wouldn't be able to take it. But the Crescent was close. And Seana—I wanted to see her. Needed to see her. To touch her. To know she was still alive. To know that I was.

All the ride there, I never looked back. I couldn't bear the thought of what might be behind me watching.

Seana had left some sort of instruction with the guards. As soon as I came in sight of the checkpoint, an escort appeared and brought me straight to her apartment.

"Ash!" Seana met me at the door, grabbed my shoulders, studied my face. "What happened?"

I studied hers. Looked for any traces of darkness in her eyes. I still didn't know where the thing had gone, but now I knew how to look for them. Now I'd felt the hollowness of Micah with the shadow inside him. Seana I knew, knew so well, and when I focused on the core of her, I saw only her. No invading monsters. "I'm all right. I think." Gods be praised, her eyes were as clear as ever.

"You're shaking."

"Micah . . . there were two . . . " I was shaking. And cold. I'd stopped moving, made it to a safe place, and suddenly everything was closing in.

Seana's lips moved, but I couldn't hear what she said. My head pounded. The cold—so much cold—closed in around me. The edges of the room went gray.

"Ash!" Seana's hands around mine, squeezing hard enough to hurt. An anchor outside my head, outside the fear trying to smother me.

I managed one deep breath. Then another. Then another. "I'm all right," I said. I thought I said.

"You're not." Seana took my arm and led me over to the living room, easing me past the hedge-walls and down the steps. She sat me on a black couch that looked all sharp angles and solid surfaces, but turned out to be soft and comfortable. "Stay here."

I didn't want to let go of her hand. She squeezed my fingers, then eased them free of her own. "I'll be right back. I promise."

I kept breathing. I leaned my head back against the leafy wall and closed my eyes and focused on air coming in and air going out. What was wrong with me? I'd held it together through the attack. I'd held it together through my escape. I got away. I was safe. I was fine.

Seana returned with a warm mug she pushed into my hands. Coffee, fresh and hot. She sat down next to me and I opened my mouth to speak without knowing what was going to come out.

"Micah's dead."

She nodded, took it in stride. I couldn't remember if I'd ever even mentioned Micah, if she had any way to know who he was. "I couldn't save him."

She nodded again. Letting me talk. Which I did.

Everything that had happened tonight. The magic, how we'd found Syed. Micah and Iris and I going after him. Micah getting taken—somehow, at some point between us leaving P&B and confronting Syed.

Her eyes narrowed as I described the shadow attacking me. Fury—as clear as any emotion I'd ever seen in her. It warmed me to see someone else angry on my behalf. I was still working my way past terrified. But as I talked, the coffee warmed me. The shaking stopped. I felt more myself. Not relaxed, not yet, but closer to functional.

"I should call Amelia," I said, once I'd run out of story. "She needs to know . . . " I didn't want to finish that sentence. Didn't know how. What could I tell Amelia, except that I'd failed, Micah was dead, and Iris was . . . Iris was . . .

Seana handed me her wireless. "Call her. Check in. Tell her you're staying the night. I don't want you back out on the street right now."

I didn't want to be out there either. I dialed Amelia's number.

"Price residence." I recognized the voice.

"Vivian? It's Ash."

"Ash! Hold on. I'll get Amelia."

Bustling sounds in the background. Muffled voices. Then Amelia. Calm and cautious. "Ash, where are you?"

"Up in the Crescent, with Seana. It seemed safer." The bright, well-lit Crescent. I still didn't know for sure the shadows had trouble in bright light, but it still gave me comfort. "Have you heard from Iris?"

"She's here."

Relief flooded through me, draining away a great deal of my remaining tension. Left me wrung out. "Good. That's good. Did she tell you what happened?"

"She said Micah didn't make it. And that she left you struggling with one of the monsters."

A jolt of understanding ran through me, why Amelia sounded so cool. What she must be thinking. "It's me. It's still me." Except how was I supposed to prove that to her? "I fought it off. Magic— that really is the key. It almost killed me, but I got away."

Silence on her end. How could I blame her for being suspicious?

"Ask me anything. I swear to you, it's still me."

I could hear her breathing over the line as she thought. Then softly, she asked, "What was my last advice to you this afternoon before you left the house?"

I looked up at Seana, next to me, saw the worry in her eyes, felt the warm drink in my hand. "Never to waste a moment."

Amelia sighed. "Don't—dammit, Ash, don't do that to me again."

I wished I could make that promise. "There's two of them out there, Amelia. At least. I don't know . . . I don't know what to do."

"Talk to Director Seana. See what progress they're making. If we can just make it rain . . ."

That was the key. The key to all of this. I didn't know if the shadows would just go away once the satellite was working, but it would certainly remove their incentive to be hunting all of us. "I'll check back in tomorrow. Once the sun's up."

"See that you do." Amelia hung up.

I gave the handset back to Seana. She took it. She took the now empty coffee mug from my hands and said, "Come to bed, Ash."

I followed Seana up to the bedroom. It was surreal to think I'd been here just this morning. So much had happened.

So much still to think about. "I don't know how to keep safe from these things. If there are more than Syed—if they can be anywhere. Or anyone—"

"Stop." Seana turned, her expression as serious as she'd been when I'd first walked into her office. "You do no one any good by working yourself back into a panic."

"I'm not. I won't." The nervous energy had mostly drained away, although I was still too keyed up to sleep. "I'm just thinking about—"

She waited, and inwardly I cursed. Too many stories. Too many secrets to keep straight. I'd been thinking about Spark. Out of our sight, with her only protection being the fact none of the creatures knew where she was. At least, I hoped that was still true.

Secrets under secrets, and I was in over my head. Maybe we all were. With the shadows able to pick us off one by one unless we could figure out how to defend against them. We were fractured, divided by cross purposes.

But only on the surface. In the end, didn't we all want to save Miroc? Maybe to save the world?

I had to take a chance. The second risk I'd leapt into tonight. "There's something I need to tell you."

She shook her head, took a step back. "Stop. I can see in your eyes—you're afraid. You're shaken. Don't seek confession or betray a confidence you'll regret."

"It's not that." I moved to her, took her hands. "Or it is that, but not like you're thinking. What I'm telling you, it's because I trust you and because I think we're all on the same side, even if we don't realize it."

Seana didn't pull away, but led me over to the bed. She waved her hand at a panel on the wall and the bright overhead lights extinguished, leaving us with a soft green glow of panels behind the flowers that covered the walls. "Be careful, Ash. I can't stop being who I am, what I am. I have other loyalties that I can't ignore."

First, last, always. Seven years ago, that had seemed so terrible. "I understand. Whatever you do, I'll understand. But this—this is too important. You'll see it the same as I do." I hoped.

She nodded, her face a mask of caution. "Tell me."

"Your satellite. Eddis's technology. I know where it came from."

I waited for a reaction. Seana gave me none. If she was surprised, she hid it well. But then, this was a woman who lived her life in the midst of corporate intrigue. For all I knew, she was used to finding out her secrets weren't really secrets.

So I dropped the real bomb. "The Fyean who invented it—I know where she is."

A tiny intake of breath, that was all I got. It was enough. I'd surprised her. "Why are you telling me this?"

"Because we both want the satellite to work. We both want to make it rain. Your scientists are having trouble fixing what the shadows broke. Spark could help."

She stood abruptly, turned and walked away several steps. I couldn't see her face. "We knew Jansynians were hunting her. It's Desavris, isn't it? It's you."

Seana nodded without looking back.

Time to lay it all out. "My job has been to keep her safe from you. But all that was before we knew anything about Syed or the rest of his monsters. Everything's changed, and I'm pretty sure the best hope—the only hope any of us have is to all work together."

She stood quiet for a long time. Finally she asked, "What do you want from me?"

— 19 —

A Gamble

For the first time in days, I saw a clear way through all our problems. "Let Spark help you. Let her fix what's broken. She doesn't want to take it from you—she just wants to see her invention become real. There's no reason to keep hunting her. She's no threat."

Seana still wouldn't look at me. I gave her time. It was a lot to work through.

The one thing I was sure of was that she wouldn't be upset with me for keeping this secret. It was my job and she knew it and she respected that. Of course, if she decided it was still her job to find Spark, to use any means at her disposal to do so . . . things could go very bad for me.

But Seana had always been smart—smarter than me. And no one rose to the position of director within a Jansynian corporation without being able to see things from multiple angles.

"You put a great deal of faith in me, telling me this."

She couldn't see me nod, so I said, "I know."

"I could have you interrogated. Drag her location from you."

I swallowed. Held my voice steady. "I know."

Another long pause. A silence so deep I could hear my own heart beating.

"This Fyean—Spark—she's central to this project. Without her, it's unlikely we would sort out Eddis's sabotage in time to save the city." Seana turned back to face me. "I believe we can work together on this."

It made sense, and I'd expected she would see that, but—all right, yes, I was relieved. "Tonight, we should start—"

Seana touched her fingers to my lips to silence me. She shook her head. Her fingers trailed lightly up my cheek, then over my hair. "Not tonight. You're exhausted. It's too dangerous out there in the dark. Spark has stayed hidden this long. Better not to risk leading one of the creatures to her."

I closed my eyes, leaned into her hand. Her words were sweet temptation. "We don't know how much time we have."

"Miroc won't die tomorrow." Her voice went low, soft. "And I want this. Tonight. I want *you*."

I understood the desperation that simmered beneath her words because I felt the same urgency. I'd nearly died tonight. To-morrow I'd be facing the same threat. So far, I'd been lucky, standing against monsters out of legend that I still didn't fully under-stand. Who knew how long my luck would hold?

I wanted her too, this strange, brilliant woman. I needed to tell her that. "I'll stay."

She nodded and reached for the drawstring tie at the collar of my over-robe. I put my hand over hers, held it there, looked straight into her eyes. *"I'll stay."*

She closed her eyes and let out her breath. Her shoulders fell the slightest bit. "Don't," she whispered. Opened her eyes to meet mine. "No promises. Not now. Not till this is over."

Last night, she'd been the one asking for promises. But last night we hadn't understood the true nature of our foe, hadn't re-alized the enormity of what we were up against. Last night we hadn't realized how close to hopeless our situation was.

Seana pushed me back onto the bed, moved her hands to my shoulders to hold me down, and leaned over me. "Be with me, Ash, right here, right now. Tomorrow will be here soon enough."

"Too soon." I pulled her down to me. Took her advice. Right here, right now, I was with Seana. Right here, right now, together.

Later, we lay together between her cool satin sheets. My head rested on her shoulder. Her fingers traced along my chest. "No matter what happens," she murmured, "I will never regret this time together."

She was already thinking about tomorrow, about the dangers that surrounded us. I was doing my best not to. Especially if I wanted to sleep tonight.

I should have been sleepy, sore—exhausted. When was the last time I'd had a real night's sleep? Even before this craziness started, it wasn't like my nights had been peaceful.

And yet, I felt better than I had in . . . what . . . years? Yes. How was that even possible? I'd been in more fights over the last couple days than I had in my entire life, running terrified through late nights and long days.

A romantic side of me would have loved to attribute this sudden energy and well-being to the woman stretched out next to me, but I couldn't honestly convince myself of the magical healing properties of sex. Of course, sex wasn't the only magic I'd engaged in tonight, was it?

I closed my eyes, focused my breathing. I couldn't assume anything. If my suspicions were correct, there should be a way for me to tell. The same way I'd spent my time looking for forgeries and mistakes; the same way I'd discovered Eddis's attacker and dug us all deeper into this mess. If I could do it with books, with electronic files, surely I could do that same magic on myself.

In the old days, I never would have tried it. But I was finding caution, at least in this area, a less and less valuable commodity.

I had no circle here, no preset limitations. Only years of experience with the pattern of this magic. And this was me, my own body, my own self—shouldn't that make it easier to notice change?

Except that we are creatures of chaos. Living examples of change. As I sunk into myself and called up the magic, I was struck by instability, confusion, and I understood why no one talked about this. Why no one did this.

Air coming into my lungs, replaced with the air going out. Blood in constant motion, being created, destroyed. Cells dying. Cells created. Bacteria, microbes—tiny bursts of change all through me, a glittering star-field that dazzled and distracted my awareness.

Rough movement broke my concentration, snapped me out of my body. Seana sitting up, pulled away to arms reach. "What are you doing?"

I'd never done magic in front of her. I must have—something strange must have shown. "It's nothing. I was just trying something, but it didn't work."

"Trying what?" Cold suspicion in her voice.

I rolled onto my back, scrubbed at my eyes with the heels of my hands. Why couldn't anything about my life be easy?

Not that I could blame her. The way things were right now, unexpected behavior out of anyone wasn't safe to ignore. "Earlier tonight, when I was struggling with the shadow creature, I did . . . something. With magic. I called it up raw, without controls to keep it safe. It almost destroyed me."

I pulled my hands away so I could look at Seana. Her expression hadn't warmed. "I kept it from killing me by—this is hard to explain—by knowing myself. By holding onto myself. It's the same thing, sort of, that's helped me fight off Syed's hypnosis, or whatever he does. Except this time with a lot more energy. And I think somehow in the process, I may have stumbled across the thing shifters can do."

That wasn't helping. "Not exactly like they can do. But it's their kind of magic. I rebuilt myself, in a sense. The magic was tearing me apart, and when I forced it to hold me together, when I forced it to conform to *me*, it put me back together in full working order. At least, I think."

I reached out a hand, inviting her back. "All I was doing just now was trying to figure out if that happened. Seeing if I could trace the influence of magic on myself."

She lay back down next to me, but her lips still held that tight, disapproving line. "No more magic in bed. It's disconcerting."

That seemed a fair enough rule. "I promise."

I felt her relax again. We lay together, quiet and still, and neither of us reached to turn off the light.

I lifted a hand to her cheek. Midnight against ivory. "I'm sorry. With all that's happening, I should have thought about what I was doing. I didn't mean to startle you."

She mirrored my gesture, her fingertips cool against my skin. "Go to sleep, Ash."

To my surprise, I could, and I did.

Nightmares again, like a curse.

Back in the dark alley where I'd gone looking to save my fellow priests.

Back on the street where the gang had attacked Iris and me.

Back in the warehouse where I'd killed Micah and nearly died.

In the fluid unreality of the dream, I was in all these places at the same time. A board struck my head. The cold of death ran through me. A bolt of lightning, gunfire, a suffocating spirit trying to claw its way into my lungs—all these things at once.

And none of them. I was alone in the darkness. A voice from over my shoulder, whispered in my ear, "Do you know who your friends are, Joshua Drake?"

I woke in a sweat, sheets tangled around me, teeth clenched to hold back a scream. I was alone in Seana's bed.

I got up, grabbed a robe from the closet, tried not to think about the fact it had probably belonged to Eddis. Lights were on outside the bedroom, and as I came out and looked down, I saw Seana seated at the kitchen counter, her focus divided between a NetPad and a computer screen that had folded out of the wall.

"Couldn't sleep?" I asked, padding barefoot down the stairs to join her. An inane question, but I at least managed to keep my voice from shaking. The effects of the nightmare hadn't completely faded.

Seana spoke without looking up. "Our brains don't need sleep the same way yours do, and our bodies can take rest in smaller doses."

A simple enough explanation, and one I'd never heard in all the time we'd been together. "Must be nice."

I sat down next to her. Her screens were full of camera feeds, several of which I recognized. The lab where they were working on the rain satellite, the reception room at the top of the lift, an aerial view of the receiving yard below. In that last image, I saw the first hint of dawn softening the harsh glow of the artificial lights. I'd slept almost through till morning. "Is everything all right?" I asked.

"For now." She slid her hand down the screen. It went dark. "As long as you're up, we should talk about retrieving your Fyean."

Seana tapped at her NetPad and a list of Jansynian faces appeared. She slid it over to me and I glanced over the names and security clearance listed beside each face. None of it meant anything.

"This is the team I've selected," Seana said. "Men and women I trust, even above the confidence I have in all the employees of my division. They're ready to go. I just need to know where to send them."

I stared down at the list, confused. "What team? What are you talking about?"

"To bring Spark back here. As we discussed last night."

My mind was still muddled from the nightmare, but I was pretty sure we hadn't discussed anything of the sort. "To work together, yes. But this is not what we talked about."

"It's the logical next step. Why divide our resources? If Spark is going to work on our project, it makes sense to have her in our lab." Seana put her hand on mine. "It's like you said—it's in everyone's best interest to see this happen. You can trust me."

I wanted to trust her. More than anything I wanted to. But I had a responsibility to Spark, to Amelia. "It's not my call. Even if I thought sending a team of your people to get her was a good idea—which it isn't, by the way—I couldn't let you do that without talking to Amelia Price."

"Of course." She pulled her hand back, all business. "Then she is the one with whom I need to be having this discussion."

"She's the boss." I knew Seana would respect that.

Indeed, the matter seemed resolved when the next thing she asked was, "Breakfast?"

So tempting to linger here with her, to be domestic and happy and delay facing the world a little longer. But I'd avoided some very important things all night; I couldn't justify putting them off any longer. One in particular. "I have to go."

"Alone? Where are you going?"

"Not far." I tried to smile, but couldn't quite manage it. "Just down to the Web. I need to let them know about Micah."

"Let me send an escort with you."

I couldn't accept that offer any more today than I could yesterday. Even if the danger had increased since then. "They wouldn't be welcome where I'm going."

I could see by the hard set of her eyes she didn't like it. Only a few days back together and I could read the subtle flicker of Seana's emotions as easily as if she were a shifter. "They're out there, Ash. Syed. The others."

"The sun's up. I'll be careful." And if they did find me, I still had magic. I was starting to think that maybe, just maybe, that was enough.

— 20 —

False Hope

It was a little frustrating that to get to the top part of the Web where Copper had her home I had to ride the lift all the way down to the ground and then climb almost all the way back up to the top. At least it gave me time to think. Time to figure out what I was going to say.

She was going to blame me. Maybe she was even right. I'd dragged Micah into this without really preparing him for what we were up against. I hadn't watched him close enough to keep him safe. I didn't know if Copper would have been able to do anything to help, but I expected she was going to be doubly upset I didn't let her come along.

I got high enough I could actually watch the sun rising out in the desert. I leaned on a support cable the size of my torso and watched the golden glow cresting over the shallow dunes that grew out to the east. The lights of the Crescent hadn't clicked off yet for the morning, so the sun created no shadows within the Web. I closed my eyes and turned my face into its warmth, thankful for another day.

As I approached Copper's territory, I could tell something was wrong. No one was out working, or talking, or doing anything at all. A space of five platforms and twice again as many webs and hammocks and tents were empty. No sound came from Copper's workshop. Which could have been explained by the early hour, but the heavy feeling in my gut made me think more sinister thoughts.

I crept across the walkway that led to Copper's platform. Still, I saw no movement. Looking out across the Web, outside this eerie little pocket, the morning activity was frantic. People everywhere trying to finish a last few chores before the morning heat hit the city for real. Nowhere was quiet. Nowhere but here.

"Copper?"

Nothing.

I pushed the door open and immediately smelled it. Her. Spread out on the floor. Face down. I took a cautious step forward.

"Wait, mister."

I jumped, spun around to see a kid, a human kid crouched at the far edge of the platform. She'd snuck up the walkway behind me. "You're him, aren't you? The other priest? The one who's helping Miss Spark?"

I nodded, not trusting my voice to be steady. I'd turned my back on Copper's body. It was dark inside Copper's hut.

"You should come away from there," the girl said. "It isn't safe."

"No kidding." I closed the door behind me and took a few steps towards the girl, who scrambled back. Somehow, I managed a calm tone. "It's okay. I'm not going to hurt you."

She shook her head. "Not okay. You got near Miss Copper. Now you might've caught it."

"Caught it? Caught what?"

Her voice dropped to a whisper I could barely hear from this distance. "It kills without a sign. First Jared, when Miss Copper was last to see him. Then Miss Copper's dead, and the last one with her was Mr. Micah. Now Mr. Micah hasn't been back."

A pattern. A traceable path of death. Was this what I thought it was? "Who was Jared?"

"My friend," the little girl said softly.

CITY OF BURNING SHADOWS

A dead boy. Micah had said something about a dead boy, about Copper being upset. On the day Copper tried to kill me. Patterns in my mind. A narrative starting to form.

The girl continued to watch me, her body tense like a wild animal ready to bolt. "Mr. Micah isn't coming back, is he?"

"No." It was a harsh truth, but we lived in a harsh world. I bent down, sitting on my heels, as unthreatening as I could manage. "But you can help me help Miss Spark if you can answer my questions."

She crept forward a step, biting at her lip. "Mr. Micah said you would protect Miss Spark from the bad men." She glanced up, at the Crescent over our heads.

I wished I had half as clear an idea of who the bad men even were anymore. "I need to know when Jared died. And when Copper died. And did you see Copper alive after Mr. Micah left last night?" A harsh world indeed, when I had to ask a child these questions. But right now she was my only witness, and I had to know.

"Morning before yesterday." She swallowed. Her hands were clenched into fists. But her eyes were clear. No tears from the children of dying Miroc. "Jared was running messages between Miss Copper and people downtown. Important people." She gave me a sad little smile. "He was real proud of that. Said he took important messages to the folk as run the city."

The city council. Another piece of the puzzle. Another death in the line.

The girl went on. "He came back that morning after being gone all night. He didn't look sick or anything. But when he was talking to Miss Copper, he just fell over. Just died. Like that." She snapped her fingers.

A chill ran through me. "Was anyone else there with Copper when Jared died?"

The girl shook her head. "But Miss Copper got whatever he had. She was still up and about last night when Mr. Micah went to talk to her, but it must have hit her after he left. Annie found her dead, just like Jared, without any marks or signs or nothing. Then we all got scared. Scared it might be catching."

It was catching all right. Gods. Jared to Copper to Micah. A path of death, clear to see.

But if this was true—if my suspicions were right—it meant Micah had been possessed by the shadow before he'd joined us last night. Which meant the shadow had been hidden from me, even when I looked for it.

Even worse, it meant the shadow had been *convincing* as Micah. I hadn't noticed anything different about him. Had I? I tried to remember what he'd said, how he'd acted, but I'd been so focused on what we were doing, so shocked by what came after, that the conversation in our office building was a blur.

Too many questions. Too many misunderstandings. I couldn't keep on like this. I couldn't keep fumbling forward acting on half-understood truths while my friends died around me. I had to know once and for all what was going on. I had to learn the truth. And there was only one man who could explain things to me. One man who I was certain knew more about this than I did.

I stood. The girl flinched back, but didn't run. "There's no more danger from Miss Copper," I said. "She wasn't sick. The magic that killed her has moved on."

"Will it come back?" she asked softly. Still frightened.

In the world that existed before the Abandon, I might have lied, tried to reassure her with false promises of safety. But if any of us were to find hope in this new world, it would have to be honest hope. And all of us had to learn to live with honest fear. "I don't know. I don't think so. I don't think it will want anything more from this place. But just to be safe, stay out of the dark. Stay away from shadows."

She nodded, accepting my words without question. She backed away from the walkway as I crossed it, but didn't go far.

As I moved to the ladder that was my closest path down to the ground, she called out, "Mister . . . ?"

I stopped, one foot on the first rung. "It's Ash."

Timid, hesitant, she asked, "Mister Ash, would you . . . would you bless me?"

I hesitated, but only for a second. With a practiced hand, I sketched Kaifail's doorway in the air and said, "May his eyes watch you from above; may his will guide you safely through dangers; and may his heart know your story and find it worthy of retelling."

Seems I was willing to lie after all.

I went home.

I could have gone back to Kaifail's temple, used the same magic as I had last night to track Syed. If my hunch was off, that would be my next step. But I didn't have Iris with me and downtown wasn't safe. A quick glance at the news feeds as I'd been getting dressed had offered up nothing but endless chatter about the growing tensions in the city and the more desperate measures the police were taking to keep riots from exploding again.

The worst that could be waiting in my home was one of the shadows.

Syed kept popping up around me. The street outside the temple, my house, the warehouse near the Crescent. Like he was following me. And unlike the shadow in Micah last night, Syed hadn't yet tried to kill me. It was almost like he wanted to talk. Or at least, like it was information he wanted from me, rather than my death. Which worked out fine; there was information I wanted from him. Time to offer up a trade.

But if he really was looking for me, that limited the places he was likely to be. He couldn't get into the Crescent, and with Iris on watch, I didn't think he could sneak into Amelia's house either. I had to presume he didn't know where Spark's safehouse was. I'd seen no signs of him in the Web. Which only left the office and my apartment.

I rode up to find a half-dozen lizards in the street in front of my building. All armed. Two of them I recognized as upstairs neighbors. I nodded cautiously to them as I swung off the bike.

"Priest Drake," the taller one said. I'd never gotten their names. Only now was I realizing the numb, self-absorbed state in which I'd been living the last few months.

"What's going on?" I asked, hoping my informality wouldn't be seen as rude.

A shorter lizard with scales of bright bronze and black-painted horns said, "Any of us who have ever served with the city defenders are being called in to work."

"Have there been riots?" I thought the idea would terrify me. But I'd been living the past few days in such a constant state of fear the idea of open violence was almost comforting in its familiarity.

"Not yet," my other neighbor said. "But they lack the manpower to both patrol the streets and protect the reservoir."

The reservoir. So many things to worry about, I'd forgotten Amelia's meeting, the worry about an attack on the city's dwindling water supply.

"You could join us," the bronze one said. "Any help would be welcome."

Among their people, the priests were the most militant, the greatest warriors. These weren't the first lizards to assume that because of my profession, I must be capable in a fight. "I am helping. I hope."

He nodded, accepting my words as easily as the little girl in the Web had. The lizards had always been one of the more devout races, and had somehow survived the Abandon with a great deal of their faith intact.

I left them to their preparations and went inside to find, again, a dark hallway. Of course it was. If Syed had knocked out the lights before, who had the time or the resources to repair them?

I walked forward through the darkness, feigning confidence and inwardly alert for the slightest brush of cold, the first sign of a shadow's touch. Nothing happened, and I made it to my door.

Which was closed and locked. I certainly hadn't bothered to lock it when I'd fled yesterday. I fumbled in the darkness, making more noise than I wanted working the key. My door opened into more darkness. "Light," I whispered, calling on the power in my sconces.

They flared up to reveal Syed seated in the center of the room. Waiting for me as I'd hoped. And what a strange turn my life had taken when I could say that.

"Joshua Drake, you return." His words were low, even. I felt none of the grayness, his hypnotic push on my mind.

I stepped in and closed the door behind me. "Expecting me?"

"I had hoped."

Face to face and so far, he'd made no aggressive moves. "I need to know what's going on."

A thin smile cracked his pale face. A predator's smile. "What makes you think I am here to tell you anything?"

My pulse quickened, but I held my ground. "Because I think you need my help as badly as I need yours."

He laughed. An edgy, eerie laugh, not at all human. It cut off as quickly as it had started. "You still have no idea. No sense of what you're dealing with. Need your help?"

He stood, his black suit rustling like gathered darkness. "Your life to me is the brief flicker of a candle's flame. This time, this city, this world will pass. You will pass. And it is your own fault; you have brought this chaos on yourselves. It doesn't touch me. None of this touches me. Your flame will go out and I will continue on as I always have."

I couldn't let myself be intimidated. I forced my feet to take the few steps forward that put me face-to-face with the monster. By now, it took hardly any effort to work the magic that let me see the dark, inhuman shadow flickering in his cold blue eyes. "You need my help," I repeated firmly. "Or you wouldn't be here. You wouldn't keep following me. You wouldn't keep talking to me." I willed my voice steady through the next words. "If you didn't need my help, you would have killed me."

"Kill you?" The shadow danced in his eyes, like it was laughing at me again. "You're a blind fool, Joshua Drake, like all your kind. And you continue to speak of things you do not understand."

Syed was playing games with me. My friends were dying and he stood there, laughing. "I know there's more than one of you. And I know the other one wants you dead." If nothing else in that fight had been clear, that much I knew—Micah really had wanted me to kill Syed.

And not just that. "When you told me you were hunting the people hunting Spark. You didn't mean the Jansynians. You meant the other creature like you. The other shadow. It wants Spark dead." Things snapping into place. Copper suddenly wanting to be taken to her sister. That was after the shadow had been inside her. It wanted Spark.

Of course it wanted Spark. "It wants to destroy the satellite. That's what all this is about."

"They," Syed corrected me.

It was the first piece of information he'd volunteered. "How many?"

"Three of them in the city. Besides myself."

Three. Three monsters in addition to Syed. Fuck. "Do you know where they are? *Who* they are?"

He shook his head. "I know them when I see them. I feel it when they kill—that's how I tracked them to Miroc. But once they are inside their new host, they can bury themselves deep enough I can't sense them. I can't find them."

"But I can." I thought I understood why he had sought me out.

But he smiled and shook his head again. "You have, through this rare set of circumstances, gained some resistance to our gifts. But if it were truly that easy to find us, don't you think someone else would have done it before now?"

Micah's shadow had hidden from me. "Why can I see them sometimes and not others?"

"In the same way they hide from me, they hide from you, sliding deep within their hosts. You see them when they rise to the surface, ready to strike, but there is no guarantee any other time."

I'd been so sure of myself, so sure of the people around me. But there were three of those things out there, three of them after Spark, after me. "What—"

My wireless buzzed against my leg. Three quick bursts. Amelia's ring.

I answered without breaking eye contact with the monster in front of me. "Amelia?"

"Ash." Iris's voice. "Where are you?"

"At home. Trying to . . . it's complicated."

"Fine. Whatever." Impatience in Iris's voice, and a quiver of something else. "I need you at the safehouse. Soon as you can get there."

Syed stood perfectly still before me. Listening. Nothing I could do about that. "Did something happen?"

"Not yet." There it was, the tone I couldn't identify. Accusation. "But Amelia isn't listening when I tell her what a terrible idea this is."

No time to be coy. "I don't know what you're talking about."

"No? This wasn't your idea?"

"Iris, what—"

"Jansynians, Ash! Your girlfriend. Director Seana. She called Amelia a little while ago, said they should meet. So now they've

213

decided we're all working together and Seana's sending her security folks to pick up Spark and bring her someplace safer."

So Amelia had agreed to Seana's plan. It was honestly reassuring. It validated the time I'd spent with Seana. Without my involvement, I couldn't see Seana being any more willing to work with us than we would have been to work with her. "This all sounds good to me. What's the problem?"

"The safehouse, Ash. They've been on high alert. On edge for days. Seana's sending armed Jansynians in to take Spark away. You really think that's going to go smooth?"

"Are you going?" I asked.

"I'll be there, but I'm only one person. And the Jansynians don't know me at all."

True. Even if Iris could keep our guys calm, the Jansynian security people had no reason to listen to her. And if they tried to bully their way in with their usual arrogance and expectation that everyone else had to do what they said . . .

"I'll get there soon as I can." I hung up.

Syed made no pretense that he hadn't heard both sides of the conversation. "Stay away from this, Joshua Drake. This will be a perfect opportunity for them."

"The sun's up. They're not going to sneak up on me."

"Such the expert," Syed sneered. "You think we cannot do what we do in the light as easily as in the dark?"

This was getting tiresome. "You can't hide in the light. Moving shadows are pretty obvious on a sunlit street."

"Just because we cannot move about in our trueforms doesn't mean we cannot attack. What would it take to provoke a fight between the two sides? What small amount of trickery is needed? If a shootout begins, how easy for the Fyean to die?"

"All the more reason I need to be there. If I know what's coming—"

"You *cannot* know what's coming." Syed sliced his hand through the air in a gesture of denial. "You think you know, and that makes you doubly blind."

I didn't have time for this. "Then come with me. Help me find them. That's what you want, isn't it? To find them?"

"Yes."

"And Spark is who they're after. If we let them kill her, then won't they just disappear again, run off somewhere else? You'll have lost your chance."

Once more he gave that eerie, inhuman smile. "Not at all, Joshua Drake. Even after they have killed the Fyean, they cannot leave the city. You've created one more loose end for them. One more person they must kill."

"Seana?" I asked, thinking of her continuing work to get the satellite functional.

"You."

His soft, flat tone sent a chill through me. "I'm not the only one who knows about them. Amelia and Iris and Seana—"

"You are the one who can see them. You are the one who has touched them with magic. You are a threat to them. And you've proven yourself unwilling to do their bidding."

Shadow-Micah had told me to attack Syed, and instead I'd turned on him. Or was it more than that? Could I trust anything that had happened to me since Micah first came to P&B? The Jansynian security chasing us in the car. The bird-man and his gang attacking Iris and me outside Kaifail's temple. Copper trying to kill me . . .

But Copper had only tried to shoot me. And then we'd gone back to the Web to talk. If she'd been one of the shadows, why hadn't she struck then? "You're right. I don't understand what's going on." And I didn't have time for a lesson, not if I wanted to get to the safehouse before something terrible happened—and it wouldn't take shadow prompting for something terrible to happen.

I needed Syed's help. One monster on my side to help keep me safe from the rest. "Work with me. Help me keep things calm while we move Spark to safety. Help me not get killed."

"I will not follow you into stupidity."

I tried again with the one gruesome leverage I had. "If they kill Spark and me both . . ."

The leverage I thought I had. Syed shrugged and sank back into his chair. "Then it will slow me down. But I will find them, one way or another."

With or without me, he meant.

I couldn't waste any more time arguing. "I'm going to go look after my friends. This was fun, though. We'll have to do it again."

I felt, or thought I felt, the cold chill of his stare between my shoulderblades all the way out into the street.

— 21 —

The Safehouse

The lizards were gone, off to keep the city safe. Safer. But even an army of lizards would only be a stopgap. Miroc was poised to explode. I could feel it in the air. All it needed was one final push, one match lit at the wrong time and place.

Smoke. I could taste the gritty, bitter edge of it in the air. I couldn't see it, not yet. But if this kept on, soon the air would be thick with it. The fires from the bombings yesterday still burned. Miroc barely had the resources to keep them contained; dousing them was too much to ask. I remembered this smell, this taste, this tension. Miroc had survived the first round of riots. As had I, barely. I didn't imagine either of us would make it through two.

I leaned forward, pushed my bike as fast as I dared. Spark might be the one person left who could change things, who could stop this march towards destruction. Syed might believe I was heading into a trap, but what could he know for sure? He'd already fled when I fought the creature inside Micah. Fought and won. The fact I was still in this meant they didn't know everything, that they weren't as powerful, as inescapable as he had implied.

Cutting across downtown would have been the most direct route to Spark, but that would have taken me by the university fires and possibly other bomb sites. I circled wide, dodging my way through outer-city streets clogged with derelict vehicles and shanty towns. Decaying neighborhoods where I had to pull up my scarf to protect my face from the blowing sand that had claimed nearly everything.

My city. My home. Even if Seana *could* keep me safe, give me shelter in the Crescent that would doubtless survive any chaos down below, I couldn't turn my back on Miroc. I couldn't stand to the side and watch it die. The gods had abandoned these people. I wouldn't.

Which would all be a moot point if the shadows killed me.

I slowed down just enough I wouldn't die as I pulled out my wireless and called Iris back. "I'm almost there. Where are you?"

"In place. Spark and Vogg are packing up, but nobody here's happy with the news."

Just because we'd run out of good options didn't mean any of us were thrilled about the bad ones. "Who came with you?"

Iris's voice got softer, muffled. I could envision her talking behind her hand, trying to keep anyone else from hearing. "It's just me. P&B security won't add anything but trouble, and with the... situation... Amelia thought it was best to limit the number of people involved."

Limit our chance of betrayal, limit the number of potentially possessed people in the room. Amelia was on top of things and thank the gods for that. "Try to keep the safehouse guards inside. The less contact they have with the Jansynians—"

"Yes, Ash," Iris cut me off. "I never would have thought of that because, after all, I'm an idiot who's never done this before."

In some strange way, it was reassuring to hear Iris snapping at me. "Just... be careful, okay? We can assume none of the guards there are possessed—"

"Because Spark's still alive."

"Right. And since Amelia went to Seana, and no one's talked about the location over open airways, or outside closed doors..."

"It's possible the monster's still a step behind us."

Monsters, plural. And Syed had made it sound like a given they would know, like he knew they had inside information. But then he'd also seemed pretty dismissive of all of us that weren't like him.

I turned into the neighborhood at the same time two Desavris hovercars came flying over a cluster of old, wrecked vehicles. "Incoming," I said, and slid the wireless into my pocket as I leaned forward to keep pace with them.

I didn't recognize any faces in the security team. Not that that meant anything. We pulled up in front of the safehouse together. Eight of them, with guns out and ready, climbed out of their cars. The one who had been driving the lead car held up a scanner, swept it around in a circle, then looked at me. "Ash Drake."

I was still wearing the security dot. Maybe that wasn't a bad thing. It had to give me some sort of status in their eyes. I hoped. "I'm here to make sure this goes smoothly."

"Director Seana gave us no instruction regarding your status." He nodded to two of his men, who took up the easily recognizable position of watching me. "I must ask that you not involve yourself."

I had to trust Seana, trust that she knew what she was doing. That she'd sent the right men to deal with this volatile situation. And ultimately, trust that she really had called off the hunt against Spark. Not out of the goodness of her heart, but because she wanted that satellite to work. She wanted Desavris to have the technology that would change everything.

I held up my hands to show they were empty, that I wasn't a threat, at the same time that I willed the now-familiar pattern of power into my mind that let me see the presence of shadows. Just because Syed said it didn't work all the time—and honestly, was I all-in ready to trust him?—it made me feel better when all I saw were eight identical sets of icy gray eyes. "The men inside are armed and jumpy," I said. "They know me. Let me help."

He glanced at his scanner again. Checking my clearance? Looking for something else? For all I knew, he had a readout on every gun in that building. "You're an outside consultant. Not active security."

"I'm not asking for a gun. I'm just asking you to let me talk to them."

I couldn't tell if my words were persuasive or if he'd somehow asked for and received new orders on his device. His expression showed no change. "Very well. You will go inside and you will bring out the Fyean and her bodyguard. No one else."

"I can do that."

He twitched his hand and the Jansynians took up a defensive arrangement around their cars, watching all directions. Good for Seana and Amelia for warning them there might be outside interference.

Except even as I was relieved they were letting me help, I was beginning to realize the true terror of what we were dealing with. Did these men know about the shadows, about the fact anyone could be possessed? They couldn't know I wasn't one of the bad guys. Just because I'd been fine when I left Seana this morning didn't mean I wasn't . . . compromised.

Iris, for that matter. I hadn't seen her for hours. Although, like with the safehouse guards, the litmus test was whether Spark was still alive. I could trust the people who'd been with Spark—been with me, for that matter—and hadn't tried to kill us. Right?

Gods, this paranoia. It was still sinking in, the implications of what Syed had said, the fact I had no way to tell shadow from friend until they tried to kill me.

I stopped at the door, looked back over my shoulder. The Jansynians hadn't moved. No guns were trained on me, none of them suddenly moved to shoot me in the back.

Trust. If I thought about this too much, the fear, the suspicion, could paralyze me. I had to stay careful, keep alert, but I also had to keep moving. If we did nothing but cower in the corner, worried about enemies we couldn't see, the city would crumble around us. And then it wouldn't matter if we'd evaded the shadows or not.

I offered my back to the armed men behind me, took a deep breath, and pushed open the door to face the armed men in front of me.

I walked into the muzzle of Viktor's very large gun, trained on the door. He lowered it, freeing my attention to take in Iris and Vogg, crowded together in the hall, with Spark peeking between them, and two more of the safehouse guards on either side of Vik. "How are we doing?" I managed a convincing calm voice.

Vik gestured with his gun, waving me away from the door. "You sure Price signed off on this?"

"I told you already." Iris sounded impatient. Jumpy. Who could blame her?

"It's fine," I said, but was it?

Vik had talked to Iris, not Amelia. Iris had talked to me. If Iris was one of them—

But why the elaborate ruse? Iris knew where the safehouse was. She could get in anytime. Kill Spark. Get me alone. Kill me. No need for a Jansynian security team. No need to put Vik on alert. "It's fine," I repeated with more confidence.

"Priest Ash," Vogg said, "you trust these Jansynians? You would give Spark to them?"

"No one is giving me to anyone." Spark pushed past him. In a situation less dire, it would have been hilarious to watch the eight-foot-tall armored lizard man defer to the willowy four-foot-nothing woman. She held up the data stick I'd brought her. "I went through the information you brought me. The satellite, I can fix it. But I need to get in there." She smacked Vogg on the knee. "Do you hear that? I *need* to get in. I can't do any good holed up here."

"The Jansynians want this satellite to work. And Spark's the only one who can fix it."

"You sure about that?" Iris asked, her eyes locked on mine, her entire body screaming mistrust.

I hesitated, my new friend, paranoia, kicking in. What *had* Seana said? Exactly? Something about working together. The importance of the project. She'd never said straight out they needed Spark, had she? That had been my idea. Had she carefully misled me, manipulated me?

First, last, and always. No matter how much she loved me, Seana had to do what was best for Desavris. "What are our chances if they start shooting at us?"

Vik snorted. All the answer I needed.

Everyone was looking at me, waiting for me to make a decision. But it wasn't really my decision to make. To Spark, I said, "I'm not sure, not one hundred percent. I believe they're here honestly, but I want to believe that. If they're here to kill you, then someone I want to trust is lying to me. So it's your call, Spark. You think it's worth the risk?"

She nodded, her huge green eyes pleading. "I can fix it."

Good enough. "Iris, can you get out unnoticed?"

She rolled her eyes. "Again with the stupid questions?"

"I . . . right. Get out there where you can see. Follow us. Make sure, if something goes wrong, Amelia knows she's been double-crossed."

"This is a terrible plan," she said, then her body shrunk and shriveled until a sleek black rat stood in her place. It stood up on its hind feet, shook its whiskers at me, then scurried off.

"Be ready," I said to Vik.

"For what?"

Vogg answered for me. "To avenge our fallen bodies."

And then there was nothing left but to do this. "Let's go."

Vogg caught my shoulder. "Priest Ash, I should go first. Then you, then Spark behind us."

His job was to take the bullet for her. Or whatever the Jansynians shot out of their guns. "Not this time. I'm . . . cleared. I'm in their system. In the unlikely event they aren't trying to kill us, I want to make this as relaxing for them as possible."

Vogg stepped back and bowed with more grace than I would have expected from a giant armored lizard.

I put my hand on the door. Opened it. And stepped through.

Nothing terrible happened. No gunfire from the Jansynians in front of me. No gunfire from the men behind me. No sudden betrayals. No angry misunderstandings.

And most of all, no shadows.

All things considered, it was the best few minutes I'd had in weeks.

As I came out of the building, empty hands held out before me, with Vogg and Spark and no one else, about half the Jansynians lowered their guns. The others kept careful watch all around us, but I was utterly in favor of that. They opened the car door for us. Spark got in first, followed by Vogg and then me. The Jansynians settled in, and we were off.

For all that, I couldn't relax. After the last few days, anything this easy had me suspicious. I kept turning to watch behind us, around us. Eyed the Jansynians for any odd behaviors. Snuck sidelong looks at Vogg. The one person I was sure of was Spark—

Gods, unless they'd taken her already and this was what Syed had been talking about, that I'd become their target—

No. No. I had to get this under control. If they wanted me dead, there were easier ways. And while the shadows could be anyone, there were only three of them. Eight Jansynians in the car, plus Vogg and Spark, plus Iris following. They could be anyone, but not everyone. I just had to stay alert and be ready when they broke cover.

Either Seana had warned the gate security or the Desavris guards really had the best poker faces of anyone in the universe. No one blinked at Spark and Vogg in the car. Not so much as a twitch. I smiled and waved at the now-familiar security faces. It earned me a nod—the closest thing to a warm welcome I was ever likely to get.

The guards escorted us to the lift, saw that we were settled, then sent Vogg and Spark and me up. These guards stayed below, to join the base security, and I let myself relax. "We made it."

Vogg stood tense, arms crossed at the glass wall farthest from the door. "It is not over."

The fact they'd let him keep his sword and his gun, the fact they hadn't shot us all when we were in the car and basically helpless—a cautious optimism came to life inside me.

And Spark, it seemed, was thinking along similar lines. "If they wanted me dead, they could have killed me," she said. She'd pressed her fingertips and forehead against the glass, watching the world drop away below us. "Jansynians are nothing if not efficient. Why go through all this trouble unless they mean it? They could have just blown up the safehouse soon as they knew where I was."

"I'll stop worrying once rain is falling on the city," Vogg said.

"Agreed." I was already thinking ahead to the next few steps, once Spark was safely ensconced in the Jansynian labs. The terrorists. The shadows. I'd have to find Syed again. Check in with Amelia. Rain would solve most of our problems, assuming Spark could get the satellite fixed quickly, but it wouldn't make the monsters go away.

A pang of hurt struck me as we rose through the level of the Web where Copper and Micah had lived. I looked over at Spark, but of course she didn't know—I hadn't told her yet. There hadn't been a chance. And this was hardly the time, as the lift slid smoothly to a stop. We'd reached the top.

The doors slid open. The receiving room was nearly empty. Seana waited for me—for us—alone. None of the other staff I was used to seeing bustling around in here were present.

Behind Seana, the doors into the hallway were closed. And for the first time in all the trips I'd made through here—night or day—most of the lights in the receiving room were off. Other than the one desk lamp illuminating Seana, the room was dark. Very, very dark.

— 22 —

A Run through the Web

I reacted entirely on instinct. I slammed my hand against the lift controls. The doors closed and the lift began to descend. We had seconds, maybe, before Seana called down to override the controls.

"We need out!" I yelled at Vogg. Had to act quickly, had to stay in motion. Couldn't stop to think. If I stopped to think . . . "Can you break the glass?"

Vogg didn't ask questions. He slammed his fist into the glass, angled so the bony knobs over his knuckles drove directly in. It bounced off. "It's too strong."

The lift shuddered to a stop. As I'd feared. We had no time. If we got back up there . . . I knew . . . I knew . . .

"Give it a running start."

Vogg nodded, obedient. As he backed up, I closed my eyes to focus. One chance. That's all we had.

Vogg ran. Eight feet of bulky muscle and plated skin. Mass times acceleration. Velocity gathered. Rearranged. Focused. All the force of him narrowed down to a pinpoint. All that energy in a single burst.

Now.

Vogg struck the glass and it shattered. I marveled at his unquestioning trust—if I hadn't sucked away all his forward motion to break the glass, he would have kept going, straight over the edge and hundreds of feet to the ground.

Vogg wasted no time questioning his good fortune. He swept his foot, pushing shards of glass over the edge, and held out his hand to Spark as the lift started once more to ascend. "There," he pointed at a platform, twenty feet up and approaching fast. It would be close enough to jump to as we passed.

Glad I didn't have time to consider the consequences if we missed, I moved with Vogg again to the center of the lift. Another running start. Vogg scooped up Spark and swung her around to cling to his back. We ran together, his longer strides countered by the fact I weighed half as much and could move my legs faster. We jumped together.

I landed hard, stumbled forward, fell. My momentum sent me rolling across the too-narrow platform. Towards the opposite edge. My head and shoulders went over—I felt the open air beneath me—

The collar of my robe snapped tight around my neck as someone grabbed it from behind. "No you don't, Ash." Iris's voice.

As the alarms sounded above and below.

I sat up, rubbing at my neck. Vogg, Iris, Spark, they were all staring at me. Waiting for instruction. Or explanation. "It *was* an ambush. They were waiting for us."

"The Jansynians?" Iris asked.

"The shadows."

Seana. Standing there in the darkness. Ready to attack. I'd seen it in her eyes. Seen the shadow swimming in her eyes.

I wrenched my mind away from the thought. Later—if we survived, I'd have to deal with it later. "They're going to be looking for us. We need someplace safe to hide."

"We *had* someplace safe to hide," Iris snapped.

"How much do they know?" Spark asked, her voice still calm.

They had Seana. They had her resources. "Everything. We have to assume they know everything."

"The temple," Iris said. "Your temple. It's the only way. Even if they can find it, they can't get in."

The idea was brilliant, and a sure sign Iris's mind was working better than mine right now, except for the problem of getting there. As I was reminded by Vogg, who stood at the platform's edge, watching below. "They're coming up. Armed men and women on hover-platforms. We can't stay here."

They'd come from above, too, as soon as they got organized.

Iris could escape, could hide, but the rest of us—we'd never slip the Jansynians. Not without a distraction. "Further in. We're sitting ducks here."

We moved as fast as we dared across walkways of unsecured boards and swaying nets. Vogg took another flying leap between the thick pipe that had turned into a dead end to a platform fifteen feet below, then he and Iris helped catch Spark and me as we followed. We struggled through the maze, but it was obvious from the start we were losing ground to the Jansynian guards on their three-man platforms that flew them towards us. And as I'd feared, the lift was coming down again, with Kaifail-only-knew how many passengers.

No way we could escape. Not like this. "Vogg, Spark, go with Iris. She'll take you to the temple. Wait for me inside the wards."

"Ash—" Iris started to argue.

"Go! I'll slow them down."

A flush of red spread over her skin in a wave, but she jumped off the platform onto a net below, and turned to help Spark. I couldn't watch them long—not if I wanted to provide cover to their escape. I just had to hope I could do enough.

Fortunately, over the last few days I'd had a lot of practice at what I had in mind. The Jansynians thought they had a clear path of pursuit, that flight gave them an advantage. Time to see if I could even the odds.

I knelt down, tracing invisible patterns along the splintery wood. Some charcoal or chalk would have made my life easier, but easy seemed to have taken a hiatus. The gestures helped my focus, but I'd have to hold the patterns in my mind.

Five trios of armed Jansynians flying through the Web. All near-identical to my eye. I'd have to deal with them one at a time, because I wouldn't be able to keep them separate in my head.

All five had continued chasing Spark, Vogg, and Iris. I wasn't sure if it was good or bad that I was lower on their priority list. For now, it meant I could work undisturbed.

The lead group cut down, flying through a gap in the girders about twenty feet below my friends. In a second, they'd be ahead of Iris and the rest, cutting them off.

I focused in on one of the loose-boarded walkways just above them, and with a hurried gesture and practiced twist of my mind, redirected some of the momentum of the last group of guards into the boards. The walkway splintered and boards spun down, right into the heads of two of the lead Jansynians.

Another vehicle swung wide, on a route that would bring them around to flank. This time I pulled energy from the still-moving front car into a nearby net. This plan worked even better than the boards, as the netting came free and tangled around the hover-platform, fouling its engine somehow. They wobbled and sank, unable to continue pursuit.

The third and fourth guard trios broke off from the pack and turned back towards me, drawing their guns as they came. Which answered the important question about their instructions regarding me—apparently I was a legal target to kill.

I didn't have the time or the tools to do a complete energy transference like I'd used to stop the car that had been chasing us. And I didn't know enough about how the hovercrafts worked to be sure I could duplicate what I'd pulled off with the net. Which left only one choice.

I ran.

I heard gunfire behind me. Vogg handling his pursuers. I tried to look back, but one of the big support struts blocked any view of my companions, and then I had to pay attention to my own footing.

A shot from a Jansynian weapon burned through the plank I was running along. I jumped for a wide girder just below as another shot blackened the thick guy-wire above my head. The girder was as wide as I was tall, but slanted more than I'd realized. I couldn't catch my balance and fell forward. I caught the edge, stopped myself from rolling off, but the fall had cost me any chance at escape. The Jansynians rose up on either side of me.

I still had the gun in my robe. With however many bullets were left after I'd shot Micah. But what was the likelihood I'd be able to hit anything I aimed at? The Jansynians weren't going to be cowed by me waving a weapon at them. If anything, it would get me killed faster.

They were so close. Close enough I could hear Seana's voice issuing from their communication system. *Leave him! The Fyean's your target.*

They spun in the air, flew away, and I was out of tricks to stop them. No time for any magic grand enough to cause them real problems. No way to give chase. I just had to hope I'd given Iris and Vogg enough of an opening to manage their own escape.

Seana. How had they . . . I had to warn Amelia. Had to let her know what happened. I couldn't call her—didn't dare use the wireless now that . . .

The next step. I had to focus on the next step. A message to Amelia, and then get Spark safe into hiding. One thing after another, and I wouldn't stop to think. I couldn't . . . oh gods . . .

Seana.

I'd left the bike at the safehouse. Without it, there was no way I could get to Amelia's house and back. But I could make it to P&B. Best case scenario, someone would be in the office. Worst case, I could leave a message. Even if Amelia wasn't in, someone else would be able to get it to her.

My heart pounded all the way down to the ground. Halfway through the climb, the adrenalin wore off and by the time I got to the street, I was more tired than I'd ever been in my life. No choice but to push forward, and so I did. I held myself to a walk, tried not to draw any undue attention. Once I got to the tube station, once I made it downtown, into the crush of people, I'd be safer.

Safer. Not safe.

In the tube station, I tried to watch every direction at once, but didn't spot any Jansynian faces or anyone at all who seemed to be paying undue attention to me. Even once I was on the train, though, I didn't relax. The car was near empty, and no one approached me, but still I couldn't relax. I did what I could to steady myself by running through the pattern that would show me any Jansynian surveillance. I didn't see any of the telltale blue glows, but I wasn't confident of my concentration either. Possible the magic wasn't working at all.

The downtown station was packed. Late afternoon and people were on their way to their twilight destinations. I welcomed the camouflage, did my best to move with the crowd and keep my head down.

I made it safely to my building and waved hello to the security guard who was just closing down for the day. "Anyone still upstairs?" I asked him, hoping the cheer in my voice didn't sound forced.

"Most're out for the day, Mr. Drake," he answered with only a brief glance in my direction. "But Ms. Price went up a while ago, so you're likely to catch her."

So not all my luck was bad today. I thanked . . . no, I didn't.

I went straight for Amelia's office. Walked in without knocking. She sat at her desk, frowning at her computer. I didn't know how to start. "Amelia—"

She stood. Her hand came up. She held a gun. Pointed it in my direction.

"Amelia! It's me! It's still me!" The words tumbled out as my mind froze. Too many shocks today to manage any cleverness. "Don't shoot, I promise it's me."

"I know," she said, and as her thumb flicked back the safety catch, I saw it.

The shadow swimming in her eyes.

— 23 —

No Escape

"Stop!"

The voice came from behind me. Seana's voice. I scrambled to the side, put my back to the wall. Amelia's gun followed my movements, but she didn't pull the trigger.

Seana stood in the door. And beside her . . .

Shadow number three, and the final piece of the puzzle. I recognized his face. I'd seen it on the news yesterday morning. They'd flashed through several videos of protestors outside the city council building, the protesters outside the reservoir, and the crowd gathered watching the fire at the university.

Too late, I saw the whole of what the shadows had been doing. How they'd played both sides. One shadow whipping the citizens into a wild, desperate frenzy. The others working the city council, making sure the leadership gave no response to the city's pleas. And Miroc slowly pulling apart. Until Spark came along with a chance to save the city and disrupt all their plans.

None of the shadows were trying to hide from me. I saw the truth in all their eyes. I was alone in the room with three monsters.

"He had his chance," Amelia—not-Amelia—said, her voice cold.

"And I'm giving him another," Seana answered. "Put the gun down."

I got it now. I understood. Iris had said, hadn't she? Amelia went to the Crescent, met with Seana in person. *After* that, she'd agreed to the Jansynians taking Spark. I hadn't made anything of it at the time because I hadn't known Seana—

And when I saw Seana had been taken, everything else happened so fast, I hadn't taken the leap. A stupid mistake, and possibly the last one I was going to get to make.

Amelia hadn't lowered the gun. "He *hurt* me," she whispered, unmistakable hatred in her voice. No, this wasn't Amelia at all.

"You tried to kill him," Seana countered, her voice as cool as ever. "Against my orders. What was he supposed to do?"

Amelia hadn't ... no, this was the shadow talking. The shadow ... the shadow that had been in Micah. In Copper before that.

The third shadow, who'd been silent all this time, spoke. His words were soft, reasonable. "He sees us. He knows us. He's too dangerous."

Seana approached me, placing herself between me and Amelia's gun. I pressed back against the wall, but couldn't get away. I was long past any of the calm I needed to mount some magic defense. When her hand came up to stroke my cheek, all I could do was stand there and let her.

"I know this is hard," she said. "And maybe I should have told you sooner, but you must understand how much that goes against our nature."

"Sooner?" I whispered, my mind spinning around the implications of that one simple word.

"That first night, when you pushed me from Eddis—"

I closed my eyes against the sudden gray that fell across my vision. My knees had no strength. I slid down the wall to the floor.

"Leave us." Seana's voice seemed to echo from a great distance. I sat on the floor, my face in my hands, waiting. Waiting for everything to stop. Waiting for the gunshot. Waiting for the cold touch of a shadow invading my body. Waiting to wake up from this horrible nightmare.

None of that happened, and when I finally opened my eyes and lifted my head, I saw Seana kneeling in front of me, watching me. We were alone in the room.

"It isn't surprising you have the wrong idea about us," she said. "These are extraordinary circumstances and they've forced us to extreme measures. We don't like to kill, truly. There's no change greater than death, which makes it abhorrent, but what choice did we have?"

"You killed her. You killed Seana."

"I *am* Seana. You don't understand, Ash. All this time, I've been her. All this time we've been together—"

I held up a hand, shook my head. I couldn't hear any more of this.

But the creature didn't stop. "It's not death, not like you understand. Death happens when we *leave* our host, not when we join them. Everything she knew, everything she thought, everything she *was*, I am her. And she loved you. Very much. *I* love you. I never lied about that. Not once. I don't want to lose you."

She took my hand. I didn't have the strength to pull away. "This city is dying. The world is dying. The gods are gone and it's time for the world to end. Can you blame us for trying to see it happens quickly, cleanly? The Fyean technology won't save the world. It only drags out the inevitable.

"We wanted this to be quiet, simple. I took Eddis because he was the key. Without him, the project failed and the city collapsed as it should have. You took us by surprise, love, and I'm sorry, truly sorry, about what followed. I've tried to keep you safe, but . . . " She glanced back towards the still-open door. "I couldn't be everywhere. I couldn't control what happened."

I shook my head again, denying everything. It couldn't be true. I couldn't believe, couldn't accept her words. "You're not her."

"You were happy enough with us, before you knew. It's true I made a couple decisions of my own. She never would have invited you to stay that first night. She would have wanted to, but even at the pinnacle of her career she worried about appearances. But she would have regretted sending you away. I made a better decision for both of us. She loves you. I love you—"

"Stop saying that!"

The creature wasn't alarmed by my shout. Only squeezed my hand and kept talking in that soft, soothing tone. "You've seen the worst of us, and you've had Syed filling your ear with poisonous whispers. It's no wonder you're confused. But I want you with us, Ash. You see us and you know us and, yes, you are learning how to fight us. The others want you dead for that, but I see potential. You'd be an incredible ally for us. And we could be together."

I shuddered as a chill ran through me. This thing speaking now had murdered the woman I loved. How could she propose— how could she think I could stomach—"What if I refuse?"

She sighed, squeezed my hand, then released it. "I would be sad to hear it, but if there's one thing Seana and I have always been in agreement on, it's the fact that you cannot let sentiment command your decisions. If you are not our friend, then I'm afraid you are our enemy."

The safest course would be to lie, to pretend I was with her until the opportunity arose when I could stop them. But I couldn't. I couldn't look into the face of Seana's killer, of Amelia's killer, and pretend I felt anything but revulsion.

I stood up and she stood with me, a look of concern on the face I knew so well. Thought I'd known. She'd been taken by a monster and I never noticed the difference. "I need some coffee."

"Of course," she said with a curt nod. "You've had quite a day."

She followed me out into the main office. I wished I dared ask for time alone to think, but Seana had been a brilliant woman and this creature had shown no sign of being any dumber. She might claim to love me, but at no point had she said she trusted me.

The other two were elsewhere. I saw a light on in the library. Amelia had always enjoyed spending time in there. Even more than her office, it was—

The thought broke me. I fought back the sob that threatened to close my throat and ran for the stairway door.

"Ash!"

I kept running. Down the stairs. Fast as I could. In the echoing stairwell, I heard the door open again and footsteps running in counterpoint to mine. I risked a look up. The third shadow, the man whose name I never knew, was chasing.

Three floors above me and gaining. I tried the door out of the stairwell. Locked. One floor down, I tried the next. This one opened to my hand. I slammed it shut behind me, locked it, and grabbed a chair from whoever's office I just invaded to brace it.

I cut through the office, heard the door rattling behind me. On the other side of the building, the fire escape provided another way down. Hopefully I'd delayed my pursuer enough to give me a head start.

I pushed my exhausted body faster. And for the second time today, I ran for my life.

I stayed ahead of my pursuer, made it down to the street without seeing him again. I aimed for the tube station. If I could just get on a train without him following, I could disappear into the city.

I couldn't keep this up much longer. I'd pushed my body long past endurance. I stumbled as I ran, cursing every bit of trash or drift of sand that no one had bothered to clean from the streets in months. I didn't dare look back. He would catch me or he wouldn't, and I couldn't waste the energy to find out which was most likely.

I'd been in the office hardly any time at all, and the station was still packed with people. Good for me. I shoved my way through the crowd, yanking my collar open. Gaps formed as people shied away from me, so there was an advantage after all to being anathema. Lucky me.

I made it to the boarding platform and only then dared to stop, dared to look around. Time to assess my situation and figure out if I was going to live through the next few minutes.

In the crowd of dark human faces, green and brown lizards, and a smattering of other races, my pale pursuer was easy to spot. He stood three steps up from the floor, staring at me, heedless of the people trying to push by him.

No question he saw me. So much for hiding in the crowd. But the crowd was packed between us and the flashing lights above my head told me the next train would be here in moments. And with the train so close, there was no way my fellow commuters would let him through ahead of them to make the train.

I smiled and waved.

He returned the smile. And the wave. And then reached out so his hand brushed the arm of the woman slipping past him on the stairs.

I didn't understand when he collapsed. I didn't understand when she grabbed the hand of the lizard next to her and then also fell to the ground. It wasn't until the lizard touched the back of the head of the man standing in front of him, then fell over on top of two other commuters, that I realized what was happening.

The shadow was moving body by body, death by death. Coming for me. The people were no obstacle to this monster. One touch and it moved from one victim into the next, leaving a line of the dead in its wake.

A line pointing towards me.

The train wouldn't be here soon enough. Not before this horror would catch me.

A scream. Another scream. People starting to notice the growing number of dead in their midst. Any moment the panic would start. Invisible death moved through them and I was the only one who knew why or how. I was trapped, people pressed tight around me, with the shadow between me and the exit. With every breath, another person fell to the ground. More screams. People tried to get away, but they didn't know what they were running from. They had nowhere to go.

The waves of terror spread. People around me struggled and shouted and shoved. I shoved with them, my panic different from theirs only because I knew what was happening. I had to get away, but how? The people around were a barrier to me, but not to the thing that chased me.

Red light flashed, turned the station full of screaming, terri-fied people into some new version of hell. The emergency lights—someone official had noticed a problem. But as long as the red emergency lights were on, it meant no train was coming. My last hope of rescue dashed.

A shoulder slammed into my arm. Someone stepped on my foot. The crowd pushed back, away from the approaching line of deaths, but there was nowhere to go. Behind me was the edge of the platform and a five-foot fall to the electrified rails.

More screams and I couldn't tell from where. From every-where. I'd lost track of the chain of death in the mad press of bodies all around. How close was it? People pushed and tried to run and fell and scrabbled at those around them. The panic shielded the monster, covered its tracks. It could be in anyone. In any of these people around me. I jerked back from a reaching hand. Yelped as an elbow ground against my spine. Where was it? *Who* was it?

I took one step back. Another. But the crowd followed, trying to get away. Except there was nowhere to go.

Trapped, I was trapped and what did it matter with Amelia dead, with Seana dead. What could I do? What was left? Seana had said it—the world was ending. The gods had left us to this—to madness and death, to chaos and terror, and no one seemed willing to do anything about it except the ones trying to drag us down faster.

The fear that had driven me this far was draining with the last of my energy. In its place, a wellspring of despair that leadened my body and dulled my mind. When the hand reached for me, I closed my eyes. I'd run out of energy to fight. It was over. Everything was over.

— 24 —

Too Close to the Edge

The hand didn't belong to the monster. For all the good that did me.

A man, pushed off balance by the rioting crowd. He grabbed the shoulder of my robe. Spinning me around.

Too close to the edge. I fell.

Past the thick yellow caution paint. Over the concrete lip, towards the electrified rails below.

Instinct kicked in. Turned out I wasn't ready to die after all. All the practice I'd had lately meant my mind could snap into the pattern it needed. As my body curled and twisted away from the rails—as I knew it wouldn't be enough—I pushed out with magic, grabbed the energy of my fall and angled it.

It was enough. Barely. I hit the ground, bashing my head against the gravel rather than the electrified metal line that would have meant instant death. I pulled in my arms, rolled further away. My head throbbed and when I touched where it had struck the ground, it felt wet.

The good news this minute was the trains had been stopped. No immediate threat there. But I didn't think I could climb back up. Even if I wanted to. Now I was down on the tracks, an avenue of escape had opened up. If I could steel myself to take it.

The tunnel stood before me, cavernous and dark. So dark. The shadow would be invisible in there.

I ran before I could think about it too much, before I could frighten myself into immobilization again. Behind me, a closer scream and the sudden sharp smell of ozone and burning flesh. I turned, despite myself, in time to see a woman lying dead on the rails as a third person pushed off the platform landed with a sizzling jerk right next to her.

Seana had asked me to join her—to join them. They didn't like to kill, she'd said. The evidence of her lie was before me. The two bodies down here and countless above. More death than I'd seen since the madness that followed the Abandon. And if they had their way, it was only going to get worse.

If they had their way, my body would be among these. Nothing I could do for the dead. With one hand on the wall to help me stay clear of the rails, I ran into the darkness.

The noise from the platform followed me. Screams and trampling footsteps and chaos so loud I couldn't hear if anyone followed me. I couldn't see what was in front of me. I could only stumble forward, pressed close to the wall, with no idea where I was going or where I would emerge.

I had no idea how long I ran. I'd lost all sense of time, of space, of reality. There was only the darkness, the echoing screams, the crunchy feel of the gravel, step after step, and the cool concrete of the wall beneath my hand. I couldn't focus enough to count my breaths or my steps. After a time, I stopped caring.

I'd been down here forever. It was like there'd never been a time before this darkness, this surreal horror. Maybe I'd died after all. Maybe this was my purgatory. Maybe I was slated to go on like this forever.

I had all but resigned myself to that fate when a sudden light ahead blinded me and a voice called out, "Stop where you are!"

I raised my arm to shield my eyes against the glare. I said nothing, a mix of confusion and caution keeping me silent.

"Are you all right?" the voice asked. Harsh, despite the question. "What's your name?"

I blinked, trying to see past the light shining in my eyes. A flashlight—no, two—pointed at my face. Behind them, the light of an open door. A maintenance entrance.

As my eyes adjusted, the blurs resolved into three men and a woman—two maintenance workers and two station security. "You'll have to come with us," one of the security men said.

No way to tell if one of them was a shadow. Since I'd lost track of it back on the platform, it could be anywhere.

One of the guards reached for me. I jerked back. My back pressed against the wall, wedging the gun in my pocket painfully against my side.

The gun. Useless in the fight with the Jansynians. Useless against the shadows. But here, now . . .

I pulled it free, pointed it at the closest man. "Stay back."

All four pulled back away from me, hands lifted. "Easy, buddy," the maintenance woman said.

"Put the gun down," the guard who'd been reaching for me said. "You're fine. Everything's fine."

I laughed. A mad sound, even to my own ears. Nothing was fine. Nothing would ever be fine again. "Back off," I said, once I had myself back under control.

They did. With gun still raised, I moved around them, through the door they'd come out of. Up a stairway, into a hall where I startled several more scurrying maintenance people with my sudden, armed presence. They froze and I ignored them, continuing up another set of stairs, through an office where a secretary screamed and another security guard started to get in my way until he got a good look at me. I hadn't had a chance to look in a mirror in the last few hours, but it seemed, at this moment, I came across as somewhat frightening.

I made it out onto the street. I put the gun away again. Out here, it would cause more problems than it would solve. The sun had set while I'd been underground. The evening traffic was out. Any one of the people crowding the streets could be the thing hunting me.

I shut that thought down. If I hadn't evaded my hunter, there was nothing I could do about it. Not until it revealed itself. Or killed me.

With my attention focused on the much more mundane threats of assaults and muggings and general mayhem, I aimed my path downtown, towards Kaifail's temple. I headed alone down the city streets with as much confidence as I could muster.

For once, the universe was merciful. Not only did I make it safely to the temple, but I found Iris, Vogg, and Spark waiting for me there. They sat together in the ruins, deep enough in the shadow of a broken wall no one could see them from outside the wards. They stood at my approach.

Vogg had bandages around one massive, scaled bicep, and the armor plate that protected the right side of his chest was cracked, but his movements weren't slowed as he drew his gun at my approach.

"Ash?" Iris asked, caution in her tone and her posture.

"Still me," I answered wearily. "You can ask me anything. Not that it matters. Turns out the shadows, they're better actors than we realized. They know—somehow they know—" My throat closed around the words. I couldn't keep talking.

"Magic," Spark said softly. "They can't do magic."

I wasn't sure I could. Exhausted, drained, scattered, broken. But I knelt on the rough, charred ground and drew a circle of sigils by rote. A small pattern, an archivist's tool, it focused the dim starlight around us into a beam of illumination in the center of the circle. A light to read by. The best I could manage.

It was enough. All three of them relaxed. I wished I could let them stay that way. "We need to get underground, and then . . ."

I'd have to tell Iris about Amelia. Tell them the truth about Seana, about how she'd been one of them all along. How their goal was the death of this city and how, at this moment, I saw no way to stop them.

— 25 —

A Story Worthy of Retelling

We built a fire in one of the work-circles that I modified to contain the flames. A couple chairs—beautiful antiques—were sacrificed for fuel. We settled around the fire. Spark, so small and frail, with a blue and silver tapestry draped around her shoulders like a blanket. Vogg sat next to her, his massive shoulders slumped and the tip of his tail twitching against the cool stone floor. Iris was subdued, her body softer and smaller than she usually appeared, her arms crossed against the story I was about to tell.

As calm as I could, I laid out the story as I knew it, the timeline I understood. Spark's contact with the city council as the triggering event. Eddis to Seana. The Jansynians guided by the shadows all along. My terrifying experience in the tubes. The few hints and clarifications Syed had shared. Finally, the path of the shadow who had brought the most grief to the people sitting in front of me. Copper, to Micah . . . to Amelia.

After all we'd been through, Iris and Spark took the news calmly. Perhaps they'd even guessed. Spark's orblike eyes closed for a moment, and color drained from Iris until she was more gray than anything.

All three of us sat silent, overweighed by loss. Vogg, too, sat with head down. Did he mourn Copper? Micah? Others lost? Or was he, like me, overwhelmed by the simple impossibility of hope.

Without a word, Spark stood and walked away from the fire, disappeared into the far depths of the workroom. Vogg followed at a distance, giving her space, but keeping her in sight.

Iris and I stared at each other, both drowning in our own shocked loss. "If I'd figured things out sooner . . . " I started, but Iris shook her head in violent negative.

"Don't start. No rethinking, no second-guessing. You can't change it. We can't change any of it." The nest of tiny braids that was her hair today were all starting to turn red at the tips. "We all had the same information. We all knew those *things* were involved. And we still—" she bit off the end of her sentence.

It was kindness she offered, a share in the blame, but neither Iris nor Amelia had spent the last few nights sleeping next to one of the monsters. "I should have seen something. I should have known Seana was different."

"She's gone." Iris's voice was as flat as I'd ever heard it. "Amelia's gone. All we can do . . . "

I looked at Iris, waited for her to finish, but she shook her head and shifted into the small orange tabby, then slunk off to find her own privacy.

Leaving me alone. The workroom was big enough and cluttered enough with bookcases and boxes piled high and enough other stuff that we could all effectively disappear from each other.

I couldn't begrudge the others their need for escape. For isolation. It wasn't what I wanted at all, but—as I suspected was true of Iris and Spark both—the person I wanted to be not-alone with couldn't be here.

I found myself wandering back towards the mural of the Thirteen. I wanted to be angry. I wanted to blame someone. And who better to blame than the thirteen smiling faces before me. I stood before Kaifail, looked up at his handsome, joyous face. I wanted to claw the paint from the wall. "You left us here to die. You shepherded us and made us what we were and then turned your back and walked away."

"Is that what you believe, Joshua Drake?"

I didn't have the energy to be surprised. "Syed." I hadn't heard him approach, but when I looked back over my shoulder, he stood mere inches away. "How did you get in here?"

"Your misdirections are clumsy things, and the magic does not touch me."

"What about the others?" My worry was muted by exhaustion. "Can they get in? Will they find us here?" I couldn't imagine where else we could go.

"You should be safe from my father's children. Presuming you have no further plans to race into danger."

I punched him in the jaw. I was as surprised by my action as he was, but his cold, superior tone drove me to it, and the sudden violence broke something open inside me, waking a rage that burned away the daze I'd been moving through.

Whatever Syed was, he wasn't used to brawling. I hit him squarely and he fell back, stumbled over a book-filled crate and crashed shoulder-first into a file cabinet.

I'd bloodied his lower lip. His tongue ran along the split as he lay on the ground, looking up at me. "Better?" he asked in that same chilly tone.

"You soulless fucker. Heartless asshole. If you'd come to me at the start. If you'd told me . . . if you'd told me *anything*! People I love are *dead*, and you stand there and sneer at me for putting myself in danger?"

"I don't care about your friends. Would you like me to pretend otherwise?"

"You're an inhuman monster."

"Yes." He sat up, rubbed at his jaw. "And you are a buzzing insect whose life will be even shorter than the usual feeble spark of your kind if you don't start acting in a rational fashion."

"Are you threatening me?"

He smiled, his face a mask of frigid amusement. "*I* will not kill you. You don't matter enough for me to bother."

I wanted to hit him again. Except that it would probably only make him laugh at me more. "Why are you here? Why do you keep following me? If you're not going to help—"

"I never said I wouldn't help."

I couldn't do this. Whatever was to happen, however we were to go forward, right now, at this moment, I just couldn't do this. I left him sitting on the floor and went to find my own quiet corner. Now it was my turn to need to be alone.

Syed was sitting by the fire by the time I felt ready to face him again. If the others had seen him yet, no one was inclined to join him.

I didn't want to, but it was time. Time to stop flailing. Time to understand what we'd all been drawn into.

Time to fight back.

"Will you answer my questions?" I asked.

His eyes stayed locked on the fire as he spoke. "Understand, it is not recalcitrance or petulance that keeps me silent. It is woven into the fabric of my being. We are not like you, Joshua Drake, so flexible and fickle in your nature. It seems such a challenge for you humans to understand how the rest of us are different."

Iris had said something similar, back at Amelia's. I wondered if she realized there was something she and Syed agreed on. "You want to stop these other three of your kind, and you need my help to do it. You can't deny that—you wouldn't be here if it weren't true."

"I do not deny it."

"That's the price for my help. I need to know what you know."

He laughed, a dark, hollow sound without an ounce of humanity to it. "What I know? *What I know?* I have been as I am since a time when your ancestors were still huddled around fires and telling stories to keep back the night. *What I know?* I have seen empires rise and fall. I have watched the births of not just men and women, but *entire races.* For four thousand years I have served and I have watched and I have given counsel to *gods,*" he snarled the word, "and now I must speak to you, one more mortal in an endless sea of faces as disposable as tissue, and beg your help as though you were an equal and you demand to know *what I know?*"

I answered in the same calm, cool tone he'd used on me earlier. "That's about the size of it, yes."

He gave a bitter, inward-focused smile, and continued to stare into the fire. When he spoke, his words were flat and even. Syed was no storyteller, but in this case, my interest in the material outweighed any flaws in the delivery.

"Understand this is your fault—humanity. All the scrabbling, curious, intrusive lot of you. I wasn't there to see it, but I can only imagine the first words out of the mouth of the ape who first learned how were, 'What's next?' And so you've gone on, poking and prodding and *changing* things.

"My father's children were created to mitigate the changes, to keep you from rewriting the world every time you had some new whim. We couldn't stop you entirely. The other gods would have objected. The chaos gods—Ouliria, Drinion, the Twins—they loved you humans. They took delight in the way you kept trying to break the world.

"Fools. Every one of them."

"Do you know where they went?" I interrupted.

He shook his head with a thin smile. "Even I do not hold the answer to that question."

He continued. "It was a delicate balance. We had to choose carefully. A researcher, for example. A politician. One pivotal person through whom we could act, calming pockets of chaos and smoothing dangerous ripples."

253

"You killed them."

He shook his head. "Even now, you do not understand, Joshua Drake. We don't kill. We *become*.

"Death is change—the greatest change of all. It brings chaos. It drives response. No, we did not kill these people. We slipped inside them and turned them from their dangerous path. Then remained with them until their appointed time. Each intervention was a labor of years, and my father's children moved silently from one lifetime to the next."

We were going to have to agree to disagree on whether they were killing people or not. "How did this go on—you said you've been around for thousands of years—how did no one notice? How did we not know about an entire race?"

"My father made his children to be good at what they do. When I say that we became, I don't speak figuratively or poetically. When we join with a person, we gain their mind, their thoughts, their memories—everything about them. No one notices because there is no difference. If we redirect their life path, alter choices by some small amount, it is a change of heart, nothing more. Always explicable and defensible."

Maybe because we were facing the end of the world, maybe because of all the terror I'd already faced over the last couple days, I found this all fascinating. In a horrifying way. "How did you know?" I asked. "How did you choose people where no one would question that kind of change?"

"My father's children did not *choose* anything." He lifted his head, met my gaze with his pale blue eyes. "You make a mistaken assumption when you group us together, me and the others."

"But you are the same. I've seen the shadow in your eyes, just like I see in theirs."

"Oh yes, the body is the same." His eyes went black and a darkness passed over his face. "We have no physical substance of our own. We are beings of thought and shadow, as my father made us."

"So how are you different? Other than the fact they're trying to end the world right now and you're not."

He sighed, clearly disappointed. I'd failed some test. "Your question is the answer."

"You're being cryptic again."

He tilted his head, acknowledging, if not apologizing. "They are not like me. They are not like you, or Iris, or Spark, or anyone you know. They were not created to be people; they were made to be servants. Servants of my father. They had no minds of their own, no thoughts of their own. They were extensions of his will—his eyes, his hands, his power."

"Puppets," I supplied. "Except when their strings got cut, they didn't lie down."

"They cannot reason in any way you understand. Their veneer of sentience is driven by the people whose minds they share. They cannot be dissuaded or turned from their path because it is not a decision they made—their actions are driven by their nature, a fundamental instinct to continue doing what they were told."

"No, wait," I held up a hand, "that doesn't make any sense. If they're against change—if you're all against change—how can their programming be driving them to do what they're doing. They're trying to destroy Miroc—to kill everyone who lives here. How is that not change?"

"They are trying to keep Miroc on the path ordained—as they understand it—by the gods. Miroc is dying, has been dying since the Abandon. Spark's research in the hands of the Jansynians could have turned it away from that path. Could have kept the city alive."

"So preserving the city is change and letting it die is stasis." I shook my head. "That makes no sense."

"To you," he countered. "It does not have to make sense to you. I simply explain what drives them."

I wondered if, deep down, Syed understood them any better than I did. If they were as different from him as he said, it was possible behind those cold eyes he was flailing in the dark as much as I was. "You say you don't kill, and even if I'm willing to accept your definition of things, they've still been doing a lot of killing. Copper, Micah, this thing in the tube station . . . "

"I heard your description to the others, of the deaths from which you ran." He said the words with no accusation, stating a simple fact. "That demonstration concerns me more than anything else that has happened in this last week. It seems . . . it seems they are *changing.*" His voice twisted around the word, as though it were the most distasteful thing he could imagine. If I understood everything he'd told me, it probably was.

"I know it's offensive to you, but I don't see how it makes our situation any worse if they'd developed a taste for the murder they're already committing."

"Don't you?" Again, his voice held disappointment. "The fact the city still stands means it has not occurred to them yet, but consider what happens when one of them realizes that display in the underground could be repeated on a larger scale. Once they have embraced the notion of death after death after death, why bother with political machinations when they can simply flow through the city, touch by touch, body by body, until no one is left?"

No one could defend against them. No one would even know what was happening. "Can they do that?"

"It would not be an act of sanity. To go from body to body like that—I can't imagine how it would break any sense of identity they've managed to build."

"Is it uncomfortable?" I was grasping at straws, anything that might keep this nightmare from happening. Because now Syed had said it, I couldn't see any other possible outcome. "Is it hard?"

He turned his face away, back to the fire. "I do not know," he said softly.

"Excuse me?"

"I do not know," he repeated. "I have never. . . . " He sighed. "I have been the same, unchanging, for the whole of my life. I have never taken another. I have never killed."

"Except for that poor sap whose body you're walking around in."

"His life would have been harsh and brief. A struggle for survival with the rest of his primitive tribe. Because of me, his eyes have seen wonders."

"But he's not really there. You took his memories, you know who he was, but it isn't like he's still in there with you. Right?"

"Are we to debate the nature of the soul?" Syed's amusement was back. "I can't explain what it's like, to become, and it doesn't affect our situation either way." He reached out for a chair leg in the pile of broken furniture we'd made and used it to stoke the fire, then threw it on top. "Storytime is over, Joshua Drake. Summon your companions. It is time to discuss what happens next."

We were all of us still moving through something of a state of shock, which probably contributed to the fact that, after I'd introduced Syed and proclaimed him on our side, no one objected to his presence. Although Iris pointedly sat as far away from him as she could and still be in on the conversation, and Vogg kept a suspicious eye on him. I couldn't fault either one of them.

The five of us were all that stood between Miroc and utter destruction. And what was more—

"Things may be worse than we thought," Iris said once everyone had settled.

"How is that even possible?" I asked. I shouldn't have asked. I didn't truly want to know.

Iris had returned to a more natural color, but her appearance was still terribly subdued. Her hair was short and lay flat against her head; the clothing she'd created was a single shade of navy and neither it nor her soft ebony skin held any ornament. "We know now that his people," she flicked her fingers at Syed, "have been in Miroc for a while. That until Spark messed everything up, their plans were to basically keep the city pointed in the direction it wanted to go. A passive approach, rather than an active one."

I nodded. Not that the shadow's actions had been anything I'd describe as passive.

"Well now we've fucked that up for them. They're on the attack and they've got Amelia." Iris waited, staring at me.

"I still don't get it."

Her skin flushed a frustrated red. "The riots, remember? The protests? The bombs? Amelia's been in charge of security around the reservoir. With the reservoir intact, Miroc still had months, maybe, if nothing else drastic changed. Without it . . . "

This time I was able to finish her thought. "The end. Just like that. No more water. No more city."

Vogg swore under his breath.

Spark was still calm. "If we can bring the rain, it won't matter."

"And how are we supposed to do that?" Iris snapped.

"Iris—" I began.

She kept talking over me. "I'm serious. How? Should we invade the Crescent? That plan was suicidal back when we thought they were on our side."

"My sister's plans—"

I cut Spark off. "Were never going to work. I'm sorry, but I saw what Copper meant to do. She never understood how the Jansynians work, and that's not even taking into account the added difficulty the shadows present."

Vogg's ears flapped open and closed, a sure sign of agitation. "To even have a chance of getting into the Crescent, we would need time to organize and to gather more resources. We won't have that if the reservoir is destroyed."

"Can we protect it?" Spark directed her question at Vogg.

Vogg's answer was honest. "There are five of us. Between Director Seana and Ms. Price, they control most of the power in this city."

"They couldn't have chosen better targets." I heard the bitterness in my voice. One of those targets, at least, we'd handed them. I was the one who suggested Amelia and Seana work together. Oh, and I couldn't forget the fact Seana had been taken by a shadow only because I'd done the magic to drive it out of Eddis. If only I'd known—

Spark reached over to rest her tiny hand on my knee. "It isn't your fault."

"It's *their* fault," Vogg said. "Everything that has happened is their fault."

I shook my head. "Not just their fault. The shadows are taking advantage, but they didn't create this situation. They didn't abandon the world they created and leave their children scrabbling in the sand."

"This is what we have," Spark said softly. "We can't make it any better by wishing or arguing."

"We won't make it better by dying, either," Iris pointed out. "We keep rushing unprepared and uninformed and look where that's gotten us."

Not that there was any forward left to rush to. As Vogg had pointed out, there were five of us against the only organized powers left in Miroc. Amelia and Seana knew what we could do, and they had the resources to see us coming. And as if that weren't enough, there was still one more shadow out there who, since I'd lost track of it in the tube station, could be anyone.

I had to be honest. "I don't know what to do from here. I don't know if there's anything we can do. There may not be anything we can do. From here, our only two choices may be dying quickly or dying slowly. Except for you." I directed that last line at Iris. "Of all of us, you're the only one who can actually get out of the city

259

any time you want. If you left now, I can't imagine any of us would hold it against you."

For once, Iris's response was no more dramatic than a simple shake of her head. "I stayed in this dying city for her. I won't leave while one of those creatures still wears her face."

I couldn't deny how glad it made me to hear that. "Spark, Vogg, if you stay here in the church, you'd be safe from the shadows, and possibly even from any riots—"

"No," Spark said. "Whatever happens, we'll help. I'm tired of hiding while my friends and my family die around me."

I looked at Vogg. His job, even before it was mine, was to keep her safe. He smiled, an unnerving, sharp-toothed smile. "If we are to die either way, better to die taking action."

The situation was just as impossible as it had been five minutes ago, but I felt better all the same. Vogg was right. We were dead either way. We might as well die trying. This was the truth I'd known after the Abandon, the truth that had driven me out into the riots, the truth that had gotten me nearly killed once already. I'd been hiding from it ever since.

This was better. I was still afraid—I wasn't sure I'd ever not be afraid from now until my inevitable death—but this was a fear I could face. To do anything less would be to let down my friends. To let down myself.

"So we have two impossible tasks before us. We have to figure out how the five of us can a) keep the reservoir from being sabotaged by the security team protecting it and b) break into the Crescent's impenetrable security to reach the lab that hopefully will have the tools Spark needs to fix the satellite."

"No," Syed said. He'd been quiet all this time. I'd almost forgotten he was there.

"Excuse me?" Iris asked, annoyed again.

"Now you've wasted this time talking yourselves into taking the actions you knew you had to take from the start, I will not suggest we not waste anything further. The reservoir is a distraction.

The satellite is a distraction. If we do not, first and foremost, find and kill the children of my father, none of the rest will matter."

Iris opened her mouth to argue, but I spoke faster. "First of all, you're not in charge here, so don't think you get to decide anything for the rest of us. Second of all, you're going to have to accept that *our* goal is Miroc. If the city goes up in flames, I don't give a shit what happens to you and the rest of your kind."

"Why are you even here?" Iris demanded. "Why should we trust you?"

I was beginning to understand. At least I thought. "You're just as locked into your path as they are. You can't let them live because they've become something they shouldn't be. The only problem is, there are three of them and only one of you."

He glared at me and I met his eyes, unblinking. "You need us. The fact you're still sitting here proves that's true. And don't get me wrong, we probably need you too. But that doesn't mean you get to call the shots."

"So I am to follow your lead?" He barked a laugh. "Your plans have gone so well thus far."

"And yours have gone so much better," I snapped back. "You know, if you'd just come to us at the start, while the shadow was still in Eddis, we could have stopped *all* of this—"

"Ash." Spark's soft voice cut me off. I'd been yelling.

And it wasn't even true. I knew that. If Syed had tried to talk to me before I'd done the magic that had driven the shadow from Eddis into Seana, I would have been useless to him. I probably wouldn't even have believed him.

It felt like forever ago, the time before I'd known about the shadows.

Vogg's voice broke the silence that had descended. "What was wrong with Copper's plan?"

The change of subject threw me. "What?"

"You said it wouldn't work. What were the failure points? What was she doing wrong?"

I pushed a hand back through my hair, trying to organize my exhausted mind. "Jansynian security doesn't exist at a single point. Copper had found what she thought was a weak point where she could sneak in, and that's fine, but the problem is, once you're in, there's more."

"What sort of more?" Vogg pressed.

I peeled my security tab off my collarbone. Not like it was of any use now. "This, for one. Even after they let me into Desavris, I was given very specific instructions about the areas I could and couldn't go into. They track where people are and what clearance they have."

Spark held out her hand. "May I see that?"

I passed it to her. From a pocket in her tunic, she pulled out what resembled a jeweler's loupe, except with blinking lights and a lens that turned on its own. She squinted through the device at the tab. "Hmmm."

I left her to that and turned back to Vogg. "Plus there's simple visual confirmation. Only Jansynians in the Crescent. There's no way to hide the fact we don't belong."

"Maybe not for you," Iris said.

"I can hack this," Spark said, looking up. "I can make it tell security we're allowed . . . well, wherever we want to be allowed. Does that change things?"

"Are you sure?" It sounded too good to be true and we'd have no margin for error.

Spark grinned, like my question was silly. "Of course. There's nothing in this circuitry I haven't seen." Her smile grew. "There's nothing here my people didn't discover first."

Iris laughed. "It's no wonder they don't like you much. Do you Fyeans make a habit of breaking into Jansynian security?"

"Why would we? It's not like they're ever doing anything interesting." Serious again, Spark looked back at me. "Does this help?"

I thought of Seana's office, all the screens on the wall. "We'd still have cameras to deal with—"

"Cameras are not a problem," Syed said with finality.

"And the fact no one who sees us is going to believe we belong there."

"I can look like I belong there," Iris pointed out. "If I take point, I can try to steer us around witnesses."

"And if we cannot evade them, we can surprise them," Vogg said, laying a hand meaningfully on the hilt of his sword.

Call me crazy, but this was starting to sound possible. "Spark, how long will it take you to hack the security disc?"

"Hard to say." Her attention was back on the tiny badge, focused through her eyepiece. "Vogg, could you get my bag? I need my NetPad and my tools."

Iris stood. "While she's working on that, Ash, you and I need to deal with the reservoir."

"How are we going to do that?"

Her color was back to normal, and she flashed a sharp, dangerous smile. "We're going to do the last thing they'd think of. We're going to tell the truth."

— 26 —

The Right Trigger at the Right Time

The one advantage we had was the shadows' need for secrecy. They had Amelia, but she couldn't revoke Iris's and my security access without raising questions. When Spark asked if they might accuse us of being the ones possessed, Syed was confident with his no. "No one knows about us, and even as insane as those three have become, they will not break that most fundamental secret. They aren't capable of it."

I had to hope he was right. Our plan hinged on it.

Miroc sloped up on this side of the city as it reached out into the dry foothills that formed the bottom tips of a mountain range that spread halfway up the world. It meant the towering wall of the reservoir dam stood almost as high as the Crescent itself. All the lights were on, a blazing cloud of white that washed out the sky and made the arching metal roof seem to glow.

A restless crowd filled the streets and parking lots outside the two-story security fence that surrounded the reservoir. I'd never been here in person. Even when rain was a regular thing, the main water supply for our city in the desert was kept under heavy guard. No one was allowed in unless they had business.

Even so, I'd seen pictures, videos, news stories. What I'd never seen before were armed men standing atop the wall, weapons in hand. None of them were pointed at the crowd—not yet—but the situation was not stable.

Iris and I had been forced to walk here. The tubes were still shut down from the . . . disruption earlier. I'd left my Jansynian bike back at the safehouse, and it was too easy to imagine any number of terrible outcomes were we to go back and get it. Besides, I'd left my security disc with Spark, so the bike probably wouldn't work.

Approaching on foot meant Iris and I got to experience the sheer scope of the restless sea of people. Mostly human, which was to be expected, but I saw an alarming number of giants—tall enough to reach up and grab the security people on the walls—and even a few lizards. If nothing else convinced me how dire the city's situation had become, it was lizards on the side of rebellion.

Even in these early morning hours, no one was asleep. Everyone was yelling. Demanding help. Demanding water. Demanding a salvation that was in no one's power to grant. The guards on the wall looked grim. Armed or not, there weren't enough of them to keep back this crowd if things turned ugly.

Iris and I pushed through, earning hostile looks and the occasional rough shove. I apologized where I could, but I kept moving.

A barrier had been set up in front of the gate that led into the reservoir. A team of five men, rifles in hand, stood guard around it, keeping the crowd back. All five looked as edgy and restless as the people they guarded against. None of this was good.

As we reached the front of the crowd, Iris's face smoothed and shifted to one I'd seen her wear a few times around the office—any repeats with Iris were notable.

And not just to me. "Iris," one of the guards said, relief obvious in his voice. "Thank the gods. We've been calling for hours for Ms. Price to send more support."

Iris twitched her head at the people spread out behind us. "What's the situation?"

"They're restless. They've been restless. They want the government to release more water. We haven't gotten any more threats from the terrorists, but if there's an attack, these people are going to be stuck in the middle of it. A bomb like the one they set off at the university—they wouldn't even have to get it into the reservoir proper. Just set it off in the middle of this crowd . . . "

He didn't need to finish his sentence. "Molly Chambers still on duty?" Iris asked. "I need to talk to her."

The guard nodded. "She's in the security office inside." He waved his hand around three times in the air, and the gate behind him opened. "Go on through."

While Iris talked, I had watched the guards carefully for any sign of possession. Assuming the shadows in Seana and Amelia would stay put, we still had one shadow unaccounted for. But if it had infiltrated one of these guards, it was well hidden. "How well do you know Molly?" I asked Iris softly as we passed through the gate.

"Well enough to trust her to be smart and sensible. As long as she hasn't been—as long as one of them hasn't taken her."

"She's the logical target if they want things here to fall apart."

We'd discussed possible attack routes on the way over. Rational ideas like poison in the water or blowing up the dam. Crazier ideas like underground drilling to drain the reservoir or a full Jansynian military strike. The conclusion we'd reached was that unless Molly herself was compromised, we could hold things stable for the time we needed to break into the Crescent. If the security team was on the lookout for a lone saboteur, our one missing shadow would have a hard time getting around it. Molly and the rest of Amelia's people were too smart for Amelia to be able to give them new instructions that would leave a gaping hole in the security. And even Seana didn't have the sole authority to direct a full-scale military attack on the city's water supply.

I hoped.

The one person we needed, though, was Molly. If the missing shadow had her already, we were in trouble. "Has anyone from the city asked to see Ms. Chambers since yesterday?" I asked our escort.

"Nah, we've been locked down pretty tight."

"Have there been any deaths?" Iris asked. Probably a better question.

If the guard thought our questions odd, he didn't show it. "Nope. Other than the crowd outside, it's been quiet."

The riot waiting to happen. "How long have they been there?"

"Been growing for days. There've been some scuffles, and I expect we'll see more. I saw the threats the city council got. Molly showed 'em around. We're buttoned up pretty tight. I don't think the terrorists can get through us, but they can sure cause a panic and if that happens, lots of people are going to die."

The main security office was at the base of the dam, a solid-looking concrete square with bars over the windows and a reinforced metal door. Our escort stopped at the door and looked up, into the small camera that pointed down at us. A moment later, the door clicked and swung open.

We walked into a dustier version of Seana's office up in the Crescent. The city had put a lot of money into this place. A wall of screens showed every imaginable location, from the front gate to the maintenance hallways to the walkway at the top of the dam. At the desk, a woman I'd seen in passing back when I'd been moving through P&B in a daze, but had never stopped to talk to.

"Molly," Iris said.

Molly nodded back. "About time. I know it's the middle of the night and all, but Amelia stuck us here and it would be nice if she'd take our calls. I need more men. We've got the front gate protected well enough, but if this crowd takes it in their head to circle around into the hills, I'm not equipped to fight a war on two fronts."

"I'm afraid it gets more complicated." Iris grabbed for herself the only other chair in the room. "Ash and I need to talk to you alone."

"Just call me if you need anything else," our escort said, and left, closing the door behind him.

"This situation's going to hell," Molly said once we three were alone.

"More than you know." Iris closed her eyes briefly, but that was the only sign she gave of just how upset she still was. "P&B's been compromised. I can't be any more specific, but I'm going to tell you to disregard any orders you receive that don't come from me or from Amelia *in person*. Don't trust any electronic communications—not even if you get a call from someone who sounds like Amelia. It isn't her on the other end. The real Amelia will bring you instructions in person if she needs to rearrange the security from what I'm about to tell you."

Molly nodded, attentive. While she was focused on Iris, I took the opportunity to study her as deep as I could. If a shadow was inside her and left any trace of itself visible, I would see.

Pointing at the screens as she talked, Iris explained the changes she wanted, the new patrol patterns, the new schedules. The fact no employee, no matter how trusted, was to be left alone. "There's magic at work here. It's nothing we've seen before, but in short, any single person can be compromised. Anyone. Even Amelia or me—don't trust either of us unless we're accompanied by at least one other person from P&B." This was our ace in the hole. Shadow-Amelia might travel down here herself—it wasn't like they had to worry about her safety—but she wouldn't know we'd given Molly these instructions. "If you see any of us alone, we are to be put under guard—multiple guards—and you are to hold us no matter what we say."

Another of the many signs I'd ignored while I was sleepwalking through my life—signs that P&B was more than the simple investigation firm we advertised—Molly nodded, accepting Iris's instructions without question.

Or maybe she didn't have to question because the shadow inside her already knew exactly what was going on.

But hopefully, with these new instructions, even if Molly herself was compromised, this would slow the shadows down. Certainly Iris and I had no plans to go anywhere until we'd seen these new instructions put into action.

Molly tapped a button on her earpiece and started talking through the new orders. On the wall, I was able to watch the men and women of her security teams rearrange into the new patterns with reassuring efficiency. As I scanned across the screens, activity at the front gate caught my eye. "Who's that?" I asked, pointing to the tall, long-haired man who had drawn the crowd in around himself as he was speaking.

Molly tapped her earpiece again, so she was talking just to us. "One of the lead protesters. There's about half a dozen of them who periodically get up and give little speeches. Keep the people nice and angry." She rolled her eyes. "'Cause sleep deprivation is everyone's best friend."

It was like a new game—what would happen if *this* person was the missing shadow? "It looks like he's trying to get the mob riled up."

"They do that." She sighed and turned her headset back on. "HQ to gate—anything going on out there we should know about?"

She listened, head tilted, then said, "Thanks. Keep me posted." She tapped off her mic. "Like I said, nothing we haven't heard before."

Iris, too, was watching the man. "How *riled* has the crowd gotten so far? What happens if they try to storm the gates?"

"Then they're running straight into a line of automatic rifles. We're fortified and well-supplied. They're unarmed civilians. They'd have to be suicidal to try it, and I think we'd discourage them pretty fast."

Mob mentality. These people were desperate, scared, and they knew they were running out of time. The right trigger at the right time—"We need to get out there," I said to Iris.

"I was thinking the same thing."

The people on the screen were shouting, cheering, yelling. We had no sound, only the images of mouths moving and fists pumping into the air. And the tall man in the center, shouting with them, pointing at the gate.

"Oh no no no," Molly said, leaning forward. "Gate, what's happening?"

I couldn't hear their response, but I saw guns being raised towards the crowd. "Shit," Molly hissed. "He can't be—" She turned back at us. "He's yelling about sacrifice, death for the greater good, crazy nonsense. He's going to march them right into our guns."

"And if he falls, someone else will take up where he left off." Exhaustion filled Iris's voice. "And another after that. Until they've killed—"

I couldn't bear the thought. "Tell them not to shoot."

"I can't do that," Molly said.

Of course. Why would she listen to me? "Iris," I pleaded.

"Ash, we can't—"

"We can't stand here and watch these people die."

"Without this water, the whole city dies!"

"The city's dying! The city has one chance, and only once chance, and you and I both know what that is. If we minimize short-term bloodshed by letting these people get in here and just take the water they need—"

The distinct sound of an automatic pistol being cocked interrupted me. Molly had a weapon in her hand. It wasn't pointed at me, not yet, but her expression was wary. "I don't know who you think you are, but I was given my instructions by Amelia Price, and her orders came from the city council. We're defending this water. That's the end of it."

— 27 —

Watching through the Glass

I saw what was coming. And I had no idea how to stop it.

Through the video screen, I couldn't search the man's eyes for signs of possession, but I could imagine the scenario if he was, and that scenario was pretty much playing out in front of me. He yelled, pumping his fist in the air, driving the crowd around him into a frenzy. Molly was back on the line with the guards, ordering them to hold their positions, to ready their weapons. And, gods help us, to fire upon anyone who got too close.

To anyone who didn't know, he probably looked brave. This man, this firebrand who took the lead. He seemed to have no fear of death, and why should he when he was already dead? But Iris and I were the only ones who knew that.

I watched, paralyzed, as he ran forward. We had no sound from the video feeds, couldn't hear the gunshot, but I saw his body jerk and fall.

The crowd went mad. They surged forward in a suicidal madness. The guards in front of the barriers fell back as the guards on the wall opened fire.

It would have been enough. Amelia knew her business. The security teams knew their business. They had the arms and the position to turn back even this crowd. Hundreds were about to die, but they weren't going to break the reservoir's defenses.

Except for the shadows.

I saw it move. For the first time since my original vision of Eddis's death, I saw one move outside the flesh. Darkness incarnate, flowing out from the fallen body of the dead instigator. In the crowd, in the chaos, I would have missed it if I hadn't been watching for it.

"Iris—" was all I had time to say as the shadow flicked across the open space and up the wall and flowed into the body of an unsuspecting guard. How did no one see that? How could no one—

The newly possessed guard lifted his gun away from the crowd and turned it on the man beside him. Four members of the security team fell in succession. Molly's volume escalated as she demanded an explanation of what was happening. Iris and I stood silent, watching. We knew.

"We need to get out there." Iris said, her calm voice a surreal counterpoint to Molly's yelling. "We're the only ones who can stop it."

I knew she was right. I tried to nod, to agree with her, but my body felt like stone. Impossible to breathe, much less move or speak. Trapped in my own nightmare, where once again I was a helpless witness to a horror I couldn't fix.

Amelia's people were the best, but no one could have prepared them for this. For their own people turning against them with no logic or warning. The first possessed guard was shot down, but his executioner was the next to be taken, the next to turn against her own people. The shadow-created chaos was enough to give the protesters a chance to make the gate. Giants reached up, grabbed guards off the wall, and pulled them down into the rabid crowd. Weapons changed hands. Now the shooting came from both sides and I'd lost track of the shadow.

"Ash!" Iris said, sharper. She grabbed my arm and dragged me to the door.

The open ground around the security building had become a warzone. Except I couldn't see it. I couldn't hear it.

I stood on a balcony at Kaifail's temple, looking out on the chanting crowd. Demanding we come out, demanding we let them in, demanding we bring back the rain, demanding we bring back the gods.

I lay in a hospital bed, immobile from the bandages and the drugs and the pain that the first two couldn't stop, smelling smoke as the city burned.

I ran through a dark alley. Never fast enough. Never far enough. Felt hands catch me. Felt the first blow of a wooden board against the side of my face. Felt the first burning lash of a knife in my side.

"Ash!" Those hands on my shoulder. I struggled, fought back, the terror a bitter taste in my mouth.

"Ash!"

My ribs cracked. Kick after kick in my sides. Coughing blood. I couldn't breathe.

"God-dammit, Ash!" Shaking me. "I need you with me."

Iris's voice was my lifeline. I clung to it, an anchor against the waking nightmares trying to smother me.

Gunshots and screams. Real or imagined? Happening now or echoes of before? "Iris," I gasped against the weight on my chest.

"Faster, Ash," she snapped. "No time right now for you to flip out."

Iris, the irritation in her voice a thin mask over her own fear. That was real. That was now.

I closed my eyes, forced air through my lungs, focused on Iris, on her voice, her presence, her reality. I willed, I prayed that when I opened my eyes again the world would be real again.

For good or ill, it was. Iris had pulled us back against the security building, out of the worst of the fight that surrounded us. "I'm here," I tried to say, but I couldn't make any noise.

Iris nodded at the shape my lips made, searched my face. "Hold it together just a little longer. Then we'll go have a breakdown together."

"Right." My throat croaked around the word, but at least the sound came out. "Where is it?"

"How should I know? You're the one who can see it."

The calm I needed for magic was out of the question at this moment. I scanned around us, the pockets of fighting. A lizard bleeding from the shoulder wrestling with one of the guards for his gun. A giant carrying a rifle that looked like a toy in her hands, swinging it around her like a bludgeon. Three human civilians with a guard on the ground before them, kicking her over and over—

My throat threatened to close again and I jerked back against the wall. "Everything's falling apart. They don't care about any of these people. He's done what he came to do."

"No he hasn't." Iris shifted with the speed of breath. In one liquid motion, a bear lunged in front of me to deflect two rushing men carrying broken pieces from the gate barriers. She knocked them aside, then melted back into herself. "Come on."

I got it. Slower than Iris, but I understood. These people—these desperate people—they wanted in. They wanted the water, and they'd take it. But not all of it. There was still enough water in the reservoir, they couldn't take all of it. This mob, once they'd won their way through, would reduce the water supply, but they wouldn't destroy it. The shadows wanted it destroyed.

Iris dove into the fray, towards the tunnel that led into the heart of the dam. She needed me to follow. She wouldn't be able to see the monster until it was crawling its way inside her.

The first step forward, away from the wall, into the madness, was the hardest thing I ever had to do.

I made that step. Then another. Then another. And I was running after her.

Iris had studied the security plans, so I hoped that meant she knew where she was going. I followed her through the red-lit maintenance-ways, up narrow staircases, higher and higher. We weren't the first to make it into the tunnels; the floors were wet with blood and littered with bodies. Some shot, some bludgeoned to death, and a few with no visible wounds. From the shadow we hunted? If so, we were on the right track, but with no idea how far we were behind.

Voices, shouts, screams echoed around us. In a better life, this would have been a nightmare, but my bar for terrifying had been pushed pretty high these last few days and after making it through the fight outside in the courtyard, my mind seemed to have settled into a middle-gear, adrenaline-smoothed dread.

At the top of a metal staircase, Iris banged open a heavy metal door that led us back outside. We both raced onto the starlit walkway at the top of the dam. Far below, I could see the struggle continuing in the street and courtyard.

Up here, we were not alone.

A woman in a tattered robe stood about a hundred feet away, in the control booth that looked out over the much-diminished lake of the reservoir. Through the glass, I could see her frowning at the panel of flashing lights before her. As the door closed behind us with a loud *ca-thunk*, she looked up at Iris and me and smiled.

Oh how I knew that smile. "It's the shadow."

"Give me your gun."

I passed the gun to Iris as the shadow-possessed woman started pressing buttons and turning dials. It was obvious she didn't know what she was doing, but the longer she stayed in there the more likely she was to cause problems.

Iris fired a shot at the window. It cracked, but didn't shatter. The shadow-woman laughed. "You'll have to come and get me," she singsonged without looking up, safe behind the bullet-proof glass.

No. Not this time. I pushed my hand forward, the gesture a focus as I willed the cracks to grow, to spread, to separate. Energy into the fractures begun by Iris's bullet.

The glass exploded inward, turning the shadow's laugh into a shriek. Then five more deafening shots as Iris emptied the gun.

The woman slumped forward, her head and shoulders a pulpy mess. I watched the inky darkness float up and braced myself. I'd fought this creature off in the warehouse. I could do it again.

Except it didn't advance on us. It zipped away into the greater darkness of the night. "It's running away." I grabbed Iris's arm, relief so intense it made my hand shake. "We did it. We saved—"

An alarm sounded all around us, an echoing klaxon from speakers both here and at the dam's base. The people far below stopped their fighting, staring up. Iris ran for the booth as I stared down, over the reservoir side of the damn.

The shadow ran because it had accomplished its goal. The release gates were opening. As I leaned over the railing, a sound floated up that I hadn't heard for months. A sound I hadn't been sure I would ever in my life hear again.

The sound of rushing water.

Iris couldn't stop it. We didn't know how the controls worked any more than the shadow had. And luck was not on our side.

As the gates opened, the water filled the channels that led down from the reservoir and out around the edge of the city, into the desert. Designed to relieve pressure if the water got too high, the canals weren't designed to carry the full rushing weight of water from fully opened gates. First a stream, then a flood, the water filled the little canals, then flooded over the side, splashing into the courtyard, the street, and the thirsty thirsty ground.

The uncontrolled deluge of water stopped everything happening below. Greeted first by cheers, then by horrified shouts as they realized all the water was running away, soaking into the sand. All the water, Miroc's last hope, would be gone—irretrievably gone—in minutes.

I knew enough—I'd seen enough to realize what that meant. Miroc's lifespan from here would be measured in hours. Fires, riots, fights—the city would tear itself apart before the sun could rise and desiccate what was left. We had one chance and one chance alone—one last shot at averting the end of the world.

"Fly back to the temple," I yelled at Iris. "You'll be able to get across the city faster than I can. Get Spark and Vogg and Syed. Meet me at the Web. At our entry point into the Crescent."

"What if they aren't ready?" she shouted back.

I didn't answer. She knew we'd run out of time as well as I did. She hesitated only a moment longer, then ran and jumped off the edge of the damn, changing into a falcon as she hit the air. I went to the booth to retrieve the gun she'd left. We were going to need it.

— 28 —

Breaking In

Kaifail was an asshole.

He was a liar and a cheat. He stacked the deck against people and then punished them when they failed to live up to his expectations. He was manipulative. He was uncaring.

And he was gone.

I thought I'd already faced the end of the world. With the Abandon, with the deaths of the Favored Children, when the people turned against the priesthoods, when they rioted, when they tore down everything and everyone I had known.

But if these last few days had taught me anything, it was that there was always more to lose. Always more people trying to take those things away.

I'd let so much be taken. I'd run, I'd hidden, I'd compromised, hoping at some point the universe would be sated, that I would wake up one morning to a world that said *I've taken enough* and then left me alone. That it would all just go away.

Stupid. Because this was what it looked like when the world went away. It was all going—really going. My friends, my city, and the people within it.

I'd been so angry at those people, sitting around and waiting for the gods to save them, but how had I been any better? I wasn't hoping for rescue, just indifference. Hoping the bad things would stop if I lay low enough and quiet enough and didn't ever think about it too much.

I'd conceded the game before I understood the stakes. Now all I could do was keep fighting forward and pray it wasn't too late.

I ghosted my way around the outer edge of Miroc, sacrificing a direct path for one that would keep me out of habited neighborhoods and the eruptions I could hear already happening. The city smelled of smoke and dust. The skyline sparkled with flickering embers. *This* was the end of the world, and if I couldn't stop it, I was going to get to stand and watch it happen.

"This can't be how it ends," I whispered to the empty night and any gods who might still be listening.

The others made it to the Web before me. Iris met me at the base, dropping out of the sky and shifting in midair to land light on her feet. "They're waiting above."

I felt like I should say something, that the moment required . . . something. "Iris, I—"

"Come *on*, Ash." She shot back up into the air.

I climbed.

Spark already had the access panel open, and Vogg was halfway inside as I inched my way along the thick support girder that got us up here. "I see the maintenance door," he said, pulling himself out. His wide, plated shoulders barely fit through the opening, but the rest of us would have no trouble.

Syed, sitting cross-legged on the girder, looked up as I joined the group. I expected an I-told-you-so of some sort, but all he did was scan me up and down with his flat blue eyes.

"Still me," I said.

"I know."

The Iris who landed next to me was an Iris I'd never seen before. Silver-white hair, pale, angular face, simple black clothing. Usually, no matter what race Iris appeared as, I could still pick her out in a room. Little details, big details, wild colors, and a liveliness to her bearing gave her away no matter who or what she was. Not this time. Her disguise was perfect.

"Wow," Spark said. "That's amazing."

Perfectly incharacter, Iris didn't smile, only turned a cold gaze on Spark. "You think Amelia kept me around just for my pretty face?" She shivered and the faintest hint of blue washed over her skin. "Come on. I've been Jansynian for ten seconds and I'm bored already. The security chip ready?"

And all at once, I saw the flaw in our plan. "Hold on. We've got a problem."

Syed looked pointedly down at the burning city below us, then back at me with an eyebrow raised. "A problem, you say?"

And people said the Silent One's Favored Son had no sense of humor. "With the plan," I said, just as scornful. "With Iris. If she's going to be ahead of us, if she's going to be out of our sight . . . "

I was glad everyone else knew the situation well enough I didn't have to finish that sentence. Spark gave a "Dammit!" as Vogg slammed his fist against the wall.

Only Syed was unfazed. "It isn't a problem."

"Easy for you to say," Iris said, her low, even tone utterly alien.

"Iris is safe." Syed stood, waved her towards the entry. "She cannot be taken. Her kind—they have no substance. Their very essence is repulsive to us."

"Likewise," Iris said, unsmiling. "And good to know." She leaned forward so Spark could press the security disc against her collarbone. "Are we ready?"

For this? How could we ever be? But I nodded. Spark and Vogg did the same.

"In we go then." Iris shimmied through the open panel. After that, there was no turning back.

For the most part, we followed Copper's plan. It was the best we had.

Entering through the access hatch, we were able to cut into a maintenance tunnel. Security here was light—no cameras, no guards, and with my modified security tab broadcasting our right to be here to the Crescent sensors, we encountered no trouble. I understood why Copper had seen this as a hole to be exploited. She hadn't understood that perimeter security could afford to be light. They didn't mind if getting in the door was easy, because once you were inside, they had you.

Vogg led through the tunnel, sword in one hand and gun in the other. If we ran into trouble, there'd be no warning, no discussion. This was a point he and I had had to argue with Spark. We were invaders, and if we were spotted, Desavris wouldn't hesitate to use deadly force against us. We would have to shoot first.

My gun had gone to Syed. In close quarters, I couldn't be sure I'd hit one of them instead of one of us. He held the rear, and I had to fight the urge to keep looking over my shoulder. I knew he was on our side, but it couldn't keep me from being nervous with him at my back.

Spark was in front of me, a bag stuffed full of equipment over her shoulder and a NetPad in her hand displaying the schematic I'd seen at Copper's place. Spark watched it as we walked, poking at the screen when lights flashed, zooming in and out seemingly at random. I was afraid to disturb her by asking what she was doing.

Iris had the place in front of Spark, behind Vogg. Unarmed, but Iris didn't need weapons to fight. The grim expression on her

284

face was out of character, but she didn't have an audience until we were out of this tunnel.

I gave in to my urge to look at Syed, covered it with a question. "If we run up against the shadows—" I started, but Syed corrected me.

"When they find us."

"Yes, okay, *when*. How do we keep them away from Spark long enough for her to do what she needs to do?"

"We kill them," Syed said, matter-of-fact.

Ahead, Iris snorted. "You say that like it's so easy. What do you think Ash and I have been trying to do all this time?"

"The fact you've survived this long is extraordinary." Syed spoke without mockery. "Believe me when I say you are unique in all of history. No one else has learned our secrets and lived to exploit them."

"Because your god isn't around anymore to protect you," I said.

"Perhaps. Probably. For whatever reason, here you are. And you have fought one of us and lived. I saw what happened in the warehouse. I saw it touch you. I saw you drive it away."

"With magic," Iris said.

Syed nodded. "Then that is your answer."

"But how—"

He shook his head. "I don't know. Magic is your expertise, not mine."

Expert or not, in this realm, I was flying blind. Even if the beginning of an idea was forming in my mind.

Vogg stopped, placed his hand against the wall. "This is the place. This is where Copper said to break through."

Once we broke through, the race started in earnest. "Iris, you know the way?" I asked.

She nodded, lips pulled tight.

"They'll know we're coming," Syed said softly. "They'll be waiting for us."

Because Copper had been one of them. Even if this plan was insane, even if she remembered I'd said it would never work. "Will they know the minute we're in? Can they sense you? Can they sense me?"

Syed shook his head. One small thing in our favor.

Spark pulled a cutting torch out of her bag and handed it to Vogg. He holstered his gun to take it, but kept his sword out and ready. "One last time. Iris leads, we follow. Any Jansynians she can't steer us around or deflect away, I will incapacitate. Syed will keep us hidden from the cameras and Spark will manage the security sensors. We will go as directly as we can to the satellite lab, where we will barricade ourselves in and hold that space as long as we need to repair the satellite." We all nodded and he lit the torch.

No job for me except the one I still wasn't certain I could do. "If they come at us one at a time—"

"They won't." Syed wasn't going to let me have any illusions. "Or if one of them does, they'll flee from me. They'll attack three at once."

Which was why he was here with us. Syed needed us, which was for the best, because we absolutely needed him.

They wouldn't separate themselves once they saw him. But they might—at least, one of them might—for me. "Vogg, wait. I have an idea."

— 29 —

In the Shadow's Arms

I have to say this for Jansynian security: they are every bit as on-the-ball as advertised.

I was in the hall less than thirty seconds before two teams in perfect unison came around corners to cut me off ahead and behind. "Hands up," the leader of the team before me said in a cool Jansynian voice.

I complied and hands came from behind to pat me down for weapons at the same time a woman in the team in front of me ran a scanner up and down. Efficient, but not troublesome. I wasn't armed.

"Drake," the woman with the scanner reported. "Clearance four-oh-seven-C, but he's not tagged, and his entry is marked immediate delivery to Director Seana."

That had been my biggest worry, that Seana would have flagged me as kill-on-sight or something equally horrible, but I'd made the gamble based on the woman I knew and the shadow that had possessed her, both of whom had claimed to love me. "Lucky me, the director is exactly the woman I was looking for."

The team leader before me tilted his head, his eyes losing focus. Listening, I realized, when he said, "Get repair down immediately. Scout and secure the breach-point." His attention focused back on me and I was pretty sure I could read exasperation in that calm Jansynian demeanor. "They would have let you through the front gate."

I flashed the most relaxed smile I could manage. "Last time I was here, there was a bit of a problem with the lift. I was worried they wouldn't have had time to repair it yet."

The hands from behind pulled my arms down and crossed my wrists, then something cool and solid clamped around them. I didn't struggle. "Follow me," the man in front said.

I wasn't sure if I should be flattered that I rated two whole teams to escort me through the building, or if that was simply standard procedure. Not that I imagined they suffered a lot of break-ins.

As I followed my escorts, I kept my eyes and focus primed for any hint of a shadow. While I was pretty sure Seana would give me a chance to talk, neither of the other two shadows seemed to like me very much.

In the predawn hours, the Desavris halls were nearly empty. While I'd seen this before—while we'd been counting on that for our plan—a part of me was still surprised to see it. Miroc was burning below them, and up here it was quiet, peaceful, business as usual. Surely someone had noticed. Did none of these people even care about the millions of lives being torn apart below them?

They took me to Seana's office, which was exactly where I wanted to be. Seana was at her desk. Amelia stood behind her. Another Jansynian in a Desavris security uniform sat across the desk from them both. Shadows one, two, and three were clearly visible in each of them.

"Thank you, Aran," Seana said to the guard in the lead. "You may leave him with me."

I wondered what the security officers thought, Seana making friends with not just one, but two humans. Was obedience so ingrained they didn't even think about it? Seana—the real Seana—had been worried about the effect her relationship with me could have on her career, so obviously someone cared. Where were those people? Why weren't they paying attention?

They didn't remove my handcuffs, which was too bad. Bound and helpless, I stood there as the living, breathing Jansynians left me alone with the shadows.

"Well now, isn't this a surprise?" Seana leaned forward, resting her chin on her tented fingers.

"I've taken some time and reconsidered your offer." As casually as I could manage with my hands behind my back, I hooked the other chair with my foot and sat down next to shadow number three.

"Have you now? And what makes you think it's still open?"

"The fact I'm not dead yet."

Amelia leaned forward over Seana's shoulder. "Where is the Fyean? Where is Syed? Tell us that and maybe we'll consider letting you beg for your life."

I saw the flash of anger on Seana's face. It was too much to hope I'd get them actually fighting amongst themselves, but a little argument could be distracting. Could slow them down. "I don't know where they are. I came straight here from the disaster at the reservoir."

"He's lying," shadow three said. He leaned towards me, reached out a hand.

I jerked back, stumbling out of my chair. There was only so much pretense of calm I could manage.

Amelia laughed. "Afraid, Ash? Oh, very good. This will be fun."

"Stop it," Seana snapped. "Both of you. We're going to listen to what he has to say."

"Why?" Amelia asked. "Give him to Terrel. Once he's become Ash, we'll know everything."

I stood up straight again. "Because that worked so well last time you tried it."

Amelia snarled, an ugly expression the real Amelia would never have worn. And shadow three had slumped back in his chair in a decidedly un-Jansynian posture. Their facades were slipping. Or they realized there was no point playing their roles in front of me.

Seana was still Seana, in speech, in posture, from the line of her shoulders to the set of her mouth. "Be careful, Ash."

She had no idea how careful I was being. And I wanted to keep it that way. I didn't want them reaching agreement about me, one way or the other. At least, not yet.

In the video screens behind her, nothing looked out of place. Hallways, offices, labs and gardens and gyms and markets, all the living and working places within Desavris—empty in these early-morning hours. Quiet. Orderly.

Except when I unfocused my eyes just so, twisted my mind into that place I'd first found when I broke through the misdirections on Eddis's security footage. I didn't dare look too long, but I saw a shimmer on one of the screens, a sign of my friends' passage, hidden so well by whatever strange mirage Syed was able to weave.

"Miroc is burning," I said to Seana, letting a very honest desperation fill my voice. "There's nothing left for me out there."

She leaned back in her chair, forcing Amelia to take a step back. "I gave you the choice and you ran. Why should I listen now?"

"I was scared. I'm still scared. You have to understand—everything that's happened—it was too much. I couldn't, right then I couldn't deal with what you were offering. With the truth of who you were and what you were."

"And now?"

How real was the hope in her voice? I couldn't let myself think about it. I couldn't afford sympathy for the monster. "Seana left me. When she brought me up here, it was only to use me. You were the one who offered me a home. I see that now."

"Oh please," Amelia muttered.

Shadow number three—Terrel—said, "You can't possibly allow this. He's too dangerous. He knows about us. That alone should be a death sentence."

I glanced up at the screens again. If I understood what I was looking at, my friends were almost to the satellite lab and, so far, no alarm had been raised.

The lab itself was visible on one of Seana's monitors. I recognized it easily enough—I'd spent plenty of intense time staring at videos of it. From here, it looked empty. More good news. Maybe this was going to work.

"He'd have to help us find Syed and the Fyean." This from Amelia.

Seana nodded. "Yes, I will require that you help us hunt down and destroy Syed. The Fyean," she shrugged, "doesn't matter so much anymore."

"What? Why not?" I probably should have aimed for a more casual tone, but she'd startled me.

"Because I decommissioned that lab. There's nothing she can do."

I looked back up at the satellite lab. I couldn't stop myself. Horror dulled my thinking. This time, Seana saw it. She looked at the screen, back to me, her eyes narrow.

She'd been a brilliant woman. She'd fought her way to a director's position in the second largest Jansynian corporation in the world. And she'd known me well, both before and after. "They're here," she said.

The other two stared up at the screen. "Syed." Amelia's fists clenched. "He's here."

Unconcerned, Seana tapped several commands into her computer. "The two of you can handle him. I've sent two full security teams down to help with the rest."

"What about him?" Terrel waved his hand at me. "He lied. *Again.*"

"To protect his friends. Who among us can fault loyalty? Especially when it won't matter in just a few more minutes."

I tried to think, tried to whip out some clever thought. Some way to warn Spark, some way to distract Seana, some way to delay the inevitable. But I couldn't move past Seana's casual declaration that we'd already lost. "What did you do?"

"Go take care of this," she said to Amelia and Terrel. "I'll be fine."

They left us alone together. Seana still had her eyes on the screen. "A pity we can't see what's actually happening down there. I don't suppose you'd disrupt Syed's illusion if I asked nicely. I know you're capable of it."

I wanted to see, too, but it would give her more of an advantage than it gave me. "I'm surprised you haven't raised the alarm."

Her lips pressed into a thin smile. "What, and warn your friends we know they're there? What good would that do?"

I had to trust Iris, that she and Vogg could hold things together, that they were watching for danger. I had to do what I came here to do, and do it quickly. But I couldn't look anxious, couldn't let Seana see I was in any hurry. I couldn't let her start to wonder, start to worry. I had to keep her relaxed and convinced she was in charge.

"I'm sorry," I said.

"For what?"

I tried to relax once more in the chair, as comfortable as I could get with my hands behind my back. "For not understanding. For running away."

She gave up on the screen, which still showed no activity, and faced me once more. "You would never have given us Spark."

"No. But as you just said, it wouldn't have mattered."

Her gray eyes softened and her lips quirked. Not quite a smile, but the look was so *Seana* it made me ache. "We were in a delicate position. I couldn't cut off the project. It wasn't in Seana's jurisdiction, for one thing. And it would have raised too many questions. And once I became Seana—once I wasn't Eddis anymore—I couldn't remember enough to be able to sabotage it again like I had before.

"Believe it or not, you helped me when you got the Fyean away from us. You broke the lift, injured a few guards. I was able to convince my superiors the situation in Miroc was too unstable and that the project should be moved. Several other Desavris locations are fighting for the project right now. It will be months before it's back up and running."

"Plenty of time for you to figure out how to break it again."

"Terrel will go with it, wherever it ends up. It will become his problem." Seana stood and came around her desk. She reached down and cupped her fingers under my chin. "I like being Seana. She has a sense of purpose. You can't imagine what it was like for us, what we lost when our father stopped speaking to us. It feels good to be her, to feel her confidence, her conviction."

Her hand moved up to stroke my cheek. I closed my eyes and thought of Seana, the real Seana. I had to remember her, focus on her, and not on the creature wearing her skin. If this was to work . . .

Her voice was soft, intimate, close. "You were her greatest regret, that she had to give you up. And I understand, I do. You shine with that same conviction. And it's selfish of me—it would have been selfish of her—but I want you here. I want you with me. The others, they hate you and fear you because you know the truth about us. They can't see that that's precisely why I need you."

A rustling sound and her hands were on my legs. I opened my eyes to see her on her knees, face-to-face with me. "I've been alive—half alive—for so long. No thoughts of my own, no needs, no wants. Only obedience and secrecy, and one life after another that wasn't mine. But I want a life. I want to feel and be and know, and I want someone at my side who understands the whole of me."

She leaned forward until her lips were a breath away from mine. "Who loves the whole of me," she whispered.

The shadow had it all down, the voice, the look, the way Seana moved. But the words were all wrong. Every one of them. Seana would never have compromised her ideals, her people, not for anything. Not for love. Not for me. It was the truth that had come between us. And now it was the truth that helped me do what I had to do, despite the face of the woman I loved pleading for me to stay.

I closed the distance between us, pressed my lips to hers. I kissed as though it were a promise. I didn't trust myself to speak the lie. Kaifail was a convincing liar. I wasn't sure I could be. Not about this.

I counted to ten in my head, then pulled back, forged my best smile. "This would be easier if my hands were free. I swear I'm not carrying any weapons."

She breathed a soft laugh. "Even if you were, it's not as if you know how to use them." She reached around behind me, touched some hidden latch, and the restraints fell away.

I lifted my hand to her cheek, ran a finger over her smooth skin. So many times I'd done this before. Nights together, Seana and I. I remembered the way she'd lean in to me, the way her eyes would not quite close. The soft sigh as she'd relax—truly relax—and for just a little while focus on us instead of her omnipresent employer.

Seana and I. I locked the images in my head as I leaned in for another kiss. I slipped one arm around her, pulling her close. The other hand behind her head, holding her against me. Seana and I. Memory and emotion. The truth of us. Our hearts, our souls.

The magic I'd used to save myself from the shadow, the power-fueled determination to stay me. I focused that power on her, my mind and heart full of my sense of us, of her, of the Seana I knew rather than this broken copy in my arms.

She felt the magic as soon as I released it. She tried to pull away, but I held her tight. She struggled against me, bit at my lip where I held her in the kiss. I fed the power through us. Everything

I knew that was Seana—the real Seana. It burned through her, refining, purifying.

Seana and I. The hope I hadn't dared voice. Syed's claim that their hosts didn't die when the shadow invaded, but only when it left. If I could hold on to Seana, if the magic could hold her, re-create her, burn her clean the way it had me—

If I could save her.

The shadow fought back. It tried to move into me, like ice against my skin, my hands, my lips, but I held my sense of self as solid in my head as I did my sense of her. I soaked in the magic, let it define me and re-create me the same as I was doing to her.

"Ash, please! Don't. I can't. I'll do anything."

Seana would never have begged. I flared the power one more time, felt it race through me, through her.

She moaned, struggled. In my heightened awareness, I knew the shadow, felt its separate presence inside, felt it trying to flee.

My power was a cage. Seana, the shadow, and I. I held it inside her as the magic burned it from the inside. Her hands clenched on my arms. My power flared through the both of us. Seana and I. Only Seana and I. I opened my eyes, saw the clear gray of hers. "Ash!"

The shadow was gone.

And Seana was . . .

She gave one last gasp, and went limp in my arms.

Lifeless.

— 30 —

Shock

I eased Seana's body onto the floor. I was numb from the effort, from the sadness, from the shock.

I hadn't saved her. Hadn't even bought myself the time to make a proper goodbye.

One shadow gone, but two more were still out there, hunting my friends. I had no time to mourn.

Seana's desk. Seana's computer. I poked at the touch-screen, searching for some kind of familiar directory. I'd watched her do this; I just had to remember. For the first time in days, I found it a blessing rather than a curse that all the technology I was used to had first been Jansynian designs.

Too long. This was taking way too long. Where were the other two shadows? Had they reached the lab already? Were Iris and Spark and Vogg already . . .

There. The screen switched over to the view of the lab. The still-empty view of the lab. Which told me Syed, at least, was still in the game.

Volume controls at the bottom of the screen, both muted. I moved both sliders up, hoping I was right and this was the intercom. "Hello? Iris? Anyone?"

"Ash!" Iris's yelling voice and the sound of gunshots. Surreal and disconnected from the video feed showing a still-empty lab.

"Where are you?"

"Seana's office. She's been . . . I'm alone."

"Nothing works! Nothing's hooked up. There's no way for Spark to get into the system. You need to get down here. We need to—"

"No." Spark's voice. "Wait. You may be able to . . . hold on."

More gunfire. A crash. "Iris? Spark? What's happening? I can't see."

The video feed flashed, and Syed's veil dropped away. I took in the situation as fast as I could.

Piles of chairs, tables, cabinets, and even computers blocked the three doorways leading into the main room. One of those doorways held a solid metal door that looked to be holding, but the other two entrances had windows built into the doors. Windows that had been smashed out and had Jansynian security shooting through them.

Vogg crouched behind a desk in the central work area, returning fire. A wall divided the central space, and Syed and Iris were behind that wall, standing up on tables so they could also shoot back. Both of them had obtained Jansynian weapons.

Spark poked her head out from one of the side offices where she was huddled on the floor. She looked up at the camera through which I was seeing the room. That must have been where my voice came from. "You need to reconnect us!"

"How?" I winced as an explosive projectile blew a hole in the wall of the desk Vogg was using for cover. He swore and squeezed off three quick shots in the direction it had come from.

Spark dragged her bag out from the office and fished out her NetPad. She lay on the floor, typing furiously into it. I waited, powerless, separated from the action once again.

Vogg's ears were flat against his head, a determined grimace on his face. Iris was still Jansynian, but her hair had gone wild, with ends of angry red. Only Syed still seemed calm, taking one careful shot after another. "Have you seen the other shadows yet?"

"Not yet," Iris answered, ducking a sudden shower of chips from the damaged ceiling.

"Only two left to deal with," Syed said.

"How did you know?"

Another explosive hit the wall directly behind Syed. He didn't flinch. "I felt her die."

Streaks of red spread up Iris's hair. "Can you feel the other two? Do you know where they are?"

"No," he answered. Then, after a pause: "But they will come to us. Never doubt it."

"I've got it!" Spark cried, excited. "Ash, if you can get me into the system, I should still be able to make this work."

I pulled in closer to Seana's computer. "How do I do that?"

"It's just security. I need the right permissions is all." She was still typing away without looking up.

Not that she had a camera into this office, so she couldn't see me staring helplessly at the screen. "You're going to have to talk me through this. I don't know what you're talking about."

"Quickly," Vogg said through clenched teeth.

It wasn't quick. Neither Spark nor I knew the system well enough for her to be able to talk me straight through it. I opened folders and ran programs and sifted through layers I didn't even know existed, reading screen after screen out loud as Spark shook her head to all of them. While the firefight continued.

Vogg took a shot to the head. It knocked him back, shattered one of his horns. He crawled back to his feet, slower, but still moving. Still shooting.

Syed got shot as well. A bullet tore through his shoulder. He didn't seem to notice.

"There, that's it!"

My hand froze over the blinking line of text I'd just read. "That's what?"

Spark looked up towards the camera. "That's me. That's my signal. You should be able to just tap me and give me access."

I did as she said, tapped the line of text and was given a menu of security options that seemed to be in ascending order of access. I picked the very top one. "Are you in?"

"I'm in." Her attention was back on her work. "Now I just need to . . . you've done all you can, Ash."

"Could use another hand down here," Iris added impatiently.

"I'm on my way."

I shut down the computer. No reason to make it any easier for anyone who came in after me to see what we were doing. I paused at Seana's body, hesitating too long before I took her gun. Guilt twisted my stomach—guilt for everything—but there simply wasn't time to let it slow me down.

Spark had talked me through the route from Seana's office to the lab before we split up. I didn't run. That would have drawn all the wrong kinds of attention. I did walk as fast as I possibly could.

No more security got in my way. I heard no alarms. Saw no signs of trouble. Seana had wanted to keep this quiet, and now Spark was inside the system, making it work for us. I moved fast as I dared through the empty halls, preparing myself for the inevitable confrontation.

Or so I thought. Instead, what I did was run directly into an ambush.

I'd seen the security shooting into the lab, keeping my friends cornered. I hadn't thought to scan the hallways outside, to get the lay of the land before I rushed down here. Too many things going on at once. I'd been picturing the Jansynian teams all crowded up by the doors, their backs to the hall, an easy target to approach. I hadn't thought it through.

I came round a corner, still two hallway intersections from the lab, when one of the guards grabbed me by the wrist and twisted. Both startling and painful, and I dropped my gun. She shoved me against the wall and held me there. "Drake is neutralized."

I was close enough to her earpiece I could hear the command that came back. "Bring him forward. He's useful as a hostage."

Shit shit shit. I tried to pull away, but she twisted my arm up until all I could think about was the pain. After that, I went quietly. I'd have to think my way out of this one. And quickly.

Except it got worse. The third shadow, Terrel, waited in the hall with the rest of the team. His eyes narrowed as he saw me. Of course he'd be able to see I was still me, and his next question would be—

"Seana?" he asked softly. Not to me. He listened, his head tilted towards his earpiece. "Director Seana, please respond."

"What did you do?" That question, full of venom, was definitely directed at me. He grabbed me by my shirt and threw me into the wall. "Little human pissant, what did you do?"

I was tired of being pushed around, of being afraid. I rippled the magic through me, felt its hot pulse. "Would you like me to show you?"

He grabbed me again, shook me hard enough to break my concentration. He was strong, much stronger than me. I didn't know if that was his Jansynian body or the shadow giving it life. I just knew I couldn't break away. "This ends now," he said.

Holding me in front, he pushed his way through the guards in position around the door. From inside, I heard Vogg yell, "Hold fire!"

"No!" What mattered was Spark, that they not get to her.

But it was too late. My friends weren't going to shoot me. That gave the Jansynians the cover they needed to push through the door.

Terrel and I breached the doorway first, with the security team streaming in behind. Vogg had fallen back. I could just see the top of his head over the divider wall. I placed him in the doorway of the office Spark had been hiding in. I didn't see Syed.

Iris launched herself from the office on my left, gaining weight and size as she moved. Even Jansynian discipline faltered at the sight of a bear inside their space. In the moment before they could get their bearings and shoot at her, she drove her claws deep into Terrel's back. He let me go, stumbling. But his shadow-driven body didn't fall.

The lights went out.

No, it was more than that. I'd seen this office with the lights out. Blinking panels on the walls, dim glows around the light switches, and soft emergency lighting meant it was never pitch-dark. Except now it was. One of the shadows, or Syed? Did this work for us or against us?

A door slammed. Vogg. The darkness was against us if it meant they could get to Spark. How long would one office door keep the shadows out?

The shooting had stopped, the Jansynians as thrown by the darkness as the rest of us. I crept forward, trying to find a wall to put at my back. My eyes watered, straining to adjust, but no matter how much I blinked I couldn't make anything out in the unnatural blackness.

A roar, and gunfire erupted. Iris taking advantage. Bright pain seared through my thigh. One of the shots meant for her. I scrambled forward on a leg that wanted to collapse. "Iris!"

A hand grabbed my shoulder, dragged me back against a woman's body. A familiar voice whispered in my ear. "You don't need her. I want some time together, just you and me."

Amelia. Her cold fingers wrapped around my neck. I tried to shout again, but she squeezed, cutting off my breath. "Quiet, now. We have unfinished business."

I'd fought this one off in the warehouse, when it had been Micah. And now it was in Amelia. I didn't know her as well as

Seana, but still well enough to use the magic, to drive out the assaulting shadow.

If only I could breathe.

"What, no clever remark? No arrogant taunts?" Her fingers were like ice, the shadow pressing against my skin, but it wasn't trying to get in. Not yet. It had learned. As an invader, it was at a disadvantage. Like this . . .

Another gunshot, close and deafening.

The lights came back up. Dimmer than before. Or maybe that was my own vision failing. I could see enough. Terrel at the door that led to Spark, his midsection a bloody mess. Syed, ten feet away, holding one of the Jansynian guns.

Terrel slid down and the shadow seeped free of his body. Towards the door.

Vogg wouldn't be able to see it.

Amelia, too, had turned towards the shot. Which meant she saw Syed's gun turn on her. She threw me at him.

I choked, dragging air through a throat that felt full of glass. I couldn't keep my feet under me. I fell towards Syed.

He jumped to the side, but the momentary distraction was enough for shadow-Amelia to draw a gun of her own. And shoot.

Bloody red holes blossomed in Syed's chest, his stomach, his throat. His eyes went wide. The gun fell from his hand.

I had no time. I had to get to Spark.

I had to block out the sound of Amelia's laughter, of Iris's pained roars, of Syed's gurgling breath as he staggered back. I had to ignore my bruised windpipe, my torn thigh, my reeling head. Shadow number three was seeping through the door that led to Vogg and Spark. I was the only one left who could stop it.

— 31 —

Out of Time

I knew how to fight off a shadow trying to invade me. I knew how to fight off a shadow that was already inside someone with whom I was close. What I didn't know was how to fight one that was floating free, how to stop it from getting to Vogg, to Spark. How to kill it before it took another life.

Magic. That was their enemy. I'd been told—what felt like years ago—that was the key. Kill the body. Magic away the shadow. But what did that even mean? What was the pattern? What was the technique? I couldn't just throw raw energy, raw change at it.

No, that wasn't true. I could. It was simply everything I'd been taught not to do. It would be dangerous. Maybe suicidal.

I'd run out of time. I'd run out of options.

"Vogg! Cover!" I yelled. Hoping it was still Vogg in there. Hoping I wasn't too late.

I closed my eyes and summoned power. I didn't try to define it. Didn't try to control it. I anchored the energy in myself and sent it radiating out. Power. Energy. Change. Light against the darkness. Chaos against the stasis.

Burning agony as the power twisted and seared my flesh. I struggled to hold myself against the tidal forces threatening to rip me apart. The magic pushed back. Pressing out as I pulled in.

The world exploded in a burst of fire around me.
Then nothing.

— 32 —

Body Made of Pain

Hands on my shoulders, dragging me back into aching awareness. I couldn't move. Couldn't lift my head. Couldn't catch my breath.

"Hold still." Iris's voice.

I tried to tell her I had no choice, but I'd lost the sense of how to make words. How to open my mouth.

Eyes. I could open my eyes. Except that didn't help. Everything was still dark. My lungs convulsed and kicked back into life, but the air they pulled in was thick with dust and I choked.

"Ready?" Vogg's voice. I didn't know how to answer.

Iris spoke. "Do it."

The weight lifted and light flooded over my face as Vogg and Iris pulled off the section of wall that had collapsed on top of me.

I blinked, coughed, tried to make sense of what I was seeing. Iris was herself again. She and Vogg were both covered with blood and dust and fragments of the ceiling and walls. I couldn't tell how bad either of them was hurt.

I couldn't tell how bad I was hurt. My entire body was made of pain, down to the last cell. "Help me up," I choked out.

The lab was a mess. Everything not nailed down had been blown against the walls. Around me, a circle of the ceiling and floor had been stripped to a bare, black slab. The glass in the office

windows was blown, and the remaining patches of carpet smol-
dered and smoked.

I saw no shadows.

Vogg gave me a hand up, then kept his arm under mine when
my legs tried to collapse again. I pointed to the far corner of the
room. To the desk and fragment of divider leaning against the wall
and the bodies beneath it.

Syed, on the bottom, was a bloody mess. Unmoving. On top
of him, trapped beneath the desk drawers, lay Amelia. Her head
was scraped, her arm pinned beneath her in a way that had to
mean it was broken, but her chest was still moving. Still breathing.

Iris handed me the gun I hadn't noticed her carrying. Then
turned away.

Vogg helped me to move closer. Until I was standing over her.
I pointed the gun at her head.

Her eyes flickered open. She looked up at me. Her lips moved
in a bare whisper. "Joshua Drake."

I looked into her eyes. At the shadow swimming there.

I lowered my gun. "Where's Spark?"

Iris spun around. "What are you doing?"

"It's Syed, Iris. Just Syed." I transferred my weight from Vogg
to the wall. "Are they all dead? All three?"

Syed-Amelia nodded. "I was struggling with Amelia when
your—whatever you did. She took the worst of it. I felt her die,
along with the other."

To Vogg, I said, "Help him up, and tell me where Spark is."

"I'm here." Spark's head popped up in the now open window
of the office she'd been hiding in all this time. "And almost done.
But if you guys have a minute, I could use some help."

The Jansynians were dead or fled. I had no idea how long that would last, if any of them had escaped to run for reinforcements.

I didn't have to tell anyone else to hurry. We all knew. As Vogg and Iris dug through the wreckage to find the intact computer Spark needed, as Syed-Amelia and I pushed our protesting bodies to rebuild the barricades on the doors. The shadows were gone, but this wasn't anywhere near over.

"I still don't hear any alarms." I risked looking out the door, at the still-empty hall. "Do you think they haven't noticed us?"

"I think they know the value of silence." Amelia's voice, but Syed's words, Syed's cadence. "They don't want to give us warning, but they're coming."

"Try this," Vogg said behind me. He'd righted a desk on the far wall, found a screen that was cracked, but functional and an outlet that still had power.

Spark came out from the office. "Ash, I need help."

I traded places with Vogg as Spark punched codes into the screen. It flickered, went black, then switched to a screen full of numbers and moving graphs. "What's that?"

Spark flashed me a wide, cheery grin. "That's the satellite. I'm connected to it. We're in." She continued to type, her fingers a blur against the screen. "Go in the office. I'll need you to work my NetPad while I do this."

Spark really had been busy while we'd been fighting off the Jansynians and the shadows. A panel of the wall was cut away and Spark's NetPad was spliced into the nest of wires she'd pulled out. I brushed a clear spot amid splintered wood and glass shards and sat down, glad to have an excuse to be off my feet.

Which meant I didn't see the explosion. But I heard it. Heard Spark's scream. Heard the hiss of gas moving through the room. Heard a new voice, muffled behind a gas mask say, "Everyone freeze."

— 33 —

The Director

"Weapons down," the new voice commanded. Footsteps—too many footsteps. What was happening out there?

"You, Fyean, step away from that terminal."

"Just one more minute," Spark murmured. "One more—"

"Step away or we will shoot."

"Spark." Vogg's sharp voice. Protecting her to the last.

A gunshot. The sound of shattering glass, and Spark's cry. A second shot and Vogg growled. I pushed up to my knees, moving quietly as I could, keeping my head down. I still had a gun. If I could get off a couple shots before they saw me . . .

Spark's NetPad flashed. A blinking green square in the center of the screen that said *EXECUTE*.

I pressed it.

Three Jansynians appeared at the door. All wearing masks. All with guns pointed directly at me.

I knew when I was beat. I put my hands up. Let them drag me out.

The gas that filled the lab tore at my throat. I started coughing again and couldn't stop. My eyes stung. I couldn't see what was happening. They dragged me out of the lab. When I'd blinked away the tears, got my breathing back under control, I was alone, surrounded by Jansynians. They were leading me to gods-knew-where and my friends were nowhere to be seen.

They threw me in a holding cell. It was empty and far too bright for my tortured eyes, with an electric buzz coming from the door holding me in. I lay on the floor where they'd dropped me, arm across my face, body screaming with pain and exhaustion.

I lost all track of time. Minutes, hours, I didn't know. I wasn't even sure I stayed conscious. The lights, the buzz digging into my brain, they dug into my sleep-deprived brain and made the room seem to float around me. I was here. I wasn't here. I didn't know who I was. I didn't know who anyone was. The shadows were here, all around, just beyond the lights. If I listened, I could hear them humming.

The buzz disappeared and its sudden lack snapped me awake. The door opened. A woman—not armed, not dressed as security, gazed down at me with perfect Jansynian neutrality. "Mr. Drake, please follow me."

"Where are my friends?"

"Please, Mr. Drake, the director is waiting."

My entire body went cold. Was Seana still—had Syed and I both been wrong? "Waiting for what? What's happening here?"

She said nothing. Only waited.

The only way I was going to get answers was to follow. So follow I did. Bloody, limping, struggling. Two guards fell in step behind us, but they didn't grab me, or even draw their weapons on me, so it almost seemed friendly.

Once again I was escorted through the Desavris halls without any idea what I was heading to. This time, if they led me back to that familiar office, if Seana was sitting there waiting for me . . . I didn't know what I would do.

We went up an elevator and across a wide square full of market stalls and kiosks just opening for the day. This was a part of Desavris I'd never seen. I didn't think she was leading me to Seana's office. Although we ended up in an almost identical hallway full of the same row of portraits that I'd looked at on my first visit.

Despite the time I'd spent with the Jansynians over the last few days, the hours I'd been in Desavris, my kidnapping from the subway, security teams hostile and un, they still all looked mostly alike. And yet, as my escort led me into an office larger and more lush than even Seana's had been, I was pretty sure the face I was looking at was the same face that had been in the portrait at the very end of the hall. The director of directors. The man who ran Desavris.

"Director Artúr." My escort gave a shallow bow.

His office wasn't as bright as my jail cell had been, but my abused, oversensitive ears were still picking up a hiss that was going to get distracting. I smiled as well as I could, and wished I could glean any clue of why I was here from the expression on his face.

"Leave us, Ina."

She bowed again and backed out. The security pair followed. The director stayed in his chair, watching me.

I didn't have the energy for games. "I'm sorry, sir, but I've had a very long night, and I'd really like to know what I'm doing here."

He slid a finger across his desk and the wall behind him opened to reveal a screen. On it, I saw the running footage of our fight in the satellite lab. "You broke into Desavris. You and your friends killed a number of my personnel, including one of Desavris's directors, destroyed expensive equipment, and hacked into our systems. If anyone has the right to ask what you're doing here, I believe that someone is me."

"Where are my friends?"

313

"In custody." Which meant they were alive.

He made another gesture and a second screen opened. This one sliding up out of the smooth black surface of his desk. "You are Joshua Drake, also known as Ash, an employee of Price & Breckenridge in the city below. You were summoned three days ago by Director Seana Desavris and granted limited security access by her less than twenty-four hours later. You used that access to enter and exit Desavris several times, removed a vehicle from the premises, and then on your final authorized entrance, you destroyed company property and engaged in an attack on security personnel. Hours later, you led an assault back into the building that led to the crimes I've already mentioned. Do you deny any of these facts?"

I shook my head, despair a weight against my chest.

He leaned over towards the screen. "Bring in Ms. Price, please."

The hiss was growing in volume. That, along with the fact my eyes kept trying to lose focus, made it difficult to concentrate on the man who held my life in his hands.

The door opened behind me and a moment later Amelia was at my side. I looked her in the eye, saw the shadow of Syed looking back. She—he—it wasn't trying to hide. I wasn't sure how that made me feel.

The director spoke to Amelia. "I've looked over the material you provided me." The screen behind him flashed through familiar-looking files. The files Seana had given me. The files I'd passed to Spark. "There is a great deal of troubling data here, especially regarding Director Seana and her husband. Evidence they were both working against Desavris's best interest."

"Sir," I took a step forward, "what you don't understand . . . "

"Ash." Amelia barely vocalized the word. Artúr wouldn't have heard it, or even seen her lips move. But I knew, I understood.

Seana's death—they'd remember her as a traitor. She deserved better. She'd died trying to protect Desavris. She'd died doing her job and what greater legacy could any Jansynian ask for?

But if I told the truth, if I explained her actions, I'd have to talk about the shadows. Even if he believed me—and that was questionable enough—I'd be passing along a secret that had held for millennia, and possibly condemning this man to a death more horrible than he could imagine. A death no one else would notice. A death he'd never see coming or be able to protect himself from.

"Did you have something to say, Mr. Drake?"

"No, sir. I'm sorry. It's been . . . my head." I stepped back next to Amelia.

Artúr continued, addressing Amelia. As he would. She was the boss. "In light of your cooperation, your willingness to hand over all data stolen from Desavris—"

"We didn't—" Amelia drove her heel down on my toes. I shut up.

"As well as your promise to abdicate any claims of ownership for the project for which your employees oversaw the conclusion—"

"Wait, what?" I pulled my foot away. "What are you talking about?"

"The satellite," the director said patiently. "And it's completion. Have you not seen?"

Another swipe across his desk and this time the whole ceiling opened to a high, arched window that gave us an open view to the sky. The cloudy sky. Now I recognized the hiss, clearer now there was nothing between us and the glass.

Rain. It was raining. Steady and solid and real. We'd done it.

Artúr took my slack-jawed stare as an invitation to keep talking. "Given your position with the city leadership and the fact that I cannot in good conscious hold you responsible for actions driven by one of my own, I am releasing you and your employees back into Miroc. I want to make it very clear, however, that you are no longer welcome guests within the Crescent."

"We understand," Amelia said. "And we thank you for your forbearance."

"Security will escort you out."

—34—

Day by Day by Day

I lay on my bed in the dark and listened to the rain.

My apartment had no windows, but I could hear it through the walls. A soft, steady sound. The sound of life. The sound of hope. The sound of tomorrow.

Since coming home, I'd slept, I'd stood out in the rain, I'd slept, I'd filled containers full of water, and I'd slept again. I still hurt. Probably would for days. And that was just my body. I hadn't begun to sort through everything that had happened. I didn't know how to start.

A soft knock interrupted the zone of thoughtlessness through which I'd been floating. Before I could answer, I heard the knob turn and the door swing open. The lights clicked on to reveal Amelia standing in the doorway.

"That was locked."

"A minor inconvenience."

I sat up, leaned back against the wall, unsure what to say to my boss-turned-ancient-nightmare.

She closed the door behind her and walked over to sit in my only chair. "When will you be returning to work?"

"Is there work for me to come back to?"

"More than ever." Syed had settled in. Amelia's every gesture, from the angle of her head to the way she smoothed her skirt as she sat were perfect. "The city needs putting back together. My father—"

"No. *Not* your father. Amelia's father. But you're not her anymore."

She sighed. "I thought you understood better, Joshua Drake." She hesitated, corrected herself. "Ash."

"Don't. Please don't . . . don't talk like her, don't sit like her, don't *be* her. Not here. Not when it's just us."

She slumped, leaned forward to balance her elbows on her knees and rest her forehead in her hands. "This isn't easy for me. It's so strange. This body. It isn't mine. I was me for so very long." She looked up, the shadow a roiling mass of black in her eyes. "I'm not like the rest of them. I still remember who I am. And now I remember who she is. And we're not the same. We're not . . . "

She took a deep breath, straightened her shoulders, and was Amelia again. "This isn't over. There are others out there, other children of my father. I have to find them, destroy them. Before they do to others what they tried to do here. And for that, I need your help."

I hadn't been able to face yet the things that had happened here. I couldn't begin to think about hunting down more monsters. "I'm just . . . gods, what did you call me? A buzzing insect? You don't need me."

"You know what we are. You can see us. You can kill us. You are invaluable to me and a living threat to them."

I knew the truth of it, but still . . . I couldn't. "It's just magic. Surely you can find someone else with the gift, have them do whatever I did."

"I don't know what you did." The flash of anger was pure Amelia. "And even if I did, am I supposed to interview one human after another? Tell them what, exactly? Measure their aptitude for this work . . . how? It's bad enough I have to humble myself to you and ask a favor as though I were some . . . " She took a slow breath, calmed. "No, Ash. You are the one who can help me.

Iris and Spark and Vogg can also be valuable, but they can't do the things you can do."

As much trouble as I was having sitting here talking to the monster inside Amelia, I couldn't imagine what Iris would do. "Can you understand how hard it is for us? Amelia was my boss, my friend. And to Iris she was even more. And now Amelia's dead, and we know she's dead, but you're still right there, in front of me, and it's . . . well, it's awful is what it is."

"I'm sorry. I truly am." She stood. "But there is a greater cause to serve, and I know because she knew that you'll want to help. You'll come to me. You'll work with me. You won't be able to do otherwise."

I didn't answer. We both knew she was right. I'd crossed a line I couldn't un-cross. "Not today, okay? I need some time. I can't face the office. I can't face the work. I can't face . . . " I sighed, and just said it outright, "I can't face you."

If Amelia—if Syed took offense—she/he gave no sign. "When you're ready, of course." She stood. "I'll leave you to your recovery."

She paused at the door. "I did bring a gift. If you can drag yourself outside to see it."

Curiosity overcame the static weight of my melancholy. I followed her out.

The Jansynian bike sat next to the porch. The rain gave it a silvery sheen, beautiful and utterly out of place in this neighborhood of run-down apartments. I stared.

Amelia smiled. "Spark made a few adjustments. It should run for you without the need for any Jansynian devices."

I nodded. I owed her thanks, owed both of them thanks, but my mind was still too worn to summon the words.

"I'll see you soon." With that, she left me alone.

The rain continued. I spent an afternoon sitting on the porch, talking to my lizard neighbors as they came and went. The fires in the city had ceased to be a problem once the rain started, but the fights and the looting and the general chaos had taken days to calm. Now, of all things, flooding was sending the city into a panic and all the temporary employees were on sandbag duty.

No one knew how the rain had started. The bird priests were trying to claim credit, but my lizard friends said no one much believed them. I kept my mouth shut, nodded along when they said they just hoped it was a sign of good things to come. That we'd made it through our purgatory and the world was coming back to life.

The rain continued. I slept without nightmares, woke long past the sunrise we couldn't see through the clouds. And on the fifth day since we'd come down from the Crescent, I got on my bike and rode it into the city.

Not to go back to P&B, although I rode past the building. I rode past Amelia's house, past Kaifail's temple, past the safehouse where Spark had hidden. It wasn't until I dared approach the Crescent that I found who I was looking for.

Iris sat on the platform where Copper had built her home. I joined her, letting my legs dangle off the edge into nothingness. We sat and watched the rain sheet down from the Crescent above, a thin wall of water that encircled the Web and made it feel like we were all alone in the world.

Neither of us spoke for a long time. That was fine. The rain made a peaceful sound. I considered how generous the Jansynians were being, letting it go on this long. Or maybe they hadn't figured out yet how to turn it off. Although Amelia had handed over all the files, I wasn't sure if Spark had included instructions.

"I considered just flying away," Iris finally said. She spoke softly, her voice barely intelligible above the patter of the rain.

"You still could."

"Where would I go? The whole world is broken. Miroc isn't even the worst of it. And now I know . . . " She waved her hand out, towards the desert and beyond. "They're out there. More just like the ones who killed Amelia. My people's worst nightmares, and they're real and they *killed Amelia*." Her hand clenched into a fist. "I loved her, Ash. My people, it isn't in our nature to settle down, to stay in a place, or as any one thing, but I stayed with her. I would have stayed with her until the end. And those *things* took her away from me.

"I'm going to find them. I'm going to help you, and I'm even going to help *him*, that thing living behind her eyes. We're going to hunt them down. Every last one of them. And then when it's over, when we've ended that nightmare, you're going to help me. You're going to help me put her to rest."

I took Iris's hand and squeezed it. "Yes. I can do that. We can do that."

After that, there was nothing more to say. We sat together, staring out at the rain. And the city it was bringing back to life.

A new beginning. A new world. I was finally ready to see what came next.

THE END

About the Author

Growing up in a house that included a library of thousands of science fiction and fantasy books, Barbara J. Webb had no choice but to become a writer herself.

A midwesterner at heart, Barbara has lived in Missouri, Kansas, and Arkansas, but finally settled in only two blocks away from the house in which she was born. She enjoys her small-town life with her husband and her cat, and occasionally dreams of keeping horses. Or even better, unicorns.

In addition to writing, Barbara enjoys cooking (her chocolate chip cookies are always in high demand), crochet, and video games. She's been an avid role-playing-gamer since she was ten. Like most of her family, Barbara began music training when she was very young, and she currently plays first violin with the local civic orchestra.

Follow Barbara's writing news at http://barbarajwebb.com

Acknowledgements

This book has been a long time in writing, and wouldn't exist without the support I received from my friends.

Lane Robins and Kij Johnson. Nothing would happen without you two.

Leigh Dragoon, who reminds me every day of the better person I want to be.

Thanks to Chris McKitterick and the rest of the Lawrence writer crowd. My home away from home.

Thanks to Miranda Suri, Paul Genesse, Amy Sundberg, Brad Beaulieu, Don Allmon, and Heather Watson who all gave me incredible feedback on the book. If you enjoyed reading this, it's in no small part because of them.

To my Taos Toolbox classmates, Amy, Hallie, George, Jason, Lou, Lawrence, Sean, Danielle, Eric, Rich, Christian, Ada and Oz. And especially to my teachers, Walter Jon Williams and Nancy Kress. For taking the first look and helping me refine the story into something I wanted to tell.

Most of all, my husband, who believes in me.

Also by Barbara J. Webb

Midnight in St. Petersburg

Book One of
The Invisible War

EXCERPT
Chapter One
Saturday After Dark

Five minutes before she was supposed to be at dinner, Rose still had no idea what she should wear. She dumped her suitcase full of clothes onto the hotel bed and pawed through them one last time, hoping something beautiful and elegant would magically appear. It didn't. Seemed the fairy tale she'd stepped into wasn't the sort that provided evening-wear. As far as she knew, no mice had turned into horses yet either. But then, the night was young.

Hard to believe that just last Saturday night, she'd been alone in her tiny apartment in Phoenix, surfing the internet for jobs while she tried to calculate how many years it would take her to pay off her student loans at a social worker's salary and if she could afford to think about grad school. Rose had resigned herself to a future of ramen noodles and Kool-Aid when her phone rang and everything changed.

A job offer. More than a job offer. An all-expenses paid vacation to exotic St. Petersburg, Russia, including first-class plane tickets and a hotel suite all her own just to listen to a pitch. Their pitch, as in *they* wanted *her*, and not the other way around. This luxury, the posh surroundings—all for Rose, and maybe that was a little suspicious. Hell it would have been a lot suspicious if even once during the conversation they'd mentioned wanting to hire her to do social work. But the man on the phone had specifically referenced her other skills, the ones no school in the world taught, and for that alone, Rose would have made this trip if she'd had to pay for the travel herself.

Now here she was due at dinner in this fancy hotel and for the first time it sank in on Rose she might be in over her head. What if there was a dress code? What if the prospective employer who so casually tossed out thousands of dollars on plane tickets and top-floor suites expected someone more polished, more experienced? And most of all, what was it they expected her to do?

Because one thing Rose knew: St. Petersburg was wrong. It was broken. Even with her back to the window, Rose felt the city's roiling malaise like a blanket trying to smother her. A blackness so deep it overwhelmed her othersense, so aggressive it felt alive. It threatened to darken her vision and dampen her hearing until the physical world around her became a dream and the tenebrous sadness intensified to become her only reality.

In a way, that could work to her advantage. If this job was about those talents she'd never put down on an employment application, then her potential employers couldn't have a lot of qualified applicants to choose from.

After years of running different phrases through Google and a lot of volunteer work at a couple different psychiatric hospitals, Rose had found a handful of others like herself. *Sensitive* was the label bandied about in the dark corners of the internet, and oh boy were they. Every one she'd met in person had been stuck in a mental ward, crying into their pillow, withering year by year. Young or old, as far as Rose could tell, all sensitives broke down sooner or later as the constant press of other people's problems became overwhelming. And that was out in the normal world. Slap on a city that felt—what, haunted?—and Rose was willing to bet the titanic sum of her student loans that there wasn't anyone else with her gift anywhere near St. Petersburg. This city was no place for sensitive sensitives.

Rose sighed and dug out a skirt still wrinkled from packing and a matching pair of leggings. They'd just have to take her as she was. She wasn't sure how long she'd be able to stand it here, but for now, curiosity won out over caution. With one final look in the mirror to make sure nothing was sticking up or out, Rose made for the elevator.

The early-evening traffic in the Astoria's lobby was enough to distract Rose from the city's dark aura. To the naked eye, the few people scattered through the gold and marble hall were pleasantly cheerful, smiling and chattering away. But Rose knew the truth behind the tableau. She felt the desk clerk's impatience, the withered despair of the man waiting by the door, the dishonest smiles of the pretty young couple walking hand in hand, while inside the woman fumed with resentment and the man burned with jealousy. Everybody lied, and no one knew that better than a sensitive.

A tall, elegantly dressed gentleman disengaged from the concierge desk. "Miss Daziani." Rose loved the sound of her name in his thick Russian accent. "Your party waits. This way, please."

Rose followed him to a conference room that tonight served as a private dining room. An elegant meal was set out, spread across a lacy white cloth and accompanied by delicate china and spiral-stemmed crystal—definitely the prettiest arrangement Rose had ever seen. But despite Rose's earlier concern about being out of place in the high-class environment, it wasn't the fancy dining table that stopped Rose in the doorway.

It was the men who sat around it.

In the course of her research, Rose had found tantalizing hints of a supernatural world beyond the broken sensitives she'd managed to track down. Despite her every effort, the rumors and obscure references had never panned out. The community she'd been so desperate to find had remained hidden. Until now.

The three men at the table looked regular enough on the outside, but to Rose's othersense, they were alien. These weren't overwhelmed psychics cowering from a world they couldn't shut out. These were men immersed in the exotic secrets Rose had been searching for her whole life.

The concierge spoke over her shoulder, making her jump. "Mr. Rutledge, Miss Daziani is here."

The handsome young black man at the head of the table stood. His casual jeans and sweater were as reassuring to Rose as the broad grin that spread across his face as he held out his hand. "Miss Rose, so lovely to meet in person. Please, come on in."

Rose recognized his voice, the smooth southern drawl. "You're Alec Rutledge. From the phone. We talked." Rose snapped her mouth shut before she could babble any further inanity. Her brain was still trying to adjust to the sudden proof of the truth she'd been chasing.

As she shook Alec's offered hand, Rose felt . . . nothing. Her eyes saw him; her ears heard him. His skin against hers was warm. But to Rose's othersense, the sense by which she navigated the world, he simply didn't exist.

If Alec was concerned by Rose's lack of eloquence, it didn't show on his face. "I'm so glad you could join us. Let me introduce you to your colleagues. Father Mike Sullivan . . . "

Alec gestured to the old man at his left. As if Rose needed help identifying the priest in the room. And Father Mike Sullivan was serious about it too. No simple collar on top of normal street clothes—this guy was in the full black suit with the fancy button-down shirt and a Pope-approved look of disapproval on his face. Like Alec, Mike was completely invisible to Rose's othersense.

When it became obvious Mike was neither going to stand nor offer a greeting, Alec turned smoothly to the third man in the room. "And Ian Fior."

Ian, Rose could feel. And then some. He rose gracefully to his feet and took Rose's hand with a captivating smile. "Rose, is it? Delightful to meet you." His lilting tenor held a hint of Irish. Vibrant. That was the word for Mr. Ian Fior.

Alec was good looking, but Ian was something else entirely. Now Rose was paying attention, she found it hard to look away. Gorgeous was too tame a word for it. He had the inhuman perfection of a photoshopped model. His hair was a shade too red; his eyes too intensely blue to be real. And beneath his broad shoulders and angelic face was a resonance like nothing Rose had ever experienced.

Most people, Rose sensed their insides as sounds through a heavy door or the view through a window obscured by a sheer curtain. Most people, Rose could tune out once she got a sense of their overall emotional pitch. Ian's emotions were invasive, disorienting. He pulsed with a mad energy that jangled against the malaise of St. Petersburg, brilliant and whirling and intense.

Rose pulled her hand away, breaking the physical contact, and Ian's presence faded to a more manageable level. Still, Rose made for the chair next to the priest, wanting as much physical distance between her and Ian as possible. She focused on getting there without tripping, then tried to sound casual as she said, "Sorry I'm late. Did I miss anything?" Like she had mysterious meetings with weird supernatural people all the time.

"We're one person short yet." Alec waved at the wine array and leaned over for her glass. "Would you care for a drink?"

Half empty glasses on the table told Rose the party had started without her. A rainbow of open bottles poked up from ice-filled high-hats clustered at the head of the table. "Sure." She pointed at a pink wine in the middle that no one had touched yet. "That one."

The food, too, looked untouched so far, but the aromas over the table set Rose's mouth watering. From the silver chafing dishes she smelled butter and garlic and the unmistakable scent of well-roasted beef. Loaves of heavy dark bread steamed next to baskets of crusty rolls. Rose's stomach gave a rumble. Hopefully their fifth would arrive soon. Whatever he or she might be.

Rose had no idea what was going on with Ian, but Rose had a word for Alec and Mike. Sometimes the internet knew what it was talking about. *Voiders* was the label used by people who seemed in the know. The less-informed used other words with varying levels of hysteria—sorcerer, witch, wizard. Rose had read all kinds of crazy theories about voiders and the magic they supposedly wielded. A lot of them were hard to accept. The worst of the stories claimed that voiders came into their power by selling their souls to otherworldly beings. Demons, if you believed in that sort of thing.

Rose didn't pretend to be an expert on souls, but she had to admit, these two had given up ... something. Ian's whirling insides might be invasive and disorienting, but the absolute lack of any emotional energy from Alec and Mike was creepy.

Alec filled Rose's glass, then settled back into his chair. "I hope all y'all got a chance to do some sight-seeing this afternoon. St. Petersburg's a lovely city."

Mike snorted. "Yeah, sightseeing is exactly what I wanted to do after a transatlantic flight."

Rose, herself, had been more interested in a nap on arrival—even in first class, the travel had been exhausting—but the last thing she wanted to do now was agree with the crotchety old priest. "I wouldn't know where to go first."

"This hotel is in a great location." Alec refilled his own glass from a bottle of pale white wine that was near empty. "We're right in the heart of where the nobility lived, and a number of their homes have been made into museums. And of course St. Isaac's next door is one of the most famous cathedrals in the city."

Rose shivered at the mention of the cathedral. Her quick look on the way into the hotel hadn't been encouraging. "Is it safe? Everything here feels—" She broke off, looked around. Was she supposed to talk about this stuff? Even if everyone here was as unusual as she was, was she supposed to keep secrets?

"It's all right, Rose." Alec correctly interpreted her expression. "We're all friends here. You can share."

How to even describe it? Rose had never tried to talk about the impressions her othersense gave her. This was the first time she'd been around people who wouldn't call her crazy. "I just got here, so I don't have a good feel for the city yet, but if I'd come here to play tourist, I'd probably be booking my flight home as soon as I could manage it."

"You're a sensitive, then," Mike said, dismissive. Not a question.

Rose stared at him and shrugged. Not an answer. She might not be able to read Mike's inner soul, but she'd known enough men and women of the church to be wary.

Alec didn't seem concerned. "It's true St. Petersburg isn't the sort of place you want to be wandering by yourself at night. No different than New York or Chicago in that respect." He flashed a smile at Ian and Mike in turn. "But the tourist spots—"

Alec stopped as the concierge reappeared in the doorway. "Mr. Rutledge, the final member of your party has arrived."

Alec rose again. "Thank you, Vasily. Could you make sure we're left alone for a bit, then?"

The concierge nodded and stepped back, revealing an attractive middle-eastern looking gentleman in a black satin shirt with a mandarin collar and smart black slacks. Rose had to grit her teeth against the sudden dissonance in her mind. Something was . . . wrong with this man. Very wrong.

Alec's default smile was back, plastered across his face. Rose wondered that his cheeks didn't go numb. "Everyone, allow me to introduce Nazeem. He's the final member of our diplomatic party."

Nazeem stepped into the room and the concierge closed the door behind him, shutting them in together. Ian sparked friendly curiosity and held out his hand. "Just Nazeem? Like a rock star?"

"No." Mike's voice grated over Ian's welcoming tone. "Like a vampire."

In the silence that followed Mike's pronouncement, Rose couldn't stop herself from staring at Nazeem. At the vampire.

Who—just like the others—seemed normal enough on the surface. She wouldn't have given him a second glance if they'd passed each other on the street. He was handsome, sure, and like Ian, Nazeem didn't look much older than Rose's twenty-two years. But where Ian's looks—and presence—demanded Rose's attention, Rose's gaze kept sliding away from Nazeem, like her eyes couldn't find anything to latch onto. Even when she tried, she couldn't focus. Maybe not so normal after all.

Definitely not to her othersense. He clashed and jangled in a quieter way than Ian, with flavors and eddies of emotion that were like nothing Rose had ever seen.

This evening was a crash-course-wake-up-call, no question. Somehow, in all her exploration of her own psychic gifts and research into people like Mike and Alec, Rose had never taken the next leap forward to wonder if things like vampires might also be real. It wasn't like once you took your first "There are more things on Heaven and Earth, Horatio" step into the supernatural they sent you a manual. All the late-night sci-fi channel and Stephen King stuff—just how much of it did she need to be watching over her shoulder for?

And why was this the first time she'd run into any of this? One truth was becoming clear: none of these people could hide their differences from a sensitive. If there was a whole world of supernatural people running around, why had Rose never met any before tonight?

Mike shoved his chair back as he stood, one hand fisted in his jacket pocket. "Explain this, Rutledge."

"Explain?" Alec's eyebrows furrowed. Rose couldn't feel his insides, but she could see the confusion on his face easy enough.

Mike planted his feet, like he was bracing for an attack. "No one told me there would be vampires."

"As no one told me I would be working with a priest. So we are both surprised." Nazeem's voice was soft, beautifully accented, and compelling. Rose found herself unable to do anything but listen.

Alec stepped between Mike and Nazeem. "Gentlemen . . . "

Nazeem held his empty hands out to either side. "Please, good Father, we are not enemies here."

"Not enemies?" Mike pulled his hand free of his pocket, revealing a black-beaded rosary with a silver crucifix wrapped around his fist. Nazeem flinched at the sight of it.

"Stop it!" Rose snapped, jumping to her feet. Vampire or not, the last thing Rose was about to do was sit by and watch him get bullied. "We're supposed to be talking."

Ian also stood, his concern striking Rose with the force of a brick to the head. "Rose is right, and I, for one, want to hear what Mr. Rutledge has to say."

After a few tense breaths, Mike lowered his hand. Whether from lack of allies in the room or some other reason, Rose couldn't tell, but either way he returned to his seat. "Fine." Rather than putting the rosary back in his pocket, he lay it next to his plate, in easy reach. "We'll all *talk*." His voice twisted on the word.

Everyone settled back into chairs, Nazeem taking the place next to Ian, where he could watch Mike from across the table. The awkward silence grew and Rose gazed longingly at the bowl of herbed potatoes before her. Would they never get to eat? The tangy, buttery smell was irresistible, but she felt awkward about reaching for it while everyone else was so intent on giving each other the hairy eyeball. Instead she took a large swallow of her wine and tried not to stare at Nazeem.

Alec leaned back in his chair, swirling his wine. His mask was good—very good—but Rose could see muscles tensing under the dark skin of his neck. He was more nervous than he wanted to show. "My friends, the world is changing." His soothing drawl sounded confident enough. "Technology and fear make it difficult for us to go on as we have for centuries, safe from discovery.

335

My employers believe it's time for us to carve out our own space in the world."

"Space to do what?" Rose asked.

"To live. To hide without hiding. A place of safety and peace."

"Just who exactly is *us*?" Mike growled, still glaring at Nazeem.

"Us," Alec answered in a smooth tone, a wave of his hand encompassing the room. "The supernatural community."

Mike snorted. "We're a community now? I must have missed that memo."

"Of course we are. Voiders, vampires—even sensitives like Rose have special needs that are hard to provide for out in the world. My employers believe there is more that unites us than divides us and it's time our various factions reach out to each other."

Alec paused. Rose found some reassurance in the fact no one else seemed to have any idea what he was trying to say. Ian's confusion was palpable, and while Rose couldn't read either Mike or Nazeem, their silence spoke volumes.

"We brought you here," Alec continued, "because my employers believe St. Petersburg is the perfect location to put their plan into action.

"Forgive me if I'm being slow," Rose said. "But what plan?"

Alec lifted the silver lid from the large dish in front of him. "Have some stroganoff. It's a specialty here."

That was all the invitation Rose needed to reach for the potatoes. And some bread. The butter on the dish beside her plate was real and shaped like little flowers. Food was good. Rose was hungry and everything smelled very expensive. Food made sense. Rose could wrap her mind around the food. Unlike whatever it was Alec was circling around.

Ian also approached the food with enthusiasm. Mike looked as suspicious of the stroganoff as he was of the vampire. Nazeem took nothing.

Alec continued. "My employers need people to be their public face. To be negotiators, diplomats and, when necessary, police."

"Police?" Rose interrupted as she buttered one of the still-warm rolls. "What do you mean police? What law would we be enforcing?"

"Peace," Alec said through his Ken-doll smile. "The specifics of the definition and your approach would be yours to work out."

Rose chewed that over, still unsure what he was getting at. But Alec wasn't done. "All I'm asking for initially is a month's commitment from all of you. We'll cover your expenses plus fifty thousand dollars up front. You can get to know the city, get to know each other, put together a plan. At the end of the month, if you don't think this is possible or we don't think it's possible, everyone walks away friends."

Rose didn't miss the sideways look Mike gave Nazeem at the last word. She, herself, was trying not to drool over the idea of that much money. More than she could make in a year! It would mean the end of student loans and credit card debt.

"And after a month," Nazeem asked, "What then?"

"My employers are prepared to offer each of you a million dollars for a year's contract."

Rose stopped moving, a forkful of stroganoff only an inch from her mouth. Had she heard that correctly?

Nazeem broke the silence that had followed Alec's remark. "I can't help but wonder who these most generous employers of yours might be."

"They would prefer to keep their identities anonymous for now. But I can tell you they've spent years researching—they hand-picked the four of you for your exceptional talents and expertise."

A million dollars. This couldn't be real. But Alec was sincere. Rose could see it on his face. "Why are we worth so much to them?"

"Business," Alec answered simply. "To my employers, this is a small investment to create a safe haven to meet, to work, even to live."

Mike had pulled back in his chair, arms crossed. It didn't take a sensitive to see his dislike of all of this. "What gives your employer the authority to do this? What gives them the right to dictate people's lives?"

"Money and power." Rose had to respect Alec's honesty. "We're all part of the invisible war, one way or another, and no government on Earth has laws that apply. If there are organizations trying to regulate it," —Rose didn't miss the way Alec's eyes lit on Mike, Ian, and Nazeem in turn— "they're flailing beneath the weight of their own secrecy and ignorance of each other. It's time to try something new."

"An interesting proposition." Nazeem's emotions were there, pulsing against Rose's senses, but they didn't resonate in any way she could understand. Yet.

"Is it?" Mike's gravelly voice demanded. "What interest is this to a vampire?"

"As Alec said, the world is changing." Nazeem's tone was low and even and impossible to ignore. "Electronic databases, cooperation between governments, watch lists. Travel becomes complicated, especially with your American initiatives against people who look like me. The idea of a safe haven is most compelling."

"The other vampires in the city—" Alec began.

"Other vampires?" Rose interrupted, remembering Mike's reaction to Nazeem. "There's more? Are they dangerous? No offense," she added quickly in Nazeem's direction.

"Not all vampires are monsters." Nazeem's lips quirked, almost a smile. "No more than we were before we died."

That earned another disdainful snort from Mike. "I suppose you couldn't bear the sight of the cross before you died either?" Nazeem gave a mild shrug. "Exactly. Don't try to tell me you people are no different than when you were alive. I know better."

"Now Mike," Alec tried to mediate, "We won't get anywhere if we can't—"

"I need a cigarette." Mike pushed his chair back. He circled wide around Nazeem as he stalked from the room.

Alec sighed. "Obviously, y'all will need some time to think about this."

Rose still didn't understand what they were supposed to be thinking about, but she knew she wanted it. The money was one thing. The challenge—the mystery—was too interesting to walk away from. But most of all, this was her way in. This was her invitation to the world that had been hiding from her all her life. And *they* wanted *her.*

She studied Ian and Nazeem, tried to figure out what was going on in their heads. Ian was agitated. Nervous and excited and all at a pulsing, screaming volume that seemed more real than anything Rose had ever felt.

Nazeem eluded her. Even his face was inhumanly still. His gaze flickered to hers, caught her looking, and his lips curved to the barest hint of a smile. "I beg everyone's forgiveness," he said, standing with an easy grace. Nothing like the hurry Mike had shown. "As we seem to be finished with the meeting for now, I will leave you to your dinner." He bowed his head to them and left.

Ian only lasted a few minutes longer. "I'm sorry," he said. "I could use some air." And he was gone.

Rose wasn't willing to let the meal go to waste. She spooned up more stroganoff. "I guess I've got one question for you, Alec."

Alec was unsettled, wary. Rose saw it in the crinkle of his eyes. "Go ahead."

"What's for dessert?"